THE
BEAUTIFUL

THE BEAUTIFUL

RENÉE AHDIEH

putnam

G. P. PUTNAM'S SONS

G. P. PUTNAM'S SONS
an imprint of Penguin Random House LLC, New York

Visit us online at penguinrandomhouse.com

Library of Congress Cataloging-in-Publication Data
Names: Ahdieh, Renée, author.
Title: The beautiful / Renée Ahdieh.
Description: New York: G. P. Putnam's Sons, [2019]
Summary: "In 19th century New Orleans, Celine, a dressmaker from Paris,
becomes embroiled in a murder mystery that's connected to
a glamorous supernatural cohort"—Provided by publisher.
Identifiers: LCCN 2019014461 (print) | LCCN 2019017774 (ebook) |
ISBN 9781524738181 (ebook) | ISBN 9781524738174 (hardback)
Subjects: | CYAC: Supernatural—Fiction. | Dressmaking—Fiction. |
Murder—Fiction. | New Orleans (La.)—History—19th century—Fiction. |
Mystery and detective stories.
Classification: LCC PZ7.1.A328 (ebook) | LCC PZ7.1.A328 Be 2019 (print) |
DDC [Fic]—dc23
LC record available at https://lccn.loc.gov/2019014461

Printed in the United States of America
ISBN 9781984816504
1 3 5 7 9 10 8 6 4 2

Design by Theresa Evangelista
Text set in Warnock Pro

To the city of New Orleans,
for reminding me there is magic around every corner

And to Victor, always

THE BEAUTIFUL

To see a World in a Grain of Sand
And a Heaven in a Wild Flower
Hold Infinity in the palm of your hand
And Eternity in an hour

From "Auguries of Innocence"
by William Blake

J'ai voulu ce matin te rapporter des roses;
Mais j'en avais tant pris dans mes ceintures closes
Que les noeuds trop serrés n'ont pu les contenir.
Les noeuds ont éclaté. Les roses envolées.
Dans le vent, à la mer s'en sont toutes allées.
Elles ont suivi l'eau pour ne plus revenir.
La vague en a paru rouge et comme enflammée.
Ce soir, ma robe encore en est toute embaumée . . .

Respires-en sur moi l'odorant souvenir.

I wanted to bring you roses this morning;
But I had closed so many in my sash
That the knots were too tight to contain them.
The knots split. The roses blew away.
All blew off to the sea, borne by the wind,
Carried to the water, never to return.
The waves looked red as if inflamed.
Tonight, my dress is still perfumed . . .

Breathe in the fragrant memory.

From "Les Roses de Saadi"
by Marceline Desbordes-Valmore

---◆◆◆---

New Orleans is a city ruled by the dead.

I remember the moment I first heard someone say this. The old man meant to frighten me. He said there was a time when coffins sprang from the ground following a heavy rain, the dead flooding the city streets. He claimed to know of a Créole woman on Rue Dauphine who could commune with spirits from the afterlife.

I believe in magic. In a city rife with illusionists, it's impossible to doubt its existence. But I didn't believe this man. *Be faithful,* he warned. *For the faithless are alone in death, blind and terrified.*

I feigned shock at his words. In truth, I found him amusing. He was the sort to scare errant young souls with stories of a shadowy creature lurking in darkened alcoves. But I was also intrigued, for I possess an errant young soul of my own. From childhood, I hid it beneath pressed garments and polished words, but it persisted in plaguing me. It called to me like a Siren, driving me to dash all pretense against the rocks and surrender to my true nature.

It drove me to where I am now. But I am not ungrateful.

For it brought to bear two of my deepest truths: I will always possess an errant young soul, no matter my age.

And I will always be the shadowy creature in darkened alcoves, waiting . . .

For you, my love. For you.

Not What It Seemed

———◦◦◇◦◦———

The *Aramis* was supposed to arrive at first light, like it did in Celine's dreams.

She would wake beneath a sunlit sky, the brine of the ocean winding through her nose, the city looming bright on the horizon.

Filled with promise. And absolution.

Instead the brass bell on the bow of the *Aramis* tolled in the twilight hour, the time of day her friend Pippa called "the gloaming." It was—in Celine's mind—a very British thing to say.

She'd begun collecting these phrases not long after she'd met Pippa four weeks ago, when the *Aramis* had docked for two days in Liverpool. Her favorite so far was "not bloody likely." Celine didn't know why they mattered to her at the time. Perhaps it was because she thought Very British Things would serve her better in America than the Very French Things she was apt to say.

The moment Celine heard the bell clang, she made her way portside, Pippa's light footsteps trailing in her wake. Inky tendrils of darkness fanned out across the sky, a ghostly mist shrouding the Crescent City. The air thickened as the two girls listened to the *Aramis* sluice through the waters of the Mississippi, drawing closer to New Orleans. Farther from the lives they'd left behind.

Pippa sniffed and rubbed her nose. In that instant, she looked younger than her sixteen years. "For all the stories, it's not as pretty as I thought it would be."

"It's exactly what I thought it would be," Celine said in a reassuring tone.

"Don't lie." Pippa glanced at her sidelong. "It won't make me feel better."

A smile curled up Celine's face. "Maybe I'm lying for me as much as I'm lying for you."

"In any case, lying is a sin."

"So is being obnoxious."

"That's not in the Bible."

"But it should be."

Pippa coughed, trying to mask her amusement. "You're terrible. The sisters at the Ursuline convent won't know what to do with you."

"They'll do the same thing they do with every unmarried girl who disembarks in New Orleans, carrying with her all her worldly possessions: they'll find me a husband." Celine refrained from frowning. This had been her choice. The best of the worst.

"If you strike them as ungodly, they'll match you with the ugliest fool in Christendom. Definitely someone with a bulbous nose and a paunch."

"Better an ugly man than a boring one. And a paunch means he eats well, so . . ." Celine canted her head to one side.

"Really, Celine." Pippa laughed, her Yorkshire accent weaving through the words like fine Chantilly lace. "You're the most incorrigible French girl I've ever met."

Celine smiled at her friend. "I'd wager you haven't met many French girls."

"At least not ones who speak English as well as you do. As if you were born to it."

"My father thought it was important for me to learn." Celine lifted one shoulder, as though this were the whole of it, instead of barely half. At the mention of her father—a staid Frenchman who'd studied linguistics at Oxford—a shadow threatened to descend. A sadness with a weight Celine could not yet bear. She fixed a wry grin on her face.

Pippa crossed her arms as though she were hugging herself. Worry gathered beneath the fringe of blond on her forehead as the two girls continued studying the city in the distance. Every young woman on board had heard the whispered accounts. At sea, the myths they'd shared over cups of gritty, bitter coffee had taken on lives of their own. They'd blended with the stories of the Old World to form richer, darker tales. New Orleans was haunted. Cursed by pirates. Prowled by scalawags. A last refuge for those who believed in magic and mysticism. Why, there was even talk of women possessing as much power and influence as that of any man.

Celine had laughed at this. As she'd dared to hope. Perhaps New Orleans was not what it seemed at first glance. Fittingly, neither was she.

And if anything could be said about the young travelers

aboard the *Aramis*, it was that the possibility of magic like this—a world like this—had become a vital thing. Especially for those who wished to shed the specter of their pasts. To become something better and brighter.

And especially for those who wanted to escape.

Pippa and Celine watched as they drew closer to the unknown. To their futures.

"I'm frightened," Pippa said softly.

Celine did not respond. Night had seeped through the water, like a dark stain across organza. A scraggly sailor balanced along a wooden beam with all the grace of an aerialist while lighting a lamp on the ship's prow. As if in response, tongues of fire leapt to life across the water, rendering the city in even more ghoulishly green tones.

The bell of the *Aramis* pealed once more, telling those along the port how far the ship had left to travel. Other passengers made their way from below deck, coming to stand alongside Celine and Pippa, muttering in Portuguese and Spanish, English and French, German and Dutch. Young women who'd taken leaps of faith and left their homelands for new opportunities. Their words melted into a soft cacophony of sound that would—under normal circumstances—soothe Celine.

Not anymore.

Ever since that fateful night amid the silks in the atelier, Celine had longed for comfortable silence. It had been weeks since she'd felt safe in the presence of others. Safe with the riot of her own thoughts. The closest she'd ever come to wading through calmer waters had been in the presence of Pippa.

When the ship drew near enough to dock, Pippa took sudden hold of Celine's wrist, as though to steel herself. Celine gasped. Flinched at the unexpected touch. Like a spray of blood had shot across her face, the salt of it staining her lips.

"Celine?" Pippa asked, her blue eyes wide. "What's wrong?"

Breathing through her nose to steady her pulse, Celine wrapped both hands around Pippa's cold fingers. "I'm frightened, too."

A STUDY IN CONTRASTS

———◦◦◇◦◦———

Twenty-three passengers disembarked from the *Aramis*, each bearing a simple trunk filled with their worldly possessions. After consulting the ship's manifest, the officer stationed in the customhouse allowed them onto American soil. An hour later, seven girls boarded a humble equipage and proceeded through the darkened city streets toward the Ursuline convent. The rest had their futures awaiting them at the docks.

The open-air wagon trundled along the cobblestones. All around them, boughs hung heavy with brightly colored blossoms. Cicadas and click beetles droned in the shadows, whispering of a haunted history. A tropical breeze stirred through the branches of a live oak abutting a small square. The warmth of its embrace felt strange against Celine's skin, especially when contrasted with the slight chill of a late-January evening.

But she knew better than to complain. Outside her home in Paris, snow likely dotted the pavers, and it would be weeks before she could don the comfortable muslin dress she now wore. Celine recalled when she'd fashioned it last June, from the remnants of an elegant tea gown she'd designed for a wealthy woman known for hosting infamous salons. At the time, Celine imagined attending one of these gatherings and mingling with the chicest members of Parisian society. She would dazzle them with her love of Shakespeare and Voltaire. She would wear this exact dress, its rich aubergine hue a lovely contrast against her fair skin, the overskirt replete with elaborate frills and flounces. And she would style her black curls in a mass atop her crown, the latest coiffure to grace the city's fashion plates.

Celine laughed to herself, amused by the memory of the seventeen-year-old girl she used to be. The things this girl had dreamed of experiencing. The things she'd wished to have and hold: entrée into the society of elegant young women she fitted for gowns they would discard days later. A chance to fall in love with a handsome young man who would steal her heart with poetry and promises.

Now she sneered at the very idea.

After weeks at sea—buried deep in a timber trunk—the rumpled gown Celine wore tonight reflected the sharp turn her life had taken. It wasn't fit for Sunday Mass, much less a salon. At the thought, Celine adjusted her position on the wooden seat, her corset digging into her ribs. The whalebone pinched her breasts as she took a deep breath.

And was met with a scent so delicious, it left her distracted.

She scanned the square for its source. On the corner opposite the live oak stood an open-air bakery that reminded Celine of her favorite boulangerie on the Boulevard du Montparnasse. The smell of fried dough and slowly melting sugar wafted through the waxy magnolia leaves. Nearby, a set of balcony shutters slammed shut, and a trellis laden with bright pink bougainvillea shook, the blossoms trembling as if in fear. Or perhaps in anticipation.

It should have been beautiful to behold. But the lovely tableau felt tinged with something sinister. As though a pale finger had slipped through a drawn curtain, beckoning her into a dark abyss.

Wisdom told her to heed the warning. Nevertheless, Celine found herself enchanted. When she glanced at the six other girls in the wagon—seated four on one side, three on the other—Celine caught an expanse of wide-eyed gazes, their expressions a study in trepidation. Or perhaps excitement? Like the bougainvillea, it was impossible to be certain.

The wagon paused on a bustling street corner, the large draft horse at its lead tossing its mane. People in all manner of dress—from the wealthy with their golden watch chains to the humble with their threadbare linen—crossed Decatur Street, their steps focused and harried, as though they were on a mission. It felt unusual for a time of day marked by endings rather than beginnings.

Since Pippa was situated closest to the driver, she leaned forward to address him. "Is there something of note occurring tonight? Something to explain the gathering crowd?"

"The parade," the gruff man replied, without turning around.

"Pardon?"

He cleared his throat. "There's a parade gettin' started near Canal Street. On account of the carnival season."

"A carnival parade!" Pippa exclaimed, turning toward Celine.

Antonia—the young woman seated at Celine's left—looked

about excitedly, her dark eyes round and bright, like those of an owl. "Um carnaval?" she asked in Portuguese as she pointed toward the sounds of distant revelry.

Celine nodded with a smile.

"It's a shame we'll miss seeing it," Pippa said.

"I wouldn't worry, lass," the driver replied, his tongue rolling over the words with a hint of Irish burr. "There'll be plenty o' parades and celebrations all month long during the carnival season. You'll see one, to be sure. And just you wait for the masquerade ball on Mardi Gras. 'Twill be the finest of them all."

"I heard talk about the carnival season from a friend in Edinburgh," Anabel—a lissome redhead with an attractive smattering of freckles across her nose—exclaimed. "The entire city of New Orleans rings in the time before Lent with soirées and balls and costume parties for weeks on end."

"Parties!" the twins from Germany repeated as soon as they recognized the word, one of them clapping her hands with delight.

Their glowing faces struck Celine. Moved something behind her heart. An emotion she'd banned herself from feeling ever since the events of that dreadful night:

Hope.

She'd arrived in a city amid celebration. One with weeks of fêtes to come. The crowd was filled with that same spirit of anticipation she saw in the girls who now shared her fate. Maybe their expressions did not have to be about trepidation. Maybe the bougainvillea was simply jostled awake instead of trembling with worry.

Maybe Celine did not have to live her life in fear of what might happen tomorrow.

As they waited for the streets to clear of passing pedestrians, Celine leaned forward, her spirits on the cusp of taking flight. She tried to catch a bit of ivy dangling from an intricate wrought-iron railing. The clattering of footsteps to her left stole her attention as the crowd parted to allow their wagon through.

No.

It was not to allow them passage.

It was for something else entirely.

There—beneath the amber haze of a gas lamp—stood a lone figure poised to cross Decatur Street, a Panama hat pulled low on his brow, shrouding his features.

Without hesitation, their driver granted the man immediate deference, dipping his head in the figure's direction as though he were bowing . . . or perhaps keeping his eyes averted.

The man crossed the road, moving from light to shadow and back again, gliding from one street corner to another. He moved . . . strangely. As though the air around him were not air at all, but water. Or perhaps smoke. His polished shoes struck the cobblestones at a clipped pace. He was tall. Broad shouldered. Despite the evening silhouette about him, Celine could tell his suit was made of exquisite material, by a practiced hand. Likely Savile Row. Her training at Madame de Beauharnais' atelier—the finest couturière in Paris—had granted her a particular eye for such things.

But his clothes did not intrigue Celine nearly as much as what he'd managed to achieve. He'd cleared the street without uttering a single word. He'd scattered women with parasols and children with powdery beignets and men in elegant top hats, with nary a glance in their direction.

That was the kind of magic she wished to possess.

Celine craved the idea of wielding such power, simply for the freedom it would afford her. She watched the man step up to the curb, envy clouding her gaze, filling her heart, taking place of the hope she'd barely allowed purchase a minute ago.

Then he looked up. His eyes met hers as though she'd called out to him, without words.

Celine blinked.

He was younger than she'd expected. Not much older than she. Nineteen or twenty, perhaps, no more. Later Celine would try to remember details about him. But it was as though her memory of that moment had gone hazy, like oil swiped across the surface of a mirror. The only thing she remembered with distinct clarity was his eyes. They shone in the flame of the gas lamp as though they were lit from within.

Dark grey. Like the barrel of a gun.

He narrowed his gaze. Tipped his hat at her. And walked away.

"Oh, my stars," Pippa breathed.

Murmurs of assent—spoken in several languages—rippled across the rows of seated young women. They leaned into each other, an air of shared excitement passing over them. One of the twins from Düsseldorf said something in German that made her sister titter behind her hands.

Only Celine continued staring at the rapidly receding figure, her eyes narrowed, as his had been. As though she were in disbelief.

Of what, she did not know.

Their wagon continued making its way toward the convent. Celine watched the boy fade into the darkness, his long, lean legs carrying him through the night with an otherworldly confidence.

She wondered what made everyone at the crossing yield to him without question. Longed for the barest measure of it. Perhaps if Celine were someone to command such respect, she would not have been forced to leave Paris. To lie to her father.

Or murder a man.

To the Stars

————⬥⬥⬥————

I shouldn't be here.

That thought rang in Noémie's head like an endless refrain.

It was dark. Late. The water lapped along the pier at the edge of the Vieux Carré, the sound lulling. Hypnotic.

She never should have agreed to meet anyone in this place, no matter the enticement. Noémie knew better. Her parents had taught her better. The church had taught her better. She drew her light spring shawl around her shoulders and straightened the pink silk ribbon around her neck. When she turned, her garnet earbobs struck the sensitive skin along her jawline.

Earbobs and silk ribbons, on a pier in the middle of the night?

What was she thinking?

I shouldn't be here. Whom did she expect to impress with such fripperies?

Not this kind of man, to be sure.

Any young man who asked to meet her in the dead of night was not a gentleman. But Noémie supposed the kind of woman who agreed was not quite a lady either. She sighed to herself.

Martin, her erstwhile beau, never would have invited her to a clandestine meeting long past sunset.

Of course, Martin had never made her skin tingle or her breath catch in her throat.

Not like her mysterious admirer had.

But if he didn't show his face soon, Noémie would go home, sneak back through her mother's wisteria, and slip into the window of her bedroom before anyone was the wiser.

Noémie paced along the length of the pier, swearing to the stars that this was the last chance she would give him. Beneath her skirts, her booted heels struck the warped wooden boards, her bustle bobbing in time with her steps. A breeze swept along the bend in the river, bringing with it the stench of spoiling fish—remnants of the day's catch.

In an effort to ward off the smell, she pressed a bare finger beneath her nose.

I shouldn't be here. The pier was too close to the Court's lair. These streets and everything surrounding them were controlled by its shadowy denizens. Never mind that they routinely donated to the church. Never mind that Le Comte de Saint Germain had box seats to the opera and hobnobbed with New Orleans' best and brightest. The Court brought with them the worst kind of people, those without scruples.

And here Noémie was, waiting alone in the dark, in the thick of their domain.

She touched her throat, her fingers grazing the soft silk there. The color of her ribbon—pale pink, like the petals of a peony— was all the rage right now. Empress Eugénie had first ushered it into fashion not long ago. Now countless young ladies of New Orleans were keen to put their long, swanlike necks on display. Supposedly the gentlemen favored it.

With a bitter smile, Noémie faced out to the water for her final trek along the pier.

Damn her impressive admirer and all his lies. No amount of sweet words or scintillating promises should have drawn Noémie from the safety of her home.

Just as she was about to reach the end of the pier, the thud of solid footsteps resounded behind her. They slowed as they neared, moving at their master's leisure.

Noémie did not turn immediately, wanting him to know she was angry.

"You kept me waiting a long time," she said, her voice honeyed.

"My sincerest apologies, mon amour," he breathed from behind her. "I was caught up at dinner . . . but I left before dessert."

A smile tugged at Noémie's lips, her pulse racing. She turned slowly.

No one was there. The pier looked deserted.

She blinked. Her heart skipped about in her chest. Had Noémie dreamed the whole thing? Had the wind played a trick on her? "Where did you—"

"I'm here, my love," he said in her ear, behind her once more. She gasped. He took her by the hand, his touch cool and steady. Reassuring. A jolt passed down her spine as he nibbled along her earlobe. Shockingly. Teasingly.

Martin would never do such a thing.

She reached back to caress his face, the scruff on his jaw abrading her skin, the blood soaring through her veins. He kissed her fingertips. When she pulled away, her hands were warm. Sticky. Wet.

Stained bright red.

"Je suis désolé," he murmured an apology.

A horrified scream began to collect in Noémie's chest.

Her swanlike throat was torn out before she could utter a sound.

The last thing Noémie saw were the stars winking merrily above.

Your Name Is Marceline Béatrice Rousseau

———◦◦◇◦◦———

S even girls took up residence in the dormitory of the Ur-
suline convent: Celine; Pippa; the twins from Düsseldorf,
Marta and Maria; Anabel, the redhead from Edinburgh;
Antonia from Lisbon; and Catherine from Liverpool.

The Catholic Church had sponsored their passage to New
Orleans, and in return, these seven young women were expected to help run its attached hospital, teach the young girls
who attended school there, and assist in any efforts to raise
funds on behalf of the diocese. That is, until the sisters of the
convent were able to find appropriate matches for them.

For Celine, the day following their arrival was a day marked
by consternation.

A day marked by the choices of others.

More than anything, she did not want the sisters to place her
as a teacher. It was such a vaunted position, with so much responsibility. Celine had never been an appropriate role model.
She laughed too loudly at bawdy jokes and enjoyed eating at
social events at which girls were to be seen rather than sated.
She'd never understood the notion. Turn her back on a pain au
chocolat? Sacrilege.

But all too expected.

For these reasons, Celine was relieved to learn that Catherine had been a governess for a family of four in Liverpool. The spectacled young woman smiled when told she would essentially be resuming her duties.

Celine would not have minded being placed in the hospital, but Pippa informed her that Marta and Maria had assisted a midwife in Düsseldorf; thusly, they were recruited there along with Antonia, who was an expert in herbs and other natural remedies.

Soon Pippa, Anabel, and Celine found themselves in a shared predicament. All three girls proved difficult to place within the whitewashed walls, as their respective interests did not naturally segue into life at the convent. Anabel possessed a head for figures and a knack for business, neither of which was a quality to admire in a young woman.

Pippa had studied art history most of her life and was an accomplished violinist and painter, but the school already had a teacher specializing in the arts.

Though no one could deny that Celine's work with ruched silk and delicate Alençon lace was unmatched, it did her no favors here. Knowing how to design gowns for the Parisian elite was not exactly high on the list of achievements at a convent.

Which was why Pippa, Anabel, and Celine were sitting in the shade of Saint Louis Cathedral a week after their arrival, peddling their wares beneath a lace of oak leaves in Jackson Square. Despite the lovely warm day, Celine could not help but feel forlorn. Every place she went, life insisted on confining her.

Perhaps she deserved it. Her sins were many, her pardons few.

On the corner of the square farthest from Celine, beignets were being served alongside steaming cups of café au lait, the scent an intoxicating mixture of butter, sugar, and chicory. At her left, the cathedral's spires rose into a blue sky offset by the kind of clouds Celine most loved, for they resembled chiffon. To her right sat a row of artists and traders and purveyors of mystical goods, their merchandise positioned along the tines of black iron enclosing the cathedral's courtyard.

Celine wanted to stroll the lanes and peruse their many offerings. Take in the city's sights and relish this newfound chance at life. But—as she'd come to realize in the past week—the things she wanted and the things expected of her were like oil and water in a baker's mixing bowl.

The day the other girls were placed in their respective positions, Pippa, Celine, and Anabel had been instructed to raise money for the expansion of the parish orphanage. They'd devoted the following week to its preparation.

Pippa had painted delicate teacups with religious vignettes, like the time Jesus had turned water to wine or fed a crowd of thousands with nothing but seven loaves and fishes. Anabel had designed their booth and devised the best way to attract people to it. And Celine had embellished small squares of pressed linen with a scalloped edging that mimicked the finest needlepoint lace.

Since their arrival in port last week, none of them had been permitted to attend a parade. Instead, every night—once they'd completed their designated tasks—they were directed to read vespers aloud to each other before retiring to their cells.

Yes. Their rooms were called cells. It was the reason Celine had stitched a cheeky set of letters into the edging of each handkerchief she'd fashioned.

GTTAN

A nod to her favorite Shakespearean tragedy, *Hamlet*.

"Get thee to a nunnery."

Celine studied the five letters of script hidden in the complicated swirls of lace, a flicker of joy warming through her. Then she glanced across the rickety wooden table, her heart growing heavier with each passing second.

Was this all she could expect of life?

Her features hardened. Celine sat up straight, the whalebone of her corset catching her breath as it stretched across her chest. She should be grateful to be here. Grateful to have a place among decent people. Grateful for another chance at life.

Determination took root inside her. She smiled brightly to a potential patron, who failed to acknowledge her presence. Celine swallowed her looming scowl before shifting her attention to a pair of young women critiquing the glazing on a porcelain cup Pippa had completed days earlier.

"Lovely, don't you think?" the girl on the left murmured to her friend.

The other girl glanced about distractedly. "It's not bad, if you favor that sort of thing," she drawled, tucking a strand of wayward brown hair beneath her straw hat. Her voice faded to a hush. "But did you hear what the dockworkers discovered at the pier yesterday morning?"

The first girl nodded once. "Richard told me. Her name was Nathalie or Noémie something-or-other." Unease marred her expression. "He suspects the Court might be responsible, since it happened near their domain."

Court? Celine wondered. As far as she knew, there had never been an American monarchy.

"Like an animal had mauled her!" The brunette shuddered. "Poor soul," she tsked, though her eyes gleamed with unspoken thoughts, "left to rot in the sun alongside the day's catch. If the Court had anything to do with it, they've become even more ruthless than before. Not that it matters. They'll curry the right favor, as they always do."

Despite Celine's better judgment, her interest was piqued. She craned her neck toward the pair.

The brunette continued, her words breathless. "Did Richard tell you what happened to her head?"

"N-no."

"I heard it was completely severed from the poor young woman's body."

The first girl gasped, a lace-gloved hand covering her mouth. "Dear Lord."

With a solemn nod, the brunette picked up one of Celine's embroidered handkerchiefs. "Her face was all but unrecognizable. Her father had to identify her based on her earbobs alone."

At this, Pippa cleared her throat in an unmistakable attempt to dissuade the two women from continuing such salacious talk. A frown cut across Anabel's face, her look turning peevish.

"Ladies, can we be of any assistance?" Celine offered the pair of young patrons a pointed smile.

The brunette's eyes narrowed as she dropped the handkerchief with a careless flick of her wrist. "No, thank you." She reached for her friend's elbow, looping her arm around it, directing them away from the rickety table.

Once they were beyond earshot, Anabel harrumphed. "Gossiping about a murder in the shadow of a church . . ." she muttered. "Dinna they ken better than to provoke the spirits in such a brash manner?" Her Scottish brogue deepened with her disdain, her fingers batting away a fat honeybee buzzing about her brow.

Pippa sighed, then caught Anabel's hand, preventing her from swatting at the hovering insect. "That poor girl." She sat up straighter, her petite features gathering. "I hope her suffering wasn't prolonged. Who could do such a thing?" Lines formed between her brows. "What kind of monster could take a human life like that?"

Anabel nodded crisply. "I hope the fiend responsible burns in Hell for all eternity. 'Tis the only justice for a murderer."

A hint of color threatened to creep up Celine's neck. She rolled her shoulders back, calming the storm in her chest. A bead of sweat collected in the hollow of her throat before sliding between her caged breasts. "I completely agree," she said lamely. The words felt ashen on her tongue. Celine twined her fingers together, praying for an end to the discussion.

Thankfully, it appeared both Pippa and Anabel were in agreement. The trio recommenced their efforts to raise money for the church with renewed vigor, standing in tandem to greet another group of potential patrons.

Most of the passersby paused to consider the jars of mayhaw jelly and lemon pear marmalade the girls stationed in the kitchen had finished preparing yesterday. Not a soul cared to while away a moment perusing the painted cups or the elegantly folded handkerchiefs.

Gloom took refuge on Celine's shoulders, like a beast settling in the shadows. She glanced about, searching for a source of comfort. At least none of the people assembling before them mentioned the ghastly murder that had occurred within sighting distance of Jackson Square.

Celine supposed that reprieve—at the very least—was something for which to be grateful.

———◇———

After three hours of little success, Celine's gloom had become a thing with teeth. Rays of sunlight continued to slide ever closer, the heat growing oppressive, making her long for the comfort of nightfall. Even the branches above felt burdened by the weight of the sultry air, their blossoms like eyelids, growing heavier and sleepier with each passing moment. Pippa's blond curls began to frame her face like a damp halo. Anabel tightened the yellow ribbon about her brow and sighed loudly. It appeared her patience had run thin as well.

The slender Scotswoman twisted an auburn curl around her

index finger and yanked it straight, her freckled nose wrinkling. "*Och*, it's as hot as a witch's cauldron. And just how are we to meet any eligible young men when all our days are spent raising money and all our nights are spent in prayer?"

There were many things Celine wished to say in response. She chose the least offensive option. "Perhaps it would be better if our nights were spent raising money instead." Her cheerful sarcasm failed to strike a chord with Anabel. The redhead stared at her with a confused expression.

But Pippa could always be counted on to understand her friend's dark sense of humor. She shot Celine a look, her lips twitching. Then she turned her graceful head back toward Anabel. "Maybe finding a husband shouldn't be our only concern?"

"Aye, it shouldna, but I'll tell ye, a sturdy young man would be a nice distraction from all this humdrum."

"Or he could make it worse." Pippa adjusted the slender chain of the golden cross around her neck. "In my experience, sturdy young men don't always improve upon the company."

Celine fought back the urge to smile. This was precisely the reason she and Pippa had been drawn to each other before setting sail. Neither of them harbored delusions when it came to the opposite sex. Of course Celine wanted to know why Pippa did not yearn to find a match, but she knew better than to ask.

A petite blonde with a heart-shaped face and sapphire-blue eyes, Pippa drew ample notice wherever she went. Men often tipped their hat to her appreciatively. Even more importantly, she possessed a mind as sharp as a tack. It should have been the work of a moment for her to find love. But instead of settling down in her homeland, Pippa had braved the wilds of a new country, far across the Atlantic.

The day they met, this had struck Celine as highly curious. But she kept her thoughts to herself. She had no intention of taking part in the discussion that would likely follow. If she asked, they would ask in return, and these were questions Celine did not want to answer. Any interest in her past—beyond the bare minimum—was a thing to be avoided at all cost.

For numerous reasons.

The afternoon Celine had embarked on the *Aramis*, it had not escaped her notice that all the girls on board were light-skinned, most without a hint of foreign blood among them. Antonia—the girl from Portugal—possessed a complexion that easily browned in the sun, but even she had spent most of the journey below deck to ward away any suggestion of color.

If they knew where Celine's mother was from. If they knew she was not fully of Anglo-Saxon heritage . . .

It was a secret she and her father had kept from the moment they'd first arrived in Paris thirteen years ago, when Celine was scarcely four years old. Though France was not as infamous for its racial divide as America had been in recent years, it nevertheless harbored a seething undercurrent of tension. One that often implied how inappropriate it was for the races to mix. This notion proved true the world over. In areas beyond New Orleans, there were even laws forbidding people of different colors from congregating in the same room.

Celine's mother had been from the Orient. Upon completing

his time at Oxford, her father had followed his passion for languages to Eastern shores. He'd crossed paths with Celine's mother in a small village along the southern coast of a rocky peninsula. Celine had never known where, though she'd often inquired as a child, only to be rebuffed.

"It doesn't matter who you were," her father had argued. "It matters who you *are*."

It rang true then, like it did now.

As a result, Celine knew precious little about her mother. The recollections she had of her first few years of life along a Far East coast were fleeting. They flickered across her thoughts from time to time, but never fully took shape. Her mother was a woman who smelled of safflower oil and fed her fruit each night and sang to her in a distant memory. Nothing more.

But if anyone looked closely—studied Celine's features with a practiced gaze—they might notice the edges of her upturned eyes. The high planes of her cheekbones, and the thick strands of dark hair. The skin that stayed fair in winter, yet bronzed with ease in the summer sun.

"Your name is Marceline Béatrice Rousseau," her father would say whenever she asked about her mother, his brow stern. "That is all anyone need know about you."

Celine had molded this into a motto by which to live. It did not matter that it left half the pages of her book empty. It did not matter one bit.

"Is this for sale, mademoiselle?" a young woman asked loudly, as if she were addressing an imbecile. Her light brown eyes darted to one of Celine's lace-embroidered handkerchiefs.

Startled, Celine responded in a curt tone, the words falling from her lips before she could catch them. "I should hope so, or else I have no idea what in hell I've been doing here for the last three hours."

To her left, she heard Anabel gasp and Pippa swallow a snicker. Celine grimaced, then tried to smile while angling her head upward, only to be blinded by a flash of sunlight.

Undeterred by Celine's rudeness, the girl standing on the opposite side of the rickety table grinned down at her. A jolt of discomfort passed through Celine's stomach when she took in the full breadth of the young lady's appearance.

In a word, the girl looked exquisite. Her features were like those of a doll, her brunette head high and proud. Eyes the color of rich honey gazed down at Celine with steady appraisal. At her throat—pinned to a fichu of Valenciennes lace—was a stunning ivory cameo surrounded by rubies. Across her shoulder lay a delicate parasol with a fringe of seed pearls, its rosewood handle engraved with a fleur-de-lis set in the mouth of a roaring lion. It matched well with the girl's Basque-style bodice, though the entire effect proved a bit outmoded.

The girl let her lace-gloved fingers graze over a handkerchief's scalloped edging. "This is superb work."

"Thank you." Celine inclined her head.

"Reminds me of something I saw the last time I was in Paris."

It was impossible to miss the excitement on Pippa's face. "Celine studied under one of the premier couturières there."

Celine pressed her lips together, cursing her pride. She never should have shared that particular detail with Pippa.

"Which one?" The girl raised her eyebrows at Celine.

"Worth's," Celine lied.

"Along Rue de la Paix?"

Celine swallowed. Then nodded. Already she could feel the urge to run from her skin take hold, and she had not even disclosed anything of significance. Nothing that would tie her to the events of that fateful night in the atelier.

"Is that so?" the girl said. Her dainty features set with conviction. "I'll take them all." She waved a hand over the handkerchiefs, as though she were casting a spell.

"All?" Anabel sputtered, the ends of her yellow ribbon fluttering in the heavy breeze. "Well, far be it from me to dissuade ye . . . Time and tide waits for no woman, and all that."

While Anabel collected the handkerchiefs to tally the total, Celine gazed at the girl standing before them, perplexed by the sudden turn of events. Something about her unnerved Celine. Like a memory she should recall. A word lost midsentence. A thought unraveling midair. The young woman allowed Celine's perusal, her grin growing wider with each passing second.

"If you studied with a couturière, are you able to design gowns?" the girl asked.

Again, Celine nodded. "Mais oui, bien sûr."

"Merveilleux!" She leaned closer, her eyes glinting like warm chalcedony. "I've been struggling with my current modiste, and I'm in desperate need of a costume for the masquerade ball on Mardi Gras next month. The Russian Grand Duke is to be the special guest this year, and I will need something memorable to mark the occasion. Something bright white and reminiscent of the French court before the revolution, I believe." She wrinkled her nose, as though she were about to share a delicious secret. "Really—despite all the ridiculousness with the pig chasing and the perfume—I do think it was one of the finest times for women's fashion in recent history, panniers and all." The girl drummed her gloved fingers along the edge of the wooden table, her head tilted in consideration. "I suppose you would need to measure me in order to begin the process?"

Another pert retort barreled from Celine's lips. "Yes, mademoiselle. That would be wise."

The center of the girl's eyes sparkled as though she could hear Celine's thoughts. "You're absolutely delightful. Like Bastien in a dress." She laughed to herself. "That snide fiend."

Lines of confusion gathered across Celine's forehead. Was the young woman insulting her or complimenting her?

"En tout cas . . ." the girl continued, her free hand waving through the air as if to disperse smoke. "Would it be possible for you to meet me later this evening?"

Celine thought quickly. The day after they'd arrived in port, the Mother Superior had cautioned them about venturing alone into the city at night, especially during carnival season. She'd spoken as though they were all foolish little lambs, and the Vieux Carré nothing but a hunting ground for wolves. Not to mention the fact that a violent death had occurred recently along the nearby pier.

Given all these facts, it was unlikely the Mother Superior would permit Celine to go.

With this realization came a surprising rush of

disappointment. Though Celine did not feel comfortable in the presence of this rambling, oddly attired girl, she nevertheless felt . . . intrigued. Even a tad bit reckless.

When the girl sensed Celine's reluctance, her lips puckered with displeasure. "Of course I will pay you handsomely."

Celine didn't doubt it. The ivory cameo alone was worth a fortune. But it was not about the money. It was about the rightness. She owed herself this second chance. And angering the Mother Superior seemed unwise.

"I'm sorry, mademoiselle." Celine shook her head. "I just don't think it would be possible. The Mother Superior would not permit it."

"I see." A long sigh passed the girl's lips. "Thus conscience doth make cowards of us all."

"Pardon?" Celine's eyes went wide. "Are you quoting . . . Shakespeare?"

And *Hamlet*, at that.

"The one and only." The girl grinned. "But, alas, I must be on my way. Is there no chance you might change your mind? You have but to name your price."

A flicker of amusement passed through Celine. Hours ago, from a place of insolence, she'd suggested it might be better to earn money beneath the light of the moon. Here was an offer to do so. One without limit.

In that moment—listening to this strange girl quote Shakespeare and tantalize her with possibility—Celine realized she wanted to go. Badly. It was the first time in recent memory she'd felt this particular spark of anticipation ignite within her.

She wanted to create something and be a part of the world instead of merely observing it. Already she'd begun envisioning ways to fashion the wide-hooped, baroque-style panniers. To construct a manteau with dripping pagoda sleeves. Her hesitation now was a last effort to hold firm to her convictions.

To obey. Be a model of humility. Earn a measure of God's forgiveness.

"If money does not entice you"—the girl leaned closer, and Celine caught a whiff of neroli oil and rosewater—"I can promise you an adventure . . . a trek through a den of lions."

That. That was it.

It was as though the girl had found a window into the darkest corner of Celine's heart.

"It would be my pleasure to design a dress for you, mademoiselle," Celine said. As soon as the words left her mouth, her pulse was set apace.

"I'm thrilled." Beaming, the girl withdrew an ecru card with gold calligraphy in its center. The script read

Jacques'

Beneath it was an address in the heart of the Vieux Carré, not too far from the convent.

"Come here this evening, around eight o'clock," she continued. "Disregard the queue outside. When a beautiful man with a voice like sin and a ring through his right ear demands to know what you are doing, tell him to bring you to Odette, tout de suite." She reached for Celine's hand. Through the lace of her glove, her touch felt cool. Calming. The girl's eyes widened for an instant, her grasp tentative at first. She canted her head, a half smile curving up her doll-like face. "It's lovely to meet you, Celine," she said warmly.

"It was lovely to meet you as well . . . Odette."

With another simpering grin, the girl named Odette sashayed away, the train of her bustle gliding in her wake. The next instant, Anabel turned toward Celine. "I ken I'm the last to go on about making mistakes, Celine, but I'm not sure what came over ye when ye agreed to meet this Odette creature tonight. Are ye touched? Ye canna leave the convent after dinner. The Mother Superior expressly forbade it. She said the happenings in the Quarter after sunset—"

"Promote the kind of licentious behavior that will not be tolerated beneath her roof," Celine finished in a weary voice. "I know. I was there."

"There's no need to be testy." Anabel blew back a tight red curl from her face. "I'm only worried what'll happen if you're caught."

"I thought you were tired of all the humdrum," Pippa teased.

Celine smiled, grateful to her friend for disarming the tension. "Ready to meet a sturdy young gentleman."

"In my mind, he doesn't even have to be young," Pippa continued.

"Or a gentleman," Celine finished.

"*Och*, you're terrible!" Color flooding her face, Anabel made the sign of the cross. "Enough to make me take to church."

Celine feigned ignorance, a black brow arching into her forehead. "I haven't the faintest idea what you're talking about."

"Don't be the wee hen that never laid away. Not with me, Mademoiselle Rousseau." Her eyes shifted to Celine's chest. "And certainly not with that bosom."

"What?" Celine blinked.

"Don't play the innocent," Pippa translated with laughter.

"What does that have to do with my . . . bosom?"

Pippa bit her lip. "It was said in jest, dear. You must know you have a lovely figure." She patted Celine's hand like she would a child's. The motion grated on Celine's nerves. "Don't take it to heart. Gifts were bestowed on you."

Gifts?

They thought her figure was a gift? The ridiculousness of it almost caused Celine to burst into laughter herself. There'd been a time when she'd appreciated her body for its beauty and resilience. But that time had passed. What she wouldn't give to be lithe and lean like Anabel. The "gifts" these girls chortled about now had brought Celine nothing but trouble.

And they'd left her far from innocent.

A flush rose in Celine's cheeks. It flared across her skin, hot and fast, as though—even in jest—these two girls could see the truth she labored to conceal every day of her life. The worst of her past washed through her memory. Blood seeped across her vision, the smell of warm copper filling her nose, leaching the light from the air.

But this was absurd. How would Pippa and Anabel know what she had done? Why she'd fled her home five weeks ago? Celine struggled to calm her nerves.

They wouldn't. No one would. As long as she didn't breathe a word.

Your name is Marceline Béatrice Rousseau. That is all anyone need know about you.

"I would never play the innocent, ladies." Celine winked and smiled brightly. "It just wouldn't suit."

MALVOLIO

—◦◦◇◇◦◦—

Anabel betrayed Celine at dinner, barely an hour after they'd returned to the convent.

It took the Mother Superior the work of an instant to draw out the truth from the loose-lipped girl. As soon as Anabel told the gathered young women that Celine's embroidered handkerchiefs had been purchased full price in one fell swoop, the hawk-eyed nun—with her perfectly pressed habit—had delved for details.

Alas, Anabel proved to be a terrible liar. For all the stories Celine had heard about Scots, she was profoundly disappointed to have met the only Highlander incapable of spinning a tale.

Now Celine was stuck reviewing the scenery in the Mother Superior's office, her dinner of bland stew going cold on the kitchen table. She searched the space for a distraction. All the while, she tried to devise a believable lie for why she should be permitted to wander into the city past nightfall.

It was all so dramatic. So unnecessary.

Why was it that everyone Celine encountered insisted on telling her how to live her life?

Pippa sat in guilty silence nearby, wringing her hands like a character from a cautionary tale. Celine inhaled deeply, aware that Philippa Montrose could not be counted on to support anything resembling perfidy. Pippa was simply too good. It was a truth universally acknowledged by all those residing at the convent, even the nuns themselves:

Pippa Montrose was trustworthy and obedient. Nothing like the impetuous Celine Rousseau.

In fact, why had Pippa been summoned here at all? She wasn't guilty of any wrongdoing. Was her presence an effort to highlight Celine's misdeeds? Or perhaps intimidate Pippa into betraying her as well?

Her gaze darkening at the thought, Celine scanned the room. On one side of the wall was a large wooden cross that had been donated by one of New Orleans' oldest Spanish families, from a time before the French had taken ownership of the port city. Beyond the partially opened shutters, a slit of waning sunlight bathed the outer reaches of the Ursuline convent.

If only the windows could be opened fully, to let the view of the port seep onto its sloping floors. Maybe it would fill these fallow rooms with life. The second day there, Celine had tried to do this herself, but she'd been roundly chastised ten minutes later; the windows of the whitewashed convent were always shuttered in an effort to maintain the cloistered atmosphere.

As though it could be anything else at all.

The door scraped open. Pippa sat up straight in the same instant Celine's shoulders fell.

Even before the Mother Superior stepped over the threshold, the wool of her black habit filled the room with her presence, smelling of lanolin and the medicinal ointment she used each night for her chapped hands.

The combination was like a wet hound in a haystack.

As soon as the door swung shut, the lines around the Mother Superior's mouth deepened. She paused for a breath, then glared down at them, her expression severe. An obvious effort to instill a sense of foreboding, like a tyrant of old.

Though it was inopportune, a smile threatened to take shape on Celine's face. Everything about this situation was absurd. Less than five weeks ago, Celine had been apprenticed to one of the most demanding couturières in Paris. A woman whose frequent screams of rage caused the crystals to tremble in their chandeliers. A true oppressor, who routinely ripped Celine's work to shreds—before her eyes—if a single stitch was out of place.

And this tyrannical nun with chapped hands thought she merited fear?

As Pippa would say, not bloody likely.

A snicker escaped Celine's mouth. Pippa toed her chair in response.

What could have caused the Mother Superior's hands to become so worn? Perhaps she labored on some clandestine craft, deep in the hollows of her cell. A painter perhaps. Or a sculptor. What if she was secretly a wordsmith by night? Even better if she wrote entirely in asides or things laced with double meaning, like Malvolio in *Twelfth Night*.

Be by my life, this is my lady's hand, these be her very C's, her U's and her T's and thus she makes her great P's.

Celine coughed. Creases of irritation formed across the Mother Superior's forehead.

The idea that this nun in a starched habit would say anything untoward caused Celine to lock eyes on the polished stone floor to keep from laughing. Pippa nudged her again, this time more forcefully. Though her friend said nothing, Celine could tell Pippa was not the least bit amused by their situation.

Rightly so. Nothing about angering the convent's matron should be funny. This woman had given them a place to live and work. A means by which to find their way in the New World.

Only an ungrateful, troublesome girl would see otherwise. A girl precisely like Celine.

Sobered by these thoughts, Celine chewed the inside of her cheek, the room growing warmer, her stays pulling tighter.

"I expect you to explain yourself, Mademoiselle Rousseau," the Mother Superior began in a voice that was tinny and gravelly all at once.

Celine kept silent, her eyes cast downward. She knew better than to begin by offering a defense. The Mother Superior had not called them here with a mind to listen; she'd called them here with a mind to teach. It was a lesson Celine understood well. She'd been raised on it.

"This young woman you met in the square, why does she not come to the convent in daylight or consult a local dressmaker?" the Mother Superior asked. "If she wishes to hire you to design garments for her, it seems fitting for her to come here, n'est-ce pas?"

When Celine still did not respond, the Mother Superior

grunted. Leaned closer. "Répondez-moi, Mademoiselle Rousseau. Immédiatement," she whispered, her tone laced with warning. "Or you and Mademoiselle Montrose will regret it."

At the threat, Celine raised her head to meet the Mother Superior's gaze. She licked her lips to bide time as she chose her next words.

"Je suis désolée, Mère Supérieure," Celine apologized, "mais"— she glanced to her right, trying to decide whether or not to involve Pippa in this falsehood—"but, alas, her modiste is unfamiliar with the baroque style of dress. She expressed urgency in needing the garments and a schedule that did not appear to be flexible during the day. You see . . . she volunteers each afternoon with a ladies' organization that knits socks for children."

Even in profile, Celine saw Pippa's eyes widen with dismay.

It was an abhorrent lie, to be sure. Fashioning Odette as an angel with a soft spot for barefooted souls was among the more . . . colorful stories Celine had told in her lifetime. But this entire situation was ridiculous. And Celine enjoyed prevailing over tyrants, even by the barest of measures. Especially ones who threatened her friends.

The Mother Superior's frown softened, though the rest of her expression remained doubtful. She linked her hands behind her back and began pacing. "Be that as it may, I do not feel it is appropriate for you to travel through the city unescorted past sundown. A young woman not much older than you . . . perished along the docks only yesterday."

In Celine's opinion, *perished* was a rather subdued word for being ripped to pieces beneath a starlit sky.

The Mother Superior paused in silent prayer before resuming her lecture. "During carnival season, there are many revelers in the streets. Sin runs rampant, and I do not wish for a mind as weak and susceptible as yours to be lured by danger."

Though Celine bristled at the slight, she nodded in agreement. "I, too, do not wish to be tempted by anything untoward." She pressed a hand over her heart. "But I believe this young woman to be good and God-fearing, Mère Supérieure. And the money she will give the convent for my work would undoubtedly be of great benefit to us all. She made it clear—several times—that cost was not an object."

"I see." The Mother Superior turned toward Pippa without warning. "Mademoiselle Montrose," she said, "it appears you have little to offer on the matter. What have you to say about this situation?"

Celine closed her eyes, bracing herself for what was to come. She wouldn't blame Pippa for telling the truth. It was simply in her nature to do so. And who could blame Pippa for following her natural inclination.

Pippa cleared her throat, her small hands tightening into fists. "I . . . found the young lady quite trustworthy and virtuous as well, Mother Superior," she said slowly. "Of course your concerns are not without merit, especially given what happened along the docks. Would it make a difference if I offered to accompany her? We could take the lady's measurements together and then be on our way. I don't believe we would be gone from the convent for long. In fact, I see no reason why we would have to miss evening prayer."

Time ground to a halt. It was Celine's turn to have her eyes widen with dismay.

Pippa Montrose had offered to help. Had lied for Celine. To a *nun*.

"I have many misgivings, Mademoiselle Montrose," the Mother Superior said after a breath. "But perhaps if you are willing to provide escort . . ."

"I am willing to take full responsibility." Pippa grasped the tiny gold crucifix nestled at the hollow of her throat. She let her voice drop. Let it fill with reverence. "And I trust God will go with us tonight."

The Mother Superior frowned again, her lips unspooling slowly. Her attention shifted from Pippa toward Celine and back again. She stood straight. And made a decision.

"Very well," she said.

A flare of surprise shot through Celine. The Mother Superior had shifted tack too quickly. Too easily. Suspicion gnawed at Celine's stomach. She eyed Pippa sidelong, but her friend did not glance her way.

"Thank you, Mother Superior," Pippa murmured. "I promise all will go as planned."

"Of course. As long as you understand I've put my full trust in you, Mademoiselle Montrose. Do not disappoint me." The nun's smile was disturbingly beatific. "May His light shine upon you both, my children."

———◦◦◇◦◦———

I first glimpse my next victim as she passes beneath the flame of a gas lamp.

Her eyes flash in a most curious way. As though she is on edge or held in suspense. Perhaps in the midst of doing something illicit.

The sight catches my attention, even through the horde of bustling bodies, a handful of them brimming with otherworldly energy. Her unease looks strangely beguiling, for it is the opposite of performative. She is heedless of everything around her, save the task at hand. It is a difficult undertaking for a hapless mortal, to move about a crowd so blissfully unaware. So enviably unaffected.

Crowds fascinate me. They provide demons such as myself with unique opportunities. Occasions to be seen and unseen in the same breath. For are we not always—human and creature alike—performing to some degree?

I digress.

The moment I enjoy most is when I first begin scanning the masses. When I first lay eyes on my target, and they know not that they are being watched. They act without thought. Smile without agenda. Laugh as though not a soul is listening.

I know what this must sound like. It sounds . . . disconcerting. I am aware. But I am by nature disconcerting. There are moments in which I can be delightful, too. I speak many languages. I have traveled the world twice over. I can sing the entirety of Verdi's *Aida* without the need of sheet music.

Do I not deserve a modicum of consideration for these and many other achievements?

I would like to think so, though I know it to be impossible.

Demons should not be granted the indulgence of men. So sayeth man, at least.

But I'll share a secret. In my years, I have discovered it is possible to be both disconcerting and delightful all at once. Wine can be delicious though it muddles the mind. A mother may love and hate her children in the span of the same afternoon.

And a predator could abhor itself even as it relishes its evening meal.

I understand my behavior might be construed as odd. Unseemly. But I am a thing of oddity. A creature born apart from this world.

Don't fret on my account. I have never been one of those immortals who enjoy toying with their food, nor do I particularly like stalking my prey. I am not looking for their weaknesses; rather, I am understanding their humanity. There is something . . . wrong with treating a living being as though it exists purely for my own sport. Every action I undertake has a purpose. It is the characteristic that distinguishes me from many beings of the Otherworld.

My convictions.

I feel keenly the loss of any life taken. The kill last week along the pier did not thrill me in any way. It was necessarily gruesome, in a manner I typically eschew, especially for such an indiscriminate death. I brought about the girl's end simply to see what was possible. To see what kind of attention it would draw. Alas, it did not have the effect I hoped, for my enemy remains above the authorities' notice. It appears a more lasting impression must be left with my next victim. A more direct assault, upon my enemy's doorstep.

Each death to come will be felt all the more keenly. That is of primary importance.

For though I may disdain wanton bloodshed, I am not impervious to the draw of the hunt. A friend from childhood used to say she knew when an animal had perished in agony. She could taste it, and it ruined the meal for her.

I find I am inclined to agree. There is also a certain allure to knowing what will happen next, before anyone else does. Perhaps it is a result of my unconventional upbringing. Or maybe it is simply human nature.

And I was human. Once.

A part of me still longs to be.

Maybe that is what draws me to the liveliness of the French Quarter. I avoided hunting in it for many years, because its corners contained memories not soon forgotten. Images of pain and loss and heartbreak. But I've returned to my old haunt after too long a time, for I have an ancient score to settle. A final performance to give.

Sacro fremito di gloria / Tutta l'anima m'investe.

A sacred thrill of glory / Runs through my heart.

Perhaps I am still human after all.

A Touch of Violence

——◦◦◇◦◦——

C eline!" Pippa called out as Celine whirled into the crowd, her steps surefooted. Free. "Slow down. There's no need to move about so quickly."

Celine halted in her tracks, excitement sparking in her chest. The beat of a distant drum met with the clash of cymbals. Soon thereafter, trumpets pealed into the vibrant night air. A sultry breeze toyed with the ends of the black satin ribbon about her throat, caressing her collarbone. Though she kept still, her heart reached for the music, as if it called to something deep in her bones. It never ceased to amaze her, how she seemed to thrive under cover of darkness. How she fell more in love with the moon every night.

Each evening—despite the thick walls of the convent—Celine's toes had tapped alongside the melodies of the passing carnival parades. Rhythms and timbres and crescendos of sound she'd never before heard had captured her attention, stealing her thoughts from the word of God. She was not alone in this. Antonia's fingers had frozen above the pages of vespers, her mind transfixed as well. Even Pippa had smiled at the music.

And here they were now, given a chance to revel in the heart of it all.

The parade drew closer, the crowd around them spilling into the side streets of the Vieux Carré. Temporary vendors began rolling carts of food and drink onto its corners, adding layer upon layer to the sights and smells and sounds collecting about the space: spice and earth and the clash of metal against stone. Celine shifted with the sea of moving bodies, dragging Pippa in her wake. When they turned the corner, a delicious scent—unlike any Celine had ever known—permeated the air.

"Cochon de lait!" a man with a soot-caked mustache called out in a strange French accent. He hovered above what looked like a beast of iron and black smoke about the size of a large trunk. When he rolled back its lid, Celine saw meat roasting above a makeshift spit, the aroma of burning pecan wood and sugarcane wafting through it. He poured a concoction that smelled of melted butter, white wine, hot peppers, and minced garlic all over the smoked cochon. A delicious steam sizzled from the smoldering embers, weaving through and around them. Then the man with the mustache poked a large fork in one side of the meat, and a piece of cochon fell from the bone onto a waiting piece of bread. Immediately a crowd formed a queue around the man and his iron beast.

Celine desperately wished she carried with her a single coin. A single chance to partake in something so mouthwatering. She knew it was a bad idea to move closer to the merriment of the incoming parade, but it had been so long since this kind of unbridled joy had taken root in her heart. She supposed that was the way of it, when one was guilty of committing unspeakable acts like murder.

Joy did not live in a heart full of fear.

Pippa saw the look on her face. "We can't linger here, Celine," she said in a grim tone. "We can't watch the parade."

"I know." Celine inhaled deeply. "I'm just imagining that we could. That we did. And it was glorious."

A sympathetic smile curled up Pippa's face. "I want to see it, too. But if the Mother Superior finds out we disregarded her wishes—that we did not go straight to our meeting and immediately return—she'll never let us venture into the city alone again."

"Of course." Celine nodded. But her feet remained fixed to one spot.

"Please," Pippa continued, taking her hand. "Life is much more difficult when those around us do not have faith in us."

Celine sighed. As usual, Pippa wasn't wrong. In the past, Celine's penchant for recklessness had proved problematic. Disastrous on at least one occasion. The sense of joy that had bloomed in her chest only a moment before wilted like a rose beneath the hot sun.

"You're right," Celine said softly. Regretfully. She turned away from the crowd and all its delightful promises.

Pippa linked arms with her as they began walking in the opposite direction. "I just don't have the same sense of adventure as you."

"I'm not sure about that." Celine grinned. "You did board a ship sailing into the unknown." *And lie for me tonight,* she added without words.

It was impossible to miss the dark cloud passing over Pippa's features. Curiosity warmed through Celine again. It was the first time in five weeks that she'd seen a shadow descend on Pippa's face when confronted with questions concerning her past.

Was it possible Pippa harbored a dark secret as well?

It just seemed so unlikely.

"There was nothing left for me in Liverpool," Pippa began, as though she could read Celine's mind, "except my family's good name and a legacy of debt. My father . . . wasted his life and our fortunes in gambling hells and in the arms of fallen women." She winced. "It was better that I leave and make my own path."

Anyone listening would sense how much it pained Pippa to disclose these truths. A part of Celine felt honored that Pippa had chosen to confide in her. She wrapped her arm more tightly around Pippa's, but could not ignore the dread coiling through her stomach.

Pippa would expect Celine to return the gesture. To trust her with details of Celine's past. Sure enough, Pippa gazed at Celine as they made their way down the Avenue des Ursulines. Celine did not need to ask why. Her friend waited expectantly for Celine to offer her own tale of woe.

To share her painful truth.

More than anything, Celine wished to tell Pippa what had happened. But how would Pippa—her only friend in the New World—look upon her if she learned Celine had killed a man and fled Paris in the aftermath? Pippa had said it herself: what kind of monster takes a human life? At best she would stop looking upon Celine with the eyes of a friend. At worst?

Celine shuddered to think.

The result would be the same: she would have no one. So Celine kept to her story, offering Pippa a shrug of her shoulders. A dismissive smile.

"I completely understand about wanting to make your own way," she said. "There was nothing left for me in Paris. It was better for me to begin anew elsewhere, too."

Pippa said nothing. For a time she did not look away from Celine. Then she nodded, as though she'd made a decision to leave things be. For now.

———◇———

The two girls made their way down Rue Royale, on the lookout for a sign that read *Jacques'*. As they turned a corner, they passed a narrow side street that reeked suspiciously of refuse. The alleyway was unlit. Removed from the realm of civilized folk.

Celine stopped short when the suggestion of a scuffle emanated from its shadows. It struck her like a bolt of lightning, electricity sizzling across her skin. A man cried out, begging for his life in a guttural mix of French and English. His words were followed by the sound of a fist against flesh.

What if a murder was occurring only steps from where they stood?

Celine knew it was wiser to continue on their course. To remain ambivalent. Safe.

But if a monster takes a life, what kind of creature refuses to save one?

Pippa tugged on Celine's arm. Celine ignored her. Someone was being beaten to death in the alley, without recourse. The parable of the Good Samaritan rang in her ears, admonishing her to take notice. To act.

The man cried out again, and Celine took a step closer.

"Celine!" Pippa exclaimed in a loud whisper.

"Who's there?" a deep voice called from the alleyway's obscured center.

Without blinking an eye, Celine yanked Pippa into a fall of nearby shadows, her heart thudding in her chest. She peered around the corner—into the narrow alleyway—allowing her sight to adjust to the darkness.

"We shouldn't be here," Pippa whispered in Celine's ear, her eyes wide with terror, her breaths heavy. "We should leave at—"

Celine pressed a finger to Pippa's mouth and shook her head. She focused on the scene unfolding in the depths of the small side street. It took an instant to form an understanding.

A man lay on his side amid a pile of desiccated fruit peelings, his words garbled, his predicament clear. One hand was raised in supplication. His shoulders shook uncontrollably.

Two other men stood on either side of this poor soul, bracketing him like a pair of suited specters. Through the darkness, the shorter man lit a cheroot. A flash of firelight shone on a set of perfect white teeth and the bleached linen of his rolled shirtsleeves.

But it was not this man who caught Celine's notice.

It was the taller one standing to his right, watching the

violence unfold as though it were simple entertainment. A show performed onstage before a paying audience.

Atop his head, Celine recognized the tilt of a Panama hat.

Perhaps it was a coincidence. The boy she'd seen that first night—the one whose memory she'd struggled to conjure days later—could not be the only individual in New Orleans with a penchant for that style. But a deeper, more visceral part of Celine warned her not to put too much stock in coincidences.

"Please, Fantôme," the man cowering in the muck begged. "Pardonnez-moi." His voice trembled while he pleaded for forgiveness. He stretched a hand toward the figure in the Panama hat. The one he'd called the Ghost. An apt moniker for a creature so comfortable in the shadows.

"Apologies are nothing without amends, Lévêque," the Ghost said in a richly rasping tone, his broad back to Celine, making it hard to discern any of his features. Even in the subtlest of motions, he carried himself as many young men of pedigree did in Paris: without a care in the world. As though the very air he breathed were laced with diamond dust.

The thought alone enraged Celine.

Continuing, he said, "You were warned what would happen the next time you behaved with such disrespect." He nodded at the man smoking the cheroot, who rolled back his shirtsleeves to begin anew.

"Wait, wait, *wait!*" the cowering man said, his voice growing louder with each plea. He moved his forearm across his face to ward away the coming blows. "What do you want? Do you want me to apologize to her? I'll beg on my knees for Mademoiselle Valmont's forgiveness. I'll—"

"Alas, Lévêque. You have nothing I—or Mademoiselle Valmont—want." Leaning his right shoulder against the brick wall, he nodded again toward his compatriot with the cheroot.

Like a crack of thunder, a fist slammed into the trembling man's face. As the beating continued, the Ghost pressed his fingers to the side of his throat as though he were checking his own pulse, then flicked away a speck of imaginary lint from his shoulder.

The sound of breaking bones splintered through the night, causing Celine to flinch.

This was cruel. Unnecessary. Appalling.

She moved to put a halt to the thrashing, but Pippa held fast to her arm. "Don't interfere," she said. "Please. Violent men are unpredictable."

Her words stopped Celine cold.

Of course they were. She knew well what violent men were capable of doing. Her mind flashed to a late winter evening in the atelier. A wealthy young man offering to bring her hot tea and a warm blanket while she worked. The feeling of a clammy palm against her neck. How it shocked her in its uninvited wantonness. How a touch quickly turned painful. Nails digging into her arm. Fingers tearing through her hair. A roughened palm around her ankle.

No.

No.

No.

Then the smashing of a candelabra against his skull.

The silence that followed. The blood that flowed.

Celine stood frozen by this sudden wash of memory. In that moment, she'd become a murderess. The next, a fugitive. Now she lived in a convent across the Atlantic, each night sharing the word of God with other young women.

The irony.

Pippa gripped Celine's forearm. "Celine?"

Celine shook herself from her thoughts as the man with the cheroot moved to exit the alleyway, wiping his bloodied knuckles with a silk handkerchief. Pippa inhaled sharply when Celine stepped into his path without thought, blocking him from proceeding farther, meeting his hooded eyes with her own cool gaze. He quirked a brow at her.

Even without the aid of a gas lamp, Celine could see his obvious youth and the fine stitching on his expensive waistcoat of English damask. A slender gold chain hung around his neck, a monocle dangling from its center. His copper skin was unmarred—indeed almost too perfect—his hair a mass of dark waves. If Celine had to guess, his family likely hailed from the East Indies. His hazel eyes were filled with interest and not a small amount of admiration. It was almost as though he'd come across her on an evening stroll through a garden.

This was—by all rights—the look of a gentleman.

The boy's eyes wandered over Celine, up and down. He let his gaze shift toward Pippa, whom he sent a slow smile. Then he bowed before stepping back, clearing the narrow path with a flourish.

And Celine was met—face-to-face—with le Fantôme. Pippa's nails dug into Celine's skin, eliciting a shudder of fear. Another jolt of heated awareness.

Le Fantôme glided closer, his movements soundless. He stood before Celine, his features absent any discernible emotion, the set of his shoulders easy. Strong. Though he wasn't much taller than the boy with the monocle, his presence took up infinitely more space. She could well understand why their driver had yielded to him without thought. Celine stopped her eyes from widening, her lips from falling open. Were she to look upon this boy in the daylight, she would be forced to admit an unassailable truth:

The Ghost was the most striking young man she'd ever seen.

The skin above his cravat was bronzed, the muscles in his neck corded. Along his square jawline was the suggestion of stubble, its shadow accentuating the elegant symmetry of his features. It brought to light an aristocratic nose, which contrasted with his thick lashes and dark brow. Spanish maybe? North African perhaps? Regardless, he was an arresting mixture of the Old World alongside the New. A pirate bedecked in Savile Row.

He was . . . truly beautiful. Like a prince from a dark fairy tale.

Celine stood there a moment, words failing her. When she realized he'd rendered her speechless—stolen the very breath from her tongue—outrage coiled in her throat.

A glimpse of amusement flickered beside his lips. A slight indentation in his right cheek. The gesture reeked of arrogance. This boy knew full well what he looked like. Knew how to wield its power like a master of arms.

Celine narrowed her gaze at him.

When he spoke, his eyes flashed, granting his chiseled features a look of menace. "How may I help you this evening, mademoiselle?" he said in a low voice.

Since this fiend clearly enjoyed the sight of her flustered, Celine decided to ignore him, and instead turned toward the minion standing behind him, who propped one foot against the brick wall while inhaling from his cheroot.

"Does it make you proud to beat a helpless man, monsieur?" she asked him in a cold tone.

"Not in the slightest," the other boy said in a British accent, around an exhalation of pale blue smoke. "But it does keep me limber for the boxing ring."

"You dare to jest about such behavior?" Celine demanded. "You ought to be ashamed."

The boy with the cheroot laughed. "The lovely young lady might speak differently if she knew what this bastard had done."

"He is helpless. You and your"—Celine stabbed a finger in the Ghost's direction, still refusing to acknowledge him—"friend have all the power." When she finished speaking, the man in the muck squinted up at her from behind swollen eyelids. Then he slumped back down, his chest heaving from relief.

"What if we were defending a woman's honor?" The boy put out his cheroot, grinding it beneath his heel.

The unexpected question took Celine off guard for an instant. "There is no honor in beating a helpless man."

"A woman wise beyond her years," the Ghost said softly, a

strange accent threading through his speech. When he spoke, a wave of ice passed between Celine's shoulder blades, sending a shiver down her spine. "But don't presume to know everything, mademoiselle," he continued.

Celine slid her gaze to his, her heart a low thud in her chest. She lifted her chin. "I know enough, monsieur."

"Then know this: the truth is not always what you see." He paused. "Now step aside." His steely eyes narrowed almost imperceptibly. "Please."

Behind him, his friend laughed. "As I live and breathe," he murmured. "Sébastien Saint Germain . . . acting the part of a gentleman instead of a blighter."

In response, a muscle ticked in the Ghost's jaw. The slightest hint of displeasure. He glanced toward his friend, warning him without words. The boy with the monocle grinned in response, which struck Celine as odd, given their circumstances. When one clearly outranked the other.

No matter. The Ghost had a name.

"You do not command me, *Sébastien*," Celine said, her tone precise. "I defy you to try."

Sébastien took in a careful breath. "I accept your challenge, mademoiselle." With a wicked half smile, he took hold of her by the waist and moved her to one side, lifting her off her feet as though she were lighter than air.

Celine reacted on impulse—the desire to immobilize him as he had her. Her booted toes dangling above the cobblestones— matching him at eye level—she grabbed Sébastien by his silk cravat. Yanked tight, her expression determined. His eyes widened with surprise, a spark of fire burning in their depths. The indentation is his cheek appeared for less than an instant.

He was . . . amused?

Unmitigated ass.

She tightened her grip on his cravat. Felt the fine fabric wind through her fingers. Refused to avert her gaze, though he held her in the air like a puppet on a string.

"Celine!" Pippa's voice was high-pitched. Celine didn't need to guess how shocked her friend was. Pippa lurched closer, panic unfurling from her skin. "Forgive us for the interruption, sir." Though Pippa addressed Sébastien, his gunmetal eyes never strayed from Celine's.

"We need to leave," Pippa urged her.

"Put me down, Monsieur Saint Germain," Celine demanded. "At once."

To her surprise, Sébastien set her upon her feet. But he did not remove his palms from about her waist, just as Celine did not relinquish her grasp on his cravat. Even through her corset, she felt the touch of his thumb above her hip, the press of his long fingers into the small of her back. Her pulse thudded in her chest, its rhythm fast and fervent.

"She has teeth," he said quietly. "But does she also have claws?"

"There is only one way to find out." She meant it as a threat.

He took it as a challenge.

Sébastien's smile was quick. Unstudied. Unusual in a boy who obviously prided himself on control. The edge in his features sharpened, leading Celine to suspect he wasn't merely amused.

Was it possible he was intrigued?

Celine let go of his cravat, the back of her hand grazing an obsidian button as it skimmed over his waistcoat. Though it was far from the most improper thing she'd done tonight, the touch felt illicit. Stolen. Her cheeks warmed when something shifted in his gaze.

"Bastien." His friend's voice cut through their silent exchange. "We should go before someone summons the police." He stepped forward purposefully, a palm moving to Sébastien's shoulder, demanding his attention.

For a delicious instant, Bastien ignored it. Then he slid his hands from Celine's waist, stepped back, and tipped his hat at her. With horror, she realized his touch had seared into her skin. That could be the only explanation for why the air around her waist felt so chilled. When he glided past her, the scent of bergamot and leather trailed in his wake.

A flurry of emotions raced through her body. Celine settled for indignation, grasping for it like a lifeline. When she turned to ensure she had the last word, she caught a glimmer of silver in her periphery. It took less than the blink of an eye to realize its source.

The man in the mud had freed a dagger from his boot, his scarred features feral in the moonlight.

Celine cried out in warning, yanking Pippa to one side. In the same instant, Bastien whirled, withdrawing a revolver from inside his frock coat in a seamless motion. He took aim— meaning to fire—but his friend lunged for the man with the dagger, his right hand wrapping around the man's wrist.

Without explanation, the man slumped forward, as though

he'd suddenly fallen asleep, the dagger clattering to the ground beside him.

It all happened so quickly. Celine blinked once. Twice. Pippa struggled for breath, her blond curls quaking above her brow.

"What did you do?" Celine whispered to the boy with the monocle. "Is he . . . dead?"

The two young men held a wordless conversation.

"He's . . . asleep," the boy with the monocle said carefully, as though he'd settled on a version of the truth. "He'll be jolly good in an hour, though the lummox doesn't deserve it."

"But—"

"We're finished here," Bastien said, his tone cold. Forbidding.

Celine glared at him. "You are absolutely not—"

"My apologies, mademoiselle. And to you, miss." He bowed curtly to Pippa before gliding away. "Arjun?" he called over his shoulder. "I believe I owe you a drink."

"Far be it from me to refuse such a generous offer." Arjun smiled mockingly as he reached for the fallen dagger, tossing it deep into the alleyway. Then he stood and wiped his hands once more. "Especially from such an esteemed gentleman."

Celine bit down on nothing as they began walking away, struggling to maintain her composure, her fists clenched. This cursed boy had stolen much from her in these moments. The words from her lips, the breath from her tongue. Now he thought to dismiss her like a child?

"You are no gentleman, Monsieur Saint Germain," Celine said loudly.

He stopped short. Pivoted on a polished heel. "Is that what you think, *Celine*?"

Celine stood taller, her knuckles turning white. "Yes. I do."

Bastien leaned closer. A flicker of firelight caught on his gold watch chain. On the roaring lion etched into his signet ring. "I don't give a fuck."

Pippa gasped, both hands covering her mouth, her eyes wider than tea saucers.

Then Bastien continued on his way, Arjun laughing softly at his heels. Almost pityingly.

The word shook Celine. She'd never heard it said aloud. The sheltered life she'd lived in Paris had spared her from being trespassed by this kind of talk. Her father often commented that feminine ears were too delicate for such things. But Celine didn't feel as though her delicate ears had been assaulted by the single syllable. Bastien may have uttered a foul word, but he'd spoken to her as he would a man. As an equal. Blood rushed through her body, adrenaline fueling its path. Horror settled in the base of her throat, a knot slowly tightening.

She knew this feeling. Recognized it. She'd felt it when her attacker had stilled on the floor of the atelier, crimson flowing from the wound in his skull, her hand clasped around the candelabra.

Celine felt . . . powerful. A part of something bigger than herself.

And still she did not feel a hint of remorse for anything she'd done.

It was terrifying to know such a dark creature writhed beneath Celine's skin. This was not the behavior of a pious young woman, nor were these the emotions of a girl who should—by all rights—be seeking forgiveness. Salvation from a God she did not quite know or understand.

Celine blinked to clear her thoughts. Just as Pippa tugged on her hand.

"Are you all right?" Pippa said, her tone incredulous. "I can't—" she tried. "I mean, can you believe what he said to you?"

Celine nodded, not trusting herself to speak.

She could not be certain what hand of Fate continued placing Sébastien Saint Germain in her path. Perhaps it was a test. God's penance for her most grievous sin, that a boy shrouded in darkness would force her to see the light. Make of her a Good Samaritan.

But a greater fear lurked deep in Celine. Past the rush of blood, into the marrow of her bones.

No matter where she went, danger followed.

And it horrified her. Just as it thrilled her.

———◦◦◇◇◦◦———

I catch her profile in the glint of a shining brass sign.
Her fear is reflected at me, her eyes bright.

I look away. It reminds me of the young woman from last week. I do not relish the sight of fear on anyone, though I know it to be a necessary evil. For if we do not understand fear, how are we ever to cherish safety?

I turn my attention to the three-story building before me, its trellised balconies overflowing with ivy and budding blossoms. Etched into the brass sign in the center—in odiously elaborate script—is the name *Jacques'*. Above the name is a symbol I often see in my dreams. A symbol infamous among the circles of both the Fallen and the Brotherhood.

A restaurant encompasses the entire first floor of the structure, its gas lanterns already ablaze. A queue is wrapping around the corner. Someone—undoubtedly Kassamir—has thrown open the double doors, revealing a smiling crowd and the sounds of fine china and tinkling crystal. Servers bustle about in their white gloves and starched jackets.

For a moment, my senses are inundated by this symphony of splendor and decadence. It is a music I know well, both in this life and in my former one. A smile curves across my lips.

Amusing that she should lead me here, of all places.

If only these poor fools knew what lurked above them, deep in a court of lions. If only my victim knew. Then they would all understand what it meant to feel true fear.

When I glance at her again, I catch a look of hesitation on her face, as though she is uncertain about whether to proceed. Recent events have unnerved her, and it saddens me. I expected her to be stronger. She began the night with such purpose, each of her steps steady. Resolute.

Perhaps I shouldn't be too judgmental. This is not a city for everyone.

It is a snake in the reeds, beautiful and deadly, even while it sleeps.

Moreover, I feel partially to blame for her fear. I could have come to their aid. It would have taken the work of a moment to blur through the alley and silence that paltry threat. But what purpose would that have served, beyond the risk of revealing my true nature before it was time? To my knowledge, my victim was not yet in any real danger. At least not from the nephew of Le Comte de Saint Germain.

Bitterness coats my tongue.

That is a promise I do not have the strength to break. Not yet.

We are not ready for the war it will bring.

My thoughts darken in a way I do not like, so I return to my earlier musings. It's possible Arjun Desai—the boy with the immobilizing touch—could present a threat one day, but it is too soon to tell. His skill set continues to intrigue me, as it did on the day I first made his acquaintance. Without a doubt, he is a worthy member of La Cour des Lions.

Another smile spreads across my face. It pleases me that our city's society of mentalists—masquerading as something else entirely—managed to recruit him.

It should make for a fascinating turn of events.

But I cannot allow these things to distract me any more than they already have. Not tonight. There is far too much at stake for me to dwell on these incidental matters.

I return my gaze to her, the young woman who led me to where it all began, unknowingly.

Fittingly.

She pauses at the entrance of Jacques', rethinking her choices once more.

Ah, but it is too late, my love.

We cannot change the mistakes of our past. They live on, so that we may learn, if we should be but so lucky. Alas, dear girl, your luck takes flight tonight.

I am the spider. I set silken traps. I watch as you step into my web.

I wait to strike.

But do not fear. I promise I will never forget you.

THE COURT OF THE LIONS

—◦◇◦—

C eline waited for Pippa to collect herself just outside the narrow alleyway. When Celine realized she was behaving oddly—standing stock-still, her eyes unblinking—she began mimicking Pippa's motions, straightening her overskirt as if it was all that needed sorting.

It never ceased to amaze Celine how circumstances could change so drastically in the matter of a moment. One second, every nerve ending in her body was alive, crackling with unseen energy. The next, everything went silent and motionless, as if she were submerged in a pool of deep water.

"Celine?" Two lines collected between Pippa's brows.

Celine gathered that Pippa had posed her a question. True to form, Celine had not been listening. Ever since Bastien and Arjun had left them behind in the alley—a stone's throw from the "sleeping" man who'd brandished a dagger at them less than ten minutes prior—Pippa had been maintaining a steady stream of nervous chatter.

Celine's focus had been elsewhere. Lost in the delicious unknown.

"Have you heard a word I've said?" Pippa asked. She held up

her skirts and edged closer to Celine, concern seeping onto her features. "I asked if you still wished to meet Odette."

"Of course," Celine answered without thought.

Dismay touched the edges of Pippa's lips, there and gone in an instant. "Oh."

"Do you not wish to meet her?"

"It isn't that." Pippa shook her head. "I'm just . . . uncertain whether it is the wisest course of action." Her blue eyes flicked toward Celine. "This evening has not gone as I'd hoped. I thought it better to stop tempting our fates."

Of course Pippa felt uncomfortable. Most people *would* feel skittish after the events of tonight. A girl like Pippa would wish to be anywhere else. No, that wasn't right. She would wish to be home, safe in her bed, with a soft blanket and a cup of hot tea. Better yet, with a mother or a lover to offer a soothing touch.

Celine exhaled slowly, a dark realization settling amid her thoughts.

Proper young women certainly wouldn't feel so enlivened by the very idea of danger. Nor would they already be seeking out the next chance to feel their hearts pound in their ears and their faces flush as though they were too close to a candle flame.

Further proof that something was broken inside Celine.

Breathing deeply through her nose, Celine reached for her friend's hand, her touch gentle. Comforting. "I'm sorry, Pippa," she said. "I've been distracted by all that happened. Of course you don't want to meet with Odette tonight after . . . well, everything. I completely understand. We'll return to the convent at once." She was careful not to let her disappointment show, though she felt it keenly.

Her friend had risked enough this evening on her account.

When Celine moved to retrace their steps, Pippa dawdled behind her. Celine turned in place. "Pippa?"

Pippa quirked her lips to one side. "You really wanted to go, didn't you? You were happier tonight than I've ever seen you before. Freer."

Celine thought to lie. But she was wearied by the notion. So very wearied.

She simply nodded.

A warm light filled Pippa's gaze. "It was like getting a peek into who you truly are," she said softly. "It made me feel like we were really friends."

"We are really friends."

Pippa shook her head, but it was not unkind. "Not yet. But I hope we will be. I do so want to be your friend, Celine."

Celine swallowed, something clutching around her heart. "I want to be your friend, too, Pippa. Very much."

Pippa nodded. Then she took hold of her skirts once more, resolve flashing across her face. "We shouldn't keep Odette waiting."

———◇———

Less than two blocks away, Celine and Pippa caught sight of a brass sign positioned above the slender double doors of a well-lit establishment.

It read *Jacques'* in fancy script. Etched above the name was a familiar symbol: a fleur-de-lis in the mouth of a roaring lion. In the distance, the pier loomed ominously, the water around it glittering like a sea of black diamonds, ready to swallow its supplicants whole.

"Oh," Pippa said, realization dawning on her. "It's a restaurant."

A similar wash of surprise passed through Celine. It felt odd for Odette to direct them to a restaurant, especially for the purpose of a dress fitting.

Based on the long queue snaking around the front, it was clear the owner of Jacques' knew how to capture the attention of a crowd, especially for a Monday evening. But on the outside, the structure itself looked rather ordinary. Red brick and black lacquered shutters enclosing three stories. Gas lamps blazing between tall, narrow windows. Polished wooden floors stained a light caramel color. Drapes of deep burgundy damask cascading down the walls.

Yet to Celine, something about it felt . . . off. Like a picture frame hanging askew. As if the restaurant had dutifully mastered every detail of the mundane, with the intention of wearing them as a mask. Concealing what, Celine could only guess.

Each time the door opened, the crystals hanging from the chandelier beside the entrance chimed merrily like they were welcoming newcomers. Then the lingering notes turned melancholy. A clash of discordant sounds, the slightest shift to minor key.

To Celine, it rang as a quiet warning. Still, everyone in the room kept smiling, oblivious to the unseen threat. Her gaze slipped across the contented faces of Jacques' countless patrons.

How was it they could not feel it, too?

Perhaps Celine was mistaken. Perhaps these observations formed from a place of wishful thought. Maybe she sought proof she wasn't the only one forced to wear a mask. And in doing so, she'd falsely found a kindred spirit . . . in a restaurant.

How ridiculous. She chastised herself. What kind of silly fool shared a silent understanding with a structure of brick and mortar? Celine committed to casting aside her concerns like a stone lying in her path.

Pippa touched Celine's shoulder to catch her attention. "Should we seek out the gentleman Odette mentioned earlier today?"

"Mais oui. Lead the way." Celine sent a deceptively careless grin over her shoulder.

As soon as the two girls crossed the threshold of Jacques'— Pippa pausing with a twinge of trepidation—the figurative stone Celine had cast aside rolled back into her path. She must be mad, seeing and feeling things not even in the demesne of possibility. But even in the most fevered of her dreams, it would be impossible to ignore this truth:

Jacques' was anything but ordinary.

It was not about what Celine saw. It was about what she *felt*.

A strange sensation rippled across her skin, tingling through her blood, taking root in her core. Something hooked around her spine, drawing her in with an unspoken promise. Something . . . otherworldly.

Yes. That was it. It was as though she'd wandered into another realm. Not Heaven. Not Hell. But somewhere in between. A liminal space, spanning both light and dark. Whatever it was, Celine felt comfortable there.

An elbow struck Celine's right arm, snagging her from her observations. The server who hastened past them offered an apologetic glance, his features knitted along his freckled brow. In both hands, he balanced trays laden with covered dishes of gleaming silver. Celine tracked his progress through the room as she directed Pippa closer to a wall of wooden paneling near the entrance, out of the main walkway's path.

Pippa gazed about the space with purpose. "Do you see him?"

Captivated by the scene unfolding before them, Celine failed to reply.

Across the restaurant's open dining area—near a set of curving stairs vanishing up into shadowy darkness—the freckled server caught the attention of an imposing figure standing beside the swinging door to the kitchen. The silk-faced lapels of his pristine frock coat glowed in the candlelight. Even from a distance, Celine recognized him as the ruler of this culinary domain. He maintained a ramrod straight posture, his dark skin and the gold ring through his right ear brilliant contrasts to his snow-white shirt. Then he glanced at the server, flicking his black eyes toward a table closer to Pippa and Celine. His gaze was pointed. Reproving.

A flush spreading across his cheeks, the young server conducted an artful about-face, twisting back in the table's direction. He began distributing covered dishes before its four patrons, one of whom was a pale gentleman of Asiatic origin, sporting a thin mustache, perfectly groomed, and a shirt with a simple collar. Beside him sat a portly white fellow with red splotches across his nose and a smoldering cigar. Across the table was a man with skin the color of mahogany, wearing a spectacular waistcoat of gold and royal blue. Next to him sulked the younger, smaller version of himself.

It struck Celine as highly unusual. She'd never seen men of different skin color occupy the same space in a fine restaurant.

Parisian high society was not a society of mixed company. The Paris Celine knew was carefully sorted, just like its many arrondissements. As a small child, Celine was told never to traverse the narrow lanes of Saint-Denis just as its émigré residents were shown that they—and their kind—did not belong anywhere near the dazzling boulevards of Place Vendôme. She wondered if the scene taking place tonight within Jacques' was normal in a port city like New Orleans, one in which people from all over the world congregated.

She would wager it was not. It had certainly been the truth for her own family. From an early age, Celine had been taught to be grateful for her mother's absence from their family's dining table.

Sadness flared around her heart. She took hold of it. Trapped it deep within her chest. It did no good to dwell on matters she could not change. Steadfast in her resolve, Celine looked to Pippa to see if they should proceed.

It appeared that Pippa, too, had been swept away by the unearthly magic of this place. She watched rapt while the freckle-faced server finished distributing the covered dishes. Then he snapped his fingers in a dramatic fashion, and all the silver domes were removed in concert. Scented steam wafted through the air, floating toward Celine and Pippa as though it were borne on an enchanted wind. Pippa stilled, her eyes falling shut.

"What . . . is that deliciousness?" she asked Celine.

Celine leaned closer to the table, peering around the hustle and bustle of the busy restaurant.

The food smelled familiar—the same scents of butter and wine, the same perfume of marjoram, thyme, and rosemary—that Celine had grown up enjoying in Paris. But something else filtered through the air. Spices she could not readily identify.

They plagued her. Tantalized her. Intoxicated her.

The newly uncovered plates of Limoges porcelain held fillets of sole resting atop beds of fragrant rice, finished with a sauce similar to a beurre blanc, but with a twist of roasted tomatoes and a hint of sweet herbs. To the right of the flaky fish sat a tureen of pommes de terre soufflées. The delectably puffed potatoes were served alongside an intricate pyramid of roasted asparagus smothered in truffle port sauce, then garnished with slender shavings of cured meat.

At the table nearest to them, an elegant woman dripping with pearls drank from her glass of red wine before nibbling on a pillowy gougères, the salty scent of Gruyère cheese mingling with the rich fragrance of the Burgundy.

In that moment, Celine wanted nothing more than to slip into this woman's expensive shoes, just for a breath of time. To sink her teeth into something decadent, heedless of all else around her.

"Oh!" Pippa said, startled by a sudden tongue of fire leaping from another table. A white-gloved maître d'hôtel swished the burning contents of a small pan, a blue blaze dancing around its edges. The concoction appeared to be a strange kind of creamy fruit covered in mounds of brown sugar, then doused with bourbon before being set aflame. A delectable perfume of warm caramel curled into the air, countless pairs of eyes drifting toward it.

This was beyond unfair.

Celine's soul cried out in protest, her memories of the flavorless stew she'd consumed earlier taunting her tongue. What would happen to Celine if she ordered a meal right now and could not pay for it? Would she be forced to wash dishes all night? Perhaps put in a stockade and pelted with rotten vegetables, like in the time of Shakespeare?

Would it be worth it?

Resolve coursed through her. At some point, Celine would partake in a meal at this restaurant. She might even entice Pippa to join her. Maybe.

Pippa's stomach grumbled, and a smile toyed at the edges of Celine's lips.

Just then, the imposing figure positioned near the kitchen's swinging door turned his attention toward them. He cut his eyes, appraising them from afar. This man had to be the individual with the sinful voice and the ring through his right ear that Odette had mentioned at their first meeting earlier today.

Before Celine could move in his direction, the man shifted from his post, striding toward the front of the restaurant, where

Celine and Pippa stood. He moved with purpose, though his attention remained sharp, watching for signs of missteps among his staff, ready to rebuke at any turn. As he wove through the space, he pointed behind him, and another liveried gentleman stepped seamlessly into position beside the swinging kitchen door.

Celine admired his poise. The respect he commanded. Less than ten years ago, men with his skin color were held as slaves in the southern part of America, forced to work in endless fields beneath a blazing hot sun. Celine knew they still were not seen as equals, much less granted prestigious positions in elegant restaurants, directing white men in perfectly pressed jackets.

The sight of this man of color helming an establishment like Jacques' emboldened Celine in a way she could not quite understand.

He stopped before them, standing directly in front of Celine. Her eyes widened as he towered over her, his gaze a tinge unwelcoming. "May I help you, mademoiselle?" he asked in a lightly accented tone. "If you wish to reserve a table tonight, it is best for you to join the queue out front." His voice reminded her of an approaching storm. A distant rumble, a swirl of clouds.

Though Celine should have felt unsettled by his cold demeanor, she found herself unaffected. Calm.

"Hello," she began, her tone unwavering. "My name is Celine."

He cast her an arched glance. And said nothing more.

"I was told to disregard the queue," Celine continued, "and ask to be taken to Odette."

His gaze softened. "My apologies." A fond light entered his

eyes. "You should have begun with that, mademoiselle." He snapped his fingers in the air, and all around them bodies moved in concert, clearing a path.

"Je m'appelle Kassamir." He introduced himself while adjusting his golden cuff links, their shining surfaces embossed with the same symbol of a fleur-de-lis in the mouth of a lion. "I am in charge of this restaurant. As friends of Mademoiselle Valmont, you are most welcome at Jacques', and please know that all those in my employ are here to attend to your needs." He began leading them toward the curving staircase near the back.

"C'est un plaisir de vous recontrer, Kassamir," Celine replied with a smile.

"It's a pleasure to make your acquaintance, Mr. . . . . Kassamir," Pippa echoed, her voice resembling the squeak of a mouse.

A grin flickered across Kassamir's face. "Please call me simply Kassamir, mademoiselle. My surname is of little consequence, as it is not one I care to use."

Celine wanted to ask what Kassamir meant by saying that, but stopped herself after an inadvertent glance over one shoulder. The sight of Pippa bravely marching forward despite her earlier concerns sent a flurry of guilt across Celine's skin. Once again, she'd placed Pippa in an uncomfortable situation. And a friend in truth would check on her companion more often.

The trio ascended the curving staircase, trepidation rippling through Celine, starting from her toes, rising up her spine. She nearly stumbled as the steps grew narrower the closer they climbed toward the top.

Anticipation spiked around her heart when the fear reached her throat. It was a strange sensation, this mixture of emotions. For as long as Celine could remember, she'd relished this particular thrill. The boys who lived on her street had called her "une petite sotte" when she'd balanced along her balcony's ledge on a single foot. "You little fool," they'd cried from far below, safe and smug in their superiority. "Veux-tu mourir, Marceline Rousseau?"

They could not have been more wrong. Celine hadn't wanted to die then, just as she had no desire to die now. In fact, it was the complete opposite. She simply wanted to revel in the excitement that always accompanied danger.

That chance to feel truly alive.

But those little tyrants in their worn woolen caps weren't completely wrong when they called her a fool. Even then, she'd known it was the height of foolishness to court danger so openly. To crave it like a slice of warm chocolate cake. Were the Mother Superior present now, Celine knew she would urge them away from this place with all haste. Signs of peril lurked everywhere, even in the sinister coil of the wrought-iron railing.

The second floor came into view, and Celine glimpsed a multitude of gas lamps turned down low, rendering the room beyond in muted tones. The air around them condensed. Turned cooler, as if they'd passed from day to night in the span of a single staircase.

They neared the top, Kassamir continuing to move at a leisurely pace. Here, the banisters were fashioned of gleaming brass, faceted on all sides with a fleur-de-lis in the mouth of a roaring lion.

As if the symbol had intentionally followed Celine all day long.

Or perhaps led her to this place, without words.

Something began coiling through her stomach. An unseen force. It spread through her limbs like a slow shudder. Beside her, Pippa gripped Celine's arm, undoubtedly experiencing the same unsettling sensation. That feeling of hovering above the threshold between light and dark.

Kassamir turned toward them, his sharp gaze appearing as though it could bore holes into her soul. "Bienvenue à La Cour des Lions."

Welcome to the Court of the Lions.

TOUSSAINT

———◦◦◇◦◦———

T he first thing Celine noticed was the sound.

Or rather the absence of it.

The moment her feet sank into the plush carpet at the top of the stairs, the noise from below dropped to a hush. As if it were being muffled, like a heavy blanket had been drawn over the entire second floor, warding away the possibility of eavesdroppers.

But that was impossible. How could anyone manage such a thing?

Celine let her vision slowly adjust to the darkness.

Dim lighting glowed around a large rectangular chamber replete with gleaming wooden tables. Surrounding the tables stood shadowy figures adorned in silks and sparkling gemstones, cut crystal glasses flashing with each of their movements. A faint breeze tempered the air, fending off the rising heat from below. The floors and paneled walls were stained a dark mahogany, polished to resemble the surface of a black mirror. Silk drapes of a costly indigo hue, trimmed with golden tassels, framed every arched window. A long chaise sat empty in the chamber's center, like a throne meant for an empress or a goddess of old.

That same sense of a blurred reality—of a sight gone hazy along its edges—enveloped the space. Punctuating the din was the occasional clatter of ivory dice across felted baize, the flutter of glossy cards being shuffled and sorted, the occasional muted cheer.

"It's . . . a gambling hell," Pippa said, her tone a mixture of unease and anticipation.

Celine tilted her head.

It was. And it wasn't.

She couldn't ignore the feeling that she was peering at a beautiful mask. Some kind of artful illusion. That if she shook her head just so, her vision would clear, leaving behind nothing but truth. Was this place the "court" the two young women had mentioned in Jackson Square that afternoon? Could its bejeweled patrons be responsible for such a sordid crime?

At first glance, it did not appear so.

But first impressions were known to be deceiving.

Whenever Celine had heard talk of gambling hells, they'd been portrayed as dens of iniquity. Powerful men sloshed with drink, wasting away fortunes on the single roll of a dice. Powdered lightskirts plying their scented wares. Bared skin and spilled liquor, lush velvet and cool ivory. Wealth at the height of its debauchery.

The scene before Celine could not appear more civilized. Everywhere she looked, dazzling women and elegant men of all skin colors congregated as seeming equals.

As if this was not an unusual sight at all.

Just then, a cry of triumph rose into the darkness to their

right, just beyond a game of faro. The sound drew Celine toward an oval table of lustrous burl wood, the sights around it unspooling like bolts of fabric, captivating her with possibility.

Roulette. She'd heard of this game before, but never had occasion to play it.

"Celine?" From behind her, Pippa took hold of her hand beseechingly.

Celine halted in her tracks and eyed her friend over her shoulder.

"What are you doing?" Pippa asked quietly.

The question emboldened Celine. Granted her a sense of purpose. Perhaps it was the golden glow of the gas lamps. Or the heady scent of spices mixed with smoldering cigars. Whatever it was, she did not want to hide among the wavering shadows.

She wanted to soar.

"I'm playing roulette," Celine replied, her voice filled with conviction.

Shock fluttered across Pippa's features. "What?"

Celine was tired of doing nothing but watching. Tired of wearing her own mask and being a mere observer to life. "You wanted to know who I really am." She bit her lower lip. "I'm a girl who'd rather experience life than watch it pass by from my window."

Pippa exhaled slowly. Then nodded as she released Celine's hand.

Like a moth to a flickering flame, Celine glided toward the amber light surrounding the roulette table. She hovered along the edges, her skin tingling with awareness.

A croupier swiped away a stack of tortoiseshell chips, presenting them to the recent winner. He waited for the players to place their new bets, then held a small ivory ball aloft before spinning a wheel of numbers in one direction and dropping the ball in the other. The *tic, tic, tic* of the roulette wheel grew louder and faster, until each sound blended into the next.

"Rouge seize!" the croupier called out when the ivory ball landed in a red square labeled "16."

Across the table, a trio of companions—two women with dark skin and a man with a burnished complexion—grumbled in French to each other before reaching to place another bet. The rings gilding both women's fingers were immense, jagged pieces of raw stone set in pure gold.

Celine searched for a set of discarded dice. A way to join the game, despite her lack of fortune. Her gaze caught on the faces of the trio, and a strange realization gripped her stomach. They were all extraordinarily attractive. Their skin seemed to glimmer beneath the warmth of the newfangled electrical lantern hanging overhead, the centers of their eyes filled with lambent light. When they moved, the air around them shifted like smoke.

Celine blinked as if something had floated across her vision, her lashes fluttering to clear her sight, her lips parting ever so slightly.

"Lovely," a male voice murmured from her left, his thick drawl catching her attention.

"Pardon?" Celine replied, turning his way.

"You could be my good luck charm, my beauty." The young man's elbow brushed her arm as he leaned in closer, his clean-shaven features sly. He, too, was inexplicably handsome, his face like that of an angel, his expression decidedly at odds with the cherubic curls atop his brow. Again Celine was struck by how clear his eyes were. How the blue ringing their dark centers seemed inordinately intense.

Inhuman.

The thought startled Celine. She banished it with a toss of her head, restoring her senses so that she wouldn't appear to be a simpleton. "I'd rather be my own good luck charm, sir." Squaring her shoulders, she met his appreciative stare.

He rolled a set of dice between his fingers, his angelic curls falling across his forehead. "I'd wager you've never played roulette."

"You'd be wagering incorrectly, then," Celine lied. She held out her hand for the dice. "I might be the best roulette player you've ever met."

He laughed. "I can taste your deceit, my lovely little liar," he whispered.

"What?" Celine dropped her hand, stepping back, disoriented by his words.

"It's sweet on my tongue."

Again Celine took a small step back, almost colliding with Pippa.

"Boone," a feminine voice warned from the shadows. "Don't be a beast. You've been warned already."

The young man put both hands in the air in a gesture of surrender and pulled away the following instant, but not before offering Celine a wink.

"Fantastique!" the same feminine voice exclaimed from behind Pippa and Celine, as if nothing of import had occurred. "I didn't think you'd actually come." The slender silhouette lurking in a fall of shadow shifted into the light.

Celine's mouth dropped open.

"Of course I hoped you would," Odette continued, her teeth flashing in a smile as she lifted her glass of red wine in salute. "But I didn't place a bet on the outcome."

If the girl had not spoken first, Celine never would have recognized her. Gone were the dainty, demure garments from earlier in the day. The only familiar embellishment was the ivory cameo with its halo of bloodred rubies.

Odette was dressed as a gentleman. Her trousers were made of supple buckskin, and her shirt—with its ballooned sleeves—was stark white, covered by an elaborate waistcoat of pale green jacquard. The chain of a large gold pocket watch hung across the front of Odette's vest. But the pièce de résistance had to be her intricately tied silk cravat, pinned in its center by the ivory cameo. Her brown hair had been slicked back from her face and gathered at the nape of her neck in a simple knot.

A slow smile unfurled across Odette's face at their stunned silence. She swirled her wine knowingly.

"Why, you're wearing . . . trousers!" Pippa remarked a moment later, her eyes enormous.

"I find it incredibly freeing." Odette moved forward, resting one of her gloved hands in her pocket. "Some days I adore wearing corsets and bustles and layers of silk. But sometimes, it pays to wear pants."

Though Celine was still rendered speechless by the sight, a sense of delight wound through her. The grin lingering on the edges of her lips threatened to bloom.

How . . . wonderful.

Celine cleared her throat. "Of course we came," she began as though nothing were amiss. "I said I would, and I don't enjoy going back on my word." Celine shifted beside Odette, studying the lovely girl's outfit with a practiced eye. "Forgive me, but there's a stain beside your cravat." She nodded at Odette's shirt, where the tiniest drop of red wine—or perhaps rouge—had seeped onto the otherwise pristine cloth.

Odette glanced downward, tugging at her collar with a gloved finger. "Merde," she cursed under her breath. "And I thought I had been so careful."

"Both rouge and red wine are easy to remove with a bit of white wine or tonic water," Celine offered. "Otherwise you look impeccable."

"Truly?" Odette wrinkled her nose, no doubt pleased to hear the compliment.

Celine nodded. "A jacquard waistcoat is an excellent choice for someone with your coloring, and the tailoring looks flawless, though I would have selected a French seam to finish the edges instead of a standard backstitch."

"Are French seams better?" Odette asked as she set her wine on a nearby table.

"Of course." Celine didn't blink. "They're French."

Odette laughed. "You're simply delightful, mon amie."

Celine almost smiled alongside Odette, but something

stopped her. Bade her to keep her distance, at least for the time being. In the past, being too trusting of others had not done her any favors. "I've never seen a knot like that." She nodded toward Odette's cravat.

"It's a mail coach knot from the earlier part of this century." Odette's eyes gleamed pale gold. "I do think that men of the Regency era had the best sense of fashion, don't you?"

Celine thought a moment. "A part of me is inclined to agree." She paused. "Though I'll admit I've never fancied the top hat. Men have no need of the added height; they lord over everything enough as it is."

Odette hummed in agreement. "What kind of hat would you pair with this ensemble?" she asked. "An Eton cap? A bowler?"

"Frankly, I'd prefer no hat at all, but I know it's simply not done. If you were out during the day, I would recommend a straw hat with a thick band. The weather here becomes it."

"So then, a Panama hat?" Odette tapped an index finger against her chin.

Celine frowned. "No. Something . . . else."

Something that did not remind her of Sébastien Saint Germain.

Celine swallowed, wondering why her thoughts had hearkened to that particular style in that particular instant. It had never struck her as memorable before. When Celine glanced at Pippa, she noticed her friend studying her, Pippa's blond head angled to one side. As though she'd heard the lie buried deep in Celine's musings.

Discomfited by the notion, Celine decided to shift tack. "Is there a place we could begin taking your measurements?" she asked Odette.

Odette rested her arms akimbo and cocked her head to one side. "I'm fine taking measurements here, as long as you don't mind." It was almost as if she had issued a challenge.

Such a thing simply wasn't done. But then again, Odette appeared to enjoy bucking convention. Why should this occasion prove any different? Her features the portrait of apathy, Celine reached inside the pocket of her petticoat and extracted a length of measuring ribbon.

She refused to be outmatched or intimidated.

Even if Odette *did* wear trousers.

While Celine worked to measure Odette's torso, she peered through a parting in the crowd, catching a glimpse of an ongoing chess match. Neither of the players moved for the span of several breaths, their eyes riveted on the black-and-white board. Then the white king fell without ever being touched. The next instant, the entire chess set rearranged itself on its own— the pieces whisking across the checkered surface in a whirl—as the victor reached over to shake his opponent's hand, a smile curving up his face.

"Wh-what?" Pippa stammered. "What happened?"

Celine stared, her expression one of disbelief. "More importantly, *how*?"

"You needn't look so surprised," Odette said with a grin. "They're simply illusions performed by those with the skill."

Pippa glanced at Odette, a brow arched in question. "You mean . . . magic?"

"Of a sort." Odette nodded. "This is a place in which students of the occult"—she searched for the word, her hands turning through the air—"gather."

"Like a gambling hell for magicians?" Doubt crossed Celine's face as she resumed measuring Odette's arms and shoulders.

"I wouldn't call us magicians," Odette replied. "We prefer to be called illusionists or mentalists."

Pippa nodded. "I saw a performance by a mentalist once, just outside of London. He turned water into ink and transformed a bouquet of lilies into a bevy of doves." She paused. "Do your members also give performances like that?"

"Some of us do." Odette raised a shoulder, eliciting a wordless rebuke from Celine. "But most of us simply choose to meet here in safety to hone our craft." She paused. "It's a blessing we've been provided with such a space. There was a time before when things were not quite so . . ." A shadow darkened Odette's countenance as her voice faded into nothingness. Then she grinned brightly.

Celine took in a careful breath while she worked, her doubts growing. Something about the girl's explanation troubled her. It felt familiar. The kind of explanation Celine had been wont to give as of late—a skeleton of the truth. "What kind of mentalist are you?" she asked, her tone nonchalant.

"One who divines the future," Odette said matter-of-factly. "The ancients called it stargazing, but the mystics in the Quarter refer to us as soothsayers."

Pippa's rosebud lips fell open. "Then you already know everything that will happen? Everything I will do or say?" She glanced about with obvious discomfort. "Even what I might be thinking or feeling?"

Odette's shook her head. "I know what *may* happen, depending on the choices you make."

"Just by"—Pippa swallowed—"looking at me?"

"No. Physical contact is necessary for me to divine things with any measure of clarity."

During this exchange, Celine had kept silent for fear she would speak out of turn. She paused to take note of the final measurements, but disbelief flared hot in her veins when she recalled how Boone had claimed to taste the flavor of her lies. *Such things are not possible,* her mind screamed, demanding attention. Her heart, however, knew better.

Celine could not deny she'd been in the presence of something otherworldly tonight, here at Jacques'. Moreover, she recalled her first encounter with Odette this afternoon. How Odette's gaze had widened infinitesimally when Celine had taken her hand.

The soothsayer had seen something, even in that briefest of interactions.

Captivated by the prospect of such knowledge—of such power—Celine discarded the measuring ribbon, her pencil dropping from her lips. She knew it was a risk, but she simply had to know if Odette had uncovered any of her secrets. "What did you see?"

Pippa turned toward her, confused by the question.

Odette met Celine's gaze, her expression knowing. "What do you mean?" Her voice sounded deceptively innocent.

"This afternoon," Celine continued without batting an eye, "when you took my hand, what did you see?"

Odette's smile turned fierce. "I only caught flashes of possibility. The lace obstructed my view." She held up a gloved hand. "Annoying, but necessary. It's easy to lose sight of what's real when you're lost in the stars."

Celine stood taller. Then held out her hand, her gaze steady, determined to learn whether or not Odette possessed any damaging information. "Please tell me what you see. I'd like to know."

As she had earlier today, Odette canted her head in contemplation. "Are you quite certain, mon amie? Knowing what might happen is not the same as preventing it from happening."

Celine nodded. "I'm certain."

Odette removed the kidskin glove on her right hand. Without hesitation, she wrapped her cool fingers around Celine's palm and closed her eyes. Her smile softened.

"La dompteuse des bêtes," she murmured after a moment. Her eyes flashed open, laughter tingeing her tone. "Je le savais!" she congratulated herself.

"The tamer of beasts?" Celine translated, her expression one of puzzlement. "I don't understand."

Odette did not answer. Her lips began to purse as if she'd consumed something sour. She swallowed carefully, her eyes squeezing shut once more. Whatever she saw now caused her unmistakable consternation.

Pippa gnawed at her lower lip. Unease trickled down Celine's spine like a bead of slowly dripping sweat. She gripped Odette's hand tightly, noticing how much warmer her skin felt with each passing second. "What?" she whispered. "What is it?"

All at once Odette pulled away, yanking her palm from Celine's grasp. Her brown eyes flickered open, their darkened centers large, shimmering, out of focus. "I couldn't . . ." She trailed off, momentarily disoriented. Then she straightened like a soldier and shot Celine a dazzling smile. "I'm sorry, mon amie, but portions of your future were too murky for me to divine."

Celine did not believe her. "What does that mean?"

Odette shrugged. "It means the course of your life has yet to be plotted." Her laughter resembled bubbles of champagne, light, frivolous, full of air. "But don't fret. We can try again soon, I promise."

Celine swallowed her retort. Odette's brand of magic was not as impressive or as helpful as she'd hoped it would be. It was also possible the girl was deliberately concealing what she'd seen. Neither option sat well with Celine, but it would be impolite to pursue the matter further in public.

As though nothing had transpired, Odette shifted her attention to Pippa, her ungloved hand held out before her. "Would you care to try?"

Pippa took a step back. "Please don't be offended, but I'd rather my future remain a surprise."

Another round of airy laughter burst from Odette's lips. "Smart girl!"

"But," Pippa said, her features knitting with confusion, "I *am* curious about how it works. Is it a skill with which you are born, or one you must cultivate?"

Odette tilted her head from side to side, wordlessly balancing her thoughts like weights on a scale. Before she responded, she donned her glove once more. "Many of the women in my family were gifted with the second sight. This place has given me a chance to cultivate this gift without judgment or expectation. For those like me, it's the only safe haven we've ever had." Her grin turned sad before she brightened the very next instant. "Truly, this is a place unlike any other."

"Kassamir called it La Cour des Lions," Celine said.

"The . . . Heart of a Lion?" Pippa attempted to translate.

"The Court of the Lions," Celine corrected in a kind voice.

Pippa's gaze widened in understanding, undoubtedly arriving at the same conclusion Celine herself had come to not long ago. That, yet again, Celine was responsible for dragging her friend deeper through a field of razor-sharp diamonds.

Perhaps it was simply her fate to be a portent of doom.

Odette rolled her eyes. "That's not Kassamir's doing. That's Bastien's. Honestly, that boy could sell a snowball to a penguin." She snickered. "You would never suspect how dramatic he truly is." Her features turned rueful. "Ah, but if he heard me say that, he would stare at me with those dagger eyes of his until I apologized. Really, men are such infants."

Distracted by her worries, it took a moment for Celine to register Odette's words. Her blood turned cold. "Bastien? Are you referring to Sébastien Saint Germain?"

Odette's eyes went wide. "Yes, that's him. Un vrai démon, n'est ce-pas?" She sniffed. "At least he's a welcome sight for the eyes. Have you ever seen a more handsome devil?"

"No," Celine admitted. "Unfortunately, neither has he."

"Parfait! Simplement parfait!" Odette clapped her hands, her laughter lilting into the coffered ceiling. Then she resumed chattering without pausing for breath.

Somewhere high above the clouds—or deep below in a fiery pit—an otherworldly creature must be having a grand time at Celine's expense. Her shoulders fell forward, her lips thinning into a line as the words continued flowing from Odette's lips like wine at a Bacchanalia.

"Bastien's uncle owns this entire building, as well as several properties in the Vieux Carré," Odette said. "Of course you've heard of Le Comte de Saint Germain. Rich as Croesus and charming as sin. Bastien is his sole heir, a fact that hasn't gone unnoticed by the débutantes of our fair city, despite the . . . concern many in society have with regard to his parentage." Her laughter became mischievous, a sly flutter of sound. "I'd wager money solves most problems, non?" She winked. "Though I myself speak only three languages, the Count has mastered *nine* and can quote entire swaths of scripture on a whim. He's also an immense fan of the—" She stopped short when she noticed the glazed look on Celine's face. "Ah, but I'm getting ahead of myself." Odette leaned conspiratorially toward Pippa, who stood to one side, her fingers threading and unthreading through each other. "Don't believe all the nasty rumors. Bastien's uncle is a gem. After Bastien's parents died, he took him in as a boy and cared for him like his own."

Celine cleared her throat, bewildered by the onslaught of information. "This is the first I've heard of the count, and I was only . . . introduced to his nephew this evening."

Odette tilted her head. "The count is not in the city at present, but I suspect Bastien should arrive at any moment." She began scanning the plush carpet, her gaze weaving around the chair legs. "In any case, you should be on the lookout for Toussaint."

"What?" Celine refrained from shifting backward. "We should be looking for something . . . on the floor?" After witnessing chess pieces offer their own surrender, Celine did not want to be caught unawares by naughty parlor tables or stools with errant senses of humor.

"Don't be alarmed. It's really nothing at all." Odette gestured once more with her hands, a reaction Celine had come to associate with agitation. "Toussaint . . . is Bastien's Burmese python." She rushed through her next words. "Really he's completely harmless. The poor angel adores his rest and wouldn't hurt a mouse." She grimaced and bit her lip. "Zut alors. I meant figuratively, of course." Odette brightened. "Just wait. Before you know it, you'll all be the best of friends."

It took a moment for her explanation to register, disjointed as it was.

Bastien's Burmese python.

Bastien's *giant snake*.

Though the serpent in question had yet to make an appearance, Pippa stifled a small shriek and jumped backward, scrambling for a chair or something upon which to stand. Celine remained rooted to one spot, a familiar rush coursing through her veins.

Odette cast them a rueful glance. "Occasionally, Toussaint

does like to wrap himself around anything warm, but please know you have nothing to fear. I only mentioned him because—if you don't know to look for him—he can be a bit . . . disconcerting."

"A snake?" Pippa squeaked, looking for all the world as if she wanted to melt into the paneled wall at her back. "What kind of person has a pet *snake*?"

"Lucifer," Celine said in a flat voice. "Lucifer would have a pet snake."

A trill of laughter burst from Odette's lips as she reached for her glass of wine. "Ah, you simply must tell me what happened when you were introduced this evening. How delicious!"

Celine sucked in her cheeks to marshal her retort.

Pippa's blue eyes darted across the floor while she gnawed on her lower lip, her fingers toying with the golden cross around her neck. "We encountered Mr. Saint Germain on our way here. He wasn't"—she hesitated—"as gracious as he should have been."

"I'm unsurprised to hear that," Odette said. "Bastien is like a character from a childhood nursery rhyme. When he's good, he's very, very good. When he's bad, well . . . I'm sure you can finish the rest."

Celine certainly could. But she refused to waste more time contemplating that wretched boy and his ridiculous pet snake. It would take effort, but Celine intended to put a swift end to . . . whatever worrisome interest this beautiful boy had managed to wake in her.

In truth, she didn't understand it at all. They'd barely spent less than a moment in each other's presence, and a handsome face was not enough to distract her from his many misdeeds. Before the night was through, Celine intended to have a firm rein on her emotions.

Nothing good ever came from letting them run amok.

Her gaze settled on a painting in a gilt frame across the room. She let her sight distort until its edges glowed molten gold. Celine hated how much her notice of a boy like Bastien brought to light how broken she was. In one short evening, he'd become a proverbial thorn in Celine's side. A reminder that something inside her was not right.

Perhaps that was it. Perhaps it wasn't a fascination with him at all. Perhaps it was the allure of the creature that lurked within her. Not too long ago, that creature had granted her immense power over a tormenter and freedom over her life.

But it had also made her a murderess.

Celine's expression hardened. She would put an end to all of it. Immediately.

It would have worked. Later, Celine would swear she'd been on the cusp of victory, intent on shoving anything related to Sébastien Saint Germain deep into a dark abyss. To make him disappear forever.

All would have gone to plan.

If not for the high-pitched scream that suddenly tore through the room.

THE GHOST

———◦◇◇◦———

Pippa's bloodcurdling shriek echoed through the chamber, rebounding off the paneled walls, setting the golden tassels atremble. It rent the space in two, like a crack had split across the plush carpeting, Hell yawning in fiery fathoms below.

Truly it was an impressive achievement, that scream.

The moment it left Pippa's lips, every member of La Cour des Lions leapt into action, their bodies tensed and alert. Odette scrambled to Pippa's side, the glass of red wine in her hand tipping, its contents splashing on Pippa's skirts. Before Celine could blink, a stylish man from the Far East moved swiftly toward them, brandishing a mother-of-pearl dagger. He halted at her shoulder, twirling his blade from one hand to the other. Boone sauntered into view while flipping an ice pick in the air. The two women with the dangerous rings posed like panthers about to spring, their fingers forming claws, as though their opulent jewels were really weapons instead of adornments. The victor of the recent chess match simply laid a pistol on the table before him, his bearded features cool and collected.

Celine gripped her friend's elbow, yanking her back, angling her body in front of Pippa's, like a shield. "What happened?"

she demanded of her friend in a hushed voice. "Are you all right?"

Guilt pulled at the corners of Pippa's mouth. "I . . . thought something brushed across my foot," she said in a breathless tone, her expression one of bewilderment. "I must have been mistaken." She spoke louder, pitching her voice through the room. "I deeply regret having frightened everyone. There is nothing amiss. Please accept my humblest apology."

Those poised to attack did not stand down. Many of them continued staring at Pippa, their features wary, their eyes continuing to flicker in a disconcerting way. Again Celine was momentarily struck by her earlier thought:

Inhuman.

But that was impossible. Wasn't it? It was one thing to believe in magic and illusion. Another entirely to believe in creatures of childish fancy.

Pippa took in a great gulp of air, her face flushed. "I'm truly sorry," she said again, even louder, while trying in vain to prevent the spilled wine from soaking through her skirts.

"Don't apologize any more," Celine muttered. "A pox on that damned snake and its fool of a master."

Then—as if Pippa's scream had sent a message through the paneled walls—one of the two doors in the back of the chamber opened, a rush of cool air racing over the exposed skin at Celine's chest and throat. At first, nothing emerged from the entrance, but then those nearby shifted slightly, as though to allow someone—or something—passage.

"Ah, there he is." Odette beamed.

Pippa reached for Celine as a massive snake—its scales covered in dark brown spots bordered by rings of black—slithered across the carpeted floor. Fear and exhilaration wound through Celine's body. She began easing to one side as the snake drew closer, but Pippa held her in place, her fingers tightly coiled around Celine's wrist.

"They smell fear," Pippa murmured.

"How do you know that?"

"I read it somewhere."

"That's rubbish." Odette doffed her wine-stained gloves. "Technically they can't smell anything. Only taste things with their tongues."

Celine sent a murderous glare in Odette's direction as the snake passed them, vanishing under a pool of indigo silk beneath an arched window. Even after the serpent disappeared, Pippa did not stop wringing the blood from the tips of Celine's fingers.

"Oh, fiddle-dee-dee, Toussaint won't hurt anyone," Odette reassured them, stuffing her bare hands in her pockets as she spoke. "One time he wrapped himself around Arjun, but it was only frightening for a minute." She paused in remembrance. "And that crumpet-eating criminal deserved it."

"What—what did he do?" Pippa asked.

"Apparently massacred one too many crumpets," the boy in question teased from behind Pippa, his British accent slurring ever so slightly, clearly tainted by drink.

Celine turned toward Arjun in shock, noting his reddened knuckles and disheveled appearance. Not-so-gentle reminders that—regardless of how pleasantly he comported himself—this boy from the East Indies was not what he seemed. After all, he'd managed to cross the room without being noticed, like a shadow slipping through a cloud of smoke.

Pippa spun around with an unusual lack of grace, only to lose her footing. She would have fallen to the floor if Arjun hadn't been there to steady her, his arms encircling her shoulders.

"I've got you, pet," he said with a mischievous half smile.

A flash of horror rippled across Pippa's face. The next instant, she shoved him away with a startling amount of force. Arjun landed on his backside, his waistcoat askew and his monocle tangling about his neck.

Celine tried to control her reaction, but it could not be helped. She pressed her knuckles to her lips. Soon, Odette was steadying herself against Celine, cackling alongside her. Unsurprisingly, Pippa did not join in their amusement. She clasped both palms over her mouth. Flustered, she bent to help Arjun to his feet, reaching for his hands.

Only to be roundly rebuffed.

"I'm so sorry!" she said, color rising up her neck. "I wasn't expecting you to be so . . ."

"Helpful?" he offered.

"Warm," she finished, her cheeks reddening.

Arjun glanced up at her quizzically, then grinned, though he still refused to take her proffered hand. Instead he looked to his left, whistling through his teeth to catch the attention of the nearby chess champion. The next instant, the gangly fellow stepped forward to yank Arjun to his feet with an uncanny amount of strength, his ruddy mustache curling along its waxed edges.

"'Ad enough, me good man?" he said in a gruff Cockney accent. When he straightened, he towered over everyone in his vicinity, his limbs long and thin, causing him to resemble a beanpole. "Is every bleedin' maharajah as piss poor at holding his liquor as you is?"

Arjun rolled his eyes. "Such poppycock. Not every man from India is a maharajah, Nigel." He paused for effect, securing his golden cuff links. "And not every Englishman is a gentleman."

"Blighter!"

"Loathsome imperialist."

"Clumsy twat!"

"Overgrown twig."

Nigel's waxed mustache twitched. Then he threw back his head and guffawed. The sound was so filled with delight that Celine began to smile.

"¿Qué está pasando, Odette?" a rich voice cut through the mêlée, the sound resonating from behind where they stood.

"¡Hostia!" Odette startled. Her small fist darted out, thudding against a solid form. "Stop trying to scare me, you horse's ass. Te dije lo que sucedería la próxima vez . . ." She launched into a tirade Celine could not follow, the Spanish words flying from her lips with ease.

Arjun and Nigel exchanged a glance. Then promptly made their way toward the roulette table in the back of the room.

Odette continued ranting to the newcomer at Celine's back. But Celine refused to turn around. She had no need to confirm the obvious. Her pulse ratcheted in her throat when the heat of him drew closer. The feeling of being both drawn in and pushed back—a magnet made of opposing poles—gripped her stomach. Just like the night she'd first arrived in New Orleans, when he'd cleared the streets without uttering a word, Bastien's presence was a tangible thing. It made something in the air shift, like a sigh of wind.

The creature inside Celine writhed beneath her skin, stirring to life.

No. Celine Rousseau was not a weathervane. She would not be moved by the Ghost's presence as everyone else was. He was not special, just like all the privileged boys she'd encountered in her past. Another spoiled and entitled approximation of a man. She took a deep breath, determined to remain unaffected.

Celine felt Bastien's eyes settle on the back of her neck. The fine hairs there stood on end, sending a warm buzz down her spine. He was close enough that she could smell the bergamot in his cologne. The hints of citrus and spice.

This boy was dangerous. Far too dangerous. Like fuel to her fire.

She stood straight. Bade the stirring creature silent.

Odette continued chastising Bastien in a mixture of Spanish and French. Unruffled by her tirade, Bastien shifted past Celine and Pippa, his strides unhurried, his movements liquid. Since their encounter an hour ago, he'd discarded his frock coat and rolled up the sleeves of his crisp white shirt, revealing a tailored waistcoat of charcoal silk and a set of curious black markings on his inner left forearm. Disdaining the fashion of the day, he wore his dark hair shorn close to his head, resembling a bust Celine had once seen of Julius Caesar. Strapped around his shoulders was a burnished leather holster, a revolver glinting beneath his right arm. When he met Celine's gaze, he pressed his lips together, a hint of irritation pushing them forward, squaring his jaw. Annoyance riddled his handsome face. Not a trace of surprise nor a drop of pleasure at finding her here.

It emboldened Celine. Urged her to dismiss him as summarily as he'd dismissed her.

"Are you finished?" he said quietly to Odette, though his eyes were trained on Celine.

"For now," Odette sniffed. "Just don't do it again. You know how much I despise being taken off guard. No doubt that's the reason you enjoy doing it, you malquisto."

Though her tone had lightened to one of jest, Bastien did not smile. "Responde mi pregunta. ¿Por qué está ella aquí?"

"No." Odette crossed her arms. "I'm not answering your question. C'est impoli. These ladies are my guests, and I do not owe you an explanation for why they are here."

The edges of Bastien's eyes tightened, his expression darkening. Under normal circumstances, Celine suspected this icy glower engendered fear in others. Moved them to obey, without question.

She met him eye for eye, glare for glare, her heart thudding behind her ribs. Celine waited for him to ask them to leave. After all, this building belonged to his family. And no matter what anyone might say otherwise, it was clear Bastien ruled La

Cour des Lions, from its coffered ceiling to the snake slithering across its plush carpets.

Lucifer in his den of lions.

Instead, Bastien remained silent. The bronze skin around his eyes and forehead softened, the set of his shoulders unwinding. Before Celine could take a breath, charm oozed from him with the kind of natural grace reserved for nobility.

It was an unnerving sight to behold.

Bastien bowed to Pippa. "Welcome to Jacques', mademoiselle. I am Sébastien Saint Germain. C'est un plaisir de faire votre connaissance." The consummate chameleon, he reached for her hand, bending to place a kiss on it.

Though Pippa's cheeks pinked at his touch, she cleared her throat. Extricated her fingers. "We've met already, sir."

Celine smothered a grin.

"Quel charlatan!" Odette snorted as she sipped her wine. "They know who you are."

Bastien did not appear the least bit perturbed by her mockery. "But I don't believe we've been formally introduced."

"Then permettez-moi." A devious light glimmered in Odette's eyes. "The stunning young lady to your right, with the raven hair and the eyes like Egyptian emeralds, is Celine—" She stopped short. Laughed. "I just realized I don't know your proper name, mon amie."

Celine put out her hand, channeling indifference. "My name is Celine Rousseau."

Bastien took it. She sensed a hint of hesitation the moment his long fingers wrapped around hers. The slightest twinge, like he'd made an error in judgment and realized it far too late. A current of fire spread into her arm, moving slowly, as though the creature in her blood wished to savor the experience. Before Bastien could bend to kiss her hand, Celine tugged her palm from his grasp.

Something unreadable passed across his features, there and gone before Celine could take in a breath. Then his smile turned savage in its amusement. An unspoken challenge.

It emboldened Celine further. If he was going to play a game, she would simply play it better. She looked at Pippa and tilted her head, allowing a knowing twinkle to shine in her eye. Just the sort of look she'd seen countless young women of Parisian society share among themselves, as if they alone were privy to a delicious secret. "This is my dear friend, Miss Philippa Montrose."

Bastien bowed again to Pippa. "Enchanté, Mademoiselle Montrose."

Pippa nodded, her unease obvious. Though Odette tried to appear indifferent to the unfolding scene, her attention flitted between Celine and Bastien as if she were witnessing a thread start to unravel. When she caught Celine staring at her, she diverted her gaze, focusing on Pippa's wine-stained skirt.

"Merde!" Odette swore. "I'm an absolute wretch. I completely forgot about your gown. Come with me." She began walking with purpose toward the staircase.

Pippa shook her head. "Don't trouble yourself. It's not—"

"Nonsense." Odette pivoted in place. "I'm certain Kassamir will have some—what was it?" Her fingertips snapped together, the sound crackling through the air. "Tonic water to remove the stain, as Celine suggested."

"That's not necessary."

"I insist." Odette took Pippa by the hand. "If you don't allow me to fix it, then at the very least you must permit me to replace your gown. The fabric is such a lovely . . . voile, isn't it?" Her features brightened, an idea already taking shape in her mind. "We could go together tomorrow to see my modiste. She doesn't have Celine's eye or training, but she's quite adept at—"

"Please don't trouble yourself, Mademoiselle Valmont. This gown isn't worth it. It's very old. It . . . was passed down to me from a cousin." Pippa winced at this admission, and something knifed behind Celine's heart. Clearly it pained Pippa to disclose this detail, and Celine did not have the slightest inkling why.

It bothered her to realize how little she knew about her only friend.

Only an hour ago, Pippa had remarked that they weren't truly friends. Not yet. It had chafed to hear it then, but Celine could not deny its truth now. Real friends freely shared their thoughts and feelings, their secrets, their fears. In Paris—before that terrible night—Celine had had two such friends, Monique and Josephine. She wondered if they thought of her now. If they worried about her. Questioned where she'd gone.

If they knew she was now a murderess.

After Pippa's pained admission, Odette kept silent for a time. When next she spoke, her words were gentle. "Please let me help with this, ma choupette." She took Pippa's hand again, this time with less insistence. "And do call me Odette. I much prefer when my friends call me that."

In that moment, Celine decided that—one day—she would like to be friends with Odette Valmont, too. Pippa waited a moment. Then nodded once with a grateful smile. The two young women made their way toward the first-floor restaurant, on a quest to find Kassamir.

Leaving Celine in a den of lions . . . standing beside Lucifer.

DES QUESTIONS, DES QUESTIONS

——◦◇◇◇◦——

The moment their friends vanished downstairs, Celine and Bastien shared a glance. A charge hummed through the air, swirling around them like the beginning of a storm.

Their smiles faded the next instant.

A thick silence descended like a cloak about their shoulders. A part of Celine relished it. It felt honest. Absent pretense. In this moment, she could be who she was. It did not matter if she failed to adhere to the social mores of her day. Bastien would not judge her, for he was not a gentleman, just as Celine was not a lady.

His posture relaxed further, almost as if he had come to the same conclusion. He spread his feet and settled into an informal stance. Celine found she enjoyed seeing him in this comfortable light. It made him appear more like a living, breathing person, rather than a subject of salacious gossip. He was, after all, nothing but a young man.

Albeit a devilishly attractive one.

Bastien pushed his lips forward again in obvious calculation. It drew attention to his mouth in a way that made Celine avert her gaze. She swallowed, dismissing a flurry of wanton thoughts. Half of her felt angered by this proof of her attraction. The other half appreciated the stark reminder that Bastien brought the worst version of Celine to the surface. The one cloaked in vice and sin.

Another minute passed in silence. The longer they went without speaking, the heavier the charge in the air grew, until it took on a life of its own, a hooded specter looming above their heads.

Celine refused to be the one who spoke first. Under pain of death. He could wait until the sun rose high in the sky tomorrow morning, for all she cared.

"You arrived to New Orleans recently." Bastien offered this as a statement of fact, rather than a question.

"A little more than a week ago." Celine paused, wondering if he recalled seeing her that first evening near Jackson Square. "You speak Spanish."

He nodded. "Because of my father."

"Your father was Spanish?"

"No."

Celine waited for him to clarify, then sighed to herself when he didn't. Not because she was troubled by his evasiveness, but rather because she understood his wish to thread a needle with every word he spoke.

Yet another similarity.

Vexed by this realization, Celine eased back on her left heel, the toes of her right foot tapping against the thick carpet.

A smile ghosted across Bastien's lips. "I'm irritating you."

"You're enjoying it."

"I am." His mouth shifted to one side, again pressed into that maddening pucker.

Silence settled between them once more. Then Bastien took a step closer to Celine, no doubt to see how she would respond. If she moved back, she'd reveal her unease, thereby granting him the upper hand. If she shifted forward, she'd reveal her attraction . . . which also granted the fiend the upper hand.

Celine did not give ground. She was a mountain. A hundred-year-old oak. A tower refusing to bend. "I can stand here forever in irritated silence. It is no bother to me." She crossed her arms tightly, her forearms winding beneath her breasts, pushing against the boning in her corset. "You can perish wondering what I'm thinking, for I'll never tell."

"Likewise." The angles in Bastien's features hollowed further. His eyes dipped downward instinctively before he caught them, his jawline flexing, sharpening.

He glanced away.

At first Celine did not understand his odd behavior. She let her gaze drift lower, only to drop her arms as though they'd burst into flame. "If you think I used my wiles to catch your notice like a girl trying to fill her dance card at a ball, then—"

"Whatever I think has nothing to do with you," Bastien interjected. "My behavior is not your responsibility."

His response unseated her. Shocked her into silence. She'd never heard such words fall from any man's lips. Celine's father had always scolded her for wearing anything that accentuated her figure. Alas, the latest fashions sought to do just that: give life to every line, sway to every curve. Even a lady's unmentionables were designed to grant her the appearance of an hourglass. Nevertheless, Professor Guillaume Rousseau had encouraged his daughter to wear modesty pieces about her throat and dress in layers, even when the Parisian summers were at their worst.

Bastien took a deep breath, as if he were biding his time. "I made you uncomfortable. I . . . apologize."

"You might be the first man who didn't blame me for it," Celine confessed, masking her shock by arching a brow.

He nodded, his expression grim. Then he rubbed the back of his neck, the gleaming leather of his shoulder holster stretching, catching the light. "To answer the question you didn't ask, my father was of Taíno heritage. I spent several years of my life in San Juan. Spanish is the language of my childhood."

This accounted for the trace of something different in his accent. Celine didn't know what Taíno meant, but she remembered reading about a city named San Juan in a former Spanish colony somewhere in the Caribbean. She found herself wanting to know more. To learn why it was that his uncle had raised him from childhood.

Because Celine wanted to know, she asked nothing.

It was safer that way, for them both.

"Are you enjoying your time in New Orleans?" It was the first question Bastien had posed to Celine that sounded contrived, as though it were meant for polite company. It grated her to hear it, for theirs had never been polite company. She preferred it that way.

Celine tilted her head. Cut her gaze. "How long are we going to pretend what happened earlier this evening didn't happen at all?"

Bastien's laughter was quick. Caustic. "You're rather certain of your moral rectitude, Mademoiselle Rousseau."

"Just as I'm certain it benefits you to be so dismissive, Monsieur Saint Germain."

His gunmetal-grey eyes glittered. "I've irritated you again."

"Yet you still have not offered a reason why."

"I don't enjoy explaining myself. My actions speak for me. If you feel them to be heartless and cruel, then so be it; I am heartless and cruel." He spoke in a glib fashion. "Trust that I will be the last person to correct you."

"It must be quite a life, not having to explain yourself."

"You should try it sometime. It's rather freeing."

"I imagine it would be freeing to care only about oneself." She heaved a dramatic sigh. "Alas, I am not a man."

A frown touched Bastien's lips. The first sign that Celine had struck a nerve. But he did not reply. This time, the silence around them hung on the cusp of something weightier. A bolt of lightning before a crash of thunder.

"Why—"

"Are—"

They both stopped. Exchanged daggered smiles. This close, Celine could see flecks of steel in his eyes. The way the stubble along his jaw accentuated its fine lines.

"Please," he began, canting his head, giving her leave to speak first.

"Why did the man in the alleyway call you Le Fantôme?"

Celine asked. "Do you have a habit of dressing like a ghoul and terrorizing those around you?"

Amusement rippled across Bastien's face. "It's a nickname from childhood." He paused before returning the volley. "Do you have a habit of dragging darkness with you wherever you go?"

"What?" It stunned Celine how precisely he managed to strike another nerve.

"Selene was a lunar goddess. A Titan. She drove a chariot of white horses across the sky to usher in the night."

How . . . lovely. Celine had never heard the story of the goddess Selene, which surprised her because her father was a lover of the classics. Her parents had named her for a family relation, long-since dead. A great-aunt named Marceline. She didn't know when they'd first taken to shortening it. Likely when she was very young. Perhaps even when she lived along the coast of her mother's country.

"No, I was not named for a goddess," she replied. "Celine . . . is a nickname from childhood."

"I deserved that." Bastien's soft laughter filtered through the air. Those in their immediate vicinity turned to peer at them in disbelief, one of their ranks blowing a stream of pale blue smoke from an elaborate water pipe. It was the first time Celine had ever heard Bastien laugh freely. It sounded low. A rich baritone swathed in silk. She ignored the way it made her appreciate each of her senses all the more.

Celine found herself settling into their exchange, without once feeling the need to play a role. The diligent worker. The obedient daughter. The pious young woman. Someone who floated with the current, rather than making her own waves.

Did the lunar goddess Selene also rule the tides, like the moon? If so, Celine wished to go through the rest of her life channeling this deity. It was true she didn't know whether this goddess was her namesake, but perhaps she could choose to take on the mantle herself.

Celine relished the thought. The idea of being a Titan who wrapped the sky in a fleece of stars.

"Why did you leave Paris?" Bastien asked, shattering the image forming in Celine's mind.

Her pulse fluttered at the question, her nerves going taut. "I never said I was from Paris."

"You didn't need to." His grin was devastatingly charming, despite the sharp angles of his features. "You told Odette. Now even the gutter rats know."

At that, Celine laughed. It felt easy. Too easy.

Nearby, the sounds of ivory dice striking against burl wood mingled with a chorus of raucous laughter. Her attention drifted toward the roulette table. Celine smiled to herself, again struck by the realization she felt comfortable here, amid practitioners of magic and lords of mayhem. As Odette had suggested, this place was unlike anything Celine had ever known.

Bastien followed her gaze. "Have you played roulette?"

Celine did not reply.

"You should try it," he pressed.

"You're encouraging me to gamble?"

"Does that riffle your delicate sensibilities?"

"Don't be a cad." Celine narrowed her eyes at him. "Perhaps

I'm an excellent gambler," she lied again, as she had to Boone. "Perhaps you will *rue* the day you *let* me win."

A spark of humor shone in his gaze. "A fair pun, though I'm loath to admit it."

"You dislike puns?"

"Almost as much as rhetorical questions."

"There was a time when puns were the height of humor." She mirrored the angle of his head. "And are you not curious about which came first, the chicken or the egg?"

"Technically"—he sent her a wicked grin—"wasn't it the rooster?"

Celine's brows shot upward, her mouth agape. The next instant, bright laughter burst from her lips, the sound startling those nearby for the second time that evening.

Bastien smiled wider, his teeth flashing white, distracting her for an instant. They looked inordinately perfect, the points of his canines almost wolfish. Something about it unsettled her, as if Celine were gazing at a painting instead of a person. Perhaps a piece by Rembrandt, a master who always managed to catch details others missed, rendering his subjects in an otherworldly light.

A timely reminder that young men like Bastien saw the world through rose-colored glasses. Through a haze of wealth and entitlement.

"Don't fall in love with me," Celine blurted without thought. "Nothing good will come of it."

Surprise touched his features. "Then you intend to break my heart?"

"Most assuredly."

"Duly noted." Bastien appeared—by all rights—to be enjoying himself. It unnerved Celine to realize that she, too, was enjoying his company. It had been weeks since she'd looked upon a man without an air of suspicion clouding her every thought.

The next instant, Celine's smile faded.

Pippa had reached the top of the stairs, Odette in tow. The front of Pippa's simple voile dress was wet, but the stain appeared to be from water rather than wine. Celine moved away from Bastien, clasping her hands behind her, turning her attention to the floor, as if she'd been caught committing an act of subterfuge.

Bastien studied her with an odd look, his expression savoring strangely of disappointment. It was only for an instant, but a cold hand of guilt grasped Celine by the throat, making it difficult to swallow. As if her conscience believed she'd wronged Bastien in some fashion. But how could that be possible? A boy like this would not care what a girl he'd just met thought of him. He'd said it himself:

He would be the last one to correct her assumptions.

Sure enough, Bastien stepped away. Stood straight, his brow hooding his gaze, a shadow falling across his features once more.

Another stab of guilt cut through Celine's chest. She banished it the following instant. If Bastien did not believe it necessary to explain himself, then why should she? Besides that, it wasn't proper for her to be seen enjoying his company, given his earlier behavior.

They were like two trains set on a collision course. Better for all those involved if they did not relish each other's company.

At least that way they could avoid colliding at all.

Odette strode before them, her hands in the pockets of her buckskin trousers, a lock of brunette hair escaping her coif. "My, that was an odyssey. I never thought voile would be quite so stubborn a fabric." She arched her brows in question. "What did we miss?"

Celine lifted a shoulder as if she were bored. "I was merely conveying to Monsieur Saint Germain my displeasure at our earlier encounter." She squared her chin. "And especially with the display of wanton violence."

Bastien remained silent, his lips pressing forward. Celine felt the weight of his gaze upon her, the steel turning colder with each passing second.

"Violence?" Odette's eyes shifted from Celine to Bastien and back again. "Qu'est-ce que tu as fait?" she accused, her lovely face crestfallen, her hands curling into fists at her sides, the skin there resembling polished Carrara. "At least do me the courtesy of not ruining my friendships before I've had the chance to make them, s'il te plaît." Huffing, Odette drew a lacquered fan from inside her ballooned sleeve and flicked it open.

Bastien considered Celine for a tense spell. Then amusement tugged at the edges of his mouth. "Answering violence with violence *was* a courtesy, ma souris. Perhaps in your quest for friendship, you could elect to choose fewer . . . unsavory characters."

Odette's fan snapped shut. "You didn't."

He crooked a dark eyebrow at her and said nothing.

"You démon," Odette said. "I warned you not to get involved in that matter with Lévêque. What did you do?" She glanced about. "Never mind. Of course you won't tell me. I'll simply ask Arjun instead."

"Des questions, des questions." Bastien held his hands out at his sides. "Qui a le temps pour ces choses?" He sent her a devilish grin.

"You should make the time." Odette sniffed with disdain. "And I wouldn't be proud of that terrible joke, if I were you."

"There are those who find me wildly clever."

"Grâce à Dieu, I am not among them," Odette retorted, "for I have no need of your golden coffers . . . or your pretty face."

Celine laughed softly. "And every man should be master of his own time."

Bastien turned to her, his features expressionless. He nodded once. "Just as every woman should quote Shakespeare when she has nothing better to say."

Celine's cheeks grew hot. Embarrassment coiled through her as Pippa took hold of her left hand, bidding her to keep calm.

Gritting her teeth, Celine swiveled toward Odette. "Forgive me, but time has gotten away from us. Is there a place we can go to finish obtaining your measurements?" She paused, her words pointed. "A place where we can avoid *unwanted* eyes?"

Odette's petite nostrils flared at Bastien, her mouth caught between silence and speech for a breath. At any moment, Celine expected her to begin berating him again, almost as if she were his elder sister or his aunt. But Odette simply nodded.

"There's a chamber in the back, past the washroom."

With a withering glance in Bastien's direction, Odette led the way toward one of the two doors in the back, situated at opposite extremes along the wall. Between them rested an ornate wooden credenza with a white cloth strewn across its middle. Covering its surface were statues resembling Saint Peter and the Virgin Mary, painted in vivid hues. A short blade lay across the credenza's center. Positioned in a semicircle around it were carved figurines with skull faces and small dolls fashioned of bone and straw. Scattered between were assortments of wooden beads, dried fruits, and nuts, mingled with drops of hardened wax.

The arrangement looked vaguely familiar to Celine. Lingering traces of incense and scented candles curled into her nose, painting flashes of memory across her vision. Recollections of a low table decorated in a similar fashion, the fragrances of fruit and myrrh suffusing the air.

The display spiked her curiosity, but Celine did not stop to study it further or ask any questions. She wished to be rid of anything associated with this place as soon as possible, though it troubled her to no longer feel welcome at Jacques'.

"Through here." Odette reached for the handle of an entrance intended to blend into the paneled walls, its hinges concealed by the folds of a heavy silk curtain. When she pushed against it, the door refused to budge.

"C'est quoi ça?" Odette muttered, shoving harder, lines gathering across her brow. She threw her weight against the heavy oak. Finally it began to give way.

A hand flopped through the opening.

A pale, unmoving hand.

It took a moment for the sight to register. A stutter of time before everything sped forward in a rush.

"Mon Dieu!" Odette exclaimed. Using her shoulder, she rammed through the opening with Celine on her heels. They both stopped short, Pippa trembling behind them.

A girl lay sprawled across the floor of a darkened corridor, her unbound auburn curls thrown over her freckled face. At her throat was a jagged wound. Something had torn through her flesh with razor-sharp teeth, like those of a large animal.

Her fingers shaking, Odette reached for the girl's wrist, checking for a pulse. When she jostled the young woman's arm, a lock of wavy red hair fell from her face.

Celine gasped. She knew that face. Had spent the better part of the day in its company.

Anabel.

"Is she—?" Pippa's voice broke. Then rose into a keening wail.

There was no need for anyone to answer her unspoken question.

Beside Anabel's lifeless body, a symbol had been drawn in blood:

An Aerialist on a Tightrope

———◇◇◇◇◇———

Celine had seen death before.

She was no stranger to the sight. But that did not make it any easier to bear witness to it now. Nor did it make its finality any less severe.

A life had been taken tonight.

Like that, Anabel was gone.

Many realizations gripped Celine in the moments following the body's discovery:

Anabel had died a violent death. That much was clear from the jagged maw across her throat. Celine had never seen a wound like that. For an instant, she toyed with the idea that Bastien's snake might be responsible.

Upon further consideration, however, it did not follow that a snake like Toussaint would go to the trouble of killing its prey, only to leave it behind in a darkened corridor. If memory served Celine correctly, pythons did not slash their victims' throats; instead they opted to squeeze the life out of them slowly.

And of course no snake would leave behind a calling card. Written in blood, no less.

But if the snake wasn't responsible for Anabel's death, then who was? And why? Moreover, why had Anabel come to Jacques' tonight? Clearly she'd followed Celine and Pippa here. But why had she not made her presence known?

It took only an instant for Celine to parse out the truth.

The Mother Superior must have sent Anabel to spy on them. It had to be the reason why the matron of the Ursuline convent had changed her mind so easily earlier this evening, when she'd suddenly granted Celine and Pippa permission to go, after protesting against it at length.

Celine swallowed, her ears going hot. If the Mother Superior's machinations explained why Anabel had come to Jacques' tonight, it meant all of them—Pippa, the Mother Superior, and Celine herself—had had a hand in Anabel's violent death.

In Anabel's murder.

Finally, if her death was at all related to the one along the docks, then it meant a madman—or madwoman—was on the loose.

Celine's eyes shifted around the room slowly, her breaths quickening. If someone had murdered Anabel in Jacques' tonight following their arrival, it meant anyone present now—including all the members of La Cour des Lions—could be responsible for killing her.

Odette. Nigel. Kassamir. Arjun. The man from the Far East with the mother-of-pearl blade. The two ebony-skinned women with their bejeweled claws. Boone. The harried young server below. Not to mention the many nameless individuals who'd been seated throughout the dimly lit chamber.

And of course Bastien.

With each passing second, these thoughts raced through Celine's mind, her skin tingling from the rush of blood, her foot tapping against the plush carpeting. In contrast, Pippa stared at the marble tabletop before them, her posture hollowing like an apple left out in the sun.

It was nearing midnight. Celine and Pippa should have returned to the convent hours ago. Instead they'd been sequestered in the shadowy chamber on the second floor, seated on an ornate divan in the style of Louis XIV, surrounded by a gathering of illusionists.

As well as five members of the Metropolitan Police.

Though it was the least of Celine's concerns, the Mother Superior would undoubtedly have their heads upon their return. But that could not be of issue now.

Far more pressing was the fact that Pippa and Celine were likely being counted among the possible suspects in a murder. If Celine found any humor in the irony, she would be on the floor, laughing maniacally.

But humor would not save her now.

Once the truth of Celine's and Pippa's association with Anabel came to light, it would not be easy for them to explain why they'd been unaware of Anabel's presence until the moment they'd discovered her body. Even to Celine, it sounded suspicious. Not only had they been nearby at the time of the victim's death, but they'd also known the poor young woman personally. Briefly Celine considered trying to summon the Mother Superior to vouch for them. Alas, that old bat would be just as likely to foist blame onto Celine as she would be to help her.

It was too much of a risk.

Celine knew she should reveal these truths the instant after she was introduced to the Metropolitan Police's best detective. But it might color his judgment against them, causing him to forgo looking elsewhere for evidence. If she waited, however, he would undoubtedly be suspicious.

Zut. Celine sighed to herself. When would be a good time to tell him?

Never was definitely not an option . . . was it?

Alas, Celine could not conceal these things from him forever. Resentment swirled through her like a fog tinged in red light. Pippa began crying quietly, her fingers winding around one of the handkerchiefs Celine had fashioned to raise money for the convent. One of the many embroidered fripperies Anabel had sold Odette earlier that very day.

How had it come to this?

What kind of horrible misfortune had befallen Anabel?

And why the devil had she acquiesced to the Mother Superior's wishes? Celine clenched her fists in her skirts, anger heating her blood.

Tonight, the cost of Anabel's decision had been her life.

Celine shook her head quickly, fending off the rising guilt. Wishing to banish the image of Anabel's mauled body from her mind. Her efforts proved futile. Even in the few seconds before Pippa's scream and Odette's shout had torn through the night— before Bastien and Arjun and Nigel had raced to their sides— the image of Anabel's death mask had seared itself forever onto Celine's eyelids.

She glanced about, wondering how long the Metropolitan Police's most celebrated detective would take to question them. None of those waiting had yet to speak with him. Upon arrival, he'd gone straight to the place where Anabel's body had been found, and the semicircle of grim-faced officers standing around them did not exactly afford Celine a vantage point from which to discern much else.

Across the way, Arjun sat on a tufted velvet stool with an ankle crossed over a knee, his posture easy. From his fingers dangled a crystal tumbler, the contents within it swirling around the glass in shades of amber and gold. The monocle swaying from his throat shimmered as the whiskey danced about his glass. Celine urged her mind to become lost in the warm prisms cast by his motions.

Better she lose herself in drink than look to her immediate right.

Toward the figure standing in the shadows, bereft of his revolver, glaring at nothing.

Celine feigned a cough to clear her throat.

Where was this cursed detective? Why was he taking so long to examine the scene of the crime? *And where in God's name was Odette?*

Chaos had ensued in the moments following the discovery of Anabel's body. There hadn't been time for Celine to take stock of what was happening around her. Too many flashes of movement in all directions, too many questions crowding her mind.

But now that a tense kind of calm had descended—an aerialist on a tightrope—several details struck Celine as odd. First, the only immediate reactions from the second floor had been those of herself, Pippa, and Odette. The other members of La Cour des Lions had kept strangely silent and still, as if murder was not at all a surprising event.

It wasn't until everyone below reacted to the news that a gruesome death had occurred a stone's throw from where they sat that those on the second floor took action. Screams had echoed into the rafters, carrying from the restaurant into the streets. Women and men had fled the building, swelling into the alleyways and avenues adjoining Jacques'.

In the crush of shrieking bodies, Odette had disappeared without a word. At first, Celine and Pippa had worried something awful might have happened to her. They'd raced down the stairs toward the doors, searching the crowd for any sign of a young woman dressed as a man. By the time they'd made their way to the front of Jacques', all the exits had been cordoned off by the New Orleans Metropolitan Police.

More than an hour later, Odette was still nowhere to be found. In fact, only a few members of La Cour des Lions were still present: Arjun, Bastien, Nigel, the man from the Far East, and the two women with the tantalizing rings. The rest had vanished into the night during the chaos. Celine knew Bastien could not avoid being interrogated. His family owned this establishment. It was only natural that he would be under immediate inquiry. At any moment, she fully expected his uncle, the Count, to stride into the room in a black silk cape and a plush fur top hat.

Celine's mind churned in a ceaseless barrage of thoughts.

Despite her best efforts to silence them, one continued rising to the forefront. The sight of Anabel's body troubled her immensely. Of course the gaping wound at the girl's throat would likely haunt Celine for the rest of her days. But something else plagued her. Remained just beyond her reach.

The thud of a solid object echoed from below. The noise clattered down the stairs in staccato bursts of sound. Celine started. Pippa yelped softly. No one else uttered a word. The five officers of the Metropolitan Police cinched their semicircle tighter, drawing closer, like the strings of a purse pulling shut.

Then they exchanged worried glances.

Without warning, someone clapped their hands behind the waiting officers, the sound loud and sudden, causing Pippa to cry out again and rekindling Celine's irritation. It prickled beneath her skin like a thousand tiny needles threatening to burst forth. Arjun stopped swirling his drink. To his left, Nigel's frown hardened, the sight contrasting with his curling mustache, the tendons in his fingers flexing as if to keep him from lunging into the fray.

Celine did not need to look at Bastien to know his anger had spiked, just as hers had.

"My most profound apologies for keeping you waiting so long," a man calmly intoned, the sound disparate with the circumstances. "But I promise only one among you will be truly inconvenienced."

The officers standing in a semicircle parted without preamble.

Revealing New Orleans' best police detective.

One of Us

---◇◇◇◇---

The young man who stepped forward was not at all what Celine expected.

Firstly, he looked to be only several years older than she. His clean-shaven skin was tawny, in contrast to the pale features of the other officers present. He was not wearing a uniform. Instead it looked as though he'd left an elegant gathering, his collar impeccably starched, his champagne-colored cravat tied in a pristine knot. His wavy hair had been tamed into the latest fashion, full on all sides. Something about his appearance struck Celine as almost professorial. A touch awkward.

Save for the undeniable air of authority around him.

Before he spoke again, he offered them a forced smile, his teeth straight and bright. Then he adjusted his shirtsleeves until the perfect amount of white peeked from beneath the edge of his deep green frock coat.

"I am Detective Michael Grimaldi of the New Orleans Metropolitan Police," he began in a clipped voice, each word racing to overcome its predecessor. "I'm hoping to have your utmost cooperation as we work together to find the perpetrator of this horrific crime." He took a step closer, moving alongside Arjun, who flinched, his features souring.

At the sight of Arjun's discomfort, satisfaction passed across Detective Grimaldi's face. Now that he stood next to Arjun, Celine noted a similarity in their coloring, though Detective Grimaldi's features did not bear the same look of the East. Perhaps he was Italian, as his name suggested.

Detective Grimaldi's light eyes swept around the room again. Undoubtedly scanning the crowd, searching for an opening. In short order, he settled on Celine. His head tilted ever so slightly, his gaze appraising. Celine lifted her chin automatically. Defiantly. She didn't know what possessed her to do it, but she refused to be seen as anything but formidable. With a knowing smirk, the young detective moved along to Pippa. Whatever he was searching for, he found in her.

Pippa gasped in awareness. Celine reached for her friend's hand to offer her a measure of strength, just as Pippa had done for her countless times today.

The detective crouched before Pippa. "I apologize for having to detain you, miss," he said. "I promise not to keep you long. I heard you were one of the ladies who found the poor young woman's body." He paused. "That must have been terrible for you." Detective Grimaldi extended a hand her way, as though he meant to help her to her feet. "Would you mind speaking with me apart from the crowd for just a—"

"No," Bastien interrupted, his tone low and harsh. Brimming with unmistakable anger. He remained in shadow, refusing to comply in even the simplest of terms. Behind him, the curtains bristled as though a breeze had ruffled their edges.

"No one will answer any questions without a witness, in full view of everyone present." When Bastien finished speaking, the menace hanging about the space thickened. Constricted, as if it were being caged in a shrinking vessel.

Detective Grimaldi stood. He rolled his shoulders back. A trace of fury crossed his face before he flattened his features once more. "Mr. Saint Germain." He quirked a brow. "If you wish to have an attorney present—"

"That will not be necessary." Bastien pushed away from the wall and glided past Celine toward the police detective. He deliberately took his time, pausing to move a butter-yellow handkerchief from the pocket of his waistcoat to the pocket of his trousers. When he stopped a stone's throw from where Detective Grimaldi stood, the curtains at his back rustled once more. The unmistakable hiss of a serpent curled into the air.

Toussaint slithered from the darkness, slowly weaving into the light.

Celine stiffened where she sat, the blood icing through her body. Cries of fear burst from the lips of several police officers. One even attempted to draw his revolver, but Detective Grimaldi stayed his hand without a word. Bastien offered them a scythe-like smile, and it reminded Celine of a character in a book she'd read recently. A cat from Cheshire who enjoyed speaking in verse.

Toussaint coiled around Bastien's feet, his forked tongue flicking over the plush carpet, his head moving in a lazy sway. Though knots of tension had pulled tight around him, Detective Grimaldi eased his stance, shifting back onto his heels.

"I gather you already have an attorney present?"

Bastien lifted a glib shoulder. "It's possible."

Celine forced herself to relax while she searched the sea of faces around her, trying to determine which member of La Cour des Lions also happened to be well versed in the law. But none of its ranks met her gaze. Nor did a single one of them move a muscle. It was as if they were all chiseled from stone.

"Amazing that you would have the foresight to do that, Mr. Saint Germain." Detective Grimaldi clicked his tongue against the roof of his mouth. "Truly I envy your sources."

"I learned from example, Detective Grimaldi." Bastien's eyes pulled taut around the edges. "The mind is a sword. Knowledge is its whetstone."

"Of course." Detective Grimaldi snorted. "If you prefer, I'd be happy to oblige you and move everyone to our headquarters before I continue questioning the young lady." A knowing gleam took shape in his colorless gaze.

"I am equally happy to comply." Though Bastien kept his voice cordial, the menace swirling between them thickened further. "However, I cannot speak as to whether everyone here will be as . . . amenable."

Celine swallowed. Something had altered, shrinking to a point. Though the two young men engaged each other civilly, it was impossible to miss the sentiment underlying their exchange.

The mutual, unadulterated hatred.

True danger—the kind that hinted at bodily harm—swirled around them. Bastien stepped from the circle of scales around his feet, moving closer to Pippa. As though he were making a silent threat. Daring the detective to press further.

What followed was subtle. Nigel, Arjun, the man from the Far East, and the two women with the dangerous rings glanced at Bastien in unison, their bodies rigid with awareness.

Waiting for something to happen.

It should not have worked. But the police officers waiting on the periphery mumbled among themselves. The youngest of the five—a boy of barely eighteen—slid his gaze from Toussaint to Bastien. He shuddered the following instant.

What was it about Bastien—about this place—that made them all quail in their boots?

One of the officers—an older gentleman with a ruddy nose and rheumy eyes—stepped forward. "Eh, Michael," he began in a thick drawl, "listen, my boy, perhaps it would be—"

"Detective Grimaldi," the young detective corrected without even glancing at the man who spoke.

The officer coughed once, but failed to conceal his resulting frown. "*Detective* Grimaldi . . . perhaps it's best if we conduct our interviews here, *sir.*"

Displeasure flickered across Michael Grimaldi's face. Celine sensed he wished to protest, but recognized the tides were turning against him. "Very well, Sergeant Brady."

In that instant, it became clear that everyone present—save for Celine and Pippa—knew something about Jacques' and its peculiar denizens that was not apparent at first glance. Sébastien Saint Germain did indeed wield a strange kind of power within these paneled walls. Not once had he issued any direct threats or raised his voice. Nevertheless he managed to hold everyone present in an invisible vise.

The hint of this kind of power—the mere suggestion of it—sent Celine's blood on a tear through her body, her mind spinning with possibility. The possibility that she, too, could wield this kind of influence over others.

That she, too, could crush her detractors in a vise.

Appalled by this reaction—by her growing obsession with power of any kind—Celine stood suddenly, wishing to run from her own skin.

It was a thoughtless move. Her heart sank like lead in her stomach when she realized she'd drawn attention to herself in the worst possible way.

The young detective turned toward her, letting his gaze settle a moment. "May I help you, miss?" he intoned.

Celine considered her options before responding. She watched Detective Grimaldi's eyes flicker over her. From the shining curls of her dark hair to the faint sheen of sweat along her brow. To the bit of black ribbon about her throat and the blue gabardine dress fastened tightly across her bust. She minded how his brows arched. Took note of the rise and fall of his chest. Observed how his expression sharpened with admiration, though he tried to conceal it.

Young men were predictable. Especially young men who appreciated life's finer things like Detective Grimaldi did, as evinced by his manner of dress.

It was a truth she'd realized at the age of twelve.

Celine lowered her eyes and stepped forward. Then she lifted her lashes slowly, offering him a tentative smile. "I'm so sorry to trouble you, Detective Grimaldi, but might I beseech you for a favor?" She tilted her head in a coy fashion.

His pale eyes widened. "As a rule, I tend not to agree to such requests until I hear the terms, Miss . . ." He waited for her to offer her name, a distinct rasp in his voice.

"Please call me Celine." She tucked a black curl behind an ear. "And could I implore you to make an exception to your rule, just this once?"

"Against my better judgment, I might be persuaded."

From her periphery, Celine swore she heard Nigel snort. She disregarded it, not even allowing herself to consider how Pippa might perceive her behavior in this moment. How . . . others might perceive it. She smiled brightly, then leaned closer, as if she wished to tell Detective Grimaldi something in confidence. "It's terribly late, and our . . . guardian will be looking for us. Would it be possible for us to conduct these interviews tomorrow, in the light of day?" Celine paused for breath, her green eyes imploring him without words. She considered reaching out to touch the young detective's arm, but that would be too forward, and she did not wish to mishandle the small amount of magic she'd managed to conjure in this moment, all in an effort to achieve a greater goal.

Celine desperately wanted to leave. To give herself an hour to collect her thoughts and speak with Pippa in private. A chance to tell the right story to themselves, so that they could offer it later as the unswerving truth.

"Us?" Detective Grimaldi asked.

Celine nodded. "I'm here with my dear friend Pippa."

The young detective glanced over her shoulder. Then returned his gaze to Celine. "I'd wager your guardian must be quite concerned about your welfare, given the hour."

Celine nodded again. "I'd hate to worry such a good woman, especially if she hears about the unfortunate events that transpired tonight."

"Of course," he agreed, his expression filled with concern. "It would be terrible for her to think something might have happened to you both."

Celine sensed he was on the cusp of acquiescing. Could it really be that easy?

Detective Grimaldi leaned closer. Almost too close. "You know," he began, his voice low and husky, "you're a very beautiful young woman. Perhaps the most beautiful young woman I've ever met."

Celine blinked. Then laughed airily. "Thank you, Detective Grimaldi."

"In fact . . . you might be too lovely for your own good," he murmured.

"Pardon me?"

He bent toward her right ear. "Sit down," he directed her, "before you embarrass yourself any further."

Outrage flared through Celine's body, hot and cold all at once. "How dare—"

The young detective turned his back on her before she could finish admonishing him. That time she could not ignore the chortle that escaped Nigel's bearded mouth, nor the look of puckish glee Arjun passed her way. Celine dared not glance at Bastien, though she desperately wished to glower at the figure standing nearby in silence, taking up too much confounded space.

Bastien had come to Pippa's defense. Why had he done nothing to help Celine?

The very next instant—as if she'd heard Celine's unspoken plea—Pippa shot to her feet in a rustle of voile. "Detective Grimaldi, I would kindly ask that you not forget there are ladies present." Her voice shook on the last word, but her fists curled against her sides. "Furthermore, I would also request that you make your inquiries in an expeditious manner. We've been waiting here for quite some time and are likely to incur the wrath of the Mother Superior at the Ursuline convent."

Detective Grimaldi pivoted on his heel. "You reside at the convent?" He looked to Celine first for an answer. She held her tongue, refusing to reply, humiliation still rippling through her veins.

"Yes," Pippa answered, moving closer to Celine in solidarity. "We do." She inhaled through her nose. "So does"—she swallowed—"so *did* Anabel."

"Anabel?" He cast Pippa a searching glance.

"The young woman who perished tonight," Celine offered in a quiet tone.

Michael Grimaldi stared at her for a breath before nodding. "Then you knew this poor girl?"

Celine balled her fists, her nails digging into her palms. "Yes. She is one of us. One of seven girls who recently took up residence at the convent. Her name is Anabel—" She turned to Pippa.

"Stewart," Pippa said, her voice cracking. "Anabel Stewart, from Edinburgh."

"I see," the detective mused. "Did Miss Stewart accompany you here tonight?"

Pippa eyed Celine sidelong. "Well—"

"We didn't know she followed us," Celine said, her words filled with resignation. Now that Pippa had disclosed their associations, it was better they reveal everything at once, rather than prolong the matter by forcing him to wring from them every last drop of information.

Though Celine would not have been unhappy to watch him struggle.

Another bout of shame clawed up her throat. How could she be pleased to thwart the young detective charged with bringing about justice for Anabel? After all, Celine was partly to blame for what had happened tonight.

The moment she'd pondered earlier—the moment in which she'd realized she was making the wrong choice—crushed her with its finality. Even then, she'd known she would regret her actions, though she never could have conceived of such a terrible outcome. Celine despised feeling this way. Like a cog in a wheel, powerless to her fate.

Better to be anything else.

To be a ghost in the night, commanding those around her without words.

In that instant, Celine thought she had an inkling of what it must be like to be a monster. To commit monstrous deeds. To wish for monstrous things to come about.

To revel in the dark.

"Miss?" Detective Grimaldi said loudly, as if he'd tried to catch Celine's attention several times already.

She shook her head, forcing her raging thoughts to quiet.

"Celine?" Pippa whispered beside her. "The detective asked you a question." She reached for Celine's hand and squeezed it, their wordless affirmation that each of them was not alone, no matter what happened. More than ever before, it strengthened them both.

Detective Grimaldi studied Celine, his pale, almost colorless eyes unnerving in their focus. "Do you know why Miss Stewart followed you here without your knowledge?"

"I am not privy to anyone's real thoughts but my own, Detective Grimaldi."

"True." He paused. "But perhaps"—he shifted closer, bearing down on Celine with his impressive height—"you would indulge me for just a moment."

Incredulity settled across Celine's features. The brashness of this boy, to make requests of her after humiliating her so publicly! "Of course, Detective Grimaldi," she said through clenched teeth. "I would be happy to oblige you."

"Charming," he pronounced in a flat tone. The next breath, his expression grew stern. He stood even taller, an unspoken threat emanating from his broad chest. "I must insist you answer my questions honestly, without further delay, or I will be forced to use the full breadth of my office to—"

"That's enough, Michael." Bastien's words were a dangerous whisper.

Finally, Celine seethed to herself. Lucifer had finally seen fit to extend his magnanimity her way.

Bastien shouldered past Celine, stepping before Michael Grimaldi, standing much too close for comfort, matching him toe to toe.

Detective Grimaldi eased back. A dark satisfaction coiled in Celine's chest. How she longed for the ability to frighten someone with nothing more than her presence. To live in Bastien's skin for just an hour. To know what it felt like to have that kind of power.

"As Celine already said, neither she nor Miss Montrose was privy to Miss Stewart's actual thoughts and could, therefore, only speculate about the latter's reasons for following them," Bastien continued in a measured tone. "Any further questioning on your part insinuates that the lady is withholding the truth."

The detective nodded once. "Which is simply a kinder way to say the lady might be a liar."

A muscle jumped in Bastien's jaw. "You still haven't learned your lesson."

"And you still fancy yourself a knight in shining armor. Some kind of dark prince." He sneered. "Do you plan to call me out again? Shall it be pistols at dawn or sabers in the square?"

"That depends." Bastien paused. "Are you going to beg your cousin to save you again?"

A glimmer of rage passed across Detective Grimaldi's features. "Very well. I'll dispense with the formalities." He spoke to all those present, the tenor in his voice reverberating off the paneled walls. "Everyone here is a possible suspect in a murder. All of you might be lying to me." His lips coiled into a smirk. "In fact, I expect it. Know that I will not relent until I uncover the truth. The Court of the Lions does not hold more authority than the New Orleans Metropolitan Police, despite the lore surrounding it. As an officer of the law, I am duty-bound to pursue any course of action to determine how this poor young woman came to be found murdered, drained of all her blood."

At this revelation, a block of ice settled around Celine's heart, the cold burning into her throat. "Someone . . . drained Anabel of her blood?"

Swiveling toward her, the detective nodded. "And used it to write that mathematical symbol beside her body."

"Actually . . . I don't think it has anything to do with math-ematics," Celine said, awareness giving her voice life. "It makes far more sense that it would be a letter or a character." A different kind of power threaded through her. A kind unlike any she had ever known. "Perhaps even one from an ancient text."

Detective Grimaldi's brows arched before he managed to wipe his face clean of all emotion. "Interesting. And how did you come about this hypothesis?"

"My father is a professor of linguistics. He had a chart on the wall of his office, showing the evolution of the English lan-guage." Exhilaration flared through Celine. *This* was the detail that had troubled her for the last hour. *This* was the thing that had remained just beyond her reach.

"Do you know what the symbol stands for?" the detective pressed.

"It looks similar to the letters *L* or *C* in Latin or Greek, but it isn't written correctly. It's as if it's been turned askew or written by the hand of a drunkard."

"I see." He pronounced these two words slowly. Contemplatively.

Celine cut her gaze at the young detective. "It's within your purview to suspect everyone here, but you can't possibly think I would tell you these things if I had anything to do with Anabel's death. It would be tantamount to confessing that I am the murderer."

Sergeant Brady stared at Celine as if she'd sprouted wings and a horn. "Well, I'll be damned. Has the girl gone and confessed?"

Michael Grimaldi peered over his shoulder, his expression wry. "In the future, I would take the time to listen fully before coming to conclusions, Sergeant Brady." He focused once more on Celine. "I will say, however, that I'm intrigued by the notion. Would you mind—"

Bastien cut him off before he could finish. "If you wish to continue this line of questioning, I insist you arrange a time to meet at your headquarters tomorrow, so that Miss Rousseau is afforded the chance to secure her own representation."

Though Bastien obviously wished to aid Celine, it grated her to appear helpless in anyone's eyes. "While I appreciate your efforts, Monsieur Saint Germain, I do not need you to defend me."

Like the other members of La Cour des Lions, Arjun had

stayed silent during this exchange, but he stood now, laughing quietly. "He's not defending you, poppet. He's doing what he does best: negotiating."

At that precise moment, a breathless Odette appeared at the top of the stairs. She gripped the railing with a gasp, then swiped her disheveled hair from her brow, leaving a smudge of red dirt across her forehead.

Celine was not prepared for what followed in Odette's shadow. At her booted heels—breathing heavily from exertion—stood the Mother Superior of the Ursuline convent.

Celine's erstwhile savior . . . as well as her possible executioner.

———◦◦◇◦◦———

Tonight was both a failure and a success.

I freely admit the girl's death was unfortunate. As I said before, I do not relish the taking of a life. But ultimately I cannot dwell in remorse. In the grand scheme of things, she is no more than a cog in a clock.

And my enemies have lived on borrowed time long enough.

With her death, I've left my intended message. But still I failed to achieve the whole of my purpose. The greatest enemy of my kind walks free, his reputation intact. Without a hint of suspicion trailing in his wake. This knowledge enrages me. The thieving wretch does not deserve to slither about unscathed— to occupy positions of power and influence—after all the things his family has done to mine.

I could kill him. Break his neck. Bleed him dry. It would be simple. Deserved. After all, he is the reason I walk this world bereft of light. Because of him, I lost everything. My very humanity, even.

I could do it. I could bring about his demise.

But his death at my hands would incur war and ruination to those around me. Would deepen the rift between the Fallen and the Brotherhood. Between my family and his. First I wish to see him suffer. I wish to see them all meet their maker and be sent to the fiery pit where they belong.

I pray you not judge me too harshly for this. I know these kinds of petty considerations are unbecoming of an immortal such as myself, but there is a thin line between justice and vengeance. That line is the edge of a blade.

One day I will plunge it into his soul.

The girl, however, did intrigue me. Not the one with the mild-mannered expression and the heart-shaped face. I know there are those who are drawn to people like her. They seek tranquility. A place to rest their heads.

I seek nothing of the sort. I have rested far too long.

But that girl . . . that girl with the unflinching stare and the knowing expression. She possesses the look of someone who has met Death on a field of battle and managed to live another day. I am intrigued by her. I am curious about the scars Death left behind. I want to know who she is. What she's done.

What role she will play in this tale of woe.

My interest consumes me in a dangerous way, for demons like me are predisposed to obsession, and I do not have the time for any distractions. Once, years ago, my sister in the night lost herself chasing after an unremarkable human, trying to find answers to questions she should have known better than to ask.

I could not save her. The light of the moon betrayed me that evening. My heart still bears the wounds, years later. I should know better than to be consumed by curiosity. I should not care what this enchanting creature thinks. What she does, or what she feels.

And yet . . .

I must care. No matter how fragile she is—how delicately her life hangs in the balance—she is a tool to be used and discarded. A hammer intended for a very specific nail.

She will be the one in the end. The one who sends my enemy deep into the pits of Hell, where he belongs. I can see it, as true as I can sense the moon at my shoulder, high at its peak, its light as much a source of comfort as it is a source of pain.

My enemy is just as enthralled as I. Even more so because he desires her in actuality, not simply as a pawn in a grander scheme. The thought fills me with delight. Perhaps I have finally found something of his with which to toy. Something to make him squirm. To take from him for everything he—and his kind—have taken from me.

For never was a story of more woe.

Soon he will know what it feels like to be unmade.

A Silhouette in a Dream

———◆◇◇◆———

T'es une allumeuse, Celine Rousseau."

You're a tease, Celine Rousseau.

Rivers, rivers, rivers of blood. The smell of warm copper and salt. The gentle swirl of her thoughts as her focus escaped her, as she began slowly drowning in her own mind.

This was the way the dream always started.

"T'as supplié pour mon baiser, n'est-ce pas?"

You've been begging for me, haven't you?

His harsh whisper beside her ear. The feeling of his clammy hand against her skin, his palm slicked with sweat. The sickening twist of her stomach.

He'd been the younger brother of one of the atelier's best clients. A wealthy wastrel, used to having whatever—and whomever—he wanted. Accustomed to spending his father's money as though he alone had earned every franc. He'd stared at Celine for the last three months, a greedy light in his gaze. It had unnerved her then, but she'd known better than to anger him by drawing attention to it.

Weeks later, she still recalled how his hands did not seem like the hands of gentleman, for they were callused and worn.

In truth, nothing about him—despite his breeding and his wealth—indicated he was a gentleman. His hands were roughened by horseback riding. Indeed, he was one of the finest riders in his elite circle of friends.

With these hands, he'd offered to soothe her. Offered to bring her something warm to drink. Asked if he could keep her company. Celine had not known what to do when he'd come to the door of the atelier long after dusk, his fine cloak about his shoulders and his breath reeking of wine. She'd asked him to return home, but he'd been insistent, barreling into the workshop as though he owned it.

In her dream, Celine observed the scene from above, as though the conscious part of her had separated from her body in sleep. She witnessed the events unfold with punishing slowness. Watched herself make mistake after mistake, as though God Himself wished to teach her a lesson.

A dull thud sounded in her ears.

Her striped chambray dress tore from her shoulder when the young man tried to stop her from fleeing. Everything after that was a haze. Celine counted herself lucky that he'd barely managed to take hold of her skirts before her fingers had flailed about, scrabbling for anything with which to defend herself.

The candelabra had not been a choice. It had been the best weapon she could grasp.

Celine often wondered—in moments to herself—if she'd meant to kill him. Surely she could have struck him using less force. Surely she did not have to aim for the side of his head. Surely she could have prevented his death.

But no. In the darkest of her dreams, she'd known the truth.

In Celine, evil had found the perfect vessel.

She'd meant to destroy the young man, as surely as he'd meant to destroy her. While she'd watched the blood seep from his body, she'd searched her soul for a drop of regret, a hint of remorse. She'd found none. She'd clutched the candelabra tighter. Prepared the lie to tell her father, knowing she could not stay where she was.

Once more, a muted thud vibrated in her skull.

Who would believe Celine had been the victim? After all, she was not the one lying cold and motionless on the atelier floor. The dream version of herself stared at the growing circle of crimson. Stepped back so it would not stain the hem of her skirts.

And then . . . something new and curious began to take shape in the blood pooling about her feet. Usually Celine was barefoot in this memory, her toes sliding across the cold marble, trying to avoid any contact with the boy she'd killed.

Tonight, a symbol formed beside her toes. The same symbol she'd seen earlier, smeared in the wood next to Anabel's body.

Something soft brushed across the tip of Celine's nose. She looked up. A flutter of golden-yellow petals cascaded around her, settling into the widening pool of blood, turning into hundreds of embroidered handkerchiefs the instant they touched the marble floor. Then the lunar goddess dragged her chariot across Celine's dream. The thudding in her ears grew louder. More insistent.

Everything dissolved in a sea of black.

Celine woke with a start.

Though her room was dark, all was not still.

The thuds were sharper now. No longer muffled. A clatter of wood against stone. She flinched as a cool mist dampened her skin. The shutters outside her window had blown open. A storm raged beyond them, sending sheets of rain sideways, driving water into her tiny room until everything it touched felt alive.

Celine stood. Almost slipped as her bare feet slid across the wet stone floor. She took the few short steps to the window of her cell. Then sighed.

"Merde," she cursed to no one.

It couldn't be helped. If she was to secure the latch once more, she would have to lean forward and be drenched.

Celine considered wrapping herself in a shawl. It would be appropriate to do so. Her nightshift was fashioned of thin cotton. If rain soaked through the garment, it would be inappropriate for her to stand beside the window and risk being seen.

Her expression hardened when she realized her shawl was nowhere within reach. The wind continued beating at her shutters, the rain gusting through her room.

Propriety be damned.

Celine battled a particularly harsh gale, then reached over the windowsill to grasp the wooden latch.

Signs of motion caught her eye. She froze, though the rain continued bearing down on her, soaking through her hair, seeping through to her skin. Celine blinked back the drops. It looked as though a figure hovered in her periphery, positioned beside a pillar near the gate of the convent's wrought-iron fence. She blinked again.

The silhouette vanished.

Celine's heart crashed through her chest, the blood thinning in her veins.

She yanked the shutters closed, latching them together in a seamless motion. Then she reached for a length of thick cotton. The blood continued pounding in her body as she stripped off her nightshift and pulled a clean chemise from her meager chest of clothing.

One thing was certain: something had shifted tonight.

Ever since that evening in the atelier nearly six weeks ago—when evil had taken refuge in her bones—Celine had felt torn. Certainly, between right and wrong. But more than that, between who she was and who she thought she should be.

Celine Rousseau was a girl who believed in justice. That young man had meant to rape her—to destroy her, body and soul.

Was it wrong for her to destroy him instead?

She knew the right answer. The one the Bible taught. Because Celine was also a girl raised on the Ten Commandments, and it was wrong to kill.

But were there ever times it could be right?

Could Celine Rousseau be a girl who valued life, as well as a girl who had taken it from someone, without a shred of remorse?

It was like walking the edge of a cliff. If Celine fell to one side, she would be good evermore. If she fell to the other? She would be consumed by evil and lose all chance at redemption. Celine knew it sounded silly, but to her it felt true.

It wasn't possible for good and evil to reside in the same person.

Was it?

Celine blinked hard into the damp darkness. After the events of this evening, she shouldn't be concerning herself with such things. She should be trembling in her nightdress, poisoned by a different kind of worry.

Tomorrow—despite her best efforts—Celine's world could crumble like a castle made of sand. In the afternoon, Detective Grimaldi would come to the convent to finish questioning them. It had been his favor to the Mother Superior, a woman well acquainted with his family. Celine had watched in quiet shock as the elderly matron had advocated for her and for Pippa. Begged the young detective's forbearance.

"Miss Rousseau and Miss Montrose are fine, upstanding young women," she'd said. "They will be more than happy to cooperate. Of course they will answer any question you pose to them. But please grant them this night to mourn the loss of their friend. To reflect on the actions that brought about this unfortunate turn of events."

Celine had looked away when she heard those words, her shame a dagger through her heart.

Not a trace of guilt could be found on the Mother Superior's face. But the wizened woman had spared Celine. Offered her a pardon on the steps of the gallows.

Tomorrow Michael Grimaldi would renew his inquiries.

What if the detective looked into Celine's past with his eerie, colorless eyes? What if he asked why she'd journeyed across the Atlantic?

What if he learned she was a murderess?

It could be her undoing.

Celine's hands shook as she wrapped the length of thick cotton around her hair, trying in vain to wring the waist-length strands dry. Her dreams taunted her. Her memories failed her. Her desires had become reapers in the dark.

She struggled to marshal her emotions. If she did not take control of her life—of these fears—they would be sure to control her. She could not allow this to happen. Succumbing to fear was the surest way to lose her footing.

Celine made her way back to her narrow rope bed, determined to fight for a measure of peace, so that she could prepare for what tomorrow might bring. When she reached for the coarse linen sheets at the foot of her mattress, she froze in her tracks. The golden petals. The embroidered handkerchiefs.

She blinked once. Twice. The length of thick cotton wrapped around her hair unraveled to the stone floor at her feet. Her body trembled.

Bastien had tucked away a folded piece of fabric in his trouser pocket. In the warm glow of the gas lanterns, it had looked like a buttery silk handkerchief.

In the bright light of day?

It would be yellow.

Like the ribbon missing from Anabel's hair.

A Surprise Visit

———◦◇◇◇◦———

Celine's dreams continued haunting her well into the waking hours. For the rest of the night, her sleep came in fits and starts. Amid the disquiet, she imagined she saw the silhouette outside her window draw closer, a splash of black in a sea of grey.

As a child, these kinds of indistinct dreams came to her in waves, often in times of turmoil. In them, everything seemed vivid and alive and possible, even her most twisted nightmares. Twice, she imagined her mother had visited her in the dead of night. Once, she'd been cloaked in lambent fox fur, her eyes aflame. The following occasion, she'd been accompanied by the briny scent of the ocean, a pearl glowing between her teeth.

Tonight Celine dreamed her mother whispered in her ear. She felt her draw near, the scent of safflower oil and incense thick about her.

"Kah," she said, her breath a cool wash on the shell of Celine's ear. *"Bhal-ee."*

Celine shouldn't know what these words meant. But her body froze, her eyes wide.

Flee. Her breath came in a gasp. *Quickly.*

As luck would have it, the next morning brought with it the clearest sky Celine had beheld since coming to New Orleans two weeks prior. As a result, the sun's rays seeped unfiltered into every nook and cranny.

By ten o'clock, the temperature had become sweltering.

On top of that, one of Celine's worst fears had come to pass.

She was stationed at the front of a classroom, gazing down at twelve smiling young faces, the eldest no more than ten. To her right stood Catherine, her hands folded before her, the bespectacled epitome of a genteel young woman.

Celine was expected to assist Catherine in teaching the young girls about proper comportment in society, in addition to instructing them on correct French pronunciation. *S'il vous plaît, merci beaucoup, je vous en prie, pardonnez-moi,* and the like.

She supposed this was all a carefully orchestrated attempt on the part of the Mother Superior to shame her. To remind Celine of her place in life and in the world.

"Ladies!" Catherine clapped. "Pay attention to Mademoiselle Rousseau. She's here to teach you exactly what to do to impress, say . . . a handsome young gentleman sometime in the near future?" She sent a kind smile Celine's way, but in its depths Celine detected a stab of resentment. Of course Catherine knew what had taken place last night. All the young women at the convent had been informed, the truth spreading like wildfire through underbrush.

Unsurprisingly. One of their ranks had perished in horrifically violent fashion.

Perhaps Celine should not fault Catherine for the condescension shaping her brow this morning. If Catherine had been linked to Anabel's untimely death, Celine would surely be sending her a judgmental look as well.

In an attempt to channel the confidence Celine lacked in this moment, she offered a toothsome smile to the roomful of waiting innocents. "Of course it is lovely knowing what to say and do in society, but you should also pay attention simply for the sake of learning how to speak another language," she said in a heedless tone. "We wouldn't want to feel like everything we do is an attempt to catch a young man's notice, now would we?" She laughed softly.

A handful of the young girls in the room giggled with Celine, though most of them squirmed in their seats, their faces pinched in confusion.

Fury shaped each of Catherine's features before gathering above her brows. "Mademoiselle Rousseau, may I speak with you for a minute?" she ground out from between her teeth.

Celine looked to the wooden beams along the ceiling, counting down from ten. She'd known it was a mistake for her to be teaching anyone anything. Especially a classroom of children under the watchful gaze of a former English governess. Jokes about Puritans and the Tower of Terror abounded in Celine's mind before she silenced them the following instant.

"Celine?" Catherine said even more softly. Even more heatedly. She eyed the exit sidelong.

Wincing all the while, Celine nodded. As she followed Catherine toward the door, a bell-like voice piped up from the back of the room. "Mademoiselle Rousseau?" asked a girl with cat eyes and a mop of unruly hair.

Grateful to have evaded the impending lecture, Celine swiveled around. "Yes?"

The girl fiddled with a corner of her slate. "Is it true you're from Paris?"

"Yes, it is."

Murmurs of admiration rippled through the space.

"Why ever did you leave?" asked another girl near the front of the classroom.

A stream of silent curses barreled from Celine's throat. Briefly she considered repeating the foul word Bastien had used last night at their first encounter. Simply to see how it would feel to shock everyone present with nothing but a single syllable.

Celine squeezed her eyes shut. "Because I wanted an adventure." Another bright smile took shape on her face. "What kind of adventure would you like to have?"

"I'd like to see the pyramids," the first girl replied.

A girl with blond pigtails tapped a finger against her chin. "Maybe travel on a boat one day?"

"I want to try . . . squid!" still another called out from the right.

Sounds of mirth mingled with their exaggerated disgust. Girlish laughter lilted into the plaster ceiling. Catherine eyed Celine suspiciously, but returned to her judgmental corner without a word.

Once more Celine was spared on the steps of the gallows.

Less than an hour later, a knock resounded at the door.

Catherine answered as if she'd been waiting for it all along, her blue-grey skirts a soft swish against the polished stone floor. The young woman waiting on the other side inclined her head of mousy brown hair regretfully. "Miss Rousseau?" she said to Celine. "Apologies for disturbing your class, but there is a gentleman waiting for you and Miss Montrose in the lemon grove leading to the vestibule."

Celine steeled her nerves while following the bonneted girl outside. On a bench near a row of carefully tended tomato vines sat Pippa in a lavender day dress, her gaze hollow, dark shadows looming beneath her eyes. Like Celine, it was obvious she had not slept well. When Pippa saw they had come to collect her, she offered them the smallest of smiles. The sight of it soothed Celine, though it troubled her that Pippa had been placed—once more—in a precarious situation.

If only Pippa hadn't volunteered to accompany Celine last night.

If only Celine hadn't been so insistent.

If only the Mother Superior hadn't sent Anabel to spy on them.

If only.

Celine's heartbeat thundered in her chest as she prepared to face the young police detective in earnest. To give the performance of her life.

When they rounded the final bend—their escort leaving

them to their fates—Celine was shocked to discover it was not Detective Michael Grimaldi waiting beneath the canopy of citrus-scented leaves.

It was Arjun.

He stood in the shade of a lemon tree, a navy bowler hat in hand, his monocle perched atop his right eye. He appeared engrossed in conversation with the gardener, a hunched gentleman whose tanned and wrinkled skin had aged him beyond his years, giving him the appearance of a wizard, replete with a long, wispy beard. The gardener offered Arjun a cutting of some sort, its vibrant green stem and tiny fronds wrapped in a length of dampened linen. Bending from the waist, Arjun reached to touch the top of the gardener's foot, as if in gratitude. Then he took the cutting before turning to Celine and Pippa and offering them the most disingenuous of smiles.

Not to be outdone, Celine responded in kind. "Forgive me," she began, "but I'm somewhat confused. Might I inquire as to—"

"It's coriander," Arjun interrupted. "An herb often used in East Indian cuisine. I missed its scent, and William generously offered me a cutting for my garden."

Celine blinked twice. "That was kind of him."

"And not at all the question you meant to ask." Arjun grinned. "Bastien requested that I come here today. I advise him on legal matters, and he did not want you or Miss Montrose to be questioned by the police without someone advocating on your behalf."

Understanding settled on Celine. In addition to being Bastien's lackey—delivering blows to poor fools in rancid alleyways—Arjun was also the lawyer mentioned in passing last night. Bitter amusement warmed through Celine's body. She was not surprised to know Bastien kept among his closest acquaintances an attorney, undoubtedly at all hours of day and night.

"Then . . . you're a barrister?" Pippa asked, a breeze playing with the ends of the blond curls framing her heart-shaped face.

"Of a sort," Arjun replied without missing a beat. "I know the law inside and out, even if I'm not permitted to practice it."

A quizzical expression passed across Pippa's features. "I don't understand."

"More's the pity." Another punishing grin took shape on his face. "My skin is not the right color, Miss Montrose, nor is my parentage. Surely you of all people understand that."

"Excuse me?" She blinked, consternation clouding her gaze.

"Based on your accent, I'd wager you're from Yorkshire. A proper English girl, through and through."

Color flooded Pippa's cheeks. "Yes, I'm from Yorkshire."

"Then you're no doubt well aware that a scrapper from East India would never be permitted to work as a barrister in any circle of significance." Tucking his bowler hat beneath his arm, Arjun stored the coriander cutting inside the breast pocket of his grey frock coat. "That's by design, in case you didn't know." He laughed to himself.

"Not all of us believe in such notions," Pippa said softly.

"That may be true," he said, "but all of you definitely benefit from it."

Pippa paled as she struggled to respond.

Knowing full well this conversation was not going in her friend's favor, Celine interjected with a small curtsy. "Thank you very much for going to such trouble on our behalf, monsieur . . ." She waited for Arjun to offer his surname.

"Desai." He looked away from Pippa and cleared his throat. "But please feel free to call me Arjun, as I do think we're past those kinds of formalities." His hazel eyes twinkled.

"I appreciate you coming here today to advocate on our behalf, but I'm afraid we lack the means to pay you." Celine fought the urge to squirm under his steady gaze. "And I would not want to take advantage of your valuable time."

He snorted. "It appears we both dislike being indebted to others. And though my time is indeed valuable, you needn't concern yourself with payment. Bastien will handle all the expenses."

The sheer arrogance. Of *both* men. Celine's gaze narrowed. Pippa glanced at her sidelong, wearing a look of supreme unease.

"And why would he do that?" Celine pressed.

Arjun tilted his head from side to side, considering. "I couldn't speculate as to his reasons. A wise young woman once told me we are only privy to our own thoughts." A half grin curled up his face as he reminded Celine of her words from last night.

Celine could feel her lips starting to pout. She kept quiet, letting her eyes answer for her.

"Brava, Miss Rousseau," Arjun commented. "I'd advise you to maintain that indignation throughout the course of today's inquiry." He took a step closer to Pippa, narrowing the gap between them in one fell swoop. "Keep silent unless you are absolutely certain the next words you speak are beyond reproach. Make the quiet your friend. Bask in it."

It was Celine's turn to snort. "Simple enough. You're merely asking us to behave as the ladies we've been raised to be."

"I'd wager that to be an easier task for some than for others."

Celine bit her tongue, refusing to let him incite her.

Pippa frowned. "There's no need for you to make such slights, sir," she said. "It's unbecoming of you."

"The truth is often unbecoming. But that does not make it unwarranted."

"In your opinion." Pippa raised her elfin chin, prepared to do battle.

Celine did not want Pippa to fall prey to Arjun's provocations, so she decided it was best to change the subject. "You still haven't answered my earlier question, Monsieur Desai. Why would Monsieur Saint Germain take on the expense of providing us with legal representation?"

"I told you last night, Miss Rousseau," he replied. "Bastien is merely doing what he does best. Don't see it as anything else. He would have done as much for anyone in need of assistance, as he's done for countless other young ladies in the city."

"How magnanimous of him," Celine countered in a cool tone.

A smile ghosted across Arjun's lips. "Trust that he is most concerned with putting a swift end to anything that might negatively affect his family's businesses."

Well. Celine sniffed, her indignation mounting. It bothered her immensely that Bastien had taken it upon himself to make decisions for them, without even consulting them first. Not to mention that if her suspicions were correct—if Bastien did indeed have something to do with Anabel's untimely death, as the yellow ribbon in his pocket suggested—he was in essence pouring drinks for them from a poisoned well.

Moreover, Celine hated the idea of owing him anything.

She could refuse. But that would be foolish and prideful. The benefit of having a legal mind present for the events to come should outweigh her concerns for what the far future might bring.

Arjun dusted the brim of his bowler hat. "I believe the detective is waiting for us inside the Mother Superior's office," he said. "If you would care to take advantage of the boon being offered you, please lead the way. But if you'd rather be damned fools, I'll bid you both good day."

Celine bristled further. At least she would not be guilty of selfishness or arrogance in this instance. "Pippa," she said, turning toward her friend, "what do you think we should do?"

Pippa glanced from Arjun to Celine and back again, her expression thoughtful. "Even though we have nothing to hide, I do think it would better to have a barrister with us, don't you?"

"I agree." Celine nodded. "We thank you for your assistance in this matter, Monsieur Desai. Please convey our appreciation to . . . your employer."

For I certainly won't, Celine finished in her head.

Dark amusement glimmered in Arjun's gaze. "Shall we?" he

said to Pippa and Celine, indicating they should lead the way inside.

Neither of them dared to step forward. Arjun's thick brows tufted together as he turned toward Pippa. "Don't worry yourself too much, Miss Montrose," he said softly. "You have nothing to hide. To quote Launcelot, the truth will out."

Pippa nodded. Then she proceeded through the lemon grove, her posture rigid, her chin held high.

Steeling herself, Celine inhaled deeply before following her friend, hoping against hope that Shakespeare—in this instance—would be proved utterly wrong.

Her truth must remain in darkness. No matter the cost.

The Performance of Her Life

———◆◇◆———

In the light of day, Detective Michael Grimaldi did not seem quite as intimidating as he had the night before. Nor did he appear quite so professorial. He almost looked . . . handsome.

Unfortunately this shift in countenance did little to ease the tension building in Celine's body.

She adjusted her seat on the creaky wooden chair positioned before the Mother Superior's desk. Then she smoothed the overskirt on the drabbest dress she owned. The color of dirty dishwater, this particular gown had been relegated to the times Celine had fiddled with fabric dyes in the atelier. Her ears still burned from how Detective Grimaldi had coolly rebuked her for using feminine wiles to sway him to her side. Today her attire had been chosen to make the point that Celine cared not a whit whether the sneering, self-important young detective found her attractive.

The most beautiful young woman he's ever met, my foot. Celine seethed to herself.

Then she heaved a great sigh.

Her temper could not get the better of her today, as it nearly had last night.

From the opposite side of the Mother Superior's desk,

Michael Grimaldi observed her in studious silence before considering Pippa, who was seated between Celine and Arjun. Celine's palms turned clammy when Detective Grimaldi leveled an icy look at Arjun, who crossed an ankle over a knee before removing a small leather notebook and laying it on the desk alongside a graphite pencil.

The immense wooden cross on the wall before Celine seemed to loom larger with each passing moment. Jesus Himself appeared to lock his tortured gaze on hers and say, "I suffered like this for *your* salvation?"

Celine looked away.

It was important she keep her wits about her. That she not lose sight of Arjun's earlier directive. If she remained demure and silent, then perhaps Michael Grimaldi would leave them all alone.

But if worse came to worst, Celine knew of a way to turn his attentions elsewhere.

The location of a missing yellow hair ribbon, to be specific.

Detective Grimaldi cleared his throat. "Thank you for agreeing to meet with me, Miss Rousseau and Miss Montrose," he intoned.

"Of course," Pippa murmured. "We wish to help in any way."

Celine canted her head. Cut her gaze. Refrained from sharing her thoughts, though she was certain her expression spoke volumes. To Pippa's left, Arjun grinned, then produced a slender blade to begin sharpening the point of his graphite pencil.

The *snick, snick, snick* of metal against wood was as comforting as it was infuriating.

"Were you able to rest at all, Miss Rousseau?" Detective Grimaldi asked Celine directly.

She inhaled through her nose. "It's kind of you to ask after me, Detective Grimaldi. I slept as well as can be expected."

Placing his tweed fore-and-aft cap on the desk, the detective leaned back in his wooden chair. "Then I suppose you did not sleep well at all."

"I'm not certain how to respond to that, sir. Are you making an indirect inquiry as to whether I slept as a guilty person would? If so, you must know . . . it won't work."

The *snick* of the knife against the pencil ceased midstroke.

Michael Grimaldi arched a brow. "You share your thoughts quite candidly, Miss Rousseau."

Celine considered baring her teeth in a fierce smile. The cursed wretch was deliberately trying to provoke her. Again. She smoothed her skirt, locking her attention on a faint green stain along its hem. "I suppose you'd prefer if I kept my thoughts to myself."

"No. I appreciate your candor. I hope you continue sharing it with me."

In response, Celine said nothing.

Utterly unruffled, Detective Grimaldi turned to Pippa. "A good night's rest is something I value highly. As the first of five children, it was a luxury we could ill afford when I was a boy. How many siblings do you have, Miss Montrose?"

Pippa startled at his question. "How do you know I have siblings?"

"A simple deduction. The inner sleeve of your dress is worn through. The color is no longer fashionable, though it was made for a young woman not too long ago, suggesting it didn't belong to your mother." He peered at her intently. "Stands to reason you're not an only child."

Outrage caught in Celine's throat the instant Pippa's face flushed crimson. Celine opened her mouth to rebuke the detective, but caught herself, looking to Arjun for guidance.

Their attorney finished sharpening his pencil. He rested his monocle atop his right eye and cracked open his small, leather-bound notebook. Without a word, he started writing in it, the scratch of graphite to paper the whole of his contribution to their inquiry.

Infuriating man, Celine thought.

"The dress was given to me by my cousin," Pippa replied, her voice clear. Guileless. "And I'm also the eldest in my family."

"Of how many?" Detective Grimaldi asked as if they were sipping afternoon tea at Claridge's.

"Three. I have a brother and a sister."

He considered her for a moment. "You must have been an excellent role model for them. Undoubtedly far better than I."

Pippa looked away. Swallowed. "I did my best, Detective Grimaldi."

"You don't feel comfortable being candid in my presence, Miss Montrose?" A furrow marred his forehead.

It was . . . unexpected of him to accuse Pippa of being disingenuous.

"I *am* being forthcoming," Pippa said.

"Would it help if I told you I don't harbor any suspicions toward you, Miss Montrose?"

Pippa took a careful breath. "It would help, most definitely."

She bit her lower lip. "But that must mean you don't have suspicions about Celine either, since we were together the whole time."

Arjun glanced up from his notebook.

The detective inclined his head, his colorless eyes unblinking. "Are you quite certain you were in Miss Rousseau's presence for the entirety of the evening?"

Celine's heart thrashed about her chest like a caged bird.

He'd trapped Pippa in a lie. So easily.

Pippa paled. "I . . ." She glanced at Arjun, who continued scribbling in his notebook, offering her not a single word of advice. "There was a brief time in which I left her side. But it could not have been for more than fifteen minutes," she finished in a hurry.

"During that time"—Detective Grimaldi looked to Celine—"did you interact with anyone else, Miss Rousseau?"

Celine didn't even bother glancing toward Arjun for cues. It was clear Detective Grimaldi already knew the answers to the questions he was asking. He was trying to trip them. To muddy the waters. To what end, Celine could only hazard a guess.

"I believe you know that answer already," Celine said primly.

Nevertheless he waited for her response.

With a small sigh, she continued. "During that time, I shared a brief conversation with the owner of the establishment."

"Mr. Saint Germain."

Celine nodded.

"And was he present throughout the entirety of your visit to Jacques'?"

Awareness flared through Celine, hot and fast. Detective

Grimaldi was after *Bastien*, not them. She should have realized it earlier, based on their mutual enmity from last night. Relief flooded through her like cool water on a parched day. Her mind whirled as it considered whether to disclose her observations about the yellow ribbon.

But every word she spoke needed to be above reproach. And she lacked incontrovertible proof.

"No," Celine replied carefully, "he was not."

Arjun stopped writing, his pencil stilling above his notebook for an instant. Then he grinned to himself before resuming his scribblings. But that breath of time had revealed his hand. The truth of why the erstwhile attorney was here at all sharpened into sudden focus.

He wasn't here to help them. He'd come to protect Bastien. To make sure his employer was not implicated in anything untoward. These blackguards had inserted themselves into Pippa and Celine's unfortunate situation to safeguard their own interests, proving they cared not a whit about anyone else. Even though Arjun had said as much to Celine, her anger rose in a sudden spike. The revelation about the yellow ribbon threatened to burst from her lips in a spate of uncontrolled fury, lack of proof be damned.

"Is something wrong, Miss Rousseau?" Detective Grimaldi asked.

Curse him for being so observant. Celine cleared her thoughts with a toss of her dark curls. "Apart from the fact that I'm being questioned by the police, I can think of nothing that might be wrong."

"I meant that you seemed piqued all of a sudden. As though something of note had captured your interest."

"I only came to a troubling realization. That's all."

"May I inquire after it?"

Pointedly, Celine slid her gaze to Arjun. He met her glare, then leaned back in his seat, the wood beneath him creaking at the shift in weight. The corners of his hazel eyes narrowed, his monocle glimmering as if in warning.

"It is with respect to Monsieur Saint Germain," Celine said.

Michael Grimaldi did not move a muscle, his stillness belying his interest.

"Though I only saw it for a moment," Celine began, "the image of Anabel in death will forever be seared onto my mind, and I wanted to be certain you'd caught every detail."

The detective nodded.

Arjun tapped the end of his pencil against the black leather of his notebook, a serene smile upon his face, though he kept his attention locked on Celine.

Wordlessly, she dared him to stop her.

"Her pallid skin," Celine continued. "Her eyes frozen open in terror." Beside her, Pippa shuddered. "Her *unbound* hair across her face . . ." She watched to see if Arjun had any reaction. Save for the continued tapping of his pencil against his notebook, he was devoid of all emotion.

"And"—Celine paused—"that horrible, jagged wound."

The detective waited.

"A kind of wound that would have produced a great deal of blood, no doubt," Celine said. "It would be all but impossible for anyone present last night—including Monsieur Saint Germain—to have committed such a heinous crime, then drain their victim of blood and remove all traces from their person in time."

Detective Grimaldi steepled his hands before him. He stared at Celine thoughtfully. She could not tell if he was impressed or irritated. "I came to a similar realization myself, Miss Rousseau," he said. "But precautions can be taken. Stained clothes can be changed. Coats and gloves can be doffed just as easily as they are donned." He bent over his joined hands. "To that end, did either you or Miss Montrose encounter anything you might deem suspicious?"

Bastien had discarded his frock coat. Numerous members of La Cour des Lions had carried weapons on their persons. Knives, guns, ice picks, even *rings* that could double as instruments of torture and violence. Suddenly the small red stain on the collar of Odette's shirt did not seem quite so innocuous.

Odette, a *murderess*? Celine almost laughed to herself. Then her blood ran cold.

Celine was a murderess.

Anyone was capable of committing ghastly deeds. And everyone in the Court of the Lions appeared to possess otherworldly gifts. Some could taste the flavor of deceit. Could make chess pieces move about, bidden by the mind. Could foretell the future, with naught but a touch.

Arjun himself had stilled a man into a stupor, simply by grabbing his wrist.

Celine looked about, fear seeping into her soul. All these individuals were beyond the ordinary, their abilities extending far past parlor room tricks. But to what extent? Again she recalled what the two young women had revealed earlier in the square, about "the Court" likely being responsible for the decapitated girl along the docks.

The Court. La *Cour* des Lions.

Celine did not believe in coincidences.

And only a fool would provoke creatures with untold appetites and unknown abilities.

If Celine wished to keep herself safe—to keep Pippa safe—she needed to bend with the wind, no matter the bitter taste it would leave on her tongue. Suddenly she understood why the other officers of the New Orleans Metropolitan Police had granted Bastien such a wide berth.

Cognez au nid de guêpe, et vous serez piqué.

Strike a wasp's nest, and you will be stung.

Celine smoothed her apron overskirt. She met the detective's penetrating stare, refusing to flinch. "I'm sorry to say I saw nothing of note, Detective Grimaldi."

Disappointment flashed across his face. He looked to Pippa.

Surreptitiously, Celine reached under the table for Pippa's hand. Squeezed it tightly.

"I'm sorry, Detective Grimaldi," Pippa said in a clear voice. "But I didn't see anything either."

———◇———

"It's a shame my clients couldn't be of more help to you, Detective Grimaldi," Arjun said as he held open the door of the Mother Superior's office.

To his credit, he did not look the least bit smug.

Nevertheless, a hollow kind of rage spiraled through Celine's stomach.

"It is indeed a great shame," Detective Grimaldi replied coolly. He moved back to let Pippa pass, then waited just beyond the oaken door.

When Celine crossed the stone threshold into the cavernous corridor, the young detective shifted his tweed hat to his other hand to walk alongside her.

He'd been waiting for Celine. Perhaps for another chance to take her off guard.

Before Detective Grimaldi could continue probing any further, Celine decided to wrest control of the situation and catch him unawares first.

The quickest solution would be to needle the detective as he'd needled her.

"It appears you know Monsieur Saint Germain well," Celine said, expecting this to provoke him, based on the charged exchange between the two young men the evening prior.

Michael Grimaldi surprised her. He did not seem perturbed in the slightest by her inquiry. "Yes. We were schoolmates as children. The best of friends." He offered this with a knowing expression. As though he were interested to see how this news affected her.

Celine frowned. "Friends? Then why are you—"

"I thought I was supposed to be the one with the questions."

Celine bit down on the inside of her cheek while they walked. "My apologies for asking," she said, though she did not feel sorry at all.

The suggestion of a smile touched his lips. "It might be odd for me to say this, but you would have made quite a detective yourself, Miss Rousseau."

Celine snorted dismissively. While they followed Pippa and Arjun down the corridor toward the double doors leading outside, she recalled what Arjun had said earlier this afternoon. About being the wrong kind of person in the wrong kind of skin. "Even you must be aware that those of the fairer sex could never strive for such a lofty position, Detective Grimaldi."

"Alas, you are not wrong." The detective paused in contemplation. "Did you know the New Orleans Metropolitan Police is one of the only police forces in our country to allow men of color to serve in its ranks?"

"I did not." Another spark of surprise warmed through Celine.

"It's a rather recent development. Most likely a twisted experiment of sorts." He sighed to himself. "But as the grandchild of a slave, I suppose it is a thing for which I should be grateful."

A few steps ahead of them, Pippa and Arjun neared the massive double doors, Arjun reaching for a wooden handle to tug it open. He paused to glance Celine's way, and the ribbon of widening light to his left caused his eyes to flash silver for an instant, as though he were a predator crouched in the shadows.

Inhuman.

Unnerved by the recurring thought, Celine returned her attention to Michael Grimaldi, taking a moment to peruse his features. "When we first met, I thought you were Italian. Are you not?"

"I am." The detective placed his hat beneath his arm and

grasped hold of the other handle. "My father's family hails from Sicily. But my mother's family is of mixed blood, as are many longtime residents of New Orleans. Beyond the Garden District, that is." Detective Grimaldi moved aside to let Celine pass into the sunlight.

"I see," Celine said slowly. Having the choice to conceal the truth of her own blended heritage meant she'd been spared this kind of cruel judgment. "It shouldn't be revolutionary to think one's skin color should have no bearing on one's place in society."

The detective held open the door while Celine emerged into the blinding brightness of the afternoon sun. "I agree," he said. "You may not be aware of this, but New Orleans society— indeed, society throughout the South—bases much of its notions on the one-drop rule." He followed in her footsteps. "If you possess a drop of African blood, you're granted little in the way of consideration."

Celine pondered this, her vision straining to adjust to the harsh white light. She squinted up at him. "It's the land of the free in idea only, then."

A smirk took shape on his face. "My father's family were humble cobblers in Palermo. They often struggled to put two sticks together to start a fire. A chance for a better life brought them to the Crescent City fifty years ago." He raised his right hand to shield his gaze from the sun. "What brought you to the shores of the New World, Miss Rousseau? The Mother Superior told me you arrived by ship less than a fortnight ago."

Celine gripped the worn fabric of her skirts. "The same thing that brought your family here, Detective Grimaldi." She grinned into the light, her expression fierce. "Opportunity."

The detective shifted, placing Celine in shadow, sheltering her from the worst of the sun's glare. "You're very good," he whispered.

"Pardon?"

"You're very good at hiding how smart you are."

"And you're very bad at trying to be charming."

His lips twitched. "You don't find me charming?"

"You're *still* interrogating me, Detective Grimaldi. Would you find yourself charming in this instance?"

He swiped a large hand through his wavy hair. "Point taken. And please," he said, "call me Michael."

"I . . . don't know that that's appropriate."

"I find such beliefs tedious. It's appropriate if we decide it can be."

"If only life were so simple. If only we all were smart enough to shun tedium as you do."

His colorless eyes—so light a shade of blue as to appear almost white—shone oddly for an instant. Almost as if he were amused.

Nearby, Pippa coughed as if to clear her throat, and Celine pivoted toward her. Arjun and Pippa waited just outside the iron gate, their expressions incongruous. Pippa looked alert and studious, her eyes wide, but not in a disapproving way. In contrast, Arjun appeared unconcerned with the happenings around him, save for the sharp light still glinting in his gaze.

If Celine had to guess, the young lawyer looked . . . cross.

An idea took shape in her mind. A simple way to impress

upon Arjun—and his employer—that she would do as she pleased, despite their attempts to interfere.

Celine offered her right hand to Michael. "Have a good day, Detective Grimaldi. Please see that you do not return here any-time soon." She sent him a teasing smile.

He offered her an awkward, almost forced grin, then took her hand to press his lips to it. They were warm and soft. Despite intending to assert the advantage, Celine felt her cheeks start to redden.

"Do I make you uncomfortable?" he asked without warning.

"Not at all."

His fingers tightened around hers. "You're lying."

"What?" Celine blinked in dismay. Was she *that* bad at it?

"It's of little consequence to me if you are. You see, the heart"—Michael lifted her wrist, where Celine's pulse pounded in her veins—"doesn't lie."

Without a word, she extricated her fingers, her cursed face enflaming further with every passing moment. Then she pivoted on a heel, intent on fleeing to the safety of the convent at once.

"May I offer you a word of caution?" Michael asked, just as she began retracing her steps.

Celine turned back, waiting expectantly, knowing full well that Arjun was listening to their exchange, all with the intention of informing his employer.

"It is with respect to Bastien," Michael said loudly, placing his tweed hat before him as if it were a shield.

Celine said nothing in response, struggling to regain her composure.

"When we were children, we called him the Ghost, because everyone around him seemed to perish without explanation, leaving behind nothing but specters," Michael began. "First his elder sister, Émilie. Then his mother. Finally his father." He paused. "It didn't end there. When he turned sixteen, his uncle bribed a spot for him at West Point. Then one of Bastien's roommates was killed in a barroom fight. Bastien attacked another boy, blaming him for his friend's death. He beat the boy within an inch of his life. Not long after that, he was asked to leave the military academy in disgrace."

"I . . . think I understand what you mean," Celine said. "Thank you for the information," she said in a cold tone while Arjun bristled beyond the tines of wrought iron.

"Bastien destroys everything he touches," Michael continued in a strident tone, "unless it's something as soulless as money. With money, he is indeed a dark prince."

"I appreciate the warning, but Monsieur Saint Germain and I are unlikely to spend time in each other's company, as I have no interest in having anything to do with him."

"I wish he shared the sentiment."

Celine chose to ignore that comment. She glanced toward the gate, where Pippa gazed at her with an expression of undisguised curiosity. Arjun, meanwhile, shot daggers at Michael's back, then tilted his head at Celine in a spuriously lighthearted fashion.

"I'd very much like to see you again, Celine," Michael announced, as if he had something to prove.

Shocked to her core by this open admission, Celine nearly

lost her footing. *This fool,* she wondered, *believes I would af-*
ford him notice after he mocked me and harangued me about a
murder *for two days straight?*

Celine thought quickly, wondering what he hoped to achieve
by making such a spectacle. It couldn't be as simple as annoying Bastien, could it? God save her from the pettiness of young
men. Or perhaps . . .

"I'd like that as well, Michael," Celine replied.

It would be smart to keep in Detective Grimaldi's good graces.
Not to mention that it would irritate her traitor of an attorney
immensely. Celine caught herself on the verge of grinning. Arjun had witnessed her chumming with Bastien's enemy. She'd
bet anything the wily lawyer would be sure to add that particular detail to his collection of useless scribblings.

Bully for him, Celine thought with dark delight.

How she wished she could see Bastien's face when Arjun informed him of today's developments. It served them right.

The next time, they would know better than to use Celine
Rousseau as a pawn.

A Murderess at Sunday Mass

—◦◦◦◦—

Mon amie,
I've discovered the perfect silk for my ball gown at a
shop that imports fabric directly from China. It glows
like a pearl and feels like water against the skin. I've
already purchased bolts and bolts of it. I can't wait to
show them to you when they arrive at Jacques' later
tonight.
Bastien plans to meet this morning with the monsignor.
Look for me after Mass.
I'll be the one with the devil.
Bisous,
Odette

Celine read Odette's letter three times. Even upon multiple readings, its contents failed to sound any less ridiculous.

Only a ruthless fiend like Bastien would attend Mass at the church near the Ursuline convent a mere week after one of its residents perished in his establishment. And only a fearless creature like Odette would insist on accompanying him simply so she could speak with her new modiste about a gown for the masquerade ball.

At the mere thought of Bastien, Celine harrumphed.

But Odette—as always—delighted her.

Would the warring dualities within Celine ever cease?

She sighed. As more time passed, it seemed increasingly unlikely.

Celine stood naked in the center of her cell, cold dread coursing through her at the thought of what today would bring. Her skin was damp, the air around her perfumed by the lavender castile soap she'd used in her recent bath. It was a joy afforded her on rare occasions, this chance to bathe in the large copper tub shared by all the young women residing in the convent. Most evenings, she was relegated to a bucket of cold water and a half ration of unscented soap.

Breathing deeply of the soothing lavender fragrance, Celine donned a clean pair of drawers and laced the ties of her chemise below her collarbone. Then she secured the front of her stays across her midriff and made a face before pulling the ties tightly behind her until her waist appeared outlandishly small in comparison to her bust and hips.

As always, it took a moment to regain her bearings after cinching herself into her corset.

Celine fastened the white ribbons of her linen camisole over the whalebone stays. She turned in place to study the three garments strewn across her narrow rope bed, trying to decide which of her shabby gowns was the least shabby.

She'd worn the blue dress to Mass last Sunday, which meant the striped one was her next best option.

With an exaggerated sigh, Celine reached for the salmon-colored gown. She'd be hot in it, but it was the least rumpled and still held a trace of its former luster.

Celine stepped into the cage of her crinolette and adjusted the bustle behind her. She knotted the strings of her best petticoat about her waist before jumping up and down to straighten the skirt over the narrow expanse of oval hoops.

Finally she tied the striped foundation skirt and its matching apron overskirt atop the linen petticoat before reaching for the coordinating bodice and beginning the arduous task of fastening all the tiny buttons up the front.

When Celine was finished, she gazed down at her dress, wishing the convent had a mirror of any kind somewhere close by. A way to determine whether she looked as foolish as she felt.

Celine supposed her gown appeared . . . serviceable. When she'd first made it more than a year ago, it was pretty and fashionable. Weeks in the sodden hold of a ship on a transatlantic crossing had altered the fabric irreparably.

Celine sucked in her cheeks.

It was fine. Serviceable was not terrible.

And her appearance did not matter to God, so why should it matter to anyone else?

Poppycock. Of course her appearance at Mass mattered. Celine couldn't very well march through the checkered nave of Saint Louis Cathedral in nothing but her chemise and drawers.

Though that would be a spectacle indeed, behaving so brazenly within such hallowed halls. It would likely have her banned from the convent—an idea that both terrified and intrigued her.

No matter.

Celine smoothed the front of her dress, the vibrant pink stripes flattening beneath her palms. It was scarcely ten o'clock, but the day sweltered like a bathhouse in summertime. The thick heat of New Orleans never ceased to amaze her. This city in late January felt like Paris in July . . . if the streets of Paris had been drenched by the sea. Beside her foot lay the remnants of a small puddle, likely from when she'd unwound her damp hair before getting dressed.

Absentmindedly, Celine drew a symbol through the puddle with the tip of her booted toe. The same symbol that had been found beside Anabel's body soon took shape along the stone floor. At once, Celine swiped her heel through it, banishing it from view.

What would New Orleans feel like in July? Hell on earth?

Celine winced.

She guessed it would feel a lot like a murderess at Sunday Mass.

———◇———

Celine sat beside Pippa in an oak pew halfway down the right side of Saint Louis Cathedral. A bead of sweat dripped down her neck. Makeshift fans fluttered alongside expensive contrivances of silk and lacquered wood. Faded whispers carried into the frescoed ceiling above. Heads began to droop even before the start of the homily, eyes falling shut an instant before the person was elbowed awake.

"Mercy," Celine murmured to Pippa. "It's even hotter than last week. How are we to endure the summer months?"

Pippa sat beside her in a gown of pale blue organza. Not too long ago, it had been the height of fashion. Pains had been taken to maintain the delicate lace detailing, but several small tears could be seen along the sleeves. In some places, it had been meticulously mended.

"You look lovely," Celine whispered.

Pippa nudged her shoulder good-naturedly. "I look like a soggy handkerchief next to you. That bright color is wonderful against your skin."

Celine tsked. "You shouldn't speak ill of my friend. Especially not in a church."

Pippa smothered a grin.

Behind the immense marble altar, the monsignor moved into position to begin his homily, switching from Latin to English to properly address his congregation.

Celine scanned the crowd until her gaze fell on a well-dressed pair positioned on the opposite side of the aisle. Bastien sat in a pew at the end of the first row, Odette beside him in a cream-colored gown of duchess satin with a matching bonnet.

Admittedly this was not the first time Celine had stolen a glance in their direction.

She'd been surprised to note that Bastien appeared well acquainted with every aspect of Mass. He recited things in unflinching Latin. Knew when to sit and stand and kneel. Bowed his head with the kind of reverence Celine would swear to be genuine.

It had taken her off guard, to say the least. She'd half expected a bolt of lightning to strike him the moment he dipped his fingers in the basin of holy water beside the entrance.

"When tragedy befalls the Lord's flock, we must look to the lessons to be learned. Tragedy is what comes of disobedience," the monsignor droned. "As He divulged to us in the book of Revelation . . ."

Celine closed her eyes, trying to ignore his words, even as fire and brimstone rained down around her.

". . . and we must be thankful for the acts of penance arising from such tragedies. We must offer blessings to the favored sons of our fair city, for their boundless generosity and their unswerving attrition," the elderly man intoned, his hands open at either side of his gold vestment. "Our God is forgiving. So must we be."

Attention in the church shifted toward Bastien, who kept his gaze averted, his head bowed in prayer.

It took Celine only a moment to understand.

That fiend had paid for his sins today. With "boundless generosity," he'd bought the church's absolution. This had to be the reason he'd met with the monsignor and made a point to attend Mass today.

Celine sank back in her pew and crossed her arms, fuming.

First he'd sent his minion attorney to cover his tracks with the Metropolitan Police. Then he'd traded gold for absolution like he would a coin for a loaf of bread. If these weren't the actions of a guilty conscience, Celine would eat her hat and swallow the striped ribbon whole.

She glared at the back of Bastien's head. Though she was loath to admit it, she had to admire him for his efficiency. Had to envy how he floated about the world so unscathed.

If Celine possessed a tenth of his power, there would be no limit to what she could do.

———◇———

"Celine!" Just beyond the steps leading into the cathedral, Odette waved from her seat in a shining black phaeton matched with a pair of midnight stallions.

Inhaling through her nose, Celine made her way down the stairs toward the open-air carriage. She put a hand to her brow to shield herself from the noon sun. "Bonjour, Odette," she said reluctantly.

"Bonjour, mon amie." Odette opened her creamy silk parasol with a flourish, the rubies around her ivory cameo winking in the filtered light, her gaze appraising. "I adore how you wear such bright hues. It's ever so much more intriguing than this sea of simpering pastel." She waved a gloved hand around the square. "One day, you must tell me what inspires you."

Celine thought for a moment, her hand still sheltering her from the uncompromising sun. "Paris often had melancholy skies. They were always beautiful—especially in the rain—but I longed for splashes of color, so I thought to wrap myself in them."

"Bien sûr," Odette murmured with a knowing smile. "Come sit with me." She patted the bloodred leather beside her.

"I shouldn't," Celine replied, glancing around at what she guessed to be a goodly portion of New Orleans' high society, exiting the church on their way to Sunday barbecue.

"Ah, would it seem untoward?"

Celine wrinkled her nose. "Not untoward. Only . . . indiscreet."

"Too soon after that unfortunate incident." Odette nodded. Celine simply smiled.

"Well," Odette said, "I suppose I can issue my invitation from here."

"Invitation?"

"To join me for dinner at Jacques' tonight, you goose. We still have much to discuss with respect to my gown for the masquerade ball. And don't worry," she added almost as an afterthought, "it won't be near where the . . . incident occurred."

"I—don't think that's wise. I'm certain the Mother Superior—"

"—has already granted the request, despite her initial misgivings. The monsignor spoke to her before Mass."

"Of course he did," Celine murmured, disbelief flaring through her.

The devil at work once more, no doubt.

Then—as if he'd been summoned by her thoughts—footsteps pounded down the hewn stairs behind her, moving rhythmically. Efficiently. Celine turned in place just as Bastien brushed past her in a suit of dove-grey linen, his Panama hat tilted atop his brow, the scent of bergamot and leather unfurling in his wake.

He did not pause to acknowledge her, so Celine returned the gesture.

"The carriage will come to collect you this evening at seven o'clock," Odette said as Bastien settled into the phaeton in a single fluid motion. "And don't trouble yourself with respect to your appearance. What you're wearing now is lovely." Without warning, she struck Bastien's arm with the carved handle of her parasol. "Don't you think Celine looks lovely?"

Bastien pursed his lips and glanced Celine's way. "C'est une belle couleur." He took hold of the reins, his expression dispassionate.

Odette cut her eyes in his direction, then smiled at Celine. "It is indeed a beautiful color. But I wasn't talking about—"

The pair of gleaming black horses took off before Odette could finish, their hooves clattering across the cobblestones, scattering any poor soul still milling about the white cathedral.

In the ensuing ruckus, Celine heard Odette screech through the courtyard, her words a jumble of French and Spanish, her outrage aimed at a precise target.

Celine smiled to herself, her features sobering the next instant. She watched the elegant phaeton turn the corner, her back to the church. A moment later, her gaze snagged on the unremitting stare of a familiar figure standing on the opposite end of the steps, studying Celine intently. The Mother Superior frowned, her censure plain, the sun casting half her face in shadow.

It did not take the work of a genius to deduce the source of her irritation. Once again, she'd been thwarted in her attempts to control Celine, this time by the monsignor himself. With a huff, the matron of the convent continued down the steps, her posture stoic, her strides unwavering.

Sighing to herself, Celine tarried for a while in front of the cathedral until the spired structure emptied of its patrons and Pippa joined her.

"Did the meeting go well?" Celine asked Pippa.

Pippa nodded. A warm breeze tugged at her organza skirts. "As well as could be expected. It's the first ladies' organization I've ever joined. Are you certain you don't want to accompany me next time?"

"I know little about music and art. I'm afraid I wouldn't be able to offer much in the way of conversation."

"You know as well as I do that conversing about the arts isn't really the objective."

Celine grinned, a black brow curving up her forehead. "How many of the society dames tried to foist their horrible sons on you?"

Pippa paused, her expression grim. "Three. One of them might not be . . . terrible." She turned to Celine, her eyes forlorn. "His name is *Phoebus*."

Laughter burst from Celine's lips. "I gather he doesn't resemble his namesake, the Sun God."

"I'm meeting his mother for tea next week." Pippa exhaled in a huff. "After all, we can't remain at the convent forever." A line formed along the bridge of her nose. "And it's up to us to make the best of our lives."

Celine said nothing in response. With a kind smile, Pippa linked arms with Celine, and they began the short journey back to the convent.

As they walked, Celine's thoughts wound through her mind.

She shouldn't go tonight. She wouldn't go tonight. Even if it meant forgoing a meal at Jacques'. Even if it meant she had to join a few ladies' organizations of her own. Associating herself with any member of La Cour des Lions was a terrible mistake. They were dangerous. Beyond the ordinary. Something dark writhed around whatever they touched.

It was a fool's folly to consider anything else.

Celine resolved to do what she had come here to do. Begin her life as a proper young woman. Find a proper young man. Have a passel of proper young children.

And that would be the end of it.

Celine sighed to herself once more.

Her own lies were starting to taste bitter on her tongue.

What was it her father liked to say?

We must taste the bitter before we can appreciate the sweet.

Tonight Celine supposed she would do just that.

You may wonder why I hold so much hate in my heart.

As tellers of tales often say, it is a long story. Hundreds of years long, in fact. It begins as many things do, with a love lost and a trust broken.

I could spend hours telling you what I lost. What my kind has suffered. How the plight of the Otherworld has sifted like grains of sand onto this mortal coil, forever threatening our survival. It is the cause célèbre of our kind, so to speak.

As our survival has long been a bone of contention.

Once, all creatures of the Otherworld existed beneath the same enchanted sky, through doorways concealed from the realm of man. Those of us who thrived in the light basked in the glittering woodlands of the Sylvan Vale, a place of perpetual springtime, the air forever bathed in the golden warmth of the sun. Those born to darkness took refuge in the Sylvan Wyld, a world of unending night, frosted by wintry stars.

But that was before our elders committed their original sin. Before the Banishment.

Now creatures such as I exist in a place between light and

darkness, without a home to call our own. Rootless. Untethered. Alone.

For our elders' crimes, we were cursed to walk in the shadows of mankind. Soon—as is wont to happen—a rift occurred, dividing our ranks between those of the Fallen and those of the Brotherhood. Through the centuries, our lore spread around the world. Humanity bestowed on us—on all these immortal night-dwellers—many names: wode; wearh; dhampyr; moroi; undead; revenant; lycanthrope; alukah; vardalak; lamia.

The name the locals of New Orleans often use is vampire, no matter that it is a bit of a misnomer, as not all of us survive solely on the blood of others. To the Brotherhood, the name is an insult. To the Fallen, it is a badge of honor. As with many things, its origins lie in the Old World. In a time of perpetual darkness and war, when those in power drank the blood of their foes and impaled the conquered on wooden pikes driven deep into the mud.

The title was granted to night-dwellers by superstitious codgers. Sad beings who believed such demons could be thwarted by cloves of garlic or sprinkles of holy water. By whispered prayers and flashing mirrors, wooden stakes and blessed crosses.

Utterly laughable. Nothing contrived by man could ever control such beings.

Creatures of the Otherworld have enjoyed propagating such notions, as it keeps our victims enthralled with the belief that their gods can save them. Fey beings—both light and dark—have always enjoyed toying with the minds of men in such a fashion.

There is only one thing that can destroy a vampire.

The light of the sun.

And there is only one thing that can subdue it.

Pure silver.

But ultimately these details don't matter.

What matters is how I feel now. How those I hold dear have felt for centuries. How we've managed to endure.

Even more important is what I plan to do. It is no longer enough to ruin my enemy and dismantle everything he's built over the years. He took me from my family. Stole the very breath from my lungs. I will hurt him as he and his kind have hurt me. With a love lost and a trust broken.

With justice finally done.

Many would say this story is not about justice. It is about vengeance.

To me, there is simply no difference.

Tonight I will test my suspicions. I will see if the girl matters, as I've come to suspect.

Before dawn breaks, I will know the scars Death left on her soul.

WORDS ARE WEAPONS

—◦◦◇◦◦—

I'm standing at the top of the world!" Ashton Albert—elder son of the shipping magnate Jay Ballon Albert—crowed into the deep purple skyline. "And I like what I see."

His voice sounded smug in its drunkenness. Despicably self-assured.

Bastien hated it, though he sent the arrogant weasel an approving smile as he stared up into a fleece of clouds.

Ashton's younger brother, Arthur (a shitcan in his own right), elbowed his way onto the steel scaffolding, standing perilously close to the edge for a seventeen-year-old boy recently conquered by drink. "Make room for me, Ash. I want to see what it feels like to stand on top of the world."

"Technically"—Phoebus Devereux, youngest grandson of New Orleans' current mayor, interjected in a nasally monotone—"you're standing on a half-built hotel along the coast of Louisiana. You're nowhere near the top of the world."

Bastien wanted to laugh. Instead he grimaced. He could swear he'd seen Phoebus adjust his spectacles while speaking. Like a gazelle who'd limped onto the Serengeti at the exact moment the lions decided to feed. Ash and Art would not be kind to him for this transgression.

"Shut your sniveling mouth, you little rat," Ash yelled over his shoulder.

"No one cares what you have to say," Art echoed like the good little sycophant he'd been raised to be.

Bastien crossed his arms and leaned against a steel column. He took a moment to check his pulse, pressing two fingers of his left hand against the side of his throat. Though he desperately wanted to take these spoiled bastards to task (or at least imagine what it would feel like to do so), he held his tongue and allowed the scene to unfold.

Bastien hated this bullshit.

That raised the question: why was he here at all?

His lips pushed forward, his eyes panning across the silhouette of New Orleans.

Because Sébastien Saint Germain loved money. In his nearly nineteen years, he'd discovered there were only two things he loved more: his family and his city. Money made all manner of grievances disappear. It erased sins and paved pathways into palaces of power and influence. It made what had been impossible, possible.

It was the greatest lesson his dead parents had ever taught him. With money, you could buy anything and everything. Even a way to save your own life.

It was a shame his parents hadn't learned that lesson in time to spare themselves.

Or Émilie.

Bastien pressed away from the metal column, drawing closer to the edge of the unfinished structure. "So what do you think?"

Ash spun around, grabbing hold of a steel cable to maintain his balance. "I think it's precisely the kind of project my father would love."

"He's been telling us for some time that Marigny is in need of a fine hotel," Art added. "It's in a perfect location, so close to the Quarter."

"He knows that," Ash spat at his younger brother. "It's why he picked it, you fool."

"Why my uncle picked it," Bastien corrected, keeping his tone mild. Good-natured.

Decidedly unmurderous.

"I'll definitely discuss it with him," Ash said. "It's the perfect project for me to whet my appetite."

"And put that expensive Princeton education to good use," Art teased.

"Trust me, I've put it to good use. Just ask the whores on the other side of Rampart." Ash chortled like a drunken hyena.

Even the way he laughed made Bastien want to deck him. To stop and watch the blood drip from his nose.

To relish what happened next.

"The city planning committee might present a problem, however," Phoebus interjected yet again. "They haven't granted anyone permission to build a hotel this tall in . . . forever."

Art shoved Phoebus in the arm, the slighter boy stumbling into a steel column. "Who gives a rat's ass about them?"

"You and your brother seem to have a disturbing fixation with rodents," Bastien replied. "And you're not wrong, Phoebus. I was hoping to consult with you about that." He shifted alongside the boy, careful to keep his posture light. Unthreatening. A feat in itself, as he stood nearly half a head taller than the youngest Devereux. "Your opinion on how to go about this would be much appreciated."

Bastien didn't need his opinion. He needed a member of the politically connected Devereux family in his pocket. Phoebus was as good a mark as any. He'd recently returned from a stint at Oxford, and rumor had it his mother had grand plans for him in the way of a political future.

Politics was the next great frontier.

Bastien patted Phoebus on the shoulder as if they were old chums. Shrewd business was about identifying an opponent's fatal flaw . . . and exploiting it. "You'd be of great help to me in this matter. I'd appreciate it immensely."

Phoebus swallowed, his brown eyes bright behind the rims of his spectacles, betraying how flattered he was to have garnered Bastien's notice. "I'll look into it."

"Good man." Bastien struck his shoulder again, this time a little too hard.

He needed Phoebus to stand up straighter. Speak with conviction. If he did, he would be a force to be reckoned with one day. Worth at least four of Art and eight of Ash.

Art tugged a leather-wrapped flask from inside his frock coat pocket. He took a long swig and passed it to his elder brother. "I don't know if the Sun God is going to be any help to you on this,

Bastien. He's too busy scaring away all the wenches his mother keeps tossing his way."

"Now she's even trying to recruit from the dregs at the Ursuline convent." Ash guffawed again.

Bastien gritted his teeth and checked his pulse a second time.

A wicked light flashed in Art's eyes. "I heard there are a few choice morsels among the latest arrivals."

Ash laughed even louder, the scent of stale liquor spoiling the balmy night air. "Maybe I should have a look." He sneered at Phoebus. "Would you even know what to do with a honeypot, Devereux?"

Rage swirled in Bastien's fists. A bloodlust longing to be slaked.

He needed to mind his temper. It had often been his undoing as a boy. It had cost Bastien the thing his uncle had desired most for him: an education at West Point and all that it entailed. Now Uncle Nico insisted he marry well to remedy the loss, a prospect Bastien despised. The tittering débutantes of New Orleans—as well as their meddling mothers—wearied him past the point of reason, a fact that amused his uncle a great deal.

"Being bored by them is far better than being enamored," Uncle Nico would say. "Never fall in love with a mortal, for love is an affliction. It always ends in blood," he'd warned countless times, in countless tongues.

Anger had also cost Bastien his sister, a young woman with a fiery temper and a ferocious heart. A lump gathered in his throat, as it always had for more than a decade. He swallowed it the next instant, disdaining any sign of weakness. Any chance for an opponent to best him.

Though Bastien fought it, his thoughts drifted unbidden to another young woman with a fierce soul. To her unflinching nerve and rapier wit. To the darkness that lingered in her gaze. To hair that glistened like a raven's wing and eyes the color of envy.

Bastien wanted to slide his fingers into that hair. Loosen it from its bonds. Let it cascade around her shoulders in a waterfall of black ink. Pause to grip the silken strands before savoring the salt on her skin.

Love is an affliction.

Frustration heated through Bastien's veins.

He had no time for such nonsense, despite what Odette had to say. Managing his uncle's affairs consumed most of Bastien's waking hours. Following General Lee's surrender at Appomattox seven years ago, Nicodemus Saint Germain had begun buying land in port cities throughout the South with a plan to one day own the largest collection of luxury hotels in the country. Most of the year, Uncle Nico traveled between his holdings in New York and Charleston, leaving control of their New Orleans operation largely to Bastien. As such, there was always someone who needed something, be it a word in the right person's ear or an intervening handful of coin. Countless decisions to be made at the drop of a hat.

Celine Rousseau was an unwelcome distraction. She brought with her nothing but trouble, as she'd proved several days ago during Michael's interrogation at the convent, when she'd attempted to bait them both. A silly attempt that, by all rights, should have failed.

Alas, it did not. It was as if she held Bastien by a spell, even at a distance. As if he'd been told not to think of the color red. Now all he saw were its vibrant hues. In the sunrise and the sunset. In every trembling flower. In the splash of wine into a crystal glass.

It always ends in blood.

Bastien already had too much to lose. This beguiling girl—with a sense of humor to match his own and a story begging to be told—would not be yet another casualty. Not if he could help it.

"I'll be sure to speak with my father about this tomorrow," Ash said with a toothsome grin.

Bastien countered with an equally obnoxious smile. "Excellent. Then I suggest we return to terra firma and grab ourselves a plate of the best sole meunière in the city, along with a chilled bottle of Chateau d'Ygeum."

Art howled into the sky while clomping drunkenly toward the suspended platform system positioned alongside the structure, Phoebus trailing in his footsteps.

Ash lingered behind for a second. "The only thing is . . ." He pulled Bastien closer by gripping his forearm, an action that sent the ball of latent anger from Bastien's chest into his throat. "I know my father isn't going to cotton to some of your . . . associates."

A cool wash of surprise unfurled down Bastien's spine. Either Ash was far more reckless than Bastien had first surmised, or he was a complete fool. Neither boded well for the bastard. Nevertheless, they'd reached a critical juncture in their conversation. A decision needed to be made. Bastien knew what Ash meant. He simply wanted to hear him say it.

So he raised a brow in question.

"Come off it, Bastien, you know of what I speak," Ash continued.

Bastien widened his smile. It appeared his bloodlust might be slaked tonight after all. "I haven't the faintest clue which of my associates troubles your father. You'll have to be more *specific.*" His voice had gone quieter with each word, until the last was no more than a whisper.

"A man like Jay Ballon Albert can't be seen doing business with Chinamen and ni—"

It took less than a second for Bastien to draw his revolver from beneath his frock coat. He leveled it before Ash could take another breath.

Slow to react, Ash remained stock-still, his mouth agape, his eyes blinking sluggishly. Behind them, Art stumbled to his brother's aid, only to be knocked from his boots by something he neither saw nor heard. A ghost in the wind.

To his credit, Phoebus knew better than to interfere or so much as utter a whimper.

Indistinct shapes melted from the lines and shadows of the skeletal building, moving too quickly to track. They scuttled down steel columns soundlessly, blurring through the darkness until they sharpened into focus, forming a circle of cloaked figures around Bastien and Ash.

"What the devil?" Ash's voice shook.

Bastien stared him down, a smile of supreme pleasure taking shape across his face. "Allow me to introduce you to some of my associates, Ash." He aimed the revolver at the shocked boy's chest. "They'd like a word with you."

———◇———

Before the night was through, Ashton Albert was going to piss his pants.

Bastien wouldn't relish the sight. Or the smell.

No. That was a lie.

He'd relish the sight immensely.

It was time for this insufferable creature to be laid low. To know what it felt like to have nothing, not even a mother or a father nearby to save their son from the demons lurking in the darkness.

Tension raked across Bastien's shoulders. With a subtle twist of his neck, he forced his muscles to relax. It had been almost a year since unremitting anger had taken hold of Bastien when he thought of his parents' untimely demise. Of all things, he wished it wasn't a whimpering Ashton Albert to serve as a reminder of what he'd lost.

Yet another reason to relish this weasel's comeuppance.

It was just as well. Bastien supposed he could make do with the sight of Jay Ballon Albert's elder son dangling horizontally over a metal platform, eight stories above New Orleans.

A burst of feminine laughter barreled into the night. Hortense took hold of Ash's polished boots and spun the boy around once more, the uncut jewels in her massive rings flashing through the darkness, her ebon skin radiant against the velvet sky. When the pulley suspending Ash above the platform creaked, he cried out, begging for reprieve.

"Dis-le plus fort, mon cher," Hortense cooed. "I can't hear you."

Boone laughed heartily, his cherubic features filled with delight. At the building's edge, Jae twirled his mother-of-pearl dagger between his fingertips, his black hair coiling in the breeze.

Hortense's sister, Madeleine, rolled her eyes. Near the hem of her cloak—stricken silent by fear—sat Art, who proceeded to vomit on the platform a second time, his chest heaving, his face soiled by snot and tears.

"Wha-what do you want?" Ash wailed.

Bastien intended to answer him. Eventually.

"Oy, Bastien," Nigel said, his Cockney accent gruff, his expression severe. "Don't descend to his level, gov. S'unbecoming of an honorable leader."

Bastien snorted. "Which fool said I was honorable? Depravity has no bounds."

"Amen to that," Boone interjected in an exaggerated drawl.

Grunting, Nigel adjusted the ties of his cloak. "S'enough." He sliced a hand through the air. Arjun shifted closer, his lips wrapped around a smoldering cheroot, his expression one of shared agreement.

Bastien studied them in amused silence. Like Odette and Jae, Nigel Fitzroy had been at his side from the beginning, Boone,

Hortense, and Madeleine following soon thereafter. Arjun Desai had arrived to New Orleans less than a year ago, but he'd joined their ranks quickly, becoming much more than a mere colleague or acquaintance. Bastien prized the counsel of these seven strange individuals above most things, though he would only admit it under extreme duress. Thumbscrews, boiling oil, and the like.

"I really should find some new friends," Bastien mused.

Arjun exhaled a plume of blue-grey smoke. "If you can afford it." His hazel eyes glittered with amusement.

"Spoken like the bloody maharajah himself." Nigel guffawed.

Annoyance flashed across Arjun's face. "In many of your beloved Crown's circles, a maharajah is no better than a mongrel."

"I would never—"

"Dogs and Indians not allowed, Master Fitzroy. Right at the entrance to your beloved Astoria."

Anger darkened Nigel's features. "If it had been left to me, none o' that tosh would've happened. I know better, just as I know my betters."

"A benevolent imperialist," Arjun said around another cloud of smoke. "How refreshing."

A feeble cry cut through the night, returning their attention to the matter at hand. Bastien gripped Ash by the rope around his waist, bringing an end to the slow torment of spinning in a circle. "I'm telling you this because I suspect you didn't know," he began in a conversational tone. "My mother was a quadroon, a free woman of color. Those *associates* your father couldn't be seen working alongside? They are me. They are my family." He paused, dropping his voice to a whisper. "No one insults my family."

"I didn't intend to—"

"Shut your mouth, you miserable swine," Boone interrupted. "God is speaking."

Bastien silenced him with a look. Then turned back to Ash. "Such a shame. I was going to share a bottle of wine with you, Ashton. Now . . . you'll have to partake in a meal with those who prefer a very different kind of drink."

When Bastien finished speaking, the tension in the air pulled taut like a string about to snap. Ash blinked away his tears, forcing himself to focus. Whatever he saw in the faces around him caused his lips to quiver and his shoulders to shake.

Bastien knew what he saw. What Art saw. What Phoebus had hidden from in the precious moments prior. Demons. Creatures of blood and darkness.

Death, made flesh.

Bastien's family, for better or for worse.

Art heaved again beside Madeleine's feet, choking as he struggled to calm himself. Bastien glanced at Arjun, sharing a wordless conversation. The next instant, Arjun reached for Art's wrist. The boy slumped forward a moment later, granted a blessed pardon.

Tears streamed sideways down Ash's face. "All I said was—"

Bastien stepped back. Cocked his revolver. Took aim.

"Please!" Ash begged. A suspicious stain darkened the front of his trousers, the acrid smell of urine suffusing about him. "I'll give you whatever you want. I won't say anything. I'll forget this ever—"

"No," Bastien said. "Never forget this as long as you live. Words are weapons. And nothing else matters when the devil has you by the balls." He fired a single shot.

Ash screamed. The rope dangling him above the platform snapped, his bound body crashing against the metal with a resounding clang. When he rolled over, blood dripped from his nose, its scent curling into the air, warm copper mixed with the salt of the sea.

Hortense and Madeleine stopped moving. Stopped breathing. Jae sheathed one of his blades with a *snick*. Boone threw his head back, inhaling deeply, his eyelids squeezed shut. Frowning with obvious frustration, Nigel crossed his arms while Arjun ground out his cheroot beneath his heel.

Bitter amusement wound through Bastien's chest. Another wish granted.

Today might be his lucky day.

Ash fought against his bindings as the cloaked figures around him drew closer, their eyes silver coins beneath a crescent moon.

Then Madeleine, Hortense, and Boone fell on Ash like whips cracking through the night, his cries of terror muffled by the heavy fabric of their cloaks. By the sounds of ecstasy rising into the air high above New Orleans.

Nigel watched the frenzy in cutting silence, his long arms crossed, the judgment on his face plain. "You're better than petty revenge, Bastien. Your uncle wouldn't be pleased."

"I never claimed to be a saint," Bastien replied, his expression cool. "And Nicodemus isn't here tonight, is he?"

"Gomapgae," Jae muttered in gratitude before wandering back toward the edge of the unfinished building, twirling a butterfly knife around his fingers with insouciant ease.

"A fine shot," Arjun interjected, deftly changing the subject. "Severing the rope with a single bullet. Bravo."

Bastien said nothing, his eyes tightening around the edges.

"What?" Arjun blinked. "Was it something I said?" He swayed unsteadily on his feet.

"You're weak."

"It happens. It took a lot of effort to subdue the brother. Unlike you, I'm not God," he joked.

A dark smile ghosted across Bastien's lips. "See to it you have something to eat."

"But of course, old chap." Arjun bowed with a flourish.

Despite his best efforts, guilt kindled in Bastien's chest, threatening to catch flame. He battled the feeling, refusing to be troubled by their judgment. Then he called for Madeleine, who blurred to his side with the stealth of a shadow, her cloak trailing behind her like smoke. Not a trace of blood could be seen anywhere . . . until she opened her mouth, showing white teeth stained crimson and canines as long as those of a wolf.

"Make sure no one dies tonight, Mad," Bastien said softly. "We have too many eyes on us as it is."

"Mais oui, Bastien." Madeleine nodded, her features serene. "And what should we do with him when we are done?"

"Leave the trash with his younger brother, in the alley near their favorite watering hole. See to it they remember nothing. As always, my trust is with you."

Madeleine nodded, then whirled back to resume her meal.

Exhaling slowly, Bastien glanced about the open space until his gaze settled on what he'd been searching for: Phoebus Devereux, huddled in a corner, his knees pulled to his chest, undoubtedly praying he'd been forgotten for the first time in his life.

When Phoebus caught sight of Bastien gliding his way, he wrapped his arms around his knees, clasping his hands together until his knuckles turned white.

Making a point to move with care, Bastien crouched in front of Phoebus. "I'm genuinely sorry you had to see any of that."

"What are you going to do to me?" Phoebus trembled like a dying leaf in a breeze.

"That depends," Bastien said, "on what you want me to do."

"I—I don't understand."

"I can simply let you go."

"You . . . could?" Phoebus' eyes went wide behind his smudged spectacles.

"If you wished it."

Phoebus nodded. "You don't have to worry. I won't say anything, Bastien."

"I know you won't." A half smile curved up Bastien's face. "Who would believe you?" Sympathy laced through his features. "Just another tantalizing story about the Court, which I've found to be far more helpful than hurtful, for reasons I'm certain you can understand."

Shuddering, Phoebus looked away.

"Conversely, I can help you forget." Bastien paused. "I can

make it so the events of tonight never haunt your dreams."

Phoebus swallowed. "Are you going to . . . kill Art and Ash?"

"No. They won't remember anything either." His expression hardened. "But they don't have a choice. You do. I never take away the choice from someone I respect."

"You . . . respect me?" Phoebus' voice was hoarse.

"You're a good man. See to it you stay that way." Bastien unfurled to his feet with the grace of a jungle cat. "And make your decision."

Phoebus pushed his spectacles up the bridge of his nose, his fingers trembling. Conviction settled across his sweating face. "I . . . want to forget."

"And so you shall."

High above the Crescent City, the youngest grandson of the mayor began to scream bloody murder into a sky bruised with clouds.

CHAMPAGNE AND ROSES

—◦◦◇◇◇◦◦—

Celine leaned back into the jewel-toned damask of her gilded chair. "I have nothing."

"Nothing?" Odette laughed. She reached for another morsel of quail, pulling the tender meat apart between her delicate fingers.

"There is nothing I can say," Celine continued. "Nothing I can do. No way to convey how amazing this meal was. Simply beyond belief." She let out a protracted sigh. "Perhaps if I could dance like a winged fairy, I could better serve this cause."

Another bout of laughter lilted into the air. "That is my favorite thing you've ever said, mon amie."

"Also the truest." Celine breathed in deeply, then reached beyond her golden cutlery for the crystal stem of her wineglass.

Celine had spent most of her seventeen years in Paris. As such, she'd lived a stone's throw from some of the finest culinary establishments in the world. Unfortunately the cost of frequenting these establishments had been too much for her family. Far too out of reach for most people she knew.

But on special occasions, her father would take her to a bistro around the corner from their flat. The shiny-faced cook helming the kitchen was famous for her decadent roast chicken, served with small golden potatoes bathed in duck fat for hours on end. As a child, Celine loved popping a perfectly round pomme de terre into her mouth when it was still too hot, the crispy skin crackling on her tongue as she blew around the potato, struggling to cool it and consume it all at once. Her father had scolded her for being so unladylike, though he'd fought to conceal his smile.

It had been Celine's favorite meal.

Every year on her birthday, her father would bring home a single mille-feuille from a well-known bakery in the eighth arrondissement. A cake of a thousand leaves. Paper-thin layers of puff pastry separated by whipped crème pâtissière, crushed almonds, and thin dribbles of chocolate.

These were some of Celine's fondest memories. Despite her father's sternness and austerity, he'd managed to show his love in simple ways. Ways she'd often brought to mind during some of her darkest moments on the transatlantic crossing, for they'd given her comfort when she most needed it.

But they were all pale shadows when compared with tonight.

Tonight—at seventeen—Celine was certain she'd consumed the best meal of her life.

Langoustines poached in butter, white wine, and thyme. Pistachio-encrusted turbot garnished with flakes of white truffle. Roasted quail served with a crème d'olive alongside root vegetables sautéed in herbes de Provence, then topped with edible flowers. Not to mention the little delicacies and perfect wine pairings offered throughout.

All of it, sublime to the last drop. The fanciful side of Celine dreamed of one day bringing her father here. Of sharing this meal with him, too.

Odette dabbed at the corners of her lips with a silk napkin before gesturing to one of the waiting maîtres d'hôtel, who set a large brass bowl filled with rose petals beside her on a marble pedestal. Then he filled the basin with bubbling champagne so Odette could rinse her hands. So indulgent. So wasteful. Once her fingers were clean, Odette smoothed her bodice of duchess satin, her thumb grazing the ivory cameo at her breast, tilting it askew.

"You wear that brooch often. It must hold a great deal of meaning to you," Celine commented while the maître d'hôtel poured an entirely new bottle of champagne and roses. The bubbles tickled her wrists, the heady perfume of the petals curling into her throat.

"Mmmmm," Odette hummed in reply. "It does indeed." She straightened the cameo, her gestures careful. A mischievous gleam shone in her eyes. "Would you believe me if I told you it was enchanted? That it kept the most shadowy of my secrets safe?" She winked.

"After this much food and wine, I would believe just about anything." Celine groaned as she tried in vain to slouch in her chair. "Tell me, Odette, why must we wear corsets even while we eat?"

"Because men enjoy keeping us in cages at every waking hour." Odette swirled her wine. "That way we're *contained*. They're afraid of what would happen if we were free." She grinned. "But perhaps if I looked as you did in a corset, I would be singing a different tune. Alas, we can't all be blessed with a tiny waist and a naturally heaving bosom," she teased.

"It . . . isn't as wonderful as you would expect." Celine winced, the wine causing her thoughts to spin. "Ever since my twelfth birthday, I've dreaded the way men look at me. As if I were something to eat."

Odette canted her head, an odd light in her gaze. "I never thought of it that way." She paused in consideration. "Forgive me for speaking out of turn." Conviction flashed across her face. "C'est assez! None of us should have to wear corsets unless *we* decide to wear them. In the meantime, I say we take to the square and burn them all."

Celine's eyes sparkled. "The corsets?"

"No, the *men*, of course."

A peal of laughter burst from Celine's lips. "You do talk scandalously."

"I merely speak the truth. Men are wretched, my dear. I've sworn off them entirely. I'll keep them as friends, but they remain forever unwelcome in my heart."

Delight flared in Celine's chest. "Please share your secret with me. I wish to be rid of them as well." She could think of one or two in particular.

"It isn't a secret." Odette pushed aside her plate of Limoges porcelain to rest her elbows along the scalloped table's edge. "I simply have no interest in them." She paused, her expression thoughtful. "In truth, I much prefer the company of women, in all respects." Odette pronounced this plainly, watching for Celine's reaction.

It took Celine a moment to comprehend the full meaning behind Odette's admission. Her eyes went wide the next instant, color creeping up her neck. "Please know how flattered I am, but—"

Odette snorted. "I don't mean you specifically, you delicious narcissist. Though you are genuinely beautiful . . . and would undoubtedly prove to be a genuine nuisance as a result. Years ago I swore never to love anything more beautiful than myself." She heaved a dramatic sigh. "Thankfully that leaves my options wide and varied."

Laughter caught in Celine's throat just as she took a sip of wine. It burned at the back of her tongue, causing her to cough like a silly young woman in her cups.

"But let's not lie to each other, mon amie," Odette said above Celine's coughing. "You don't wish to be rid of *all* men, do you?"

"I do." Celine cleared her throat and wiped the tears from beneath her lashes. "They are nothing but a bother."

Odette wagged a finger at Celine. "Menteuse. I see the way you look at Bastien." She leaned closer, her expression sly. Knowing.

Celine startled, her hand jostling her water goblet. "What are you—" She sat up, her heart hammering in her chest. "How do I look?"

"Parched, mon amie. Like you wandered the desert for forty years, seeking the Promised Land."

"I look . . . thirsty?" Celine groaned, her cheeks reddening. A mixture of anger and embarrassment washed through her veins. She considering denying it. Tried in vain to conjure a plausible explanation. Then lifted her chin in defiance. Why should she have to lie?

"Very well," Celine announced. "I won't deny it. I'm attracted to Bastien. I think he's . . . too beautiful to be real."

Odette clapped as if she'd just heard the world's foremost soprano perform her favorite aria. "*This* is now my favorite thing you've ever said." She proceeded to giggle in a way that reminded Celine of being a small girl. She didn't know anyone who giggled like that anymore. "Now"—Odette paused to tap an index finger along her chin—"what to do about this situation . . ."

"Nothing," Celine said determinedly. "There is nothing to do. I have no intention of pursuing anyone like Sébastien Saint Germain, Odette," she warned. "Nothing will come from your rather naked attempts to interfere. You know as well as I do that Bastien isn't a proper young gentleman."

"And you require a proper young gentleman?"

"I do." Celine nodded with conviction.

Her expression dubious, Odette pursed her lips. "We'll discuss this later." She shifted tack with the ease of a dancer. "Tell me what you think about my idea for the masquerade ball."

Grateful that Odette had changed the subject, Celine did not hesitate to reply. "I think you shouldn't go as Marie Antoinette. I daresay there will be at least fifteen other women dressed accordingly for the occasion. Because it's expected. I say you do something unexpected." A shrewd gleam alighted her gaze. "Don't go as the wife. Go as the mistress."

"Pardon?" Odette let out a burst of laughter. "This, from the girl who requires a proper young gentleman!"

Celine waved a dismissive hand. "Never mind that. You should go as Madame du Barry."

"Scandaleux!" Odette clapped gleefully. "The society matrons will be positively bug-eyed!"

"And it will be the dress no one forgets," Celine promised.

"I'll do it . . . but I must insist you accompany me to the masquerade ball, as well as another soirée I'm keen to attend." Odette toyed with the silk ribbon about her neck. "Rumor has it the host—a member of a new krewe known as the Twelfth Night Revelers—plans to decorate his gardens after *A Midsummer Night's Dream*."

Though both ideas tantalized Celine with possibility, she shook her head. "I don't think that's wise."

"Not even if Bastien is there, in all his impropriety?" Odette winked.

"Especially not if he's there."

"Ah, don't be so difficult, mon amie." Odette paused meaningfully. "You already admitted he's . . . how did you say it?"

Celine groaned, regret blooming in her stomach. "Too beautiful to be real."

Something clattered to the floor behind her.

The blood drained from Celine's face in a sudden rush. She froze in her seat, her eyes wide. It took only a glance in Odette's direction to confirm the obvious.

Sébastien Saint Germain was standing behind Celine.

Listening to every word she'd just said.

———◇———

"Je suis désolée." Odette wrinkled her nose, clearly not sorry at all.

Celine considered balling up the silk napkin in her hand and hurling it toward Odette's doll-like face. She reconsidered in the next instant. Although it might prove satisfying in the moment, it would do little to help her situation. Her pulse wreaking havoc through her body, Celine turned around.

And immediately wished she could shrink into nothingness.

Bastien stood at the top of the curved staircase, as striking as ever, his Panama hat in hand. Flanking him were several members of La Cour des Lions, each sporting varying degrees of amusement.

Before anyone could speak, Arjun bent to retrieve his leather notebook, an apologetic expression on his face. If Celine had to guess, he'd dropped it on purpose.

She tamped down a flare of gratitude. He'd dropped the notebook too late, that traitor.

A hero was only a hero if he managed to save the damsel in time.

Mortified, Celine stood at once, the legs of her gilded chair catching on the plush carpeting, her salmon-striped skirts a tangle about her feet. Gritting her teeth, Celine allowed her embarrassment to mushroom into anger. She curled her hands into fists and lengthened her neck so she could peer down at the recent arrivals with unmistakable disdain.

One of the elegant women with the rings laughed. "Comme une reine des ténèbres."

Like a queen of darkness.

Easy laughter rippled around the room. Bastien kept silent, his gunmetal eyes unflinching, his handsome features unreadable.

Celine's heartbeat drummed in her ears like the wings of a hummingbird. It would not do for her to appear weak. She would never be able to show her face again in this place if she succumbed to mortification.

Her fists gripping the striped fabric of her gown, Celine nodded once. "Hello."

In response, Bastien bowed low, his hat held out at his side. When he stood once more, the suggestion of a smile played across his lips.

"Good evening," he said, his voice silken. Sinful.

Celine wanted to stomp her foot and flee. To scream like a bean sídhe, loud enough to damage her own hearing.

"Bonsoir, Bastien," Odette replied with a simpering grin.

Before another word could be spoken, the carved longcase clock along the wall began tolling the hour in furtive tones, its weighted brass pendulum swinging back and forth.

The interruption afforded Celine the perfect opportunity. "I'm afraid I must be going." She pushed past the table, her face flushed.

"Not yet!" Odette stood, her sable eyes round, beseeching. "You must at least taste the îles flottantes."

"Floating islands?"

"It's a dessert Kassamir has been keen to add to the menu. We were to be among the first to try it. Clouds of perfect meringue floating in a decadent sauce of crème anglaise."

Celine smiled sadly. "While that sounds heavenly, I'm afraid the hour is late. My friends at the convent will worry."

Odette pouted, tucking a brunette curl behind an ear. "Then at least wait while I call for the carriage."

"No," Celine replied, straightening her skirts, keenly aware of their audience. "I'll be fine. It's only a few blocks to the convent."

"I'm afraid I must insist," Odette countered. "You simply can't walk home alone, not after everything that's happened recently."

Frustration gripped Celine's stomach. She needed to leave *now*. "Very well, then. I'll hail a hired conveyance."

"But that's not necessary," Odette protested. "Not when—"

"Odette," Celine said through gritted teeth. "Thank you so much for the wonderful meal and the consummate hospitality. I'll find my own way home."

"I can't in good conscience—"

"Let her be, Odette," Bastien interrupted softly, the sound of his voice causing Celine to stiffen where she stood. "Tu ne peux pas tout contrôler."

Odette moved from her side of the table. "Mais, Bastien, elle ne—"

"I'll be fine, mon amie," Celine said with another smile. "Please tell Kassamir the meal was a work of art. I'll begin fashioning your gown for the masquerade ball immediately. Feel free to send the bolts of fabric and all the supplies to the convent first thing tomorrow."

With that, Celine lifted her chin and made her way toward the stairs leading to the first floor of Jacques'. The members of La Cour des Lions—who'd stood silent and watchful throughout the entirety of this humiliating exchange—moved aside to grant Celine leave, though she could feel their eyes following her as she descended the steps, Boone inhaling deeply as she passed by.

Her hands trembled in her skirts, but she did not falter. She was a mountain, a tower, a hundred-year-old oak in the—

Behind her, soft laughter rose into the coffered ceiling.

Damn them all to Hell.

MEET YOUR MAKER

—◦◇◦—

Celine regretted the decision to walk home the instant after she made it.

Less than a block from Jacques', every shifting shadow and unfamiliar sound caught her attention, heightening her awareness, lending itself to a creeping kind of fear.

If only the Court could see the queen of darkness now.

It was Celine's pride that wouldn't allow her to admit she lacked the means to hire a hack. And it was her arrogance that forbade her from taking anything else from Odette. Or Bastien. Or any member of La Cour des Lions.

But now that the fervor over recent events had subsided, regret unfurled down Celine's spine. She'd been too hasty. She should have taken advantage of the offered carriage instead of allowing her pride to get the better of her.

Celine sighed to herself.

No. It wasn't just her pride. She was simply tired of being told what to do.

Steeling herself, Celine decided to let the beauty of a New Orleans evening distract her from her thoughts.

A balmy breeze riffled through a magnolia tree to her left, its downy white blossoms swaying in the sultry wind. The breeze coiled closer, carrying with it the sweet perfume of honeysuckle and lavender, the tiny flowers peeking from between the tines of a wrought-iron fence in front of a stately, four-storied mansion. Overhead, wraparound terraces and hanging baskets overflowed with waxy vines and brightly colored blossoms. A row of blue cypress trees dripped with Spanish moss, forming layers of scent and shadow. Somewhere in the distance, an unseen man with a beautiful voice began to sing, his words a mixture of French and something Celine could not quite discern.

In only a few short weeks, Celine had learned to appreciate how the city seemed to come alive the moment the sun dipped below the horizon. Not a normal kind of alive, like sunshine and laughter. But a sinister, sensual kind of alive. A warm caress and a cool whisper.

Despite everything, Celine found herself falling a little bit in love.

As she continued making her way toward the convent, footsteps shifted in line behind her, clear and crisp against the blue-grey pavestones. Heavy footsteps, like those of a man.

Celine listened as they drew near. Then straightened her spine. There was no reason to fear the person at her back. Pedestrians took to the streets of the Quarter at all hours of day and night. It was irrational to think this might be anyone—or anything—else.

Nevertheless, she could not help but be reminded of that

awful night in the atelier, when her naïveté had betrayed her, changing the course of her life.

Celine turned onto the next street. The footsteps lingered in her shadow.

Fear prickled the nape of her neck. That feeling of being followed.

She refrained from turning to confront the man, lest she appear foolish for the second time in a single evening or, worse, provoke him into taking action. Instead she decided to conduct a test. She slowed her pace to a leisurely stroll, expecting the pedestrian to pass by.

He did not.

Instead he, too, slowed his footsteps to match hers.

Celine fended off a wave of panic, her memories of that terrible evening taking flight in her mind. She glanced about without moving her head, looking to see who might be around her. A lone gentleman strolled on the opposite side of the street, his walking stick striking the pavers, his gaze focused on the path before him, heedless of all else.

Would he bother to help her?

For an instant, Celine considered dashing across the lane and coming to stand alongside him, irrespective of these concerns. Then she made out the sounds of a parade in the distance. A place in which countless people undoubtedly gathered. She decided to speed up in order to make her way toward the crowd, no matter that it was in the wrong direction of the convent.

The footsteps behind her stopped midstride. Then Celine

swore she heard something take to the wind in a flutter of leaves, the sound clattering against the bars of an iron balustrade.

Panic taking hold, Celine halted in her tracks. Dared to look over her shoulder.

Nothing was there.

Her heart dropped into her stomach, its beat thundering loud and hard through her body.

"Celine," a voice whispered behind her. A voice of nails grating across slate.

Fear lanced through her, keeping her immobile for an instant. Then she whirled around . . . to find nothing.

"Mon amour," it rasped at her back, its words an icy brush against her skin. "You smell divine. Come with me to the heart of Chartres. *Die in my arms.*"

Celine lifted her skirts and ran, her feet racing above the grey pavestones. She sprinted to the nearest corner, rounding it, her teeth chattering in her skull.

Footsteps battered against the walkway behind her, then dissolved in a rustle of dried leaves. She continued running toward the noise of the parade in the distance, refusing to stop until she reached the crowd.

A hand shot from behind an alcove to her left, grabbing Celine by the arm, yanking her from her intended path, causing her to nearly stumble.

Celine screamed, forcing every bit of air from her lungs. A cool palm covered her lips, bidding her silent. Then strong arms shoved her behind a wall of bergamot-scented muscle.

Bastien.

Positioning himself before her, Bastien leveled his revolver into a fall of darkness beneath a nearby awning. A strange muttering could be heard in its depths, almost like the chittering of insects or the gnashing of teeth.

"Be gone," Bastien said, his words punishing in their precision. "Or stay and meet your maker, for I'll grant you no quarter."

Celine pressed her face into his shoulder, her fingers digging into his back.

The chittering ceased, the cloaked creature scuttling up the side of the building before vanishing into the night.

For a beat, Celine and Bastien stood there unmoving, their bodies tensed, their breaths rising and falling in tandem. Then Bastien turned toward her, his expression cut from stone as he holstered his gun.

Something within Celine was on the brink of shattering. Her legs felt boneless, her body felt stretched thin. Energy pounded through her veins, causing her hands to shake.

Bastien's fingers tightened around her arms at the exact moment Celine's legs started to give. He held her in place, his gaze locked on hers.

Her vision hazy, Celine blinked. Then exhaled slowly.

"Celine," Bastien said, his voice soft. Careful.

She nodded. "I'm . . . fine." Celine continued staring at Bastien's face, tracing its lines in an effort to calm herself, her throat dry, the words a jumble on her tongue. "How did you . . . I mean, you don't need to—"

"Celine," Bastien said again. Tentatively, he shifted a hand to the side of her face.

She kept still, though she wanted to lean into his touch.

"Tu vas bien?" he asked quietly, brushing his thumb along her cheek in a soothing caress.

Celine nodded. "But . . . please . . . stay."

"I will." Something glinted in his gaze. "I promise."

"What—*was* that?" she whispered.

He hesitated, his thumb grazing the edge of her lips.

"Don't lie to me," she said softly. "I'm tired of all the lies."

He inhaled through his nose. "It was . . ." He searched for the right words.

"Something inhuman," Celine finished.

Bastien considered her for a moment. Then nodded.

"Did that . . . thing kill Anabel?" Celine asked.

"I can't be certain. It's possible." His words seemed to ring of truth. Or maybe Celine simply wished to believe him. To dismiss the yellow ribbon. To ignore logic and listen to the whispers of her heart.

Fickle little fool that it was.

"It knew my name. Told me to come with it to the heart of Chartres." Celine shuddered. "It asked me to *die in its arms.*"

A trace of rage rippled across Bastien's face. "It's gone now."

"It might come back."

"I'll find it first." Bastien's fingers slid down her face, his palm framing her chin. His features took on a dangerous edge, his steel-flecked eyes bright and intense.

He looked . . . vicious. Like an avenging angel. Or a demon from Hell.

Celine wrapped a hand around his wrist. The way he spoke

in this moment—the way he gazed at her—should have frightened her. But it didn't. Instead Celine bowed into his caress. Tightened her grip around his wrist, the creature in her blood restless, feverish.

Bastien bent closer, his breath a cool wash across her skin, his lips close enough to touch. To nip. To taste.

He was going to kiss her. She was going to kiss him back.

And—for a blink of time—nothing else would matter.

A pair of footfalls across the street shattered their reverie. A well-dressed couple around her father's age had stopped in their tracks, pausing to stare at Bastien and Celine, their expressions filled with shared disapproval.

All at once, Celine's sense of propriety returned. She knew why the other pair looked upon them with such disdain. To anyone passing by, Bastien and Celine appeared to be two young lovers caught in a passionate embrace on a darkened street corner. Unknowingly, Celine's fingers had twisted around the fine fabric of Bastien's waistcoat, as if to tug him closer. The palm of Bastien's free hand was pressed against the small of her back, dragging her against him.

She felt the heat of him through her bodice. Through her skirts. Felt it caress past her skin, into her soul.

Wanton. Sinful. Perfect.

With a gasp, Celine pushed away.

Bastien's fingers fell from her throat. He stepped back. The fire in his eyes faded the next instant, replaced by amused indifference.

Celine swallowed, gripped by a sudden despondency.

"Thank you . . . for coming to my aid this evening, Monsieur Saint Germain."

Bastien nodded. "Of course." He rubbed a palm against his neck, pausing to check his pulse, for reasons Celine could not begin to fathom.

Straightening stiffly, she looked about, seeking her own distraction. A few short blocks away, the noise of the carnival rose in her ears, the revelry drawing closer with each passing second.

"We should make our way back to the convent," Bastien said above the rising din.

Celine nodded in agreement. But unease took hold of her at the thought of marching through the darkened corridors of the Ursuline convent. Of trying to fall asleep amid its lurking shadows.

She could not be alone right now, though she refused to say it aloud.

"I appreciate your offer to accompany me to the convent," Celine said, her voice shaken by uncertainty. "I just . . ."

Bastien's expression softened. Her heart stuttered when he moved toward her, only to catch himself midstep. "Would you rather walk someplace else first? Perhaps a nearby café for some coffee or a cup of tea?" he asked, his tone bordering on formal.

Celine hated to hear the distance in his words. Another wash of inexplicable sadness hollowed through her. How she wished she could ask him for what she truly wanted. How she wished she could admit it to herself.

The creature inside her rattled its cage, demanding to be released.

As if to mock her further, raucous laughter pealed in the distance, its echo cheerful. Unencumbered. Celine resented it greatly. More than anything, she wanted to feel as free as that ribbon of laughter. To remember what it felt like to feel safe in her own skin.

Darkness wrapped around her like a shroud, reminding Celine of her truth. How could she dare to wish for such a thing? She'd killed a man and run away, flouting French law. If the truth ever came to light, she could be hanged for it.

Did a murderess deserve to feel free?

A new strain of music unraveled into the sky, its melody bright. Effervescent.

It beckoned to Celine, all but making the decision for her. Still she hesitated.

Then—as if he could read her mind—Bastien said, "Perhaps we should venture in the direction of the parade and walk with the crowd for a few minutes."

Celine nodded, the gratitude plain on her face.

Maybe a girl destined for the gallows didn't deserve to feel free. To drown her dark sorrows in something light. But neither did any young man who tried to force himself on a young woman.

And Celine still wasn't sorry for what she'd done.

MÉFIEZ-VOUS DU ROUGAROU

—◦◊◦◊◦◦—

The crowd pulsed around Celine and Bastien, ebbing and flowing like a capricious tide. Cheers and wild laughter suffused the air, putting to rout the worst of her fears. Celine's pulse thrummed beneath her skin, her blood rising in a heady rush. If she closed her eyes, she could almost feel as if she were floating with the crowd, being carried on an errant wave.

She'd never experienced a more welcome distraction.

Bits of colored paper rained down around them, collecting in Celine's hair and against Bastien's skin before littering the ground. Music pounded into the sky, brass trumpets blaring, screeching through the night as if their joy could not be contained. Revelers gathered beneath eaves and along street corners festooned with vibrant streamers, many with their hands or arms linked, all sense of propriety lost beneath the light of the crescent moon.

A papier-mâché tableaux car trundled down the lane, moving at a snail's pace. Men clothed in jackets trimmed with golden epaulettes—as if they were foot soldiers in Napoleon's army—laughed as they threw coins, painted buttons, and wooden beads into the crowd.

Each of Celine's senses were aflame. The sweat and the smell of overturned earth mixed with powdery clouds of sugar to form its own unique fragrance. She soon found herself caught up in the commotion, her fears further dulled by the sight of the ongoing spectacle.

She whirled around, stepping back when members of a dancing troupe bearing torches pressed through the center of the crowd, their skirts spinning in a blur about their slender bodies. Shirtless, barrel-chested men with waxed mustaches and scandalously tight trousers performed acrobatic tricks in the middle of the street.

The chaos of the crowd threatening to separate them, Celine reached for Bastien's hand without thought. He threaded his fingers through hers as if it were natural. As if the only thing that made sense amid the confusion was the touch of his skin to hers.

Celine drew alongside Bastien, her eyes wide-open, a smile threatening to take shape on her face. Swallowed by the sea of moving bodies, they were soon carried past a narrow alleyway where a young, well-dressed couple shared an ardent kiss in the shadows, as though they were the only two souls in existence, her fingers winding through his hair, his hands gripping her hips.

Her cheeks flushing, Celine averted her gaze. It was wrong to watch something so intimate.

To watch them. To want to be them.

"Faites attention!" a man yelled as the crowd made a sudden surge.

"Nom de Dieu," Celine cursed as she almost collided with a

stout man clutching an empty bottle of port. Bastien pulled back in a seamless motion, spinning them about, away from the budding confusion.

Before they could take in a breath, three young women turned the corner, pulling short a hairsbreadth from Bastien and Celine. Blue ostrich feathers fanned about their heads, their wide belts fashioned of satin and sparkling beads in an array of rainbow colors, their skirts constructed of layers of translucent tulle. Fabric rosettes covered the centers of their breasts.

The rest of their pale skin was bare.

Bastien laughed as the women harrumphed at a stunned Celine, rounding her with ease.

"Faites attention," he whispered in her ear, his tone teasing.

She glanced over her shoulder—armed with a retort—when a tall figure wearing a terrifying mask lunged for them, the fur around its face trembling, its walnut-shell claws nearly grazing their shoulders.

Celine stifled a cry as she stepped back into Bastien, who wrapped a steadying arm around her waist.

The man in the furred mask angled his head to the sky. Bayed once. "Méfiez-vous du rougarou!" He drew out the last word into another howl, then spun about in an awkward dance.

Celine's eyes went wide. Though her heart still pounded, a smile tugged at the edges of her lips. Bastien laughed, then bowed at the masked man, who proceeded to lope in another direction.

"Beware the . . . what did he say?" Celine tilted her head, struggling to be heard over the commotion.

"The rougarou."

Celine blinked. "What is a rougarou?" she asked loudly.

"A creature of darkness meant to instill fear in the hearts of children." Bastien sent her a lighthearted grin, his gaze glittering. "Half man, half wolf, it prowls the swamps and forests beneath the light of the moon, hunting for its next kill."

Though he spoke in obvious jest, Celine could not ignore the strange pull in her stomach. Something inhuman had attacked her less than half an hour ago. The worst of her nightmares had become very real possibilities. Was this a creature of fact or fiction?

Bastien's features softened with understanding. "Don't worry. A rougarou exists only in our imagination."

"And in your imagination, what does it kill?" she asked carefully.

"Bad Catholics."

A rush of unexpected laughter burst from Celine's lips. "You can't be serious."

He peaked a brow. "Make sure you keep all your promises during Lent." He leaned close, electrifying the skin beneath her ear, sending a chill from her neck down to her toes. "Or méfiez-vous du rougarou."

Celine laughed again, shoving him away.

"Regardez!" a throaty voice commanded nearby.

Bastien and Celine followed the directive, turning to look to one side.

Four elderly women with dark skin stood in a semicircle, the eldest at its center waving a hand in Bastien's direction.

"C'est un *beau* diable," she declared, the other women around her chortling in response. "Do you not agree?" she asked Celine.

Celine answered with a humorless nod. Bastien was indeed a beautiful devil.

The lady held out her wrinkled hands. "Dance with me, beau diable," she ordered Bastien.

Without the slightest hesitation, he swept her up in his arms as the beat of a festive quadrille blared into the night sky, the drums and violins soaring in tandem. Soon other couples joined in, until a small corner of the street moved in a familiar pattern, changing partners, weaving in and out of each other like the reeds of a basket coming together.

Celine found herself pulled into the mêlée, brushing past hands and shoulders, flashing around blurring faces, the sweat dripping from her brow, the hem of her salmon-striped skirt kicking up a whirl of red dust around her feet.

When the quadrille ended—a new melody quick to take its place—Celine laughed loudly and clapped with the dispersing crowd. Then she glanced across the way to find Bastien watching her, a strange look on his face.

They held each other's gazes as they all but collided in the center of the street.

"You dance well," Celine said with an awkward smile.

"As do you."

She made a face. "I was a bit uncertain about the steps. There haven't been many occasions for me to dance."

"We should remedy that." Bastien brushed the settling dust from his shoulders. "And dancing well isn't about knowing the steps. It's about knowing yourself."

"That's a bit trite, don't you think?"

His lips pushed forward. "Trite? Why would it be trite to know oneself?"

"I only meant—do we ever truly know ourselves?"

"I should hope so. Knowing who you are is necessary in order to determine who you want to be." Bastien looked to Celine for cues on where to proceed. Without a word, she began winding through the fringes of the crowd, moving in the direction of the convent, reassured by the feeling of his palm against the small of her back.

Once they'd cleared the parade, Celine shifted beside Bastien, at ease for the first time since leaving Jacques', when her chief concern had been the recent humiliation she'd suffered at Odette's hands. Celine almost laughed at herself. To think that had happened less than an hour ago.

But none of it mattered now. Not much, at least.

Her fingers no longer trembled. Her ribs no longer constricted her heart. She didn't yet feel entirely safe, but at least she no longer felt afraid.

And she was thankful.

For the length of the next city block, Celine considered the last thing Bastien had said. "If knowing who you are is a necessary part of knowing who you will become, then who are you, Sébastien Saint Germain?"

He snorted. "I should warn you, turnabout is fair play."

Celine paused in deliberation. "Tonight, I agree. From this point onward, let's deal only in truths."

"And tomorrow?"

"We'll return to cloaking ourselves in comfortable lies."

Bastien laughed, the sound rich and resonant. "Very well, then. Who am I?" he mused. "I'm . . . a man." Something glinted in his gaze.

Celine eyed him sidelong, her expression sardonic.

"I'm the son of people from different worlds," he continued, his smile lingering. "My mother was a free woman of color, and my father was Taíno." He paused. "For too short a time, I was also"—a shadow crossed his face—"a brother. After I lost my family, I became a nephew. My uncle brought me back to New Orleans at the age of nine, and I lived here until I was sent to the academy, where—barring a rather unfortunate incident—I almost became a soldier." A hint of bitter amusement touched his lips. "Now I handle my uncle's affairs when he is away on business." He raised a shoulder. "I suppose that's the whole of it."

Celine refrained from calling him out. Bastien may not have told any falsehoods, but he'd obfuscated the truth, distilling the whole of his life down to nothing more than a few particulars. A fount of questions gathered in her throat. Michael's admonition from days earlier rang through her mind, spurring her to press Bastien for details, so that she might understand the full extent of the Ghost's unhappy tale.

She chose to ignore this desire. It would be easier to take on those concerns tomorrow than bear their weight tonight.

"You can ask me, Celine," Bastien said. "After all, Michael didn't tell you everything." Caustic humor laced his words.

"Of course he didn't. I'm certain it hasn't escaped your notice how much he hates you."

"The feeling is most assuredly mutual." His grin reeked of arrogance.

"May I ask why?"

"You may. But I may not answer. Since I promised not to lie."

Celine's lips were caught between silence and speech for an instant. "Very well," she grumbled. "For what it's worth, Arjun is a wretched spy."

He snorted. "As well as an excellent attorney."

"For fiends and scoundrels alike." She paused. "But in all seriousness . . . what happened to your family?" This, at least, she wished to know in this moment.

A look of blank apathy settled onto his beautiful face. "My mother died six months after my sister. Following their deaths, my father took me from New Orleans to Saint Domingue. He fell ill soon thereafter, so we moved to his home in San Juan."

"And . . . how did your sister die?"

"She was killed in an accident, at the age of fifteen." Though Bastien's reply sounded indifferent, his features hardened for an instant, anger flashing behind his eyes before his artful mask slipped back into place. There was a story there. A source of immense pain. But Celine did not wish to press Bastien on the matter. Not yet. "My father succumbed to his illness a short while later, after which I returned to New Orleans," he finished.

An invisible hand gripped Celine's heart in a vise. It troubled her how Bastien spoke about loss in such a matter-of-fact tone. Perhaps that was how he talked about things that truly mattered to him, in cold, detached fashion.

"I've heard many people say tragedy shapes us," Bastien continued. "But I am not the worst thing that's ever happened to me, nor am I the worst thing I've ever done. Nothing in life is that simple." He looked across the darkened streets of New Orleans, his gaze steady. Determined.

His words were like a blow to Celine. Every day she denied parts of herself. Tried to hide the worst thing that had happened to her, the worst thing she'd ever done. Her entire life, she'd denied who her mother was, as if it were some kind of great shame. Because of this, she knew nothing about half her past. Half of her own story.

Since the age of four, she'd been told this was the only way.

"Do you ever wish you could be someone else?" Celine asked, her tone solemn.

"Often. Especially when I was a boy." Bastien turned toward her. "And you?"

Celine blanched.

"Don't lie to me." Bastien repeated her earlier words: "Tonight we deal only in truths."

"Which is . . . difficult, since my whole life is built on a lie."

It was honest. More honest than Celine had ever been with anyone in her life.

She breathed in deeply through her nose. "My mother was from a Far Eastern country. I was never told which one. But . . . I am of mixed heritage, from a marriage of East and West," Celine blurted, almost as if her own admission startled her. "I've never said that to a soul," she finished in a rush.

And yet the words fell from her lips with surprising ease.

Bastien studied her while they walked. Whatever his thoughts were, he concealed them well.

Her head remarkably cool, Celine trained her eyes on the grey pavestones ahead. "When my father and I came to Paris, I was very young. He told me to keep who my mother was a secret. He said if the world knew, I would live with derision for the rest of my life. So I listened, and I lied. And . . . I feel ashamed for it. It's as if this lie has become an essential part of my truth, like a kind of twisted keystone. So much so, that I don't know how to"—she struggled for a moment—"how to think or behave any differently, lest the whole thing crumble to pieces."

There. Several painful truths unmasked. Truths she'd been incapable of admitting even to herself. It surprised her that— of all the people she'd encountered thus far—she'd decided to share these truths with Bastien.

Celine waited in silence for a time, pondering this realization. Wishing she could ignore the meaning behind it.

"I'm sorry for your pain, Celine," Bastien said in a subdued tone. "Thank you for trusting me with your truth."

A sharp twinge cut through her chest, making it difficult to respond at first.

Finally Celine spoke, her voice a soft brush of sound. "And I'm sorry for your pain, Bastien. I think trust is a precious thing. Know that I will always treat yours as such."

He looked at her, his eyes a liquid silver. "Merci, mon coeur. From my heart to yours."

They walked the rest of the way toward the Ursuline convent with nothing accompanying them but the chirruping of insects and the whispering of palm fronds. Once they rounded the final bend—the convent looming tall in the darkness—Celine tilted her head toward the lace of stars around the sickle moon, their cool light surging through her veins. Bastien stopped beside her, though he did not follow her gaze.

"Are the stars that captivating?" he teased in a gentle tone.

"Of course they are," she said without looking away. "They're infinite. They see all and know all. These same stars hung in the sky during the times of Michelangelo and Shakespeare. Isn't that fascinating?"

Bastien sighed, the sound grim. "I'll never understand the fascination with the infinite. There is an end to everything, to good things as well."

"Chaucer was an ass." Celine glanced at him, a brow quirked with amusement. "And the infinite captivates us because it allows us to believe all things are possible. That true love can last beyond time."

He did not reply. Instead his eyes bored into hers, the lashes above them thick. Deliciously sooty. When Celine looked away, Bastien cleared his throat, pausing to check his pulse.

"You did it again," Celine said.

"What?"

"You often check your pulse. I'm curious as to why."

A sardonic smile took shape on Bastien's face. "To remind myself I'm human."

That same strange feeling gripped Celine again. That feeling of something eluding her grasp. Something . . . important. Before she could stop herself, she asked, "*Are* you?"

Her question caught Bastien off guard. He stared down at her, his perfect lips pushing forward with slow deliberation. Then he took her hand and pressed it to the side of his neck. Beneath Celine's fingertips drummed a steady heartbeat. One that began to race at her touch, its warmth tingling through her body. Bastien held both their hands there for a time, aware his pulse betrayed him. Aware and seemingly unconcerned.

The heart doesn't lie, Michael had said.

Celine let her shaking hand fall. And decided to ignore all common sense. "Since we're dealing in truths for this one night, I wanted to say I'm attracted to you."

"And I'm attracted to you." Bastien did not hesitate in this admission.

She stared up at him, her eyes unflinching. "Earlier this evening, I wanted to kiss you."

"I've wanted to kiss you since the night we first saw each other in Jackson Square."

"You remembered," she murmured. "I thought you had forgotten."

Bastien canted his head. "How could I forget? You surprised me. It had been a long time since anything surprised me."

Celine blinked. "I surprised *you*?"

He laughed. Then his expression turned serious. "One day, someone should tell you how beautiful you are in the moonlight," Bastien said softly.

Heat pooled in Celine's stomach, licking through her chest, rising into her throat. "Someone should." She swallowed. "But . . . I don't think it should be you."

"I agree." Again, Bastien did not hesitate.

"Don't fall in love with me," she warned again, her words breathless. "You're not good for me. And I'm not good for you."

"I agree, on all counts."

"Most likely, you require a young woman with wealth and pedigree. An established place in society," Celine continued. "And I require a proper young gentleman."

The angles in Bastien's face sharpened, betraying a spark of emotion too slight to discern. "Correct on all counts," he said. "You lack the right pedigree." A half smile curved up his face. "And I am not a gentleman."

"Nevertheless, I appreciate what you did for me tonight, more than words. And in the future"—Celine inhaled—"I would not be offended if you chose to maintain your distance."

"I don't think that's necessary. If you agree, I believe we're safe being passing acquaintances." Bastien paused as if he intended to say something more. Then kept silent, his lips curling upward.

But . . . who wants to be safe? Celine banished the reckless thought from her mind and held out her hand. "Thank you again. I will not forget your kindness."

"You're welcome, mon coeur." Instead of bending to kiss her hand, Bastien shook it, as he would an equal, his signet ring winking back at the stars.

A wave of satisfaction rippled through Celine. "Do passing acquaintances use such terms of endearment?"

"They do in my world."

She smiled through a flicker of sadness. "Your world is beautiful, Bastien. I wish I could stay."

"As do I."

With that, Celine slid her hand from his, the tips of her fingers lingering a beat longer than necessary. Then she turned toward the convent, surprised to realize it was possible to feel both gladdened and gutted in the same instant.

The Witching Hour

———◦◦◇◇◦◦———

From the corner of her eye, Celine watched their last candle begin to flicker and wane.

Not yet, she silently implored. *Please not yet.*

Her tongue slipped between her teeth as she hastened her efforts, basting the pieces of lustrous fabric together in a race against the sputtering light. Just as she was about to reach the end of the seam, the door to Pippa's cell creaked open. A faint breeze blew through the space, snuffing out the flame before Celine could blink, swallowing her in sudden darkness.

"Oh," Pippa said, her petite figure silhouetted by a beam of moonlight. "I'm terribly sorry about that." With her foot, she propped the door halfway open. "But I come bearing gifts." She sidestepped into the room. Between her hands rested a simple wooden tray laden with what appeared to be food and the stub of a candle in an old-fashioned brass holder.

It took a moment for Celine's eyes to adjust to the blue darkness. "Apologies are unnecessary, especially if you brought cheese."

"And ham and Dijon mustard, as well as tea, a crust of warm bread . . . and a piece of fresh honeycomb I filched earlier from a hive of glorious bees!" Pippa said triumphantly.

Celine could almost hear Pippa smiling. It was in these moments that she appreciated her the most. Philippa Montrose was sunlight and goodness. A honeycomb in her own right. Perhaps it sounded silly, but having a friend like Pippa helped Celine believe she was welcome in the eyes of decent society, despite everything that had happened in the last few weeks.

Grinning, Celine pinned her needle to the shimmering white fabric and shifted back from her makeshift workstation to stretch her arms above her head. Briefly she considered waiting to eat. It would be wise to take advantage of the tiny candle Pippa had finagled to finish the last bit of basting before retiring for the night. After all, a single week remained before the masquerade ball. Celine had never completed a gown in such a short amount of time, much less without assistance.

But she was famished. She'd already forgone dinner because she'd been so consumed with her work. When Pippa had suggested they pool their meager rations of light to make them last longer, Celine was beyond appreciative of the gesture. Ever since arriving to the convent less than three weeks ago, she'd lamented its dearth of oil lanterns.

Once the sun had set, Celine had moved her things to Pippa's slightly larger cell, where Pippa had chosen to work on her watercolors while Celine stitched by the light of their shared candle flames.

Now Pippa bustled about the space, humming a familiar melody as she lit the short taper and positioned a stool in the center of the room, placing the tray on the seat to form a makeshift table.

On the opposite side of the cell, Celine stepped back to survey her work.

It pleased her how much she'd managed to complete in only two days. As soon as dawn had broken the past morning, she'd consulted with a carpenter on Rue Bienville, who'd been recommended to her by the Mother Superior. After Celine explained how the baroque-style panniers should look—extending sideways at each hip in an exaggerated fashion, the front and back silhouettes held close to the body—he suggested they use willow branches, as they would be light, pliable, and readily available. Perfect for constructing hoops that had been out of fashion for nearly a century. To Celine's immense pleasure, he'd assured her he would have a sample for her to test in three days' time.

Celine had proceeded to pour herself into fashioning Odette's gown with a single-minded focus. It had helped distract her from the many unanswered questions spinning through her mind.

The first time Celine had visited Jacques', she'd come to the conclusion that the members of La Cour des Lions were not ordinary humans. Of course that knowledge raised the question: if they weren't exactly human, then what were they?

Celine didn't have the slightest clue. Were they goblins or changelings? Witches or warlocks? Perhaps some kind of dark fairy or ephemeral sylph? These were among the more fanciful possibilities. The kind Celine borrowed from books or stole from stories she'd heard as a child. It felt safer to believe they were tricksters like Puck or fey gentry from a shimmering forest, like Oberon and Titania. Safer to think that than believe they might be creatures so terrible, the worst of Celine's nightmares could never have conceived of them.

After all, if magic was possible, anything was possible.

The thought that alarmed her most was the likelihood that La Cour des Lions had something to do with Anabel's murder. That Bastien intended to protect the culprit when he concealed the yellow ribbon.

Or that he was in fact the culprit.

Perhaps Celine lacked the stomach for the truth. Perhaps she wished to remain blissfully ignorant, a worry that disconcerted her all the more.

Her mind a tangle of thorns, Celine ran her fingers over the pieces of cut fabric she'd stacked in a neat pile atop Pippa's rope bed. What had begun this morning as nothing more than a list of measurements and bits of scattered muslin had transformed into the beginnings of a grand ball gown.

Celine let her mind be consumed by the challenge. Welcomed the diversion.

The next part of the project could prove to be the most difficult task she'd ever undertaken. A portion of Odette's masquerade ball costume was intended to be a surprise. Thusly Celine could not rely on her help to complete it. She would have to recruit assistance from elsewhere. Perhaps Pippa would be a good option. Her frame was similar in size and shape to that of Odette, despite their disparity in height.

"Have you finished for the evening?" Pippa asked while clearing away the last of her watercolor accoutrements.

Celine stretched again, a yawn tugging at her mouth. "More or less."

"I've never seen anyone labor for such a long period of time without stopping. As if you would happily work well into the witching hour had you not been interrupted."

"It's true I'm enjoying myself." Celine sent her a tired smile. "It's been quite a while since I've had the chance to create something so grand. The masquerade ball is barely a week away. Usually I have months to make a dress this intricate. It's fortunate Odette had in her possession a great deal of lace and beadwork for me to use." She knelt before the makeshift table and poured a cup of tea for Pippa. "I didn't see you earlier this afternoon. Did you go to the market with Antonia or to the milliner with Catherine?"

Pippa shook her head. "I met Phoebus Devereux's mother for tea." She stirred a drop of cream into her tea, the pale color swirling about the cup.

"I almost forgot about that," Celine said, as she daubed coarse grain mustard on a piece of bread, then layered slices of Gruyère and salted ham on top. "How was it?"

Pippa pursed her rosebud lips to one side. "Odd. She said her son has been a bit ill these last two days. The doctors are struggling to determine what might be ailing him. Thankfully he's on the mend. She wants me to meet with him soon. Phoebus will issue an invitation when he is well again."

"If all goes according to his mother's plan, how do you feel about being courted by him?" Celine bit into the bread, savoring the sharpness of the mustard and the salt of the cheese.

Pippa broke off a piece of honeycomb, letting the golden honey dribble into her tea while she considered how to respond. "In all honesty, I'm more concerned about what will happen to me if I fail to find a match. When I can no longer reside in a convent without being a nun." She licked the honey from her fingertips, her expression morose.

Her friend's bleak honesty angered Celine. "And if you didn't have to worry about such things? Would marrying a boy like Phoebus suit your sensibilities?"

"I suppose so. It would be nice to have something of my own. A space to draw. Paint. Play music. Be myself. The Devereux family appears to be of comfortable means." Pippa paused. "I would be well cared for if I married Phoebus, should he choose to ask." Resignation tugged at the edges of her lips.

Celine sipped her tea, wishing she could speak plainly about how much this situation troubled her. That a girl as wonderful as Pippa would have to forgo her desires in order to have comfort and protection. "I suppose this all sounds reasonable and prudent." *And disheartening,* she added to herself.

"I know this frustrates you." Pippa paused again in consideration. "I'm just—I don't have the temperament to wait and hope for something better. I worry all the time what will happen to me. Even reasonable goals can be unattainable when you're a young woman without prospects," she said simply, the light dulling in her eyes. "I learned this back home in Yorkshire, when it became clear that no amount of effort on my part or the part of my mother could atone for my father's failings."

Atonement. A concept that also haunted Celine of late. "Do

you think it's possible your father could ever atone for his sins?"

"To me or to God?"

"To you."

Pippa didn't reply, a frown settling into the lines of her face, as if the thought troubled her.

Celine took in a careful breath. "I suppose I'm asking if it's possible for anyone to truly atone for their sins. To ask for forgiveness and truly be forgiven."

For a beat, Pippa lingered in contemplation. "For quite some time now, I've thought sin isn't as black and white as they'd like us to believe," she replied in a pensive tone. "I suppose there are times in which sin lies in the eyes of the beholder."

"When we first met, I would not have thought you capable of saying such a thing."

"Is that a compliment or an insult?" Pippa grinned good-naturedly.

"It's a compliment. I'm thankful you feel comfortable sharing such thoughts with me." Celine chewed at the inside of her cheek. "Perhaps you're right. Perhaps what one might consider a sin, another might consider . . . survival."

"Like when Jean Valjean stole a loaf of bread to feed his family in *Les Misérables*." Pippa nodded in agreement, then prepared a ham-and-cheese tartine for herself. An easy silence settled between them as they finished their midnight meal.

Just as Celine swallowed the dregs of her lukewarm tea, Pippa angled her head to one side. "Celine . . . there's something I've been meaning to say to you for quite some time. I might muck it up, but I hope you'll bear with me while I try."

Celine's stomach tightened with dread. "Of course." She forced herself to smile.

"I think all of us who came to the convent are here because we didn't have a better choice," Pippa began. "It's possible some of us are trying to . . . escape something from our pasts." She wavered for an instant. "But I believe you're a wonderful person, with a good heart and a warm soul. Whatever you may have done in your past life, I think that—no, I *know* that—God can forgive you."

A knot formed in the base of Celine's throat. "Pippa, I—"

"Wait, wait, there's more." Pippa took in a deep, steadying breath. "If God forgives you, so can I." Determination etched across her brow. "So should we all." She swallowed, her lips gathering sheepishly. "I made a hash of that, didn't I? It sounded much better in my head. Ever so much more poignant and meaningful."

Celine's mouth had gone dry. "You didn't make a hash of it. I . . ."

"You don't have to say anything. I just thought you should know." With a tender smile, Pippa placed the last of the honeycomb on the edge of Celine's tea saucer.

For a time, Celine's eyes burned with unshed tears. She blinked them back and averted her gaze, fighting to collect herself. "Thank you," she said in a thick voice. Then she brought the piece of sun-drenched honeycomb to her lips.

Pippa couldn't know what she'd done for Celine. What Pippa's halting statement had meant to her.

It suddenly struck Celine how the simplest words often carried the most weight.

Yes and no. Love and hate. Give and take.

For the first time since she'd killed a man and fled France, she felt understood. Seen.

Safe.

———◇———

"Ooofff," Pippa gasped as she tripped over an uneven stone in the darkened corridors of the Ursuline convent. The basket of basted fabric in her hands almost spilled across the floor, but she managed to hold fast to it.

"Are you all right?" Celine asked in a loud whisper, a few steps behind her.

Pippa's laughter was soft. Rueful. "My hands are slippery from the water and the soap. Perhaps we should have gone to wash for the night *after* returning your things to your cell." She righted herself, her motions awkward as a result of her burden.

"Or perhaps we should have saved the last taper for something besides mocking Catherine."

"I didn't mock her!"

"Well, you watched me mock her. And you laughed, which is just as awful."

"It is not." Pippa smothered a snicker.

Celine smiled to herself, her soul awash in warmth. At this point, she'd truly lost count of how many times she'd offered silent thanks for Pippa. Perhaps if she'd had a sister—as she'd so often wished when she was younger—she could understand better what it felt like to have an ally by her side through thick and thin. Someone with whom to brave the darkest of nights.

A flash of movement caught Celine's eye at the end of the arched corridor. Like a shadow stretching in a beam of sunlight.

She stopped short, her last footstep echoing in her ears.

The memory of that shapeless creature gnashing its teeth and scuttling up the side of the building flickered through Celine's mind, causing her breath to lodge in her throat. Pippa's skirts swished across the stone floor a few steps ahead, the sound reminiscent of the creature taking flight in a tangle of wind-swept branches.

Celine's skin bristled as if she'd wandered into a spiderweb. The hairs on the back of her neck stood straight. She stared at the opposite end of the hallway, half of her willing the shadows to shift once again, the other half praying they did not.

A moment later, she decided her tired mind had played tricks on her. With a firm set to her shoulders, she adjusted her grip on her wicker basket and proceeded to follow Pippa.

Outside the door to her cell, Celine rested the basket of sewing bric-a-brac on one hip, then braced herself to push open the heavy wooden door. Just before she took hold of the handle, she turned toward Pippa. "Do you have a free moment tomorrow for me to measure a length of fabric on you?"

"Of course not." Pippa grinned. "I abhor the idea of being draped in shimmering silk. It's as if you don't know me at all."

Celine snorted. "So then I'll see you at noon?" She turned the handle of her cell.

The door blew back all at once, drawn by an unexpected draft.

Pippa yelped as Celine's basket of sewing instruments crashed to the stone floor. Without pausing for breath, Celine yanked a set of shears from the pile beside her feet, brandishing the sharp point as if it were a blade.

The smell hit her first. A mixture of old pennies and the stench of a butcher's shop.

Of a place in which animals were slaughtered.

"Pippa," Celine said, her voice even, despite the fear roiling beneath her skin. "Go find the Mother Superior."

"I'm not leaving you. What if—" Pippa's words were swallowed in a gasp. A large shadow flitted from the floor of the cell to the ceiling, moving too quickly to distinguish.

"Who's there?" Celine demanded, her heart thundering in her chest.

Behind her, Pippa struggled to light a long match, the box falling beside her feet in a scatter of twigs.

"Go!" Celine demanded. But Pippa persisted, refusing to leave her side.

The creature hovering on the ceiling chittered, its teeth grating together, causing Celine's shoulders to pull back and a shudder to course down her spine. On the floor beneath her open window, another creature moaned, the sound a feeble whistle. As though it were caught in the throes of death.

It took an instant for Celine to understand. The demon in the shadows had attacked something in her cell. She moved to help the wounded soul beneath the window, but her toes slid in something wet, her right foot skidding out from under her. Gripping the wall to steady herself, Celine looked up as a dry cackle emanated from above.

Terror racing through her veins, Celine fought to stand

straight, her knees threatening to buckle out from under her. Pippa screamed and backed away.

"Be gone from here!" Celine demanded into the blackness looming above her, her fingers trembling around her shears.

The thing blurred from the ceiling to the floor like a tempest across a field of wheat. Then it stood slowly, its long figure unfolding in a beam of waning moonlight. Before Celine could blink, it rushed toward her, taking her by the wrist, slamming her back against the rough plaster wall. It drew close, smelling of blood and rain. The damp of the earth. It breathed deeply of Celine's neck, its teeth grazing the lobe of her left ear, leaving a trail of sticky wetness.

"Each time you evade me, I only want you more," it gasped, its voice like metal against stone. "You cannot escape. You are *mine*." Then it dragged its bloody fingers across her face, as if it were marking her.

A horrified scream caught in Celine's throat. She kept rigid, her eyes unblinking, struggling to detect anything of note. Anything that might help identify the creature in the light of day. But the room was too dark, the demon far too close. Pippa's footsteps pounded down the corridor, her screams jumbled and nonsensical.

"Death leads to another garden. Welcome to the Battle of Carthage," the thing whispered in Celine's ear, its words a crazed rasp, its accent refined. "To thine own self, be true."

Celine stabbed it in its chest with her sewing shears. Roaring, the demon shoved her to one side with inhuman strength, an earsplitting cry rending through the darkness. Celine's head struck the floor in a dull thud, her vision distorting from the blow. She fought to focus on the figure looming above her. All she could distinguish was the silhouette of what appeared to be a man, tall and well muscled, his chest heaving, the sleeves and hem of his coat tattered.

"I'm not afraid of you," Celine said in a hoarse tone.

The demon's laughter was a wet gurgle. "You will be."

Commotion rang through the hallways beyond Celine's cell. Doors banged open, and the cries of young women layered through the thick darkness, their footsteps pattering across the stone floors, their candles wavering over the walls.

Then the demon leapt out of Celine's window with preternatural grace.

Her skull buzzing and her vision hazy, Celine reached for the fallen box of matches. Labored to sit up and light one, her toes slipping through the pool of sticky warmth collecting by her feet. Her fingers shook as the match burst into flame, the peppery scent of gunpowder suffusing the air.

Celine's heart hammered in her temples, her limbs bereft of warmth. The moment the match's flame stretched tall to spread its light, Pippa burst through the entrance of the cell, brandishing a fireplace poker like a fencing épée. Her resounding scream turned into many, mounting like ripples across a pond. Horrified, sleep-laden faces craned for a glimpse beyond the doorway, regretting their curiosity in the next instant.

For nothing could have prepared them for the sight that met their eyes.

Strewn across the sill of Celine's open window was a man's

mangled body. One of his legs was crooked at an unnatural angle, an arm bent behind him, nearly torn from its socket. His wispy beard trailed onto the stone floor. Red bubbles frothed around his mouth as the blood from a gash in his neck trickled downward, seeping between the cracks in eerie tributaries.

Above his body—painted onto the wooden shutter—was another symbol, sketched in crimson:

THE LONELY FREEDOM
OF A MISTY STREET

———◦◦◇◦◦———

Numbness enveloped Celine, settling on her shoulders, winding about her limbs. She welcomed it. Wished it would swallow her whole.

A demon had touched her. Marked her.

Taken another life.

William, the kind gardener who resembled a wizard, had been murdered tonight in Celine's cell, on the cusp of the witching hour. He'd perished much like Anabel, his throat torn out in gruesome fashion, the blood spilling from his body as fast as his heart could pump it. This time the killer had been far less fastidious. Instead of draining William entirely of blood, he had allowed it to spatter everywhere, as if there had been a struggle. Or perhaps the demon had chosen to toy with its prey.

Neither thought was reassuring.

Celine sat on the steps beyond the vestibule of the Ursuline convent. A light rain dusted the air, sprinkling her skin, though she could not feel it, courtesy of the blessed numbness. Around her, muted speech and rapid footfalls punctuated the night, every so often laced with intermittent wails.

Thankfully—following the initial onslaught of questions—no one thought to trouble Celine or draw anywhere near. It was as if they'd come to the same realization she had. That she was a curse. A blight upon all their lives.

It could not have been a coincidence that Anabel had been killed after following Celine into a den of iniquity. Nor could it be mere chance that William had met his gruesome end in her cell. With the exception of the seemingly unrelated murder along the docks, the killer looked to be targeting anyone tied to Celine Rousseau, for reasons beyond all their ken. There appeared to be no logic to any of it, save for the victims' associations with her and with the Ursuline convent.

Was it possible the young woman along the docks was *also* connected in some way?

At this point, no detail, however far-fetched, could be ignored.

Each time you evade me, I only want you more.

You cannot escape. You are mine.

Celine winced as she stared at the granite pavers beside her feet, watching the rain glisten across their gritty surfaces. She stiffened when Pippa crouched next to her, then glanced at her friend sidelong, meeting blue eyes wide with worry. Without a word, Pippa handed her a clean linen handkerchief. Then waited attentively while Celine wiped the blood from her face, the dried bits flaking onto her damp dress, causing her stomach to churn and acid to bubble in her throat.

"Is there anything I can do?" Pippa asked, her voice gentle.

You can leave me alone. Rage coursed through Celine at how little regard Pippa seemed to hold for her own self-preservation.

By now, she should know better than to seek out the company of a blight like her.

By now, they should all have run for the hills.

"May I get you some tea?" Pippa asked.

Celine drew back and said nothing. She worried if she opened her mouth, a torrent of foul words—the worst of her fears given voice—would flow from her mouth. Things no one deserved to hear, least of all Pippa.

Though Celine had not responded to Pippa's query—or even acknowledged her presence in any meaningful fashion—Pippa kept close, hovering in a way that aggravated Celine further.

Why doesn't she know to save herself? Does she have a death wish? Celine's thoughts turned vicious. Senseless in their rage.

A wall of black wool stepped before her, obscuring her vision. As always, Celine smelled the Mother Superior before she took in the elder woman's face. That same scent of a wet hound in a haystack. Pippa stood at once, Celine remaining on the stairs, all sense of decorum scattered to the winds.

The wall of wool remained stalwart in its approach, watching and waiting. A dark streak of amusement sliced through Celine. She longed for a return to the day she'd believed the matron of the Ursuline convent to be her worst enemy. When the most memorable of Celine's afternoons had been spent trying to imagine creative ways to thwart her.

For an instant, Celine pondered whether there was a single point at which she could have foiled her fate. At what precise moment had she wandered down the wrong path? Alas, there was nothing she could do about that now. But perhaps there was a way to stop this fearful turn of events from happening again in the future.

The Mother Superior cleared her throat, wordlessly demanding Celine's attention, the wooden beads of her rosary dangling from her waist. Celine studied the small cross swaying before her. Observed the rain as it slid downward.

"Mademoiselle Rousseau," the Mother Superior began in a grim tone. "I wanted to—"

"Why did you send Anabel to spy on us?" Celine asked, her voice hollow, her eyes leveled on the wall of black wool positioned before her.

A sharp intake of breath resounded from above. Celine looked up. The Mother Superior's features were tight. Weary. Her habit had been tilted askew, rain trickling from its hem.

"You could have refused to let us go," Celine continued. "You didn't need to use Anabel as a pawn in your scheme. You sent her to her death." Her accusation was low. Pitiless.

"Celine!" Pippa chastised softly.

In the deepest recesses of Celine's mind, she knew how unfair it was to accuse the Mother Superior of being responsible for Anabel's death. But her heart demanded answers. The wound around it continued to grow with each passing moment, the pain searing through her chest, burning into her lungs. She had to put a stop to it. To all of it.

"Why?" Celine repeated.

"I—" The Mother Superior hesitated, her expression oddly uncertain. Then her frown turned severe, the lines around her mouth deepening. Celine braced herself for a harsh rebuke.

"I am human," the Mother Superior said simply. "As such, I made a mistake."

Celine shook her head. "That's not an answer. Please"—she stood at once, drops of rain cascading from the tip of her nose—"help me understand. I need to understand *why*."

The Mother Superior considered Celine, her eyes flitting to and fro. "Because I saw in you the kind of reckless spirit that craves danger, and I desired proof. A weed left to flourish is the death of the entire garden."

The ache in Celine's chest intensified. "So you sent a young girl out by herself, simply to prove I was rotten to the core? Why didn't you just ask me? Je vous l'aurait dis, Mère Supérieure!" Her hands balled into fists at her sides.

The Mother Superior took hold of Celine's left wrist, gripping it tightly, pulling her closer. For a breath of time, Celine thought the matron might strike her. But then the elder woman's grey brows gathered, her features pinching with sorrow. "You are in pain right now, Mademoiselle Rousseau," she said gently. "I, too, am in pain. I, too, long to point a finger of blame. But it serves no purpose now. I entreat you to sit with your pain. To let it pass, not to lash out. It will do you no good." She released her grip on Celine's wrist. "Trust in this important lesson I learned long ago: Rage is a moment. Regret is forever."

Celine struggled to marshal her fury. She wasn't ready to relinquish her rage and succumb to the sadness that was sure to follow. If she did, it meant she accepted everything that had happened tonight. She didn't want to accept it. She wanted to fight it. To shatter its truth into oblivion.

But the Mother Superior was right. What good did it do to rail against an elderly woman? Anabel and William had not died because of the Mother Superior.

They'd died because of *her*.

Celine blinked back the rain. Forced the tension in her shoulders to abate. "Yes, Mère Supérieure." She swallowed. Realized she was shivering and that her temple throbbed. "I apologize for my behavior. It won't happen again."

The Mother Superior nodded. "Are you in need of anything right now? Is there anything I might provide for you?"

Celine shook her head.

A sigh fell from the Mother Superior's lips. "Should you change your mind at any time—now or in the future—do not hesitate to tell me. I am here to assist you in any way." She paused to hold Celine's gaze, her features somber. "The next few days will not be easy ones, my child."

Celine nodded, already knowing what the Mother Superior intended to say next.

"Many of my fellow sisters have come to me in the last hour," the Mother Superior continued in a hushed tone. "The consensus is that it might be time for us to find you alternate lodging."

Celine kept nodding.

The Mother Superior reached out once more. This time she took hold of Celine's hand, her touch gentle and warm, despite the coolness of the rain. "I've already begun making inquiries. We will not throw you out on the street, and it is not necessary for you to leave tonight. It is simply no longer safe for you to stay here." She paused. "Please know this is not at all what we want to do. But I agree it is the best course of action. For the sake of all who remain within these walls."

"A weed left to flourish is the death of the entire garden," Celine said, a tinge of sadness in her voice.

With another sigh, the Mother Superior nodded. Squeezed Celine's hand. And let go.

Straightening her spine, Celine met the matron's wrinkled gaze. "Thank you for giving me a chance to begin my life in a new world, Mère Supérieure. I . . . don't know what would have happened to me without it."

"Of course, my dear. May God go with you. May you live a life of bounty and purpose." Then—after the slightest hesitation—the Mother Superior turned toward the convent, her cross swaying with her steps, the scent of lanolin and medicinal ointment trailing in her wake.

Celine stood in the rain for a time, Pippa waiting nearby, quietly wiping tears from her cheeks with the back of one hand. It was an exercise in futility, for the rain soon began to fall in earnest, its fat droplets plinking onto the iron railing and splashing onto their skin.

Pippa removed the shawl from her own shoulders, draping it over Celine's. "You're shaking."

"Am I?" The throbbing in Celine's head was worsening. She touched her temple and found a tender spot from where she'd struck the floor in her struggle with the killer.

"Tomorrow I'll make inquiries with some of the other women in my ladies' organization," Pippa continued. "Perhaps Phoebus' mother will know of a place you can go."

"Thank you," Celine mumbled, "but the boat to Tartarus is full." She spoke the last under her breath. *I am a Titan, after all,* she sneered to herself.

"I'm sorry. I couldn't hear you, dear." Infinite patience rounded out Pippa's response.

"I said thank you, but I will make the inquiries myself." Celine refrained from gritting her teeth, aware of how wrong it was to turn her frustrations on her closest friend.

Pippa's brows tufted together, betraying her own mounting irritation. "You don't have to do everything yourself, Celine. It's not your fault that a madman has unleashed himself on those near you. Nor is it your fault you've been asked to quit the convent."

"Even if the Mother Superior had not asked me to go, I would have left of my own will. It isn't safe for me to stay. It would be better . . . if I never showed my face here again."

"I see." Pippa blinked through the rain, her eyes shimmering suspiciously. Then she wiped her chin on her sleeve. Renewed her convictions with a bright smile. "Well, perhaps we can let a room together. Wouldn't that be lovely? I've always liked Marigny."

Her words iced the blood in Celine's body. Made her want to flee as fast as she could. She could not have Pippa anywhere near her. Of all people, Pippa should be as far from Celine as possible. Being near Celine Rousseau had become a kiss of death.

And she did not know what she would do if something happened to Pippa because of her.

To their right, the doors to the convent scraped open with yawning slowness. Two sullen officers shifted into view, bearing between them a bundle wrapped in linen sheets. Already the center of the sheets was stained red, the rain causing the blot to spread, its edges lightening to a pale pink. Celine watched in silence as they moved toward an open wagon waiting along the lane to bear the body to the station.

William's arms hung lifeless on either side of him, one of his hands still twisted in an unnatural position. They flopped like dead fish as the two officers lifted his battered body into the back of the wagon. Tears began to well in Celine's eyes.

Just a few days ago, William had offered Arjun a cutting from the convent's garden, to help remind Arjun of home. He'd shown him a kindness, expecting nothing in return.

Now he was dead, the last remembrance in his life the face of his killer.

The tears spilled over, flowing down Celine's cheeks in steady streams.

Not once had she cried in earnest since that night in the atelier. Her mind had forbidden her the reprieve. She hadn't cried when she'd realized her life in France was over. The first night aboard the *Aramis*, she'd listened to the soft sniffles of countless other young women. Still she'd failed to shed a single tear. She hadn't cried even when Anabel had been slain.

Why did the sight of William's broken body move her to tears? Perhaps the dam inside her had finally burst. Or perhaps this was one crack too many in her façade.

To thine own self, be true. The killer had quoted Shakespeare, as if he could see into Celine's soul.

Guilt seeped into her bones, burning like acid as it traveled down the length of her body. Bile choked in her throat. Celine was the reason this kind man and a lovely young woman had died.

She would not be the reason anyone else died. Ever again.

Without thought or consideration—her tears trailing down her cheeks, joining hands with the rain—Celine began to walk.

"Celine?" Pippa called out from behind her.

Celine ignored her and quickened her pace. Turned into the lemon grove, deliberately winding through the trees, pausing for a time in an effort to shake Pippa from her trail. Beneath a dripping branch, Celine took a deep breath, filling her head with the sweet scent of citrus as it mingled with the metal and moss of an early spring shower. Entreated her spirit to grant her the fortitude necessary to do what must be done.

The street lay empty through the iron gate, a few short steps and a world away.

In a moment, she would disappear and never turn back. It didn't matter where she went. It only mattered that she vanish without a trace. That no one else perish because of her.

"Celine!" She heard Pippa shout from the opposite side of the lemon grove.

Now was her best chance. Celine darted from the shade of the tree, making her way toward the gate and the lonely freedom of a misty street.

A tall man stepped into her path, his tweed cap pulled low on his brow. "Celine," he said calmly, his eyes like chips of ice.

Celine stumbled midstep, her composure on the cusp of splintering. "Yes, Detective Grimaldi?"

"Where are you going?"

"I've been asked to leave the convent." She attempted to skirt him, but he shifted once more, blocking her from reaching the gate.

Anger lined Michael's features. "You've been asked to leave . . . tonight?" His words sounded muffled to her. As if he were speaking into a void or at the end of a long tunnel.

Desperation clutched around her heart. "Let me go, Michael. Please."

"Now is not the time for anyone to be walking the streets alone, least of all *you*."

It was a cool declaration. But it seared through Celine like a brand, reminding her of the many deaths on her conscience. One by her own hand. "Get out of my way," she said, her voice dangerously close to breaking.

"No."

Celine shoved Michael with all her might. She didn't stop to watch him fall. She simply raced toward the gate, her feet flying above the pavestones, her heart pounding at a frantic pace. The memory of what Bastien had said to her the night they first met echoed through her ears. He'd likened her to a lunar goddess who dragged darkness with her wherever she went.

She would bring no more darkness here. She'd run away once to begin a new life. She could do it again, without a single glance over her shoulder.

A firm hand yanked Celine off course, gripping her forearm tightly. Then it pulled her into a solid chest, clasping both her wrists behind her, forcing the air from her lungs. Michael towered over her, caging her with his arms, effectively rendering her immobile. He was stronger than he appeared at first glance, his body shifting beneath his wet garments like sinew.

"You little fool," he snarled under his breath, fury sharpening his features. "You think you're going to run away and everything will be as it once was?"

Celine glared up at him, drops of rain catching on her eyelashes. "Go to Hell."

"Will you make sense in Hell? If so, then lead the way."

"Sense?" she cried. "Tonight I was attacked by a creature that could fly. It taunted me. Said I belonged to it. Told me death was a garden and likened its work to the Battle of Carthage. Two nights ago, I was stalked by something that crawled up a wall and *vanished in the wind without a trace.*" Celine laughed, the sound bordering on crazed. "It knew my name. Tell me, Michael Grimaldi, does any of this make sense?"

Michael's nostrils flared. He released her wrists, a veil of lethal calm descending over his face. "Why am I only now hearing of the incident from two nights ago?"

"Am I to report to you at every turn?" Celine laughed again. Pushed him away, her hands thrown in the air. "Besides, I sound like a lunatic. Like someone who lived in the dungeons of the Bastille for an age, deprived of sunlight and air and all that is necessary to survive." Her chest heaved as she took in a ragged breath.

His expression unreadable, Michael stared down at her, his pale gaze steady. "What happened when the creature stalked you two days ago? How did you manage to escape?"

"Bastien."

"Bastien?" Michael's eyes narrowed, a muscle jumping in his neck. "Why was Bastien there?"

"I haven't the faintest clue. Perhaps you should stop behaving like a belligerent child and ask him. It's possible he has a death wish, too."

Michael opened his mouth to retort, but the clatter of an arriving carriage stole his attention, sparing Celine from having to partake further in the conversation.

A glossy black brougham halted just outside the iron gates of the convent. Emblazoned on its door was the symbol of a fleur-de-lis in the mouth of a roaring lion. For a stutter of time, Celine allowed herself to hope a broad-shouldered young man would alight from its confines, his eyes like honed daggers and his jaw like hewn stone. Dared to dream he would gift her this enchanted carriage, capable of taking her to the ends of the earth. Tell her to go anyplace she wished. Swore to follow wherever she went, even to Hell itself.

Ridiculous. A man should not have to grant her this kind of freedom. Celine should be able to take it herself. But she'd already tried to take it. Tried and failed numerous times, the world reminding her at all turns that her own liberty wasn't hers to give, much less take. A woman absent money or prospects had no place in proper society. In such a society, a wife and daughter were legal possessions. Commodities used to curry wealth and favor.

Perhaps it was time for Celine to reject proper society.

As if to underscore the notion, the door to the brougham

swung open and Odette bounded down its steps, dressed in trousers and polished Hessians, a military-style jacket draped across her shoulders. She raced toward Celine's side, brushing past Michael with a look that would scald the sun.

"Mon amie," Odette said, her expression grave, her eyes reddened around the rims.

Celine steeled herself, her shoulders all but quaking with gratitude. The fairy tales of her childhood had been filled with lies. No man had come to her rescue tonight, as they always did in the stories.

But her friends had. First Pippa with her épée. Then Odette with her carriage.

And just a moment ago, Celine had almost turned her back on them forever.

Before Celine could say anything, Michael glared down at Odette, his colorless eyes seeming as if they could pierce her through her heart. "Miss Valmont," he said curtly. "Word certainly does travel fast . . . rousing even the most ardent of sleepers."

"None of your nonsense tonight." Odette glowered back at him, stone-faced. "My patience for mediocre young men has fallen dangerously low." She looked to Celine, her features softening. "I came as soon as I heard." Her gloved hands wrapped around Celine's fingers. "What is it you wish to do? I'll take you anywhere you want to go."

Michael cleared his throat. "An unnecessary offer. I will arrange a place for Celine at police headquarters. It's well insulated from potential intruders, and officers will be stationed nearby at all times." He stood tall, water dribbling from the brim of his tweed cap. "I myself will patrol the streets around it twice a night, so there is no need for this dramatic display of concern. Return to your gilded abode, Miss Valmont. Leave the real work to those accustomed to doing it."

Odette sniffed, the sound filled with derision. "Don't be proud of that rejoinder, you sanctimonious prick. It's work enough having to look upon you with a straight face." Her sable eyes tapered to slits. "And perhaps we should let Celine make her own decisions, rather than informing her of yours, as you seem so keen to do." She turned to Celine. "Mon amie, we can go wherever you like. Charleston or Atlanta. New York, if you prefer. Perhaps even San Francisco. And if you wish to stay in New Orleans, I can have a suite ready for you at the Dumaine within the hour."

Celine nodded, her thoughts racing in a whirl. She could go wherever she chose. Flee this place and all its mounting terrors. Her eyes closed as she allowed herself to dream of a new life. A slate wiped clean once more.

Footsteps splashed through a nearby puddle, drawing to a sudden halt, the sound of frightened gasps punching through the darkness. Celine opened her eyes, locking on a single image.

Pippa, the color drained from her skin, her lips trembling, her features awash in unmistakable relief. Her hem was six inches deep in mud, and a branch had scratched the side of her left cheek, tiny trickles of blood sliding toward her chin.

This entire time, Pippa had been searching for Celine, her concern for her friend causing her to be heedless of all else, even her own well-being.

If Celine ran away now, the killer might never be caught. He would likely continue wreaking havoc on the world she'd left behind. Perhaps she wouldn't have to witness it with her own eyes anymore or be terrorized by its possibility. But she would always know. Would always wonder.

And her friends would remain in danger.

Rage is a moment. Regret is forever. Celine had enough regrets on her head. Running away like a victim would not be one of them ever again. She was not a victim.

She was a survivor.

"I want to stay in New Orleans," Celine said. "But I have one condition."

The Haunted Portrait

———◇◇◇◇◇———

An hour later, Celine, Michael, and Odette stood in a corner of darkly veined marble, ensconced in the farthest reaches of a deserted hotel lobby.

Above them, crystal-and-brass chandeliers hung like silent sentinels, chiming softly in a ghostly breeze. Lanterns housed in spheres of opaque glass glowed around the room, resembling will-o'-the-wisps floating through the night. Purple orchids and white jasmine perfumed the air, the scent hinting of wealth and far-flung locales. Positioned at either end of the entrance hall were large chinoiserie vases overflowing with long-stemmed roses so deep a shade of red, their petals appeared black in the shadows.

Were Celine's exhaustion not an anchor about her shoulders, she would have whiled away a moment marveling at the grandeur of the space. Everything about it felt like it had been decorated to suit a queen of darkness.

"We've waited long enough, mon amie," Odette said, her voice scratched and weary. "Tell us your condition, s'il te plaît."

Michael stood a healthy distance from Odette, his long arms crossed, his dark curls mussed by the rain. Though his face was lined with distaste, his pale eyes blazed bright.

In a barely audible whisper, Celine informed them of her plan. Once she was finished, they stared at her in stunned silence, Odette blinking rapidly, as if her mind intended to flash through every possible outcome in the span of a single breath.

"Over my dead body," Michael announced in a flat tone.

"Here's hoping, mon cher," Odette quipped. She turned toward Celine, her sable gaze uncertain. "But I must agree with the boor's sentiment. Using yourself as bait to catch a crazed killer . . . sounds unduly foolish."

Michael sniffed with unmistakable scorn. "Finally a semblance of sense." He nodded at Odette, who offered him a mocking bow in return.

"I knew you would not agree at first," Celine replied. "But by tomorrow, I hope you will see the logic of it. How it makes sense for us to take action rather than be forced into a corner."

"Logic?" Odette snorted. "It's madness, mon amie. Sheer madness. I finally understand why you lied to Pippa before we left the convent. You must have known she would never accept this as an option."

"Pippa is . . ." Celine exhaled with great care. "I don't want Pippa anywhere near me, at least not until this ordeal is over. She's not selfish enough to worry about her own safety." The image of Pippa trembling in a puddle—her eyes shining and streams of blood trickling down her cheek—was one Celine would not soon forget.

"Failing to worry about one's own safety isn't selfless. It's foolish." Odette quirked a brow, her lips puckering in judgment.

Celine nodded. "I agree. But I don't have the patience to argue with Pippa about it. It isn't my place to dissuade her. And I'd rather be the hunter than the prey. Wouldn't you?"

A contemplative look settled on Odette's face at the same time a frown tugged at the corners of Michael's mouth.

"Then I have your support?" Celine asked Odette.

Inhaling slowly, Odette nodded. "Though I'm certain I'll live to regret this."

"You won't," Celine said, infusing her voice with a surety she did not feel. "Thank you, Odette." With that, she shifted her attention toward Michael.

His displeasure deepened at her scrutiny. "I have no intention of agreeing to this plan, so spare yourself the effort," he said, his words characteristically curt. Unfeeling. "It was folly to come here. For both of us." Michael pivoted in place and began walking toward the double doors at the hotel's entrance. "I'll send for your things in the morning, then make my way to the Dumaine shortly afterward to collect you," he said over his shoulder.

A crick in Celine's neck sent a surge of discomfort down her spine. She tilted her head, wincing all the while. "It's unfortunate you aren't willing to listen to reason, Michael," she called out after him. "But until you agree to help me, I plan to remain here at the Hotel Dumaine."

He spun around, anger sparking across his features. In a few long strides, he stood before her once more. "A foolish choice, especially when I've already arranged a place for you with full police protection."

"It isn't foolish at all," Celine argued. "If you won't respect my wishes, I see no reason to bend to your will. Besides that, no place in this city is safe if the killer is watching me, as I believe him to be." A shiver chased over her skin, but Celine kept her gaze steady.

His thick brows tufted together. "It isn't about respecting your wishes. It's about what's best for you. What will keep you the safest."

Irritation simmered at the edges of Celine's vision. "Then the New Orleans Metropolitan Police will only protect me if I do exactly as Detective Michael Grimaldi says?"

Michael said nothing in response. Soft laughter resonated from Odette.

Celine sighed. "For whatever reason, this—*thing*—has singled me out. We can either run from that fact or use it to our advantage." She took a deep breath. "I'm not a fool. I'm aware of the danger, and I promise I'm appropriately afraid. I just refuse to be a victim for a single second more." A muscle twitched beneath her left eye. Celine rubbed the skin there and found another fleck of dried blood smeared across her fingertips, the smell thick and metallic. Her stomach churned at the sight. "I only wish we knew what this *thing* was so that we might determine how best to destroy it."

"Don't believe every myth you hear. If there are no gods among us, there can be no demons," Michael said, his voice leached of all emotion. "The same logic you've already employed indicates the killer must be a man. Most killers with multiple victims are."

"It's not simply a man." Celine shook her head. "It's something . . . else. Something inhuman."

"If it lives and breathes, it can be killed like any living and breathing creature."

Exhaustion burrowed deep into Celine's bones. The strength to keep arguing with the intractable Michael Grimaldi was leaving her with each passing breath. Her fingers and toes had lost all sense of feeling. Soon it would be difficult to stand straight.

Even still, Celine did not miss the fact that Odette had failed to counter Michael's recent assertions. Nor could Celine overlook the thoughtful slant of Odette's brunette head.

Odette Valmont possessed information of value and was doing her level best to keep it from them.

Here was proof of something Celine had long suspected. The members of La Cour des Lions did have an inkling of what—or who—this demon might be. Why they chose to keep it among themselves remained a mystery. It could be because the murderer resided in their midst, and they wished to protect his identity. But their recent behavior did not follow this reasoning. In the last few days, Odette had become more than a mere acquaintance to Celine, and Bastien had gone out of his way to ensure her safety the other night. He'd even threatened to destroy the creature in a wholly remorseless manner.

Why would they go to such trouble to protect her if their loyalty lay with the killer?

Unless . . . this was all part of their plan.

An elaborate ruse to establish their innocence.

If that was true, Celine had already lost the battle. Only moments ago, she'd divulged her plan in its entirety to Odette. If Odette betrayed her, all her efforts would be for naught.

Celine's shoulders sagged.

She was tired of speculating. She needed the truth. And Celine knew who to ask, though she dreaded his answer. The lie he would offer in place of what she desired. Nevertheless, Celine planned to speak to Bastien tomorrow. She'd demand he share with her everything he knew. No more lies. No more masks. It was time for them to cast aside their façades and bare all.

Bastien no longer had a choice. If he refused to be forthcoming, Celine would tell Michael about the yellow ribbon and allow judgment to rain down upon them all.

"Give up on this cockamamie plan," Michael said to Celine, tearing her from her inner turmoil, his countenance grave. "Because I will never agree to using you as bait."

Celine scowled, desperately wishing she could throttle Michael. Just a little. "I have no intention of giving up anything. Surely you of all people must understand that." She reached for his hand in a weak attempt to channel sugar instead of spice. "Please, Michael. Don't be so stubborn. I urge you to reconsider."

He blinked twice at her touch, a vein jumping in his neck. "I won't reconsider. But . . . I *will* promise to do everything I can to keep you safe." The last was said in a fervent tone, his words jagged, his grasp rough. Celine didn't think Michael was aware of how he'd wrapped her cold hand in both of his, clutching her fingers with an odd kind of desperation.

No matter what he said or how he said it, Michael's intensity always betrayed him.

He cared for her. And that knowledge troubled Celine all the more.

For a moment, she considered taking advantage of it. If she begged him, perhaps he would relent. If she cried prettily or raged in just the right fashion, perhaps she could do what she'd failed to do before and overcome his mulishness.

But she didn't want to play the role of the coy demoiselle. Not like this. It was never a role that had suited her well anyway, as evinced by their earlier interactions. Celine needed to be cold and calculating. If Michael refused to help her, the plan wouldn't work.

That simply was not an option.

Her life—and the lives of those around her—depended on them all working together in concert.

"I don't need you to help me," Celine lied, her words callous, channeling Michael at his best. "I'll simply ask Bastien instead." She extricated her fingers from his grasp.

Dismay rippled across his face, there and gone in a flash. The next instant, Michael smiled coolly. "Ask him." His smile turned punishing. "I have no doubt what his answer will be."

"Mon cher, you don't know him as well as you think you do." Odette's retort was pointed. "That's the thing about beautiful fiends like Sébastien Saint Germain: they always do what you least expect them to do." She brushed a speck of nonexistent dust from his shoulder. "And in the end, they *always* wear the crown."

Celine could not have scripted a more perfect response. It was a loaded weapon, cocked and aimed at Michael's chest.

Sometimes it was necessary to be as cunning as a fox, even if it also meant being cruel.

Michael narrowed his gaze. His nostrils flared. "The Court of the Lions does not rule this roost, Miss Valmont. I will see this city burn to the ground before I cede control of my investigation to a band of lawless beasts." With that, he whirled toward the entrance, taking his leave, the very air around him seething.

It didn't matter. Celine had planted the seed. Odette had watered it. Now they had only to watch it grow. If Celine had learned anything in the last few days, she'd learned that Detective Michael Grimaldi was not the type of young man to allow his enemy to best him. In any way.

She was counting on it.

"Connard," Odette cursed under her breath as Michael disappeared from view.

The veined marble around Celine started to sway, the will-o'-the-wisps blurring in the background. "It can't look too obvious," she said to Odette, blinking hard. "And we'll need to finesse the details." She wound her fingers in her damp skirt and squeezed the ruined fabric in an effort to keep herself alert. "If you count the first murder of the young woman on the docks, the killer has taken one life a week since my arrival," she babbled. "Following this pattern, the next murder is likely to take place in the coming week, which should give us a few days to set our trap." Her head started to list forward. "Perhaps we should plan it for the night of the masquerade ball itself?" she thought aloud, just as the polished floor rushed toward her face.

"Ah, putain!" Odette cried out, catching Celine the moment before she struck the cold stone. "You're falling to pieces before my very eyes." She threaded one arm through Celine's and wrapped the other around her shoulders, then began leading them down a darkened corridor.

Celine braced herself against Odette, her eyes struggling to stay open. "Thank you." Her words were hoarse. "For everything." She gripped her friend's gloved hand tightly.

"You're welcome, my brave little doe. But if you want your *cockamamie* plan to work—honestly, who uses such a word?— you'll need to be more than brave. You'll need to be ruthless. After tonight, I trust this won't be an issue. It's not every day one meets a girl who stabbed a demon with sewing shears. Ah, to have seen that!" Odette's laughter was rueful, the sound chiming like bells. "Also I find it fascinating how talkative you are after bearing witness to a shocking event. Most people I know are struck silent by such things. You're unusual at all turns, Celine Rousseau." She grinned appreciatively.

Even through the haze of her exhaustion, Celine smiled. Her thoughts sobered in the next instant. "Why do they hate each other so much?" she murmured.

"Who hates whom, mon amie? I know nothing but love."

"Please." Celine nudged her elbow into Odette's ribs. "I'm too exhausted to play these games. It's a struggle putting one foot in front of the other."

"Why do *you* think they hate each other?"

"How should I know?"

"Hazard a guess. It's an age-old tale."

"Because of a girl?" Celine's eye twitched once more, her nose wiggling in response.

"Correct."

"Oh." Her shoulders fell.

Perhaps this was the young woman who possessed the right pedigree. Celine exhaled slowly. Such things shouldn't matter to her. Not anymore.

They turned a corner, their steps light over the honed marble. Celine could almost swear Odette bore the whole of their shared weight, as if she possessed the strength of an Amazon.

"Was she impressive?" Celine's voice sounded small. Tinny. Fitting for such a question.

"Very," Odette replied, at ease despite her burden. "She sang like a lark and danced in the light of the sun." She added in Celine's ear, "But don't worry, she wasn't as beautiful as you."

Celine snorted, then tripped over herself like she'd imbibed too much champagne. As inelegant as a swine in the mud, she crumpled to the floor.

A foul curse flew from Odette's lips. She repeated the word in two more languages for good measure. Tugging Celine to her feet, Odette proceeded to drag her the rest of the way. They halted before an immense lift of gleaming brass, its bars fashioned of winding vines and birds of paradise, their feathers inlaid with Persian turquoise.

"You shouldn't have," Celine muttered. "A cage of my very own."

Odette snickered. She gestured to the right, and an inordinately tall man with rich auburn hair secured at the nape of his neck and a frock coat of midnight blue with matching gloves stepped forward to unfetter a gleaming lock of pure silver. Though he was as lithe as a dancer, he managed to heave open the sliding door to the brass lift with barely a twinge of effort.

Once they were situated inside, Celine rested her head on Odette's shoulder, her eyes falling shut as the lift lurched into motion under the steady direction of its lissome gatekeeper.

"The list of those allowed access here is short," Odette said. "This lift has one destination: the top floor of the hotel. While you reside at the Dumaine, that entire space will be yours alone."

Celine considered this, even as the weariness fell upon her like a warm woolen blanket. "And if the killer can scale the walls of the hotel?" She recalled how the demon had scuttled up the building before vanishing into the wind.

"Can he also shatter iron bars and locks of solid silver?"

"For the sake of argument, let's assume so."

"Then t'es foutue," Odette swore under her breath. "As are we all."

Celine laughed softly, her eyes still closed. "Merci, Odette."

"Pas du tout, mon amie," Odette replied. "We take care of our own."

Celine's breath caught in her throat. "Is that . . . thing one of your own?" she asked, her tone halting.

Odette said nothing until the lift began to slow. "No."

But her hesitation suggested otherwise.

"You know what it is." Celine's eyes flew open. "Why won't you tell me?"

"It isn't my story to tell."

"Please—"

The lift ground to a halt, and the slender gentleman in the blue velvet frock coat unlatched the door in a seamless motion, his gaze one of supreme ennui.

"No more questions," Odette said, smoothing back Celine's disheveled curls in a soothing gesture. Then she locked eyes with Celine, refusing to blink as if she were in a trance. "I'm going to show you to your room, and you're going to sleep through an entire night, as if you're adrift among the clouds." A sad smile curved up her doll-like face. "The only dreams you'll have will be pleasant ones, filled with islands of floating meringue and sparkling glasses of champagne." Her voice sounded layered. Weighted. It resonated through Celine, reaching through to the marrow of her bones.

The last thing she remembered was the rumble of a brass cage. Of the bird within flying free.

———◇———

Celine woke with a start, her heart hammering in her chest. Disorientation gripped her, her vision struggling to find focus. Her eyes darted to all corners, searching for something familiar. Fighting for a semblance of footing.

She had no recollection of this place.

Then—like a wave crashing upon a shore—all the events of last night flooded through her mind. She was enshrined in the top floor suite of the finest hotel in the city. A brass lift festooned with gilded birds had borne her to this place.

Before she'd taken her leave, Odette had made certain Celine was comfortable. Warm and well cared for.

Tomorrow they would begin devising a trap to catch a killer.

This last thought caused Celine to sit up at once, her breath lodged in her throat, the ache in her head throbbing dully. She looked around, her gaze moving about the space once more, this time with measured deliberation.

The cream-colored sheets beneath her fingers possessed a faint luster, their surfaces smooth, their edges trimmed with delicate gold embroidery. When she ran her hands across them, they felt like cool water to the touch. As if they'd been woven from pure spider silk. Above her hung a thick canopy of golden damask, pinned in its center by an emblem entwined with intricate filigree. Tied around each of the bed's four mahogany posts were drapes of wine-red velvet.

Celine threw back the bedcovers and sank her bare toes into the luxurious Aubusson carpet, the tassels along its edge glinting in the candlelight.

Countless paintings hung on the far side of the bedchamber, extending the full height of the room, some twenty-odd feet. A few were the width of Celine's palm, others stood more than double her height. Each was rendered by the hand of a master, the details within both dark and light, as if their collector appreciated the contrast of sunlight and shadow in equal measure.

Crowning the remaining three sides of the room was a kind of narrow balcony, the like of which Celine had never seen before. Shelves upon shelves of books filled the walls along the upper half of the chamber, oiled castors and iron ladders awaiting their savant's inevitable return.

Tall scented candles had been lit around the room, as if Odette had known how disconcerting it would be for Celine to wake in a cold and unfamiliar place.

She crossed the chamber toward a pair of mullioned windows, numbness tingling along her extremities. She'd slept hard. Surprisingly so, given the shocking tenor of recent events. When Celine tugged aside the heavy curtains to look outside, she discovered two things of note: that there were—indeed—wrought-iron bars encasing every window, painted a glossy white, and that nightfall still reigned supreme on the world below. Despite Odette's final admonition for Celine to sleep until the sun rose, she'd woken in that time just before dawn, when night was at its darkest.

Celine studied the scene beyond her barred window. Noted the lack of a balcony outside. The level of security for the top floor of the Dumaine was certainly extreme. As if it were intended for a visiting dignitary or a member of royalty.

Celine retraced her steps, taking stock of every entrance and egress. The main access to the room was a set of double doors built to look as if they were part of the intricate paneling, their edges trimmed in gilt-leafed molding. Another door leading to a washroom appeared as if it were a piece of art in its own right, a thick frame concealing its seams. Inside the washroom, a large tub of hammered copper stood on a raised platform surrounded by squares of white marble tile. Every sconce in sight had been encrusted with crystals. The air around Celine smelled of irises and sweet water, the flames of countless white candles dancing along the walls and ledges.

Her feet steady on the cold marble, Celine shucked her still damp dress, not even bothering to collect it from the floor. In rote silence, she removed the hairpins from her scalp, pausing to rub the sore spots they'd left behind. Then she moved toward a porcelain bowl and pitcher enclosed by a three-sided mirror of embellished brass.

She stared at her reflection. At eyes wider than a raccoon's and hair like a murder of crows. Dried blood still dotted her skin. The red specks were especially disturbing beside her eyes, which glittered with a consumptive light, as if Celine were possessed of a fever. Without a second thought, she filled the basin with clear water from the pitcher and began splashing her face, scrubbing at her cheeks until they looked raw. Until all three versions of herself reflected in the mirrors appeared appropriately chafed.

Celine didn't pause to dry her face. She returned to the canopied bed and drew the covers to her chin, letting the wetness soak through the sheets, cooling her heated skin.

Her gaze settled above the large fireplace parallel to the foot of the four-poster bed.

It had been cut from a solid block of Italian marble, the screen before it fashioned of meshed iron and gold. Hanging above the tiered ledge was a portrait of a young man of no more than twenty-five, a devilish whorl of black hair falling across his forehead and the knowing glint of a pirate in his eyes. Though his coloring was much fairer than Bastien's—and his face possessed a distinctly European bent—Celine could detect a vague resemblance, most especially in the cut of his jaw. In the unmistakable arrogance of his amber gaze.

A gold skeleton key rested in his palm, a crimson ribbon dangling from a loop at its end. A young man of obvious means, who possessed the key to countless doors.

How droll.

But the most striking thing about the portrait was its palette. The subject's skin and features had all been rendered in believable tones, but everything else stretched the notion. The shadows were too bright a blue, the edges a blur, the corners splashed with ochre paint as if the artist had been on the cusp of madness.

Celine stared at the painting for a time. Then closed her eyes. She felt as if she were being watched. As if the portrait's gaze followed her, like the stories of the Leonardo da Vinci masterpiece, the *Mona Lisa*. She decided to focus on the taper beside her head, which dripped wax down its brass holder in steady streams, until the gleaming candelabra appeared as if it were weeping.

Another disconcerting sight. Everywhere Celine looked, something sinister sprang to life. She thought about waiting until the sun rose to return to sleep. Until the rays of white-gold light seeped onto her silken sheets. The sight of dawn should bring with it a measure of peace.

Why did Celine not feel as if it would?

Her head sank into the sumptuous pillow, her body restless, the eyes at the foot of her bed taunting.

Disturbed by the sense of being watched while she slept, Celine drew the wine-red curtains around the bed and swallowed herself in the comfort of darkness.

From my deserted street corner, I watch the expensive curtains on the uppermost floor of the Hotel Dumaine shift to one side. The face of a stunning young woman with sharp green eyes and hair the color of spilled ink peers through the opening. Only to vanish in the next breath, the heavy damask falling back into place.

I smile.

Fitting that they would take her to Nicodemus' rooms. A chamber suited for a Sun King, replete with a garish display of wealth, the kind to which he has grown accustomed over the years. An homage to Versailles at its best. Or at its worst, depending on one's perspective.

No matter. Nicodemus is rarely there now. He knows better than to come to New Orleans and tempt his fate. He has lost much in the last few years.

But I have lost more. And there is still much for us both to lose. Memories and hopes, wishes for a future that can never be replaced once it is gone. By now, Nicodemus has undoubtedly been summoned from the safety of his New York lair in response to the rash of recent murders in New Orleans.

He will return to the city soon, just as I have foreseen.

Precisely in time for my final performance.

Satisfaction winds through my limbs, causing me to drop my guard for a moment. All is unfolding according to plan. I relish this twinkle of time before I allow the rage to collect in my chest and color my vision. Then I breathe deeply of the briny air. Let the dampness fill my lungs as my heightened senses stretch, soaking in every detail in my vicinity. A horse nearby with an aching tooth, smelling of blood and sweet decay. Crumbs of rye bread swirling about in the gutter, their perfume sour and pungent. A dead rat lingering in the corner of a nearby sewer, the maggots on it wriggling beneath a beam of moonlight.

And—just around the bend—the beating of hearts. One old. Two young. If I had to guess, the younger ones are engaged in an act of lust, their hearts racing in tandem with their sighs.

The old heart thuds slowly. Steadily. Beating toward its inexorable end.

Another creature of the night draws close. My muscles tense and my teeth lengthen on instinct, like the claws of a cat. I reassure myself when I realize it is a familiar scent. One I need not fear.

I continue breathing deeply until my shoulders fall. Then I look once more to the top floor of the Dumaine. Another haunt I know well . . . down to its secret doors and hidden passageways.

Not long ago, I visited these rooms under cover of night, taking in the world of my enemies, knowing I would face them all soon. I even chose to lie upon Nicodemus' bed and admire his collection of books, the shelves of which crown the towering space like a glittering tiara. I pushed the ladders along their oiled casters and marveled at the gleaming motions before pocketing one of my favorite tomes, a first edition of *The Count of Monte Cristo*. Pity I missed the chance to bid my beloved Alexandre a final farewell.

Contentment ripples across my skin at the wash of memories.

Nicodemus' bedchamber is a fitting place to leave my next mark.

I linger in my delicious reverie along my street corner, a pleasant hum forming behind my lips. A song from a brighter, happier time.

A beggar passes by, her hands outstretched for an alm, her shawl a tattered rag flapping in the breeze. Her heart thumps in a recognizable pattern. The old soul I sensed moments ago. I reach into my pocket to offer her everything I possess, a small fortune by anyone's standards.

I have no need of money. What I need, I take. Currency is not important to a creature like me. I do not seek to rest beneath a golden canopy or bathe in a roomful of polished marble.

I seek only to survive.

No. That is a lie. I wish to thrive. To see those who would bring an end to my existence die a slow, agonizing death. After they witness everything they value crumple to pieces before them.

It is only fitting.

"Bless you," the beggar woman says, a sibilant sound whistling from between her handful of teeth.

"May the Lord keep you," I reply with a smile.

My voice catches her off guard. I'm unsurprised by this. Its rich music lulls mortals closer in a way that never ceases to amuse me. It helps greatly in salving the path toward their inevitable demise. In a way, I would argue we are among the most perfect of predators. We mime the mannerisms of our prey. We walk among them, unknown and unseen. By the time they realize they are caught in our web, it is far too late. The transformation is the click of a tumbler, the turn of a handle.

The end of a life. Here one moment. Gone the next.

There is only one other kind of creature that rivals us in such a way. Or perhaps two, though I find most woodland folk genuinely annoying, with all their talk of glamour and promises. With their gleeful tales of tricking mortals into making disastrous bargains. Why would I have need of anyone's firstborn child? A mewling infant is a nuisance, not a reward. And only true monsters would make meals of such a thing.

Besides that, I do not bargain with lesser beings. I take. After which I make the necessary amends, so that I might one day thrive. It is a blessing to even hope for such a future, given the stains of our past.

I remember the last time I watched a vampire die.

She was a vampire I loved beyond words, though I knew I should not, for I realized it would amount to nothing but heartbreak. But when one finds a kindred spirit, how is it possible to turn away? These connections are so rare, even for immortals. For me, they are the food of life.

I watched as they threw Marin into a narrow pit. Those in

my coterie bore witness from the sidelines as cloaked sentries. I buried my affection for her deep behind my heart. Locked it tightly in my chest, so that none of our ranks would know how much I loved a creature who flouted our rules and treated the gifts given to her as nothing more than tokens of appreciation from a dark god.

It was one of the things I appreciated most about her. Marin never took herself too seriously.

After they threw her in the pit, it took a moment for her to regain her bearings. Only a moment. She realized where she was the instant she looked up.

I remember seeing her face as the knowledge passed through her, thankful she could not discern me from the shadows.

She was terrified. Her eyes turned to stone, leached of all light.

But she laughed. Defiant to the end.

She called out to us, knowing we stood on the fringes under cover of darkness, safe in our self-righteousness. Secure in the cloak of our shared hatred.

Marin hurled terrible names in our direction. Demanded to know what we sought to prove by putting an end to her existence.

I call it an existence because—to this day—I do not believe what she lived was a life. Hunting under cover of night. In constant war with beasts of the Otherworld. In constant worry about whom to call friend and whom to call foe. It was not a life because Marin never longed for anything more. She was complacent. She learned nothing in all her years.

And in the end, this complacency failed her. She should have betrayed me before I betrayed her. She never should have been my friend. I never should have loved her. It brought me nothing but pain in the end. The reminder of her skin, soft and hard all at once, like velvet and steel. The taste of her lips upon mine, ever so bittersweet.

But no matter. That is a story for a different night.

Not long after Marin was thrown into the pit, the sun began to shift over the opening of the narrow chasm, slipping in place of the waning moonlight. We all watched in silence while its rays streamed toward the stone floor. We listened as Marin laughed louder, pressing her body against the stacked stones of the cylindrical chamber.

She cried for help in the last moments. Screamed through her laughter, begging for a reprieve. Howling for rescue, her song a broken melody.

Her shrieks haunted me for years. The smell of her flesh as it burned is a memory that still turns my stomach, and not much can do that anymore. Alas, fire will never be my friend. In the years that followed, I hardened myself to such sights. These punishments were necessary if my kind intended to survive. If we meant to establish our place in this world.

After Marin's death, her coven scattered to the far corners of the earth. Every so often I would hear tales of one of its ranks stalking one of ours in retaliation.

A fool's errand. True vengeance does not happen in a moment. It happens over time. The careful doling out of chips, the assiduous display of self-control. When I reap what I have sown, it will be in safety. It will be a breath to savor. And I will be far away when it finally comes.

I turn from my lovely street corner, moving toward a narrow alleyway shrouded in thick darkness. A place in which my kind have thrived for centuries, across all the continents of the world.

I sense a familiar presence though it moves without sound. I wait until it draws near. Close enough that I am the only one to hear his words.

"Master," he says, his eyes glowing like embers in the night, "I did as you asked."

I nod, my features cool. Aloof. Even through the layers of darkness, it is impossible to miss the adoration in his gaze. The almost feverish desire to garner my approval. "And the girl?" I continue.

"She is no longer welcome at the convent." He practically vibrates with the pleasure of delivering this news.

Irritating how much he craves my affection. Like a dog begging for its master's touch. "Good," I say. "And the Court?"

Amusement tinges his words. "They know of her plight. A member of their thieving ranks was sent to her rescue."

Delicious. It will make my vengeance that much sweeter. "Does he know?"

My faithful servant draws closer, the scruff on his youthful chin shadowing his inhuman speed. "I assume as much. The Valmont creature will undoubtedly tell him. She angers me, master. I wish to silence her now, more than ever. I wish to silence them all for what they stole from us."

"The girl is incidental, as are the rest. The usurper alone matters."

Silence swallows us for a breath. "Master?" he says, his voice tentative. "What is the meaning behind the Carthaginian symbols you've instructed me to leave?"

"It is the mark of my kind. Its deeper meaning need not concern you." I keep my tone flat, my rejoinder final.

When my servant shifts back in frustration, his motions send a whiff of dried blood in my direction. Immortal blood. I narrow my gaze at him. "What caused you injury?"

"She—attacked me, master."

I smirk at him. "You allowed a witless human girl to get the better of you?"

"I did not expect her to be so . . . fearless."

"I told you already; she has met Death and lived to tell the tale. Of course she would be capable of causing you harm. You are lucky the blade was not made of silver."

"Yes, master," he grumbles. "Is there anything else you need of me?"

I sense his irritation. He did not wish for me to learn of his wound. Even endeavored to conceal it by changing his shirt. More than his need for revenge, this one's pride will be his undoing. His desire to be noticed. To be deemed the savior who resurrected his fellow demons of the night—those of us banished from the Sylvan Wyld—back to their rightful place among the wintry stars.

But Lazarus was no savior, and this pathetic quim is no concern of mine. They are all expendable. Each a means to my end.

"Master?" he presses. "Is there any other service you require?"

"Not at this time." I pause. "No. That isn't true. I wish for you to take a bath."

"Master?"

His puzzlement vexes me. "You may have changed your garments, but still you reek of death. They will smell it on you before they set eyes on you." I resort to my greatest asset. The power to hold lesser beings in my thrall, with nothing more than my words. "This is your next lesson: if you wish to command respect and rise above your ranks, you must be better than your brethren. Far more cunning. Your life was stolen from you, and you have been relegated to a place of servitude far too long. But you are not a servant. You have at hand the tools to be king of this jungle. A means to bridge the divide . . . and save us all." I let my voice fade with significance, my features high in their regard.

"A lion," he breathes, his eyes luminous in their glory.

I nod. "But you must never forget. All the world's a stage."

"And all the men and women merely players," he finishes with a flourish.

I direct him to leave with a jerk of my chin. He bows before dissolving into the darkness, his steps light with his success.

Insignificant fool.

He is eager to please me. Eager to assume the usurper's role and settle into a position of power. It is why I singled him out not long ago. For I am also eager to take from my enemy what has been taken from me. To have him know what it feels like to have a love lost and a trust broken.

Briefly I recall the moment the betrayal tore through my soul. The realization hollowed me, the way a scorching of one's essence is wont to do. It took years for me to collect the embers. To remake of myself something whole. After that trying time, I no longer felt sorrow for what I had lost. I only felt anger. Hatred.

Now I feel vengeance. It tastes sweet. Sweeter than all the blood and death I could ever hope to swallow.

One man in his time plays many parts.

They thought there was no reason to fear me. That I had scattered to the winds, like ashes from an urn. They sought to steal my birthright and install a false king upon the throne.

They were wrong.

A Midsummer Night's Soirée

---◦◦◦◦◦◦◦---

No. ——B

Bastien had refused to meet with Celine. The insufferable cad hadn't even bothered to display the barest measure of civility in his response.

The first five times she read his note—his initial scrawled larger than life along the bottom of the page—rage had coursed through her veins. She'd resorted to pacing across the plush carpet of her borrowed bedchambers, seething with fury.

Then—on the sixth reading—she'd composed herself. Settled her expression.

Rage was a moment. He would regret this forever.

Coolly and calmly, Celine made plans. She sent a note to Odette via the hotel's courier, who passed along Odette's immediate reply, informing her of Bastien's plans for the evening.

He would be attending the Midsummer Night's soirée hosted by a member of the Twelfth Night Revelers. The same party Celine had declined to attend when Odette had invited her at dinner only a few days ago.

That particular evening, it had not served a purpose.

But today was a different story. Celine intended for this event to serve several purposes, all in her favor. Indeed, she would frequent every ridiculous carnival function in the foreseeable future—even the blasted masquerade ball itself—if it meant rooting out the perpetrator of these ghastly crimes, which were now occurring around her once a week.

Her plan tonight was twofold: to gain answers to her many questions from the lion himself, and to inform the killer that Celine Rousseau was not going to tuck tail and run.

That she planned to stay and fight.

She took time to make herself ready. It didn't matter that she had less than a single afternoon to procure a costume. Another quick message to Odette secured Celine a dress borrowed from a family who owed the Court "a barrelful of money."

The resulting gown did not fit Celine well, but she spent the latter part of the day remaking it to suit the occasion, an outdoor event held alongside a manse in the wealthiest lane of the Garden District. To be sure, it was in poor taste for Celine to be attending a party of any kind, mere days after she'd been cast out of the convent.

But it didn't matter anymore.

Proper society didn't hold a place for Celine anyway. It was high time she removed herself from its confines.

After she finished applying the final details of her costume, Celine placed Bastien's letter into the pocket of her borrowed gown. She planned to reach inside every so often to pinch the piece of parchment between her fingers, imagining it was his neck.

The idea alone steeled her spine. He might have avoided her earlier summons, but Sébastien Saint Germain would not be able to elude Celine tonight. Tonight she would have her answers. She would know the truth about the yellow ribbon. About his involvement in these murders. What exactly all the members of La Cour des Lions were.

Finally she would know where they all stood.

If they weren't fighting with her, they were against her. And Celine intended to use every tool in her arsenal to protect those she cared about—and herself—from whatever may come.

Even if Hell itself unleashed all its monsters on the Crescent City.

———◇———

Rapturous screams rang along the hedge of ochre rosebushes at Celine's back. A man streaked past the entrance to the garden maze, his garments covered in leaves, twigs placed strategically throughout his hair, champagne dribbling from his fluted glass. He laughed, glancing over his left shoulder while he ran. A young woman in diaphanous skirts dyed the color of palest jade almost rammed into Celine in her efforts to trail after the drunken gentleman. The girl raced into the boy's arms, and they crashed into each other before dissolving in a fit of laughter.

Celine inhaled slowly. It might have been a mistake for her to come here.

The longer she wore this gown, the more she realized how ill it suited her. Its basque of emerald silk polonaise was hot, its layers of cream-colored underskirt heavy. Worse still, its smaller size had forced her to tightlace into her stays. And—as evinced by the other "costumes" guests had chosen for a soirée themed after Shakespeare's *A Midsummer Night's Dream*—all her efforts had clearly been for naught.

The members of New Orleans' upper echelons had taken the party's theme as nothing more than a light suggestion. Already Celine had caught sight of people dressed as forest nymphs or fairy sprites, replete with paste gems, translucent garments, and twigs affixed to their elegant frock coats. At least five satyrs were in attendance. *Five* young men from prominent families dressed as randy goats. One was already too many, in Celine's opinion.

Had they even seen or bothered to read the play?

Celine had hoped to channel Hermia, a character named after the god of trade. As such, it felt fitting to don a dress the color of greed. Along her cheekbones and around her eyes, she'd stippled flakes of paper-thin gold leaf into the shape of coins, positioning them as if they were falling from the crown of ebony curls at the top of her head. Actual bills had been pinned to her coif, half of which she'd left down, thrown carelessly over one shoulder. It had been years since society had deemed it appropriate for Celine to wear her hair unbound in public.

Hang society anyway. Well, hang it halfway at least.

At Odette's insistence, a final touch of powder made from crushed pearls had been dusted across Celine's face and décolleté. "You simply must, my dear," Odette had said, as if this made a sliver of sense.

Every time Celine bent one way or leaned to reach for something, she could hear the seams of the emerald basque start to scream. She'd laced her stays as tightly as they would go, and still the rich green fabric across her bust was holding together on little but a prayer. By the end of the night, her breasts were likely to burst free from her corset, a sight that would draw a certain kind of ignominy. Though it would advance Celine's removal from proper society, it might bring about this conclusion in an abrupt manner. One with which she was not yet entirely comfortable.

But from the way the evening looked to be progressing, it might not be the most scandalous event of the night.

The moment Celine and Odette had entered the glittering foyer of this magnificent home, champagne had been poured liberally, to any and all who wished to partake. Hours later, the glitziest pillars of New Orleans society were well into their cups. Already couples were disappearing into the hedgerow deep within the impressive labyrinth, seeking shadowy corners awash in fervent whispers.

Celine fiddled with the low-cut edge of her emerald gown, trying in vain to tug it higher.

"Stop fretting over it, mon amie. You'll only draw more attention to the impressive swath of bare skin there," Odette said from beside Celine, her long sheath dress falling from her shoulders in a cascade of lavender organza, her hair cocooned in a shimmering net atop her head. She'd styled herself in Regency garb, with a hint of Greco-Roman influence. A skein of whisper-thin tulle stained a deep Tyrian purple had been draped across her chest, its ends left to trail down her back. Around her waist was a golden girdle inspired by the character Hippolyta, queen of the Amazons.

"I don't mind a swath of bare skin," Celine retorted. "I *do* mind my bare breasts spilling over the top of my dress at a party replete with satyrs."

Odette laughed, her ivory fan fluttering her loose brunette curls. "If that happens, you'll have ten marriage proposals by the end of the evening."

"I have no intention of becoming the future Madame Goat." Celine sniffed. "Besides that, I feel like a ham trussed up for holiday dinner."

Odette's laughter rang into the starlit sky. "One glass of champagne, and you're far more entertaining than the Bard himself." The edges of her lovely face crinkled as she gazed upon Celine, her expression warm. "Before I forget, you look divine in that color. It's a perfect match for your eyes."

Her words caused Celine to flinch. Her tormentor that night in the Quarter had used that word. *Divine.* Meaning "of the gods." She certainly didn't feel "of the gods" tonight.

"I should have gone dressed as a tree," Celine said in a flat tone. When her gaze ran the length of the hedgerow, she caught a glimpse of yet *another* satyr, his goat ears high on his curly head, a tail fashioned of wool and feathers pinned to the back of his gabardine trousers.

Exasperation rippled through her chest. "Have *any* of these fools actually read the play?"

Odette cackled with merriment, her long purple mantle swirling about her feet.

A familiar figure caught Celine's attention across the way. Her heart missed a beat when a pair of sapphire eyes skimmed dangerously close to where Celine stood, the smile below them sweet and serene.

Pippa Montrose was in attendance at this soirée, dressed as Titania, the queen of the fairies, if Celine had to hazard a guess. She'd arrived on the arm of a placid young man with a slender frame and large round spectacles, likely Phoebus Devereux.

Thankfully, it appeared Pippa had yet to spot Celine across the crowded expanse.

Without a second thought, Celine turned in place, positioning her back to Pippa, all the while wishing she could shrink into the rosebushes. If Pippa saw her, a confrontation would likely ensue. Pippa had sent two messages to the hotel today alone, both inquiring after Celine's welfare. In the latter part of the afternoon, Pippa had come to the Dumaine in person, hoping to check on her friend. Celine had begged off each attempt to make contact, spinning a web of white lies designed to keep Pippa as far away from her as possible, even if it meant damaging their relationship.

Better that Pippa feel cast aside than remain in the murderer's notice.

"We should leave," Celine muttered to Odette, just as another passel of jubilant partygoers hoisted a young man onto their shoulders and proceeded to cheer as if his horse had won the Derby.

Odette drew closer, her features tufting with concern. "I thought you wanted to meet with Bastien. Is something wrong?"

"Nothing is wrong." Celine struggled to appear nonchalant. "It's just been three hours since we arrived. If he had any intention of showing his face, he would be here by now."

Odette tossed a dismissive hand into the air, the jewels adorning her fingers flashing. Definitely not made of paste. "Oh, fiddle-dee-dee, he's always late to these kinds of things. The fiend enjoys making an entrance."

Despite Odette's reassurances, doubt unfurled in Celine's stomach. Madeleine and Hortense had arrived not long after Celine and Odette, dressed as ethereal fey, their dark shoulders gleaming with gold dust. Boone had trailed in their shadow a moment later, garbed in white, a literal halo about his head. A sight that had caused Odette's body to shake with laughter.

Celine was about to renew her objections when Odette waved her fingers in the air above her head, her smile bright.

"Nigel!" Odette took hold of Celine's hand to tug her along.

Closer to where Pippa and Phoebus stood engaged in conversation with the crème de la crème of the Crescent City.

"Odette," Celine gasped, trying to extricate herself from Odette's determined grip.

The damp warmth of the night and the dull roar of the festivities succeeded in drowning out Celine's protests. Nigel met them halfway, two masked figures sauntering behind him at an unhurried pace. His tall frame wove with ease around the countless bodies milling and spilling about. Like most of the other guests in attendance, he'd taken a rather blasé approach to his costume, resorting to winding a few willow branches around his arms, their leaves drooping, the overall effect lackluster, save for the laurel crown gracing his brow.

Boone appeared out of nowhere, startling Celine as he sidled next to her, his loose white shirt billowing about his trim torso, the halo of gold across his forehead tilted askew.

Grateful for the cover his closeness provided, Celine paused to peruse his attire. "And who are you supposed to be?"

"Theseus," Boone said without hesitation.

"The founder hero of Athens?" Disbelief flared across Celine's face. "Be serious. You're dressed as an angel."

Boone shrugged. "Honestly I thought this was a fête for saints and sinners."

"And you thought to go dressed as a saint?"

"Didn't you know, darlin'?" he drawled. "All the best saints are sinners."

Despite everything, Celine laughed, the sound filling her lungs, causing her tightlaced stays to stretch farther. She pressed a hand to her sternum, exhaling slowly to catch her breath. With the hunger of a seasoned sinner, Boone ogled Celine's chest, the irony not at all lost on her.

Nigel grinned as Odette shoved Boone in the shoulder, a note of warning in her eyes. The next instant, she turned to Nigel and sighed a soul-deep sigh. "Just whom are you hoping to channel in that godforsaken costume? I expected better of you, Lord Fitzroy."

"Oberon, o' course." Nigel twisted the waxed ends of his ruddy mustache, his expression mischievous, his accent thick. "One and only king o' the fairies."

"King of the overgrown trees, more like," Odette teased as she tore away a lifeless leaf along his elbow.

He peered down at her with exaggerated imperiousness. "Regardless, I lord over every'fing in my dominion. Kneel before me, Hippolyta."

"You lord over nothing, my silly, sweet boy." Odette swiped a gloved fingertip beneath his chin, a ghost of a smile lingering on her face. "Least of all the queen of the Amazons."

Nigel bowed deeply, the leaves wrapped around his wrist trembling from his motions. He sent a cheeky nod to Celine, whose attention strayed toward the two masked figures loitering in his shadow. Perhaps *loitering* was the wrong word. For neither gentleman appeared to be the least bit concerned with the unfolding spectacle.

One of them was obviously Arjun Desai. The mask of a donkey concealed the upper half of his burnished face. A felt tail had been attached to his backside. At least he'd paid the soirée's theme the appropriate due, for he obviously meant to portray Nick Bottom, the poor fool transformed into a beast of burden by the notorious trickster, Robin Goodfellow.

Arjun scanned his surroundings, his eyes falling on Pippa, his lips twitching. "Is that your friend on the arm of Phoebus Devereux?" he asked Celine.

"I believe so," she replied in noncommittal fashion. Hoping he would not press the matter further.

"Fascinating." Arjun's grin widened as he cast a meaningful glance toward the tall, broad-shouldered young man to his left. A mask covered the entirety of his face, complete with a set of spiraled horns twisting away from his brow, the profile reminiscent of a bull. His body was swathed in a leather greatcoat, its large black collar turned up, further shrouding his features from view.

His only identifier was the gold signet ring on the smallest finger of his left hand, embossed with the seal of La Cour des Lions.

Celine's gaze lingered on the ring, and Bastien's graceful fingers flexed at his sides, as if they could sense her unwavering study. It should have meant nothing for Celine to notice this particular crack in his façade. But—to her endless chagrin—it caused her stomach to tighten and her skin to tingle as if she'd stepped out into a bracing winter's night.

His awareness made her feel alive. Which meant it fell somewhere between nothing and everything. A bothersome development, to be sure. Almost as troubling as the inevitable question that followed.

Was Bastien pleased to see her, or was he irritated?

This was the first time they'd seen each other since admitting their mutual attraction. The night they'd agreed to be nothing more than mere acquaintances. Alas, the presence of a mere acquaintance would not cause a swarm of butterflies to take flight in Celine's stomach, to cluster around her heart, their wings fluttering.

Frustration warmed beneath her skin.

Odette struck a dramatic pose, her right hip jutting forward as she gestured toward Bastien. "Pray tell, just who are you supposed to be?"

"The Minotaur." A rich voice emanated from behind the bull mask, amusement rounding its tone.

"Is there a Minotaur in Shakespeare's play?" Odette queried.

Bastien shook his horned head once.

"Well, bully for you," Celine joked, wishing she could see his eyes. Wishing she could read his thoughts like the pages of a beloved book, pausing to savor every word. Her fingers moved into her pocket of their own volition, pinching his insolent note, stoking the anger in her blood, hoping the blaze would overcome the desire.

The bull's head tilted in Celine's direction, the motion filled with scorn. Then Bastien glanced away, as if he were bored with the very idea of her.

Though it was subtle, his dismissal enraged Celine beyond reason, the fire of fury swallowing everything in its path. She crumpled the note in her fist. He'd already disregarded her once today. After which Celine had gone to immense trouble to attend this godforsaken gathering, all with the intention of confronting him.

And he thought to treat *her* with derision?

Madness, to the very end. It was true a foolish part of Celine had wanted to see him and be seen in return. She deserved to feel wounded now. Nothing good ever came from succumbing to madness.

No matter. To borrow his own words, Celine would grant Bastien no quarter. He'd trifled with her long enough. These weren't the actions of an acquaintance. These were the actions of an enemy. She'd had her fill of enemies.

If Bastien was the Minotaur, Celine would be Theseus, armed with the sword of Aegeus.

Ready to slay the beast.

As if Arjun could taste the discomfort collecting in the air, he laughed, pushing his donkey mask up his face, the silk ties swiping through his unruly waves. "Well, I'd wager this event to be the height of this season's debauchery. Anyone care to name the terms?" His British accent sounded too refined for a party in which satyrs roamed the gardens with insidious ease. Too cultured for a night in which drunken fools lost their inhibitions in a maze of fragrant rosebushes, forgetting all their thorns.

As if to illustrate the point, a striking young woman with hair the color of smoldering embers poured a glass of bubbling champagne down the pale skin of her throat, letting it dribble between her collarbones and soak through the front of her bodice. It traced the shape of her breasts before she feigned outrage, as if she'd simply missed her mouth, her ensuing giggles high and false.

Whatever attention the girl sought to garner, she succeeded. Every eye—male and female alike—was locked on her slender form, equal parts scandalized and tantalized. With a smug smile, she whirled into her circle of tittering friends, safe and cosseted.

For now.

Distracted by the exhibition, Pippa's shocked gaze landed on Celine, the same realization stealing through them in the next breath. A flash of pain shimmered across Pippa's features, her lips parting in surprise. The next instant, she leaned toward her escort, speaking with him in hushed tones.

Celine knew it would take less than ten paces for Pippa to face her. Less than half that for the murderer to notice, were he present, as she suspected. And Celine simply could not allow that to happen.

Panic took root in her stomach. Maddening laughter lilted into the air around them, mingling with incessant chatter. The scent of fresh herbs and the iron of overturned soil filled her nostrils as Celine looked about, seeking an escape.

In a single, sinuous motion, Bastien removed his bull mask, his silver eyes like storm clouds, his expression guarded. As if he could sense her distress.

They locked gazes for a blink of time.

The next instant, Celine wheeled about without warning, rushing toward the entrance of the maze, her cream-colored hem snagging on thorns as she ran.

Darkness Incarnate

———◦◦◇◦◦———

Celine didn't know why she was sure Bastien would follow her.

She just knew—with the certainty of a rising moon—that he would.

When she glanced over her shoulder, the shape of his great-coat stretched behind her, and a jolt of something unseen, unheard, unfelt before this moment raced through her blood. It pulsed in time with her heart, sending her rushing down a wicked path, deeper into wicked darkness.

She *was* Theseus. Setting a trap for the mighty Minotaur in a cursed Labyrinth.

As if she led him on a string, Bastien glided in her footsteps. Celine felt him through the layers of shadow, like the night had embraced her, remaking her in its own image. The sounds of merriment faded into sighs, the smell of sweat and trampled flowers steeping in the warm air.

Celine wove past a pair of young women embracing in a corner, rose petals crushed to paste beneath their feet. A shoulder strap on one girl's gown had slid down her arm, the rouge on her lover's lips nothing more than a smudge across her cheek.

Her face flaming with apology, Celine rounded the next corner and came upon a dead end. She spun in place, her head held high. Bastien stood before her, backlit by the moon, his upturned collar concealing most of his face, the head of the Minotaur dangling from one hand.

She glared at him through the void, vowing to hold fast to her plan, though the space around them thickened with suggestion. "The Minotaur, Bastien? Really?"

"I possess a certain affinity for monsters."

"And the long black coat?"

"I enjoy making a spectacle." His face held nothing but shadows, the set of his jaw refined. As if nothing about the situation troubled him in the slightest.

It provoked Celine further. "And what of Anabel's yellow ribbon?"

Bastien took a step closer. An arctic chill emanated from his skin. "What of it?"

"Why do you have it?"

He said nothing for a time. "Why do you think I have it?" Bastien took another step closer, pressing Celine into the corner.

"Stop," she commanded.

He halted in his tracks. "Are you afraid?"

"No. I'm furious."

"I see." Bastien's response was slow. Deliberate. "You think I killed her," he said quietly.

The coal of night made it difficult for Celine to discern his features. "I don't know what to think anymore."

"If I told you I didn't kill her, would you believe me? If I said I found the ribbon on the stairwell, would that ring true?" He advanced once more, prowling like a panther, the timbre of his voice lowering even further. "Or would you believe me if I told you it belonged to someone I loved long ago?"

"I . . . don't know."

"Do you *want* to believe me?" It was as if Lucifer himself had posed Celine the question, his tone filled with dark deviltry.

Yes, her heart said. "No." Celine's hands balled into fists.

"Liar." The last step Bastien took brought his face into a beam of moonlight.

A sharp breath filled Celine's lungs. He was painfully beautiful. Not in the way of art or the way of poetry. But in the way of violence. The way the sight of it gripped you and took hold. Like a lightning storm behind a bank of clouds. A tidal wave crashing upon a shore. A reminder that life was a moment in time.

That every second of it should be relished.

"What manner of creature are the members of La Cour des Lions?" Celine asked outright, unnerved by the tremor in her chest. "Because I don't believe any of you are human."

Celine expected to see a glimmer of shock in his expression. He remained stone-faced, the hem of his long coat writhing about him like darkness incarnate.

"Odette makes all things possible. Arjun is a weaver of words. Nigel balances the banker's scale. Jae eliminates any dead weight. Boone finds things that wish to remain hidden. Madeleine puts those things to work, all while Hortense cavorts in the background. And—my love of snakes notwith-standing—I am as human as you are," Bastien said simply.

"Do you take me for a fool?" she retorted.

He said nothing in response.

"If the Court of the Lions isn't responsible for killing Anabel and William, then who is?" Celine demanded in a harsh whisper. "And how do we stop him?"

The sound of a twig snapped around the bend, crackling with warning.

Before Celine could blink, Bastien shoved her into the cor-ner, covering her with his body, the waxen leaves at her back prickling against the bare skin along her arms. All the air left her chest, the blood flooding her veins in a heated rush. For a ridiculous instant, Celine thought Bastien was going to kiss her, like the heroes in the penny dreadfuls she often purloined from her friend Josephine.

His arms encircled her as he assumed a wide stance, shield-ing her from view. To anyone looking closely, it would appear as though they were paramours lost in the evening revelry. It did not escape Celine's notice that Bastien failed to take a defensive position.

Which meant he thought only to protect.

Footsteps emanated from behind him, a cluster of indistinct figures shifting into view. With every second, they drew closer, their identities concealed under cover of night.

Unmistakable menace rolled off Bastien's body. From every sleek muscle beneath his black waistcoat to every stretched tendon in his arms. Celine's breath lodged in her throat, her pulse trilling in her ears. Again reminding her why so many people granted Bastien such a wide berth.

Standing before Celine was a young man capable of spilling blood without a moment's hesitation. A ruthless fiend who could slay an armed dragoon and attend Mass the next morning.

The intruders moved closer, as if they were searching for something in the hedgerow, their words slurring together, their bodies stumbling through the darkness. Bastien's right arm snaked around Celine's waist to place the handle of a small dagger in her palm, his left hand shifting toward the revolver tucked in his shoulder holster.

He shook his head once. Celine nodded in understanding.

They would say nothing. They would wait like coiled asps, ready to strike.

A slender form—that of a young woman—tripped into view just beyond Bastien's shoulder. "Didn't you say you saw Sébastien Saint Germain go into the maze, chasing after a young lady?" she said to the companion at her back, her words slurring from drink.

"I could have sworn I did," another feminine voice rang out from behind her.

The first girl groaned. "Which lucky mouse managed to snag herself a lion?"

"She can have him," her friend replied with an audible shudder. "He and every member of the Court frighten me. I don't care how much money or influence they peddle."

"How can you say that? He's a prize in all respects. Have you seen the way he looks when he smiles?" She sighed. "It's a face that would set a girl's drawers aflame."

A cold light settled in Bastien's gaze as they spoke. The ice of a moonless night, high in the Himalayas.

"Well, he isn't here," the second girl said. "And Maman would be furious if she knew we'd wandered into the maze. Everyone knows what happens here after midnight."

"Blast it all," the first girl said through her teeth. "I was hoping to leave the party with at least *one* good story."

"Let's be grateful we're leaving at all, given the recent murders." Her sensible friend tugged the first girl away, forcing them to retrace their steps, their words melting into nothingness a moment later.

Even after they'd wandered beyond earshot, Bastien did not shift back. He stared down at Celine, his lips pursed, his features calculating.

Celine looked up, meeting his study, measure for measure. She inhaled, taking in the spice of the bergamot in his cologne mixed with the scent of supple leather. "It appears your reputation precedes you," she said, her words soundless. Traitorous. With each passing instant, the charge in the air began to shift, the danger reshaping itself into something warmer, headier.

But no less deadly.

"At least one young woman here is wise enough to fear me," he replied, his meaning plain.

"Is that what you think?" Her brow furrowed. "That I'm nothing more than a fool in silken skirts?"

"You're nothing like them. They're leeches. You're a lion."

Pleasure riffled through her at the compliment. "And what do leeches want with lions?"

"The chance to drink from our ice-cold veins." He drew closer, his cool breath washing across her skin.

Celine considered his face, focusing on the way his mouth shaped words. The way its perfect furrow dipped in its center. How easy it would be to stand on her toes and do what she'd been wanting to do since the moment she first laid eyes on him.

She wasn't alone in her desire. Even in the blue moonlight, the naked wanting on Bastien's face unmoored Celine, setting her adrift in a stormy sea.

It was the kind of wanting that hurt.

"Celine." He pronounced her name like a prayer. "What do you want?"

"I want . . ." She saw herself mirrored in his liquid gaze.

Bastien brushed his forehead across hers. "Put an end to our miseries, mon coeur," he whispered. "Please."

Celine rose on the tips of her toes, crowding his space as he'd crowded hers. She gripped him by his pristine lapels, his knife still entwined between her fingers, the blade gleaming white beneath the stars. The front of her basque pressed to the hardened planes of his body, Bastien's heart racing against hers. He looked down, then steadied himself.

Their lips were a hairsbreadth from touching. "I want"—Celine's tongue was a taste away from his—"you to answer my goddamned questions."

It took a moment for her words to register. A shadow crossed Bastien's brow, a muscle working in his jaw as he unwound himself and took a careful step backward. Celine's hands slid from his chest, her heels returning to earth once more, the dagger's handle hanging limply in her palm.

She expected his anger. From an early age, Celine had known boys did not take well to girls who toyed with their desires. She was prepared for his anger. Prepared to unleash some of her own in return.

Rich laughter rumbled through the night. It began in Bastien's chest, then barreled from his perfect lips, the sound unabashed with appreciation.

Celine stood frozen, stunned silent.

Why did he never behave as expected? And why did it make him even more damnably attractive?

Bastien continued laughing as if no one was there to listen. His lips crooked into a half smile. "Celine Rousseau, you're—"

"—brilliant," she finished, refusing to admit how unsettled she was by his reaction. "An absolute joy to behold."

"I was going to say impossible." Bastien shook his head, looking bemused for the barest stretch of time. Then his expression smoothed, ever the consummate chameleon. "But I suppose I'd be willing to consider other options." He straightened. "If you want me to answer your questions, then name your terms."

She blinked, resenting how he donned his guises with such ease. "You wish to negotiate?"

"If you'll sheathe your weapon." Bastien motioned toward the dagger in her hand.

Unbeknownst to herself, Celine had lifted the small blade into the air, brandishing it between them. Blinking like a deer caught in the crosshairs, she turned the iridescent handle toward him.

Instead of taking it, Bastien passed its mother-of-pearl scabbard to her. "Keep it on you at all times. The blade is solid silver. In these times, such a weapon is a necessity, not an option." His tone would not brook any reproach. "And if need be, always aim for the throat."

Celine swallowed. "Thank you," she murmured. "Do you . . . truly promise to answer my questions?"

Bastien checked his pulse. Nodded once. "Not here. Every hedgerow in this cursed maze contains at least five spies." He rubbed at the side of his neck. "Come with me."

TREAD CAREFULLY

———◦◦◇◦◦———

Sébastien Saint Germain loathed what he was about to do. But his feelings could have no bearing on his decision.

It must be done. Tonight. Without a shred of mercy.

Celine Rousseau suffered from many misguided notions. The first of which was that she could be part of this world and not suffer the consequences. That she could stand toe to toe with creatures who would tear her to shreds without blinking an eye . . . and live to speak about it.

If there was anything Bastien had learned in his eighteen years, it was that humans—no matter how formidable or resilient—did not belong in an Otherworld filled with demons and beasts. In the shadowy underbelly of creatures who held nothing but scorn for the fragility of life.

The world in which Bastien had been raised.

It didn't matter that Bastien wanted Celine in his world, more than anything. She was the first mortal girl to stand toe to toe with Nicodemus Saint Germain's heir and not flinch. And perhaps—if these murders had not come about—it could have been possible.

Love is an affliction.

For the span of a breath, Bastien allowed himself to dream. The next instant, the dream coiled on itself like a snake, wrapping his heart in a vise. He needed to silence this foolish desire. His uncle had said it to him before. *We forget our dreams, but nightmares linger with us evermore.*

Celine was the precise opposite of what Bastien's uncle desired for him in a wife. She was stubborn in her pursuits. Uncompromising in her approach. Characteristics his uncle refused to tolerate in any mortal. Not to mention that she lacked the cachet of a distinguished family. Bastien's union with a pillar of New Orleans society was of tantamount importance to Uncle Nico. His marriage should be nothing more than a business transaction, and Celine Rousseau was not a wise choice in that respect, for countless reasons.

But these matters did not have bearing on Bastien's decision tonight. Celine's single month in this world had already caused her irreparable harm. The kindest thing for Bastien to do would be to cast her from it, so he would not become a nightmare lingering evermore in her mind.

He would rather be a dream she once had. Beautiful for a time. Meant to be forgotten.

It always ends in blood.

Bastien wasn't a noble fool. Far from it. There was nothing noble about what he intended to do. It was purely selfish on his part. He could not watch Celine die, as he'd watched his family die. The image of her life draining from her body—of the spark in her eyes fading before him—stole the breath from his chest.

He was doing it for himself. Not for her.

Bastien stood taller, then sank his chin into the collar of his greatcoat, his expression morose. Celine leaned against the bars of the brass lift as they rode to the top floor of the Dumaine. When Bastien glanced sidelong at her, he tried to disregard the lovely shade of pink in her cheeks. Struggled to ignore the strange electricity pulsing between them.

In vain he fought to banish the memory of her body against his. Of the way her green eyes tempted him into sin. She was too close now, her skin smelling of lavender and honeysuckle, the scent parching his throat, beckoning him closer.

Just for a taste.

As always, the lift lurched to a halt at precisely the right moment. "Thank you, Ifan," Bastien said to the dark fey manning it. An outcast from the Sylvan Wyld to whom his uncle paid an obscene fortune every month for the express purpose of guarding this post. With a single touch of his hand, Ifan possessed the ability to ice an intruder in their footsteps.

Ifan nodded, his features cool. If not for the fey's binding promise to Nicodemus, Bastien had no doubt Ifan would sneer at any human who deigned to look him in the eye. It likely curdled his nonexistent soul to serve a breather in such a fashion.

Bastien waited for Celine to exit the lift, knowing it gave her comfort to lead rather than to follow. He needed her to feel comfortable.

So that when he took the feeling away, it would hurt that much more.

He discarded his bull mask in a corner while Celine strode past the mirror hanging along the damasked wall of the narrow corridor, oblivious to what it was. On the surface, it shone brightly, nothing more than a simple looking glass. But the silver had been spelled to see past the naked eye. To uncover the truth lurking beneath a prowler's skin.

Bastien had learned at the age of five how most appearances were designed to deceive.

Celine paused in front of the double doors leading to his uncle's chambers. Again Bastien was reminded of how much she did not know. How the wards spelled into the molding around the doors—cleverly concealed within the elaborate carvings—would burn the flesh of an unwanted intruder.

Oblivious to all the magic around her, Celine's fingers wavered on one of the gilded handles. She turned in place. "Is something wrong, Bastien?"

"What do you mean?"

She frowned. "You keep looking at me as if I owe you money."

Bastien's immediate reaction was to laugh. He held the sentiment in check, though it pained him to do so. One of the things that enchanted him most about Celine was her wit.

It didn't matter. Nothing about her could hold him in thrall anymore.

Before he had a chance to reconsider, Bastien glowered at Celine with a look that would send lesser men running for their mothers. On the force of this scowl alone, he pressed her back against the double doors, his right hand coming to rest on the English oak beside her head. Though Celine's eyes widened, she did not falter. Instead she bristled, cautioning him without words.

Tread carefully, Sébastien Saint Germain.

Damn her audacity. For matching him in all ways.

"You don't owe me anything," Bastien said, his tone imbued with warning. "Just as I owe you nothing in return."

"When are you going to—"

"You wanted answers. All you need to know is this: there are demons in the night that want nothing more than to drain you of your blood and leave behind a lifeless husk." Bastien cut her off before she could say anything. "It doesn't matter what they're called. It doesn't matter how they are killed. It only matters that they *will* kill you. The best advice I can give you is to stay away and leave these matters to those equipped to handle them."

Celine choked through a bout of dark amusement, her pulse fluttering beneath the thin skin along her neck. "If you're equipped to handle this demon, then why is it still wreaking havoc on us? I deserve to know how to defend myself. Odette would—"

"Did you not hear a word I said?" Bastien drew himself up to his full height, intentionally towering over her, though he continued speaking in a measured tone. "Stay away from everyone in the Court of the Lions. Don't trust me. Don't trust anyone around me, including Odette. Whatever you hear, believe none of it. Whatever you see, believe less than half."

"You—promised me the truth." Her eyes narrowed to slits.

He lifted a dismissive shoulder. "I lied."

Fury mottled Celine's face, the flakes of gold along her cheekbones flashing. To Bastien's eternal frustration, it made her appear even lovelier, her eyes like gemstones, her teeth bared like weapons. "Then you brought me here just to—"

"You should have run away when you had the chance. There is—"

"Stop interrupting me, you fils de pute." Celine shoved him, her palms like brands against his chest. "And for your information, I already tried to run."

"Liar." Bastien brushed aside her hands as if he were swatting a fly. "If you meant to run, you would have fled this place long ago. Don't tell me you tried. Selfish bastards like you and me don't try. We *do*." The words felt like acid on his tongue, the truth searing through to his soul.

Celine recoiled from it, her lips parting. A look of understanding smoothed across her beautiful face. "You're trying to scare me. It won't work."

Bastien wrapped a careful hand around her throat, pulling her closer, her unbound curls tickling his wrist, distracting him for another maddening instant. "Then you're a fool."

"Why won't you help me?" Celine's voice cracked at the last, the first sign he'd caused her demonstrable pain.

It struck Bastien like a battering ram to his stomach. "You worry about the creature who *might* kill you?" A cold spate of laughter fell from his lips. "You should worry about the demon who will. For I'll kill you myself if you don't stay away."

"Liar. You wouldn't hurt me." Despite everything, Celine Rousseau still refused to retreat.

Bastien could not admire her for it. He *would not* admire her for it.

"You don't know anything about me," he said. "I've killed before, Celine. Countless times. And relished in doing it, never once asking for forgiveness." He meant to terrify her with this admission. To seal their fate once and for all.

Celine exhaled slowly, her breath shaking as it left her lips. "So have I."

Bastien's hand dropped from her throat, tension flowing from beneath his skin, his chest tight with surprise. He thought about accusing her of lying. But she wasn't lying. He knew her well enough to realize a revelation like this could not be a lie. It was too brutal, like truth often was.

Celine raised her pointed chin. Angry tears welled in her eyes. "I killed a man with my own two hands." Her fists balled at her sides. "It's why I ran away from Paris." She inhaled, her body trembling. "And I don't feel sorry for it, not in the slightest. I'm not afraid of death, Sébastien Saint Germain. Nor am I afraid of you. It is *you* who should be afraid of *me*." She shoved him once more, the tears spilling down her cheeks.

Bastien grabbed her hands. Steadied her as she took in another ragged breath. His thoughts roiled through his mind, questions collecting on his tongue. "Who?"

"I killed the boy who tried to rape me."

The fire left his body in a soul-stealing rush. It was the same as always. Whenever Bastien was about to destroy something, he felt ice, not fire. "Good," he said, not trusting himself to say more.

"Maybe we're not so different, you and I."

It was so far from the truth. So close to what his heart longed to believe. Bastien couldn't help himself. He shifted a palm to her face, brushing away her tears with his thumb.

"Tell me why you have Anabel's ribbon," Celine said, her green eyes shimmering. "Please."

Bastien's grip tightened, his hands cradling her chin. He abhorred the need to explain himself. Despised the meaning behind it. "Reach into my left breast pocket."

Her brow furrowing, Celine withdrew a length of butter-yellow silk from its place over his heart. Stitched on one corner of the worn handkerchief was a set of initials:

ESG

Confusion gathered along the bridge of her nose. "What—"

"It belonged to my sister, Émilie," Bastien said. "She gave it to me the day she died." He took a breath, the air burning through his lungs the instant he uttered her name. "I carry it with me always. It gives me strength."

A moment passed in silence. Celine waited for him to speak, as if she knew no pithy words of condolence would make a difference, even after more than a decade.

"She died for me." He fought to conceal his pain, as he always did. To make light of it, so no one would know how the memories of his past still haunted his present.

Celine cast him a searching glance. "You shouldn't hide how you feel, Bastien. Not from me. I promise never to judge you for it."

"And why would you make such a promise to a boy you barely know?"

"I think you know why." She did not look away.

Again he was held in thrall. *Here* was true power. The power to captivate without a word.

In that moment, Bastien no longer wished to hide from Celine. Not anymore. With her, his pain was not a weakness for an enemy to exploit. It was a strength, just as Émilie would have wanted.

"I feel . . . shattered when I think of my sister," he said, his voice graveled with unchecked emotion. "Like my heart is made of glass, the pieces splintering through my chest." Each word was an unburdening. A truth longing to be set free.

Celine nodded, her expression wistful. "Wouldn't it be wonderful if we could all have hearts made of diamonds?"

"Unbreakable." Bastien's lips crooked into a half smile.

In her eyes, he saw an answered question.

Love is an affliction.

"We shouldn't," he said softly.

"But we will."

"No." Still Bastien could not stop himself from touching her. From letting his fingers slide along her heated skin. "We won't."

"Yes, we will. Just like you'll help me set my trap at the masquerade ball."

"I will not."

Celine leaned into his caress. "Such a liar." She pressed the full length of her body to his, a flame igniting in her gaze. "And a coward," she breathed beneath his chin, the sensation curling down his spine.

Before Bastien could offer a rejoinder, Celine surged onto her toes and slanted her lips to his. The instant they met, she softened in his arms, molding against him. He surrendered, the rest of the world melting away. When her tongue brushed across his lips, Bastien groaned, no longer capable of restraint.

This was not a kiss of curiosity, nor was it one of tentative exploration. It was wild. Reckless. And Bastien could do nothing but respond in kind. He'd wanted this the first night they met. When Celine had grabbed his cravat. When she'd stared him down—expecting Sébastien Saint Germain to cower in fear—she'd stolen his splintered heart.

All in one perfect instant.

Bastien lifted her from the floor, his hands hardening as they wrapped her legs about his waist. He pushed through the double doors with Celine in his arms, swallowing them in sudden darkness. Barely aware of his surroundings, he crossed the room toward his uncle's four-poster bed. Amusement flared through him, hot and fast. Uncle Nico would no doubt rage about this lack of respect.

It would be worth it.

They sank onto the cool sheets. Bastien kissed Spanish words into the skin of Celine's throat, promises no mortal man could keep, vows of a poetic fool. His fingers loosened the pins buried in her crown of midnight curls, the metal pieces flying free, her hair coiling about them like a cloak of darkness. She tore at the buttons of his shirt, the sound of rending fabric causing Bastien to smile into her bared shoulder.

"I liked that shirt," he rasped beside her ear.

"Then say a prayer for its immortal soul."

Bastien laughed. Every touch of her skin, every brush of his hand, sent another wave of desire coursing through his veins.

In the farthest reaches of his mind, Bastien considered what this would mean. He risked little by taking Celine to bed. She risked everything. Her reputation, her future, possibly even her well-being. It was something Odette often remarked upon. The injustice of it all.

He thought about stopping, even as he gathered her skirts in his hands. "Celine."

"Bastien." She arched into him, her nails raking down his arms, the sensation turning his sight black. He gripped behind her knees, relishing the shock in her gasp.

He should put a stop to this. He knew he should. "Is this all right?"

"Yes."

His hands grazed higher. "This?" The blood roared through his chest.

"Yes."

His thumbs brushed across the soft skin between her thighs. "And . . . this?"

"Bastien." Celine's head fell back, her body trembling. "Please, I . . . what?"

The question in her voice caught his attention. She sat up abruptly, squinting through the shadows on the opposite wall. Then she pushed Bastien away, a bloodcurdling scream ripping from her throat.

Bastien whirled to his feet, reaching for his revolver in a seamless motion. Then he followed her gaze.

The darkness across the way was thick and deep. The contrast of light streaming from the open doors at the entrance of the chamber made it difficult to see past the end of the bed. It took a moment for Bastien to detect the source of Celine's scream. To realize what tore a wrenching sob from her now.

Bastien stumbled to his knees, his revolver clattering onto the Aubusson carpet.

It always ends in blood.

There—along the balcony of books high above head—lay the remnants of an arm wrapped in broken willow branches, blood dripping from its torn socket. Resting atop the banister sat the crimson remains of a severed human head, its features mauled by the claws of an animal.

But it didn't matter. Nothing could hide the truth of his identity. Not from Bastien.

Nigel.

On the wall above the pool of blood was another symbol:

———◦◦◇◦◦———

The ice grows thinner beneath my enemy. Beneath all his kith and kin.

Now he knows I will take from him those he holds dearest in the world. I will show them no mercy. I will take and take and take until there is nothing left for them to lose.

Soon they will understand there are no limits to my reach. For I have breached Nicodemus' wall of protectors. His last remaining bastion. Now there can be no succor. Not from my wrath.

He will endeavor to protect his family—as he has for centuries—but there can be no doubt who will emerge victorious in this battle. I alone hold all the cards. No doors are barred to me. There is no mountain too high to climb. There are no reaches in this Hell.

I stand in the shadows, staring up at the Hotel Dumaine. I watch his Court of the Lions skulk through the darkness. Bear witness as an impotent force of police officers descends on the stately edifice. I listen as they speak. As she cries and he rages. As they all wail for what once was.

The loss stings, does it not?

No more than it stung when I lost everything I held dear. When all I valued shattered to pieces, trampled to dust beneath their feet.

My skin is electrified by their torment. My soul flies free.

He knows it is personal now. When his trust is taken from him—when the one he most loves is marked by Death's lasting kiss—he will know why it was done. Whom to blame.

There is no way for us to turn back. The tinder has been collected. The match has been struck.

Only one of us can survive the fires of Hell.

THE PIANTAGRANE

———◆◇◇◇◆———

Celine sat on the edge of the rickety cot in Michael's office at police headquarters. The ticking of the nearby clock reverberated through her brain, the sound growing louder with each passing second. Rays of filtered light cut across the wooden floorboards beneath her feet, the sun warming in preparation for its grand finale.

Her pulse thudded in her ears as she studied the large slate chalkboard across the way, covered with endless lists and meticulous diagrams Michael had constructed since the night of the first murder along the docks less than one month ago. She paused on the weather-beaten map affixed to a corner of the smooth grey surface. Peered intently upon the details she'd shared of the evening the killer had trailed her down a darkened city street. The things the demon had said to her, both that night and the night William had been killed. The threats the creature had snarled in her ear:

Welcome to the Battle of Carthage.
You are mine.

Death leads to another garden.
To thine own self, be true.
Die in my arms.

She shuddered at the memory of how the demon's cool breath had rippled down her back. Of the warm copper scent he'd left behind after raking his bloodstained fingers across her face. Celine looked away, her eyes catching on the chalkboard's most recent addition: the one pertaining to Nigel's murder last night in the suite at the Dumaine. The tallying of another horrific clue to their collection of symbols.

She sighed, her shoulders bowing forward as if burdened by an invisible weight.

It was the same as it had been for the last few hours.

Celine could make neither heads nor tails of it.

The letters themselves could be as they appeared at first glance: an *L*, an *O*, and a *Y*. But strung together, they held no meaning for Celine, nor did they appear to resonate with Michael or any other member of the Metropolitan Police. They could be initials. Or directives. Or utter nonsense meant to worry them to distraction.

If they were in fact another kind of script altogether, their significance remained beyond Celine's reach. The first letter could be a backward or sideways *L*, in either ancient Greek or Latin. Or perhaps even a *C*? Maybe the killer had written it incorrectly, or perhaps the perspective had been skewed. The second letter was arguably an *O*, if it was indeed a letter at all. And the last? It could be any number of letters. *A* or *Y* or *W*.

Perhaps a *U*, depending on its origins. It could even be from a language that predated ancient Greek.

Maybe they weren't letters at all, and Michael had been right to assign them mathematical meaning.

It was exhausting. All the unending possibilities had plagued Celine well past dawn. As the hours had passed, the events of last night had tangled through her mind, leaving behind an eerie mélange of memory. What struck Celine most was the contrast of coldness and warmth. Of darkness and light. The way the air had felt in the maze, thick and heavy. The remembrance of the young girl spilling cool champagne down the skin of her throat, the sparkling glass in the garden silhouetting her shape. The way Celine's nerves had iced at any threat, her bones pulling taut as if she'd stepped into a bracing winter's night. The feel of Bastien's hands searing across her skin, his lips a brand in the hollow of her throat. The delicious warmth pouring down her body even now at the thought. That horrifying moment when a scream had frozen on Celine's tongue.

The warm smell of blood.

The bitter cold of death.

She clutched the silly note tighter in her palm. The one handed to her in passing by a stone-faced Odette a mere minute after Michael had separated Celine and Bastien upon his arrival to the hotel, intent on squirreling her away to the tristoried police headquarters in Jackson Square beside Saint Louis Cathedral.

Wherever you are, I will find you at midnight.

— B

It shouldn't have mattered to Celine that Bastien had thought of her moments after discovering his murdered friend. But it mattered more than she could find the words to say. The note she held in her palm proved they were not simply the "passing acquaintances" they'd agreed to be only days before. They were beyond such inanities. Perhaps it mattered to someone somewhere that Celine was not a proper match for Bastien, nor was he at all the proper suitor she'd envisioned for herself.

But it no longer mattered to them.

Celine saw past Bastien's masks. He looked beyond her lifetime of artful lies. And when confronted with these truths—the worst things that had happened to them, the worst things they had done—Bastien did not flinch nor did Celine turn away.

These were the only truths that made sense amid such chaos.

Hooking an errant curl behind an ear, Celine strode toward the slate chalkboard to take a closer look at the worn map, pockmarked with metal pins from prior investigations. Again she struggled to understand what had made the killer shift his attentions to her. What had driven him to murder that poor girl along the docks weeks ago. Whether everything was connected and, if so, what the killer's next step might be. Her gaze caught on the name of the street running in front of the police station, Rue de Chartres.

Come with me to the heart of Chartres.

The phrase was missing from Michael's collection. Evidently Celine had neglected to mention it to him. Did it matter? Did it hold any meaning? Who *was* this madman, and why was he killing people around them? Where was he hiding, in plain sight or in a shadowy labyrinth of his own? He could be among so many of the people she had met thus far. Or he could be none of them at all.

One thing was clear: Celine was finished waiting for him to make his next move.

Frustration clutched at her throat, the heat of barely checked rage warming across her skin. Her resolve hardened further. She would bait the killer into a trap the night of the masquerade ball, when he believed her to be preoccupied by drink. She would appear to indulge herself in the carnival festivities, and then leave the ball to wander the Quarter alone, just as she had the first evening the killer had followed her, a mere fortnight ago.

The fiend wouldn't know that members of the Court would be lurking nearby in an ever-tightening circle, waiting for him to reveal himself. To finally make a misstep.

And if it didn't work?

Celine would simply set the trap again at a different time and place.

Perhaps it was ridiculous to think she could outwit such a villain. But at least it was *something*.

Beside her feet, the rays of sunlight stretched long and lean as dusk began to descend on New Orleans, the sky catching fire along the horizon. Celine huffed, the echo unspooling into the plaster ceilings.

"What a waste of time," she murmured to no one. Stopped herself from kicking the corner of Michael's inordinately tidy desk like a child denied a sweet. There were so many other things she could be doing. Should be doing. Her glance fell on the skirt of Odette's ball gown, strewn across the end of the rickety cot. For several hours this morning, Celine had worked to persevere and put the finishing touches on it. The masquerade ball was only two days away, and she still needed time to complete her own costume. But the needles had fallen from her shaking fingers, her nerves frayed from the prior evening's events. No matter what Celine did, she could not silence the riot of her thoughts.

Militant footsteps rounded the corner just beyond the locked door. Celine listened, glancing at the clock to verify—once more—the time the guards patrolled the corridors outside Detective Grimaldi's office.

Being quarantined like a cholera patient had been a waste of precious hours in many respects, but at least it had helped Celine gather the information necessary for tonight's venture:

A midnight prison break.

By her count, guards patrolled the impressive brick edifice beside Saint Louis Cathedral every fifteen minutes. In two-hour increments, someone knocked on the door of Michael's office to check on Celine or deliver something for her to eat. If she wished to attend to her physical needs, an officer stationed just around the nearest bend in the hall was there to make sure she returned to Michael's office immediately afterward.

Michael himself had come twice to check on her since daybreak.

As he'd promised, Celine was well attended. It would be quite a task indeed for any intruder to make his way past the impressive squadron of guards surrounding the building, up its winding staircases to the third floor, and into its slew of hallways, patrolled as they were at all hours.

But she would wager none of them had considered whether Celine would wish to break *out* of this makeshift prison.

Of course it was wild and irresponsible to attempt such a thing. Alas, Celine suspected that if she even asked to leave the premises, Michael himself would be there to thwart her every move. Besides that, Celine did not think he would take kindly to her request to meet with any member of La Cour des Lions at police headquarters, let alone Bastien.

Merde, she thought to herself. *I never should have told him anything, least of all my plan to use myself as bait.*

Celine sniffed. It grated on her to be shackled to one place in such a manner, like a princess kept in a tower, awaiting a white knight. She wasn't a complete fool, after all. No undue risk would be taken this evening. At all times, Bastien's solid silver dagger would be close at hand. And she had no intention of wandering beyond earshot of police headquarters. Instead she'd wait for Bastien in the heart of Jackson Square not a minute before midnight, less than forty paces from the front doors of the cathedral.

What kind of foolish killer would try to strike her down a stone's throw from a garrison of armed police officers?

Several sets of footsteps neared the door, pausing just outside. A fist pounded lightly on its oaken surface in three successive knocks. Then waited a breath before rapping four times more.

The signal Michael had devised to convey he was outside and all was well.

Celine unlocked the door to find the young detective standing there, a storm brewing in his colorless eyes. Over his shoulder loomed a jolly giant of a man carrying an incongruously small basket and a stooped woman with a woolen shawl draped across her shoulders and a covered dish between her wrinkled palms.

The elderly woman peered past Michael with a wry expression. "Step aside, caro." Her accent was threaded with rolling *r*'s and richly rounded vowels. "And be sure to introduce me." A twinkle shone in her watchful gaze.

When Michael failed to cross the threshold or utter a single word, the elderly woman elbowed him aside with an amused snort, the looming brute laughing under his breath, the sound like the barking of a large hound.

With a world-weary sigh, Michael followed them into his office, his motions uncharacteristically awkward. "Nonna, this is Miss Celine Rousseau of Paris." He paused. "Miss Rousseau, I'd like to introduce you to my grandmother."

Celine's eyes went wide. She stood straight while tucking Bastien's letter into the pocket of her petticoat. "It's such a pleasure to meet you, Madame Gri—"

"None of that nonsense. Call me Nonna." Her smile crinkled every line in her brow, the effect more soothing than a mug of hot tea. She shuffled past Celine. "I brought you some ribollita." With a *thunk*, Nonna set down the covered dish on Michael's desk. "It's a soup my mother taught me to make when I was a child. You see, I was a bit of a piantagrane in my youth." She made small circles with her hands, her gestures punctuating her words. "Always destroying things and getting into mischief. So my mamma would give me old bread to tear into pieces, then we would wait until they soaked up the delicious broth before having a feast! Have you ever had ribollita?" she asked Celine as she waved her immense escort closer, his steps mincing, as if he'd incurred a recent injury.

"No, ma'am." Celine smiled, a fond warmth settling in her stomach.

"You will love it." Nonna beamed. Every time she moved, the smell of cinnamon and sage suffused the air. "Luca, per favore, where are the bowls?" She turned to the jolly giant, a stern expression on her face. "And, Michael, why are you standing there as if you were struck by lightning? Muoviti!" She flung her hands to one side, shooing him away.

For the first time since Celine had met Michael, she glimpsed a look of utter bewilderment on his face. He started to step forward, then stopped, clearing his throat and adjusting the cuffs of his sleeves.

Despite everything, a bubble of dark laughter threatened to burst past Celine's lips. Michael's diminutive grandmother had ripped the proverbial carpet from beneath his feet, and Celine relished every second of watching him stumble.

Nonna continued, "I can only imagine how little my grandson has thought of providing you adequate food, since he himself often forgets to eat." She spun around, her shawl falling from one shoulder. "Let me look at you." Without warning, she seized Celine by the chin, turning her face to and fro. "Bella, bella, bella," she murmured. "Where did you get those eyes and those cheekbones, cara?"

"My mother."

"Ovviamente," Nonna said with a nod. "Your mother must have been a great beauty." She winked at the man she'd called Luca. "Not unlike myself in my heyday."

Luca laughed, the sound dancing about the dimly lit room as he stepped forward. "Since my cousin is clearly tongue-tied, I'll have to apologize for him and make my own introduction." He dipped his head into a small bow. "Luca Grimaldi, at your service." When he smiled down at her, Celine noticed the similarity in the line of his jaw and along his tousled brow. But instead of lending him the scholarly look it did Michael, it made Luca appear quite rugged. Like a man who toiled with his hands in the outdoors for long stretches of time. His eyes brought to mind the color of melting chocolate, and—when he took Celine's hand to press a polite kiss on it—the solidness of his grasp made her feel even more at ease.

Celine grinned up at him, marveling at how tall he was. "A pleasure to meet you, Luca."

"Get the young lady a chair, caro," Nonna chided Michael while spooning the hearty soup into small bowls she removed from Luca's basket. Celine moved closer to help, but was brushed to one side without preamble. "No, no. You are our guest here." Nonna handed Celine a bowl, and the steaming ribollita heated through Celine's palms, winding toward her heart. A strange flutter took shape in her chest. She couldn't recall the last time anyone had prepared something especially for her, with their own two hands. At home in Paris, she'd done most of the cooking. And Celine had never known either of her grandmothers.

She cleared her throat. "Thank you, Nonna."

"Of course." Nonna served bowls of soup to Michael and to Luca. "Sit, sit, before the food runs away from you." She snorted. "Can you believe my grandson didn't want me to come here today?" Nonna said as they all gathered around Michael's desk for a makeshift meal of ribollita. "He protested most ardently. So of course I made Luca bring me." She tucked away a silver curl. "Though the circumstances are less than ideal, I was eager to meet you, dear Celine." Her eyes sparkled. "Michael speaks well of you."

"All the time," Luca added in a teasing tone.

Michael's gaze pierced into his cousin's skull with the precision of a lance. "Christ Almighty, let this end soon," he grumbled as he stirred his soup slowly, his features morose.

Quicker than a bolt of lightning, Nonna smacked the back of his head. "Non pronunciare il nome del Signore invano, Michael Antonio Grimaldi!"

Michael closed his eyes and gritted his teeth, all while Nonna continued eating as if nothing at all had transpired. As if she hadn't just struck New Orleans' premier police detective for daring to take the Lord's name in vain.

Celine's lips twitched. She coughed. Then snorted in a most unladylike fashion. "I'm deeply sorry." She cleared her throat.

"For what?" Luca asked, his question tinged with amusement.

"That I can't watch that happen over and over in my head."

Luca barked, a meaty fist pounding against the desk, jostling Celine's soup. "She'll do nicely, cousin." He howled. To his left, Nonna tittered, her slender shoulders shaking with laughter.

"I suppose it doesn't matter that no one asked your opinion," Michael replied, his words coolly cutting.

"Not at all." Luca slurped his soup and leaned toward Celine. "I'd tell you awful stories about him, but I fear we've already pressed my proper cousin too far by gracing his doorstep un-announced."

Celine curved a brow. "Was he as trying a child as I suspect? Lots of sanctimonious questions and smug answers?"

"Worse. Next time I'll tell you about his fifth birthday, when he stabbed me in the side of the neck with a newly sharpened pencil." He bent closer. "I still bear the scar right here." Luca pointed at a small dark spot just below his left ear.

Celine tsked, delighted to sense Michael's ire flare hot from beside her.

"Basta, Luca," Nonna commanded. "You deserved it for breaking his other pencils as you did, and I think Michael has suffered enough for one evening. Let's speak of pleasant things." Her spoon clattered into her bowl. "Such as when you plan to bring that young woman to see me. The one who keeps writing you those lovely letters. It's time I met her. You know I'm not getting any younger, Luca Grimaldi."

Luca guffawed, choking around a mouthful of ribollita. "I thought you wanted us to discuss pleasant topics, Nonna."

"She meant pleasant for herself," Michael interjected.

Nonna harrumphed. "I will resort to all manners of shame if it means I get to hold my great-grandchildren before I die."

"What about you, Michael?" Luca eyed his cousin with a devilish smirk. "Didn't you tell me only last week that a young lady had caught your attention?"

Celine expected Michael to glare at his brawny cousin in response. But he merely glanced back at Luca with a look of unchecked annoyance.

"Who has caught your eye?" Nonna demanded, her outrage clearly feigned. Far too dramatic to be real. "And why am I only learning of this now?" Her tiny hand slapped the edge of the desk. "Rispondetemi."

Luca laughed softly, crossing his arms and leaning back in his chair while Celine stared into her bowl of soup, praying for someone to change the subject.

Michael wiped his mouth with a linen handkerchief, his words measured. "I haven't told you about her because I'm still trying to prove I'm worthy of her notice." He leveled his gaze at the clock along the wall with a determined stare.

Celine refrained from squirming in her seat.

"Any young woman who fails to see what a wonderful man you are must be a fool," Nonna said, her words pointed. "My Michael has always been the smartest boy in the room. So hardworking. And handsomer than any young man has any right to be."

The color rose in Celine's neck with unbridled ferocity. A part of her wished to say something to disrupt the course of the conversation, but she lacked the right words. No matter what she said or how she said it, she was bound to offend someone.

And Michael's family had been so kind to her. Kinder than she deserved.

"She isn't a fool," Michael said with great care. "Far from it, in fact. She's sharp and quick-witted. Notices details others would miss. Despite her own difficulties, she manages to be warm and selfless. Moreover, she refuses to bow at the altar of money," he continued. "But she *is* stubborn, and a bit distracted."

Celine's jaw almost dropped. She'd never heard Michael speak of anyone so highly, least of all her.

"Well, you'll simply have to get her to focus," Nonna said, the side of her hand slicing toward the table as if it were a knife. "Turn your charms on her."

Luca laughed. "His charms? No young lady wants to be inundated with useless facts, or be forced to contend with starched collars and ungodly hours of work." He slid his attention to Celine, his expression shrewd. "Might you have any suggestions for my cousin, Miss Rousseau?"

"Pardon?" Celine sat up straight, her spoon jangling to the desk, the delicious broth splashing in its wake.

"You're a young woman," Luca pressed. "What would a young man need to do to catch your attention?"

The outlandishness of his request nearly unseated Celine. Only the daftest fool would fail to see what Luca and Nonna were trying to do. When she peered in Michael's direction, he looked just as uncomfortable as she felt. "Perhaps"—Celine firmed her tone—"Detective Grimaldi should start with a poem?"

"Do you hear that, Michael?" Luca braced both elbows along

the desk, an eager spark in his chocolate eyes. "You should send the young lady a poem."

Michael considered his cousin's suggestion, as if nothing at all were strange about this conversation. Then he turned toward Celine, watching her intently while he spoke. "I'm partial to Blake myself. Or perhaps Byron?"

Celine swallowed. "I favor Shakespeare, though I do enjoy Blake on occasion." She didn't know what possessed her to say it. Perhaps it was Michael's compliments still ringing in her ears. But even if he recited her favorite sonnet by memory, it wouldn't give life to a sentiment she did not hold for him. What she felt for Bastien was not yet love, but it was . . . something. A feeling Celine could no longer ignore.

"Shakespeare." Michael nodded once, his brow resolute. "It's worth a try."

A THOUSAND TINY CUTS

———◦∞◊∞◦———

N ow was her chance.

The booted footsteps outside Michael's office faded as they turned the corner. If Celine made a dash for it, she could sneak down the corridor and make her way outside.

The clock on the wall began to chime, tolling the midnight hour in dulcet tones.

One. Two. Three.

With a steeling breath, Celine removed her shoes. Unlatched the door. Twisted the knob.

Seven. Eight.

She glided down the hall, careful to walk on her stockinged toes. When the guard posted near the necessary looked in her direction, she ducked in an open doorway, her eyes peeled for the moment he turned back.

A battle charge drumming through her veins, Celine flew down the shadowed steps, careful to pause at each landing, ensuring not a soul was within sight. The moment she reached the ground floor, she stole a glance at the portly sergeant manning the front desk. Watched while he took a sip of coffee from a stained mug. Listened to him cough and clear his throat before he poured a splash of whiskey into his cup.

With a small smile, Celine crept along the wall until she arrived at a bolted side door. Taking great care to unlatch the brass lock without so much as a sigh of metal, she slipped through the opening and into the night. Once more, she waited beneath an eave, on the lookout for prowling gazes. Triumph settling on her face, she took a step onto the darkened path, her ears filled with the sound of chirruping insects and her eyes locked on the elegant expanse of saw palmettos in front of Saint Louis Cathedral.

"Marceline."

The voice at her back was low. Accented. Unthreatening. Nevertheless it frightened Celine to her core. It had been months since she'd heard her full name spoken aloud. Though she did not recognize the voice offhand, its owner pronounced the three syllables with unmistakable purpose. As if he knew how she took her tea, as well as the last occasion she'd prayed to anyone for anything.

Celine froze midstep, her heart galloping through her chest like a spooked horse.

"N'aie pas peur," the voice reassured from behind her, its baritone rich and clear. "I am not here to harm you."

For a rash instant, Celine considered running. But something told her she would not get far. The fine hairs on her neck stood on end, as if she'd been sighted through a rifle's lens, eyes surrounding her on all sides. Though her fingers trembled, Celine managed to unsheathe Bastien's silver dagger before pivoting on a stockinged heel.

From a fall of nearby shadow emerged a slender gentleman wearing a felted top hat and a suit of darkest blue. The walking stick in his left hand was crowned by a solid gold lion, his pocket watch fashioned of gleaming Spanish bullion. When he removed his hat, Celine stifled a gasp.

She recognized this man.

It was the young man in the oddly colored painting above the fireplace in the suite at the Dumaine. The one that had haunted her from beyond the four-poster bed.

He gazed at her, his expression calm and collected. Then a slow smile unfurled on his cultured face. It startled her, for it was like watching a statue come to life. One second, his expression looked still and smooth, as if honed by the hand of a master. The next second everything softened, making him appear almost human.

Almost.

Like Arjun and Odette and all the other members of the Court, this man was not entirely human. Celine would bet her life on it.

She said nothing as he appraised her in silence. Despite the disbelief flaring through her, Celine knew at a glance who he was. Who he must be.

Bastien's uncle. Le Comte de Saint Germain.

With nothing to do but return his unflinching study, Celine scoured his features for similarities, as if it would calm her.

The count stared down at her with the same exacting precision as his nephew, the line of his jaw no less cutting. His brow was as dark and expressive as that of Bastien, the tone of his skin several shades lighter.

Celine took in a sharp breath of warm night air. The count must have been no more than a boy himself when he assumed the task of raising his nephew. The painting in the suite at the Dumaine could have been completed yesterday, for Bastien's uncle did not appear to be a day over twenty-five.

Impossible.

"I am Nicodemus Saint Germain," he interrupted her thoughts. His accent was difficult to place, though his words were lyrical and precise, as if he'd been an elocutionist in a past life. When he shifted into the faint glow of a distant streetlamp, a current of fear chased across Celine's skin.

Even the way he moved took her off guard. Like he was limned in smoke. Or deliberately moving slower than usual, as one would with a cornered animal.

On instinct, Celine lifted the silver blade in her hand, as if to ward him away.

A breeze blew past her, shocking her still, riffling the loose tendrils of her hair and the hem of her wrinkled skirt. Before Celine could blink, a figure came into focus. One second, nothing was there, save a swirl of darkness. The next breath, a man stood in its place, fully formed. As if he'd always been there, a watchful specter in his own right.

Jae. The member of the Court Bastien said "eliminated dead weight."

Whatever that meant.

The graceful young man from the Far East loitered between Celine and the count, short blades in either hand. When he twirled one dagger across his fingers, Celine caught sight of something she'd missed before: countless tiny scars on the backs of his hands, the markings raised and faintly white. Her gaze traveled upward to note the same scars on the side of his neck, reaching just above his starched collar. There did not appear to be a design to the markings, for they'd been sliced at random, some of them crosshatched, every one of them painful to behold.

"In ancient China," Nicodemus Saint Germain began in a conversational tone, "there was a time when capital punishment was inflicted by a means known as *lingchi*, or the Death of a Thousand Cuts."

Celine shrank backward a single step. Then stood straight, determined to hold her ground, despite the fact that every fiber in her body wanted her to flee.

"Jaehyuk was caught some years ago on an errand in Hunan," Nicodemus continued. "He barely escaped with his life. I am thankful every day he is by our side."

Jae stared into nothingness, unblinking and unbreathing, as if he had no desire to feign even a semblance of humanity.

"I prize loyalty above most things," the count said, "and Shin Jaehyuk possesses this quality in spades."

Inhaling to quell her nerves, Celine said, "Monsieur le Comte, I'm not certain what—"

"Sébastien is not for you, Miss Rousseau," Jae interjected, his voice no more than a whisper. "Have a care with your heart . . . and your life."

The first cut.

Indignation took shape in Celine's chest. She opened her

mouth to retort when a noise resonated from the darkness at her back. The thud of approaching footsteps. She fought the urge to shudder the instant a pair of willowy figures glided past her.

The two young women with the unforgettable rings. In the starlight, their gems sparked like wildfire, their skin lustrous and dark, their silk skirts immaculate.

Bastien's uncle watched Celine as they passed. "Madeleine de Morny is the most gifted tactician I've encountered in my life, a rival of Napoleon himself. Her younger sister, Hortense, sings like a songbird and dances like the wind." The count leaned on his walking stick, gripping the lion in his palm. "But above all, I prize their candor. Madeleine is honest to a fault, and Hortense incapable of deceit."

Celine gnawed at the inside of her cheek as the two women came to stand at the count's right hand.

Madeleine de Morny stared at Celine without batting an eye. "Bastien est trop dangereux pour la santé," she warned. "Be smarter than this, mademoiselle."

A wicked smile unwound across Hortense's face. "À moins que vous souhaitiez jouer à l'imbecile."

Cuts two and three.

Another gust of wind blew from Jae's back, fanning through his long black hair.

Whistling from the shadows, Boone sauntered toward them, his hands in his pockets, his cherubic curls splayed across his forehead. "Ah, darlin'," he began when he met Celine's gaze. "I was hoping it wouldn't come to this."

"Let me guess," Celine said. "You're here to tell me to stay away from Bastien."

A rueful expression crossed his face. "I would avoid it if I could. I like you, Celine Rousseau. You vex Bastien greatly. Bet you cut your teeth on it." He grinned, then his features soured all at once. "But we just lost Nigel. We can't afford to lose anyone else."

"An excellent point, Monsieur Ravenel. The loss of one among us is indeed an agonizing blow," the count agreed in a soft tone. "As always, I appreciate your support and your wisdom." Again he returned his attention to Celine.

The fourth cut.

Despite her rising irritation, Celine felt herself start to curl inward, the fear threatening to overcome all else. The next instant, she forced herself to rally. To channel the goddess Selene, who lorded over the night sky and all its countless stars. "Monsieur le Comte, I've heard much about you over the past few weeks. It's a pleasure to finally make your acquaintance." Though Celine tried her best not to sound cheeky, she knew she'd failed the moment Boone snorted and Hortense cackled.

"Comme une reine des ténèbres." Hortense repeated her words from that evening at Jacques', amusement coiling across her features. Celine almost laughed at the absurdity. If she was a queen of anything at all, she was Marie Antoinette, on her way to meet the guillotine.

To his credit, the count merely smiled, his amber eyes gleaming. "And a pleasure to make yours, ma chérie."

In an ideal world, Celine should be striving to charm Bastien's uncle. But that chance had vanished like smoke in the wind. After all, only a fool would try to charm a man whose first inclination was to threaten her.

Nicodemus Saint Germain had, without a doubt, succeeded in frightening Celine with this show of bravado. But she had no intention of cowering in his shadow. "I do not wish to be disrespectful, Monsieur le Comte, but you claim to prize candor, so I submit that there's no need to belabor your point." She glanced pointedly at his gathering retinue. "It's clear you don't find me a suitable companion for your nephew. But in fairness, you know very little about me."

"On the contrary, I know a great deal about you, Marceline Béatrice Rousseau."

Again her full name echoed in her ears, the sound carrying high above the soughing treetops. And again her heart raced behind her ribs in response.

Soft laughter fell from the count's lips, as if he could sense her mounting fear. "Until recently, you resided with your scholarly father on the third floor of a small flat in Montmartre." He took another step forward. Celine could not help it when she eased backward in tandem. Her body made the choice before she could reason with it.

Nicodemus continued, "And worked under the tutelage of the famed Camille de Beauharnais." He paused with meaning. "In the uppermost floor of her atelier . . . beneath a lace of shimmering chandeliers."

The thudding of Celine's heart clawed into her throat.

He knows. Her worries invaded her mind. *He knows.*

The two words raced through her brain in time with her pulse. She fought to maintain her composure, her fingers gripping the silver dagger, her nails digging into her palms to the point of pain. "It's clear you've learned much about my past, monsieur. You obviously have great resources at your disposal. But these details do not necessarily inform my present."

Nicodemus' smile was punishing. "I've heard you also enjoy being reckless. Venturing to places you've been forbidden. Lying through your teeth and flouting the rules."

Color flooded Celine's cheeks. "To which rules do you refer?"

"The only ones that matter. *Mine.*" His last word was the point of a knife in her back.

Celine refused to be intimidated, though her knees shook beneath her skirts.

A new emotion crossed the count's face. One she could not recognize. As Nicodemus studied her, a line formed across the marble of his forehead. The next instant, it smoothed, vanishing from sight. "I admire your fearlessness, Celine. More than anything I could learn about your past, I can appreciate why my nephew is so taken with you. Not many young women would dare to hold their own in the company of so many who could kill her without a second thought." He stepped forward again, the end of his walking stick striking the pavers beside his feet with a decisive *thwack.* "Who would kill you at my command, without a moment's hesitation."

The trembling took hold of Celine. She bit down on nothing to prevent it from reaching her teeth. There was nothing for her to say in response. Bastien's uncle had just stated in no uncertain terms that Celine continued to breathe at his leisure. A cheeky retort would serve no purpose here. The only thing she could do was stand firm. Refuse to quail or beg, though her jaw clenched tighter with each passing second, her muscles tensing in preparation to fight or to flee.

After all, Celine Rousseau was not a mewling calf marked for slaughter. She could hold her own, if need be. The boy she'd killed for daring to treat her like a conquered thing was testament to that fact. Her last breath on this earth would not be tinged in regret, of that Celine was certain.

The count glowered into the night as if he could read her thoughts, his posture immovable. A mountain beneath the moon. "I, too, have heard the whispers of how you're not afraid to spill blood. But you must know that I, too, have no qualms about destroying something in my path."

"Why do you persist in threatening me, monsieur?" Celine gripped her skirts, the handle of Bastien's dagger cool in her palm. "What do you hope to accomplish?"

Another flash of that same unreadable emotion. If Celine didn't know better, she would have sworn it to be admiration. "I don't threaten people, ma chérie," Nicodemus said. "I trade in favors. If there is something I can do for you, you have but to ask."

Celine almost laughed. Now he was offering her his good favor? It appeared that Bastien had learned his chameleon ways from his uncle. "I don't want your money, monsieur."

"I would not insult you by offering something as uninspiring as money."

"May I ask what you want in exchange for earning your favor?"

The count did not hesitate. "I want you to reject my nephew. Cast him aside. Better still if it is for someone else."

Celine blinked. "Why do you object to me so?" Her gaze narrowed. "Is it my lack of fortune or family?"

"As I said, I am not so uninspiring. Your lack of fortune is indeed a nuisance, but not of the insurmountable kind, were you suitable in other respects." His words blistered Celine's ears, mortification thrumming through her body. "In truth, I am most concerned by two things: you are far too inquisitive, and you have already become a weakness. I dislike seeing weakness in my nephew. Especially for something as inane as human emotion."

Celine chose her next words with care, aware her cheeks had started to flush. "It is not a weakness to feel, monsieur. I—am not a weakness."

"It *is* a weakness the moment one's feelings override one's judgment. And love of any kind is a weapon to be used against you, when wielded by the right hand."

A part of Celine agreed with him. There were many times in life when she'd fallen prey to her emotions and erred in judgment as a result. Then she recalled the threads of hope she'd clung to during the long Atlantic crossing. "You should want your nephew to find love, my lord. When life becomes difficult, the only source of strength we have is love. Love of others, love of self, love of life in its entirety."

Nicodemus nodded. "And what is love, ma chérie, a choice or a feeling?"

Taken aback, it took a moment for Celine to respond. "It is . . . a feeling." She angled her head upward, biding time while searching for a better answer. As if it had been waiting for this moment, the moon emerged from behind a cloudbank, surrounded by a bevy of stars. Celine stared at the count with determination. "Love is looking at someone as if the stars shine in their eyes."

He nodded again. "A beautiful notion. But you are wrong, ma chérie. Love is not a feeling. It is a choice. Contrary to popular opinion, there are many paths to happiness. I must ask which one you will choose, for the path you are on now will bring you only pain." The count took a final step closer, until he stood just before her. Close enough that she could see the colors swirling in his amber eyes and smell the strange, icy scent emanating from his skin. Like frosted mint. "You do not belong in this world, Celine. It may be beautiful—intoxicating even—but beauty is a danger to behold, for it often masks the decay lurking beneath. Et ça fini toujours dans le sang."

And it always ends in blood.

"I am not so captivated by the beautiful, monsieur." Celine met his gaze without wavering. "For I know beauty is only a moment in time."

"How right you are," Nicodemus murmured. Then he placed his walking stick before him, both hands braced on the golden handle. "Nevertheless I must send along my nephew's regrets. He will be unable to meet you tonight as planned."

"I gathered as much, Monsieur le Comte," Celine said.

"Don't take it to heart, mademoiselle. My one goal in life is to protect my legacy. Do as I ask. Reject Sébastien. Hurt him once now to spare you both a life of pain. If you abide by my wishes, I will grant any favor you ask. And you'll find there are no limits to my reach in all matters." He paused, the line marring his forehead once more. "Defy me, and you'll find your worst fears have become your reality. I will make sure you are left utterly alone, Celine Rousseau. Left to face everything you've run from, with no one to blame but yourself."

His words struck Celine like a blow to the face. As if the count had peered into her very soul and unmasked her greatest fear of all. She flinched when a final gust of wind preceded the last arrival. The one she'd been expecting for quite some time. She'd braced herself for it, knowing this wound would cut her to the quick. But that did not lessen the sting. She felt it keenly, like a string snapping on a harp, the sound reverberating deep in her bones.

Odette did not meet Celine's gaze as she moved into position at Nicodemus' left. Her shoulders were rounded, her features somber. But still she came to stand beside Bastien's uncle, her steps unfaltering.

"I'm sorry, mon amie," Odette said, her sable eyes downturned. "You are my friend. But they . . . are my family."

With this final cut, the count drew an invisible line in the sand.

Celine could trust no member of the Court. It was laughable to think their loyalties could ever be with her. If Nicodemus ordered them to leave her to her fate—to fend for herself, no matter the circumstances—they would do as he asked.

Michael had already refused to use Celine as bait. If Nicodemus prevented Bastien from helping Celine, she would be utterly alone, as the count had promised.

With a killer lurking in her shadow.

Perhaps I'll resort to praying once more. Her thoughts turned grim. *In the premier pew of Saint Louis Cathedral, where all the best sinners take refuge.*

Awareness prickled through her limbs.

Come with me to the heart of Chartres.

Knowledge kindled within Celine, its cool light surging through her veins. She knew where to set her trap. And the devil take her if she would wait for a boy to defy his family before she made plans. She would do as she always did: whatever needed to be done. In Paris, Celine Rousseau had struck down her attacker in his prime, with no one to depend on but herself. She'd traveled half the world to start a new life, with not a single promise on her horizon.

And no one—human or demon alike—would stand in her way now.

I believe tonight will end in blood
and I alone know for whom.

Maybe she will trap me, with her
evil little
Masque, her clever little mind.

It will all be for naught, for she knows not what she does.

Love is proof that blood alone means nothing.

I am thankful my blood is thicker than oil
Et brille plus fort que le soleil (And burns brighter than the sun).

Beautiful Decay

———◦◦◇◦◦———

Celine had lived and breathed French fashion for the better part of five years.

In Paris she'd learned the importance of one's choice in garments. How it spoke for a girl, perhaps before she was able to speak for herself. Clothes opened doors as surely as they closed them. On a practical level, the way a young lady chose to dress indicated not only her station in life, but where she wished to go.

There was an art to dressing. Of all the reasons to love fashion, Celine had fallen in love with this one the most. The idea that she could drape her body in colors to match her soul. How a simple dress could convey her hopes and fears and dreams. How bolts of silk could be molded into armor in the right person's hands.

This was the spirit that had inspired Celine to create the gown she wore now. It was completely unsuitable for the event in question, yet perfect in all other respects. The battle regalia of a lunar goddess. Or perhaps an homage to a queen of darkness.

Celine smiled to herself. Sometimes a girl must make her own magic.

She filled her lungs with the sultry air of a warm evening. The last of the afternoon showers had ended just before the sun sank below the horizon. All the packed streets of New Orleans glimmered like newly polished silver, the air smelling of iron and smoke. Her hem swept over a pool of mirrored water, the black taffeta whispering in her wake.

Just beyond the arch of the main entrance to the Orléans Ballroom, Celine paused midstep. For an instant, she imagined it to be the exact spot the Marquis de Lafayette himself had once stood.

Though it was unlikely he would have arrived to a fête two hours late.

Celine had needed the time. She'd spent most of her waking hours sequestered at police headquarters, finishing her costume. Just yesterday she'd managed to complete Odette's ensemble. She'd even attempted to deliver the garments to Jacques', only to be rebuffed at the door by the same Titian-haired individual who manned the lift at the Dumaine. After confiscating her parcels and rendering payment in full, Ifan had turned Celine and the officers in her company away, a self-satisfied sneer on his face. Consequently, she'd been denied the opportunity to see Bastien or perform a final fitting on Odette. Her first glimpse of the finished costume—a daring hat tip to Madame du Barry—would be tonight when she saw Odette at the ball.

Celine hoped her friend would delight in her surprise as much as she had delighted in creating it.

From dawn until dusk, Celine had poured her efforts into the black taffeta confection she wore now. It had begun as a gown of mourning, the kind readily available in any dress shop. She'd taken it apart and pieced it back together in a nod to the baroque silhouette. Within the gown's skirts, she'd incorporated the first set of wide pannier hoops the carpenter on Rue Bienville had fashioned.

The overall effect wasn't perfect. Perhaps if she'd had more time, Celine would have added more flounces. She might have trimmed the black lace dripping from her pagoda sleeves into something more dramatic. But even in its imperfection, it was *her*, for better or for worse. Reckless, incomplete, and inappropriate.

But here all the same.

Celine rested her right foot on the bottom step, taking a moment to steel her spine.

Bastien's uncle would undoubtedly be present tonight, as would several members of La Cour des Lions. Still, Celine was uncertain if Bastien would be in attendance, so soon after Nigel's death. The masquerade ball at the Orléans Ballroom was to be the soirée of the carnival season. His absence would be noted among those in society. Would this be enough to ensure his presence?

Celine hoped it would.

All the best and brightest of the Crescent City were sure to make an appearance. This year's theme had been announced at the culmination of last year's event. Twelve long months of anticipation for a tribute to the dazzling courts of Louis XV and his son Louis-Auguste, in that glimmer of time just before the

French Revolution. Every invited guest had been instructed to garb themselves in white, from head to toe.

And here Celine stood in nothing but black, from the domino on her face to the tips of her dyed slippers . . . save for the silver dagger concealed beneath her skirts, of course. This should have frightened her. In Paris, it would have been shocking to contemplate such a thing. But Celine was not in Paris anymore. Nor was she the same girl who'd fled the atelier that terrible night, her hands bloodied, her features frantic. That girl was a creature of distant memory. One unsure of her place, her toes lingering on a step leading into the unknown.

Celine mounted the stairs. Tonight she wasn't a girl afraid to face her choices. She was a goddess, baiting a trap to catch a killer.

Her shoulders back, Celine glided beneath the arched doorway. Just beyond the entrance awaited two liveried gentlemen wearing powdered wigs and buckled shoes, their white stockings gartered at the knee, just beneath their tight breeches.

"Password," the one to the left said, his eyes glazed with boredom.

Celine did not waver. "Capetian."

While the other guard opened the heavy doors, the man to the left sent Celine a quizzical look. As if he wished to say something and lacked the right words.

She smiled to herself. That was the truth about proper society. They made all these rules, never planning to apply any consequences to themselves. Never expecting any of their ranks to stray from the established course.

With an imperious tilt to her chin, Celine turned sideways to accommodate her wide-set hoops, then breezed through the doorway into what could possibly be her last night on this earth. It had been her first thought when she'd decided to remake a dress intended for mourning. If this was to be her last evening among the living, she wanted it to be the most glorious night in memory.

She would live one night as Selene, a Titan who dragged darkness with her wherever she went.

The jet beads along her bodice shimmered as Celine swept beneath the domed ceiling of the ballroom, ignoring the looks of surprise and distaste flashing nearby. She marveled at the countless chandeliers reflected in the polished marble at her feet, filling the room with a buttery glow. A makeshift court had been positioned around an ornate throne, festooned in ribbons of purple, green, and gold. In its center stood a bearded gentleman in his early twenties, his white regimentals embellished with braided brass, a smile of smug satisfaction winding across his lips. Celine supposed him to be the fête's honored guest, the Russian Grand Duke, Alexei Alexandrovich. Under normal circumstances, she might have been impressed by his imposing mien. But tonight she was a goddess.

And a goddess did not concern herself with the triflings of men.

All around Celine, couples floated in dazzling circles, whirling in the familiar triple time of a waltz. Their white garments lent them the appearance of pillowy clouds spinning through a golden firmament. The best of New Orleans society had powdered their wigs and faces, the scent sweetly suffocating alongside the towering bouquets of hothouse flowers, all chosen for their angelic hue. Even the servers bustling about with their trays of bubbling champagne had rouged their cheeks and lips, black beauty marks affixed beneath their right eyes.

Celine watched the Crescent City's finest dance in their powdered costumes, feeling their eyes upon her. The whispers behind the ivory fans. The looks of male disdain, along with the occasional wink of sly approval.

None of it mattered. This was a different kind of freedom from the one Celine had longed for on the journey here. A different kind of power. The ability to see through a beautiful veneer and appreciate the decay beneath it.

Now that she'd had a taste of such power, she never wanted to go back to before.

Was the killer lurking among these dancing clouds? If he was, Celine had made certain he would notice her. She was counting on it.

Her gaze snagged on a figure across the way. A young man who'd stopped in his tracks, his gunmetal eyes fastened on hers. He stood above the crowd, his black hair shorn against his scalp like Julius Caesar. The gold filigree trimming his mask contrasted with the dark bronze of his skin. His ivory jacquard waistcoat shone in the warm candlelight, as did the intricate soutache around the gilt buttons of his silk frock coat. He took a step forward and stopped, his satin breeches clinging to the sinew of his body, his head angled with admiration.

Heaven forgive her, but Bastien was beautiful. Dangerously so.

At his back stood a handful of preening young ladies, their papillote curls perfect, their expressions covetous.

But he had eyes for one girl alone.

A low hum resounded in Celine's ears. It heated through her veins, the blood coloring her cheeks. Bastien bowed slowly, one foot in front of the other, his right hand swooping downward in tribute to the period. When he stood once more, Celine could not help but smile.

Bastien returned her smile without hesitation, his eyes like glittering coins, an unspoken promise on his face. Then he melted into the crowd, unconcerned with those around him.

If Alexei Alexandrovich presided over this heavenly court, then Sébastien Saint Germain was the prince of its shadowy counterpart.

With this thought, the last of Celine's fears dissipated. She knew Bastien would help her catch the killer tonight, in defiance of his uncle's wishes. She was certain of it. Lucifer was hers the moment he returned her smile.

Was this love, then?

If it was, Celine wanted to bathe in it. To luxuriate in this feeling of knowing—without being told—that someone saw *her*, amid the beautiful decay. Saw her and stood by her side, against the very world itself.

The next instant, her shoulders tensed. Through a parting in the crowd, Celine caught sight of Pippa's unmistakable profile. Again her petite friend wandered through the ballroom on the arm of Phoebus Devereux, amid the crème de la crème of New Orleans society.

Pippa met Celine's gaze. Then turned away, her expression cold.

Though it stung, Celine was grateful. It was better for Pippa to be angry with her. Anger kept her far from the killer's line of sight.

Odette spun past Celine on the dance floor, laughing as she careened in Boone's arms, her skirted mantle swaying on the ingenious panniers. When they turned, Celine noticed the matching breeches she'd designed as a surprise, the gown of Odette's costume split in its center, revealing her figure as she swirled to the music. Her ruby-encrusted brooch sparkled in the candlelight, pinned in the middle of a gentleman's cravat. A mixture of the masculine and the feminine. A perfect representation of both Odette Valmont and Madame du Barry, the courtesan who helped rule a kingdom.

Again Celine smiled to herself. Even if Odette never said another word to her, Celine knew her friend was grateful.

"Mademoiselle Rousseau," a familiar voice announced behind her right shoulder.

Celine twisted around to meet the amber eyes of a tall masked figure. The black domino across her face shifted, obstructing her vision. She took a moment to straighten it, her pulse thudding through her body.

"Monsieur le Comte," she replied with a curtsy, her nerves tingling in her fingers.

Bastien's uncle held out a white-gloved hand. "May I have this dance?" A knowing smile ghosted across his lips, as if he were the serpent offering Eve the apple. Celine slid her hand in his.

The next moment the world blurred around her, candle flames streaking along the edges of her vision.

Nicodemus danced as if he'd been born to it. To all of it. The wealth, the debauchery, each of the glittering chandeliers. When he reeled them around the first bend—his steps smooth and precise—Celine closed her eyes for the briefest of instants. Wondered what it would be like to put her trust in an other-worldly creature like this.

Her eyes flew open. This world of dark magic might intrigue Celine, but she knew better than to take a bite of its fruit.

"A daring choice," the count commented, noting the way her black skirts rustled around them in time with the music. "I appreciate young women who turn up their noses at society."

"All evidence to the contrary." Fear would not dictate her actions tonight.

"Sébastien must treasure your sharp wit."

"As they say, monsieur," she replied. "One man's treasure . . ."

Another smile rippled across his face, his teeth blindingly white. "Touché, ma chérie. Touché."

They danced in silence for a spell.

"Have you had a chance to consider my offer?" he asked.

"I have," she replied in equally noncommittal fashion.

Something glinted in Nicodemus' golden eyes. "Tell me, Mademoiselle Rousseau, have you ever heard of a game called shatranj?"

Taken aback by the odd question, Celine missed a step. "I'm afraid I have not, Monsieur le Comte."

"It's a Persian game of strategy, not so dissimilar to chess.

Legend has it that it was among the favorites of the famed storyteller Shahrzad."

It troubled Celine to realize he'd stolen the upper hand with such a seemingly innocuous question. "I've played chess before, but I am not proficient. My father always let me win."

"Shatranj is one of the precursors to chess. I'd be pleased to teach you how to play." His grin was sharp. "You may rest assured I will never let you win."

"Merci, Monsieur le Comte. I accept your generous offer . . . and hope to prove you wrong in all respects."

Nicodemus laughed, the sound savoring strangely of fatherly approval. "If you've taken time to consider my offer"—he spun them in place—"what request do you have of me?"

Such arrogance. Such presumption. Celine pretended to hesitate before answering. "After much consideration . . . I think it would be best for me to leave New Orleans." She did not have to be proficient at chess or shatranj to know that gifted players anticipated their opponent's moves and planned accordingly.

The count's grip tightened on her hand. "You would leave the city without a glance back?"

"It's possible I could be persuaded," she demurred. "There was a moment last week in which I wished I could forget everything and simply disappear."

The count considered her for half a turn around the ballroom. "If you mean that in earnest, I could help you."

"I'm certain you would be more than happy to help me disappear, monsieur," she joked.

His expression took on a thoughtful bent. "I meant I could help you forget."

"You could help me . . . forget?"

Nicodemus nodded once. "It is the work of a moment. You would feel nothing, nor would it cause any lasting damage." He spoke as if he were inviting her to a picnic on the lawn of his country estate.

It unnerved Celine beyond words. "And how would you explain this sudden bout of amnesia?"

"I do not keep secrets from my nephew. Sébastien would know it was your choice. As such, he would come to respect it."

The strains of music died down, the bodies spinning around the ballroom slowing to a halt. Her mind in turmoil, Celine laughed with false abandon, joining in the applause as the song came to an end.

Bastien's uncle was a man with the power to steal memories.

The thought alone frightened Celine more than anything he'd said thus far. It forced her to change tack, for if she lied about leaving New Orleans, what would stop him from robbing her mind with a snap of his fingers? Moreover, if she were to "disappear" afterward, not a soul would question her absence, given her decision to quit the city. She would be alone and adrift once more.

No. It would be safer to negotiate a way to remain in New Orleans.

Celine took Nicodemus' proffered arm and strolled with him toward the fringes of the ballroom, taking time to construct a new plan. "Monsieur le Comte, I must apologize. When I said I thought the best thing for me to do was leave the city, I meant it, for it *is* the most rational approach." She paused. "However, as you've already pointed out, my emotions are a weakness. I found that I've come to love New Orleans, and I do not wish to leave." She shuddered as if a wave of fear had passed between her shoulder blades. "But I have no desire to relinquish my memories, nor do I wish to engage in battle with you. So I have an offer . . . if you'll allow me to stay."

The count folded his gloved hands before him, his expression unreadable. "You would not demand Sébastien choose between us?"

"Bastien has already lost most of his family," Celine said. "I would not wish for him to lose you." She bit at her lower lip. "So I will reject him, as you have asked."

Nicodemus said nothing for a time. "And what request do you have of me in exchange for rejecting my nephew?"

"I have three." Celine hoped her greed would convince him of her sincerity. "I would like a finished pied-à-terre in the Quarter. As well as a dress shop nearby for me to earn a living."

"And the third request?"

Celine focused on his amber eyes, fighting to convey a sense of earnestness. "I want to tell Bastien myself, without any of your spies or henchmen nearby."

"Why would you think I would agree to such a sentimental request?"

"Because despite everything, you like me, Monsieur le Comte," Celine replied without flinching. "And you love your nephew. Bastien is *your* weakness. I'd wager it must pain you to cause him grief."

Another unreadable emotion crossed his face, the silence stretching thin for several breaths. "When did you wish to tell Sébastien?"

Here was the most important question he'd asked yet. Celine maintained a flat affect while answering. "I suppose it depends on how soon you wish to see this matter at an end."

"Tonight, then?"

It was just as she'd hoped. "If you wish, Monsieur le Comte."

Nicodemus sent her a wry look. "Love is, indeed, a weakness." He leaned toward her right ear. "And I do like you, Marceline Rousseau. Most especially when you do what I want." The brush of his threat curdled her spine, sending spiders scurrying across her skin.

Celine smiled to mask her fear. "I understand."

"Sébastien will meet you on the terrace in twenty minutes."

Two Sides of the Same Coin

—◇◇◇◇—

The scent of dying flowers wafted past the open doors, weaving toward Celine. It reminded her of the praline vendor who idled on the corner of Rue Bourbon and Rue Toulouse every Saturday, Christmas bells on his wrists and ankles, a homemade pipe dangling from his lips. Beneath the moonlight, the travertine balustrade at her fingertips glowed a pale shade of pink, spidered with veins the color of dried blood. Vines of bougainvillea and peach begonias wrapped around the terrace railing, dew glistening on their downy petals.

From this vantage point, Celine considered her next move.

She'd successfully secured what she most wanted: a moment alone with Bastien. As a result of the count's efforts to keep them apart after Nigel's murder, Celine had yet to share what she'd realized while studying the clues on Michael's slate chalkboard.

Come with me to the heart of Chartres.

At the very least, it was possible she'd learned the location of the killer's lair. What they should do with this information remained to be seen. She'd considered taking it to Michael, but he'd already refused to help her once, and the New Orleans Metropolitan Police had thus far been stymied in all their attempts to catch this otherworldly demon.

Celine didn't know how much time Nicodemus would give them now. Would it be enough to secure Arjun's or Odette's help as well? The prospect seemed unlikely. Bastien might be willing to defy his uncle to catch Nigel's murderer, but it would be foolish of Celine to expect the same of anyone else in the Court, especially given their recent encounter outside police headquarters several nights ago.

No matter. Celine intended to use every second of her borrowed time with Bastien, especially if it meant they might lure the killer into the light.

Several other couples mingled at the edge of the balcony. A trio of young women huddled together, laughing at bawdy jokes. Their levity brightened the tenor of Celine's thoughts. For an instant, she even considered joining them. Especially when she overheard one of their ranks speaking in animated tones about Odette Valmont's costume. How Sébastien Saint Germain's scandalous lover had dared to wear fitted breeches beneath her open mantle, as well as *a gentleman's cravat*.

Mischief gleamed in one girl's brown eyes. "Whom do you suppose wears the trousers in bed?"

"Neither of them, if they're doing it correctly," the young woman next to her replied.

"Zut alors!" the last girl cried with delight.

Despite everything, Celine could not help but laugh. She'd meant it when she'd told Nicodemus she liked it here. New

Orleans was a world of contrasts. A city of life and death. A raw and rich tableau.

It suited her.

She traced her fingers along the stone balustrade, sketching through the thin layer of moisture collecting along its surface. A pair of footsteps came to an abrupt halt over her shoulder, too close to be by chance. She turned at once, her words swallowed by a gasp.

"Pippa." Alarm scalded through Celine's body.

Anger pinched her lovely friend's features. "I came here because I wanted to tell you something."

"Please, you can't be seen with—"

"No," Pippa interrupted. "This time, *you* will be the one to listen."

Celine tugged her deeper into the shadows, glancing about wildly, her features tight. "You don't understand, I—"

"No!" Tears pooled in Pippa's eyes as she wrenched herself free. "I don't want to give you a chance to offer me an explanation. You've . . . *wounded* me. Immensely. I've worried about you every day. A single word or note would have sufficed. But you've cut me out of your life, and I won't pretend to know why." She gesticulated as she spoke, her lace sleeve snagging on the elegant silver frogging across her baroque stomacher. "Oh, bother," she moaned.

"Let me help," Celine said, reaching for the lace.

Pippa moved to stop her. The next instant, her shoulders fell, her sigh one of defeat. "Blast it all," she muttered. "I came outside intent on making an impression, yet here I am in your debt." Her wig of powdered sausage curls slid down her brow, the cross on her golden chain catching on a loose tendril. "And to make matters worse, I look like the Ghost of Christmas Past."

"Don't fret." A smile tugged at Celine's lips. "I'll be sure to heed your warnings, no matter how portentous."

Cutting her gaze, Pippa sighed once more. "I need you to know how angry I am . . . and that it doesn't matter if you ignore me or push me away. I'll always be here, Celine. I love you dearly, and that doesn't change simply because you're behaving like a wretch." She yanked her wig straight, a cloud of powder diffusing about her head.

Celine detangled the last of the snarled lace. "I love you dearly, too, and I'm beyond sorry for behaving like a wretch," she said in a soft voice. "Please know I have my reasons for keeping my distance. One day soon, I'll tell you everything."

"I'll hold you to that promise." Pippa nodded. "But never forget that I am here, if ever you need me."

A lump gathered in the base of Celine's throat. "I won't forget. Ever."

Pippa nodded again, her expression turning morose. "I suppose I should return to the ball. I sent Phoebus for some refreshments, and only a total lummox would get lost on his way to the punch bowl."

"Is Monsieur Devereux such a lummox?" Celine teased in a gentle tone.

"I'm sure I don't know what you mean." Pippa cast her an arched glance. "But if you meet me for tea next Thursday, I'm sure—together—we can divine the truth."

A part of Celine desperately wanted to be the kind of girl who could make plans next Thursday with a dear friend. But she had no idea what the next hour would hold, much less the next few days. It seemed that, no matter where she went in the world, these two warring sides of her were destined to come to an impasse. Two sides of the same coin. For Celine was every bit the girl in a jewel-toned dress who longed for the love and laughter of an afternoon tea. Just as she was every bit the girl in black, her heart filled with murderous designs, intent on bringing about a killer's demise.

Could two such opposing forces ever coexist in the same soul?

"I'd love to have tea with you next Thursday," Celine replied with conviction.

The best she could do was hope. After all, hope was its own kind of magic.

—◇—

The sky darkened to a deep purple as the minutes passed. Celine waited at the edge of the balcony, staring up at the stars. She didn't know when she'd first realized how much the sight of the moon soothed her. Perhaps it had something to do with her mother.

In the far reaches of her mind, Celine recalled walking along a rocky shore as a child, hand in hand with a lithe figure whose black hair fell past her waist in thick waves. In this memory, her mother sang to a full moon, the melody carrying over the inky water, unfurling into the vast sky above.

Perhaps it was a dream. Nothing more.

A branch snapped in the treetops to Celine's left, drawing her from her thoughts with a sudden jolt. Molten energy coursed through her veins, her skin growing hot like embers stoked to flame. Celine's eyes flitted in all directions, fear making her aware of every breath. Every scuttle. Every sigh. She focused on the grove of looming oaks, her heart careening in her chest.

A lone owl burst from the shadows, its wings beating in time with her breath.

She almost laughed. Her fingers trembled as they moved to the bare skin of her throat in an effort to soothe her raging nerves.

The next instant, silence fell around her like a hammer on an anvil. The birds stopped stirring in the treetops, the cicadas ceased with their droning. A dull roar echoed in Celine's ears when she twisted toward the open double doors at her back, intent on making her way inside.

Before she could take a single step, the suddenly mute individuals along the balcony crowded her path. They turned to leave in concert, their expressions blank, their footsteps rote. The trio of girls from earlier linked hands, their eyes glassy as they filed toward the double doors, the last of their ranks pausing to latch them shut behind her, the locks falling into place with an ominous click.

Was this Nicodemus' doing?

Panic thrummed through Celine's body. What kind of dark magic was this?

Had Nicodemus lied to her? Was he toying with her? Had he

made false promises of his own, all along intending to rid himself of Celine at the first opportunity?

Suddenly each of her memories became that much more precious. She thought about hitching up her skirts and fleeing. Considered racing toward the latched doors and pounding on their oaken surfaces, bellowing for help.

How badly would she injure herself if she were to jump over the balustrade?

Celine had planned to lure the killer to the location of his first murder. To hem him in along the docks, taking advantage of the open spaces and the stretch of water at their backs, thereby thwarting his attempts to escape. And if that didn't work, she was determined to root him out of his hiding place in the heart of Chartres.

He was not meant to trap *her*.

Was Nicodemus the killer? Had Celine quite literally waltzed into his clutches?

Her chest rose and fell in rapid succession, the whalebone of her stays laced tight. The only recourse Celine had was that if she screamed loud enough, someone inside was sure to hear her.

But would they reach her in time?

Celine planted her feet, rooting her convictions. If this was to be her one chance, she would take it. Her fingers moved toward the hidden pocket at her hip, pausing a hairsbreadth from the handle of Bastien's silver dagger.

A murder of crows burst from the branches to her right. She spun around, watching them soar into the moon, wishing with all her might that she could sprout wings of her own and take flight.

Just then, Celine noticed a strange set of markings along the edge of the balustrade. Her feet carried her closer before she had a chance to think.

Four symbols had been inked into the travertine stone, their edges dried to match its veins, their centers a wet, brilliant crimson:

$$LOYD$$

L, O, U . . . P?

A strangled sound emitted from Celine's throat. She backed away, colliding with a wall of stone. Shock took hold of her when a pair of long arms reached around her waist, gloved hands running up her rib cage.

"Mon amour," he rasped behind her ear, his cool breath washing across her nape. "You are mine forever."

Celine opened her mouth to scream. Something sharp tore into the side of her neck, and she was consumed in a dark void.

A Pound of Flesh

———◦◦◇◇◇◦◦———

Something was horribly wrong.

Bastien had known it the instant his uncle had come to him, a warm smile on his face and an unsettling light in his gaze. The moment Nicodemus had offered Bastien a chance to speak with Celine on the terrace in private.

No member of the undead granted such a boon without first exacting an excruciating price. Especially a theatrical immortal like Nicodemus Saint Germain. Once, years ago, Bastien had witnessed his uncle take an actual pound of flesh from an enemy, peeling the man's skin back slowly, relishing each of his screams. Bastien had been a boy of nine then. And in fairness, the enemy in question *had* killed his father.

Unease gathered in the base of Bastien's throat. His uncle's sudden change of heart was sure to be an ill omen. Nevertheless, he murmured his thanks and crossed the ballroom, pausing only to nod at those who vied for his attention. To beg their leave, with promises to return in a trice.

All Bastien could think was reaching Celine. Of reassuring her that his uncle's wishes had no bearing on his heart.

Not that she needed any man's reassurances.

An appreciative smile curved up one side of Bastien's face when he thought of how she'd burst into the ballroom two hours late, garbed in a gown of mourning, a devil-may-care attitude in each of her steps. It was one of the things he loved most about Celine. How little she gave a damn about anyone's good opinion.

Bastien paused before the solid oak double doors leading onto the terrace, puzzled to find them locked from the inside. Tension banding in his arms, he unlatched the doors to step onto the balcony . . . and was met with a sight that iced the marrow in his bones.

No one was there. Not a single soul lingered beneath the violet sky, taking in the night air.

Celine Rousseau was nowhere to be found.

His teeth clenched and his jaw rippling, Bastien glided toward the empty railing, his eyes scanning every which way. He did not possess any of his uncle's preternatural gifts. He could not see through the darkness unimpeded, nor could he smell the scent of blood from a vast distance. And he most definitely could not blur through time and space in the blink of an eye.

But Bastien had learned as a boy to notice things most mortals would overlook. Like the smear of blood along the ledge, the color camouflaged in the veined travertine. And the four smudged symbols nearby, written in macabre ink, smelling of copper and salt.

There had been a struggle. And it appeared the killer had taken Celine from the balcony.

Rage spread through Bastien's veins. The rime of unmitigated rage. Always ice. Never fire.

Bastien ripped the ridiculous mask from his face. Without a glance back, he returned to the double doors, stopping at the threshold, his mind in a calculated turmoil.

First he looked for his uncle. Studied the crowd for the tall figure dressed in a long white opera cape. Thankfully Nicodemus no longer appeared to be mingling among the Crescent City's unofficial gentry. It was likely he'd joined some of New Orleans' most influential gentlemen in a nearby antechamber to partake in a glass of cognac, a cigar, and a well of secrets. One of the Vieux Carré's most cherished rituals.

Which meant Bastien had less than half an hour before his uncle noticed his absence.

Without pausing to think, Bastien slid among the couples weaving across the ballroom floor, stealing Odette from her partner before the foolish young man could form a protest.

She did not miss a step. Nor did her smile falter at any moment, despite the fact that a single glance at Bastien's face told her something was terribly amiss.

Odette Valmont represented the best of Bastien's found family. She, Nigel, Hortense, Madeleine, Jae, and Boone had surrounded him not long after he'd arrived on the city's docks almost a decade ago, an angry boy filled with loss and pain, whose haunted features had granted him the moniker Le Fantôme.

This strange collection of immortals had been tasked with only one thing: guarding Nicodemus' lone surviving heir. Protecting their maker's greatest legacy. For nearly ten years, they'd stood at Bastien's back, helping him blaze a trail through the city, all while keeping him safe from the terrors that had torn him from his parents and his sister.

"Take a turn with me on the balcony," Bastien said to Odette through a winsome smile, his words more breath than sound. With that, they reeled through the crowd—scattering the couples lingering on the periphery—before spinning through the double doors and into the velvet darkness.

As soon as they were beyond earshot, Bastien stopped moving, his arms dropping to his sides. "Celine is gone," he said quietly, aware that anyone—or anything—could be listening.

Odette's sable eyes flashed black, her features sharpening, her canines lengthening past her rouged lips. Piercing the elegant veil and bringing the world's most perfect predator to the surface. She paused to fill her lungs with air. "I can smell her blood. She was here not five minutes ago."

"How can you be certain it's hers?"

She sniffed once more, her powdered head cocking to one side. "Her blood sings an unusual melody."

Bastien's eyes narrowed, his lips pursing. "Have you ever looked in her future?"

"Only that one time." Odette hesitated. "But it showed me nothing about this, Bastien. It simply told me what I shared with you weeks ago. A truth that has already come to pass. She will be the tamer of—"

"I remember." The fury had reached Bastien's fingertips, his fists clenching and unclenching at his sides. It took all his control not to break something with his bare hands. He knew better. The greater the anger, the more destructive its force. It would be of no help if he lost his head to it. "Can you track her scent?"

Odette's eyes returned to their normal shade, her nostrils no longer flaring like those of a jackal. "I'm not sure. The rain makes it difficult for me to track things by scent. Have you asked the Hellhound for help? He's our best hunter."

"You know as well as I do that Boone won't lift a finger in defiance of Nicodemus," Bastien replied, ire sharpening his tone. "He's too afraid."

"Our little hound has always been a lamb at heart," Odette rejoined softly. "He took Nigel's death the hardest. Tonight was the first time he's come home in days."

Bastien glared at nothing, a twinge piercing through his chest. Time had become such a treasured commodity to them all. "Can you give me an hour?"

Alarm flared across her lovely face. "Your uncle forbade—"

"I don't give a damn what Nicodemus said," Bastien all but snarled.

She reached for his hand, her gloved fingers cool to the touch. "Every member of La Cour des Lions is under express orders to prevent you from going anywhere that involves Celine Rousseau. Please," she entreated, "Nigel *died* because we all failed to take this threat seriously. If something happens to you, I don't know what we'll all do."

"I'm not the boy you met years ago."

"I know, my dearest," she said. "Only Jae is a quicker draw

394

than you, and we've all seen you shoot a man through the eye at sixty paces. But the killer is trying to force us out into the open. Pick us off, one by one," she continued, her eyes swimming, her tears turning pink. "The devil only knows why. This was supposed to have ended years ago."

"Odette." Bastien gripped her by the shoulders, willing his expression calm. "You're the only one I can trust. I know you care for Celine deeply. If we don't help her, she could die." His insides twisted at the thought, the words burning in his throat. "I cannot allow that to happen. You've spent years obeying your maker. Tonight, will you not help your friend?"

Odette studied him, her lips pressed in a line, a single stream of blood-tinged tears sliding down one cheek. "I can't stop them from looking for you, Bastien."

"Can you at least give me an hour?"

She wavered, fighting to maintain her composure. "I'll . . . try my best. But the Hellhound *will* find you, Bastien, as he always does. And we will all face the consequences."

"Thank you, Odette." He kissed her forehead.

Then he vaulted the balustrade and vanished into the darkness.

———◇———

Bastien kicked through the door of Michael's office at police headquarters without pausing for breath. He'd fully expected to find his childhood friend looming over his desk. Just as he'd fully anticipated an altercation the moment he demanded that the detective share all his notes on the killer. Who he might be.

What he might be. And—most importantly—where he might be.

The only sign of life Bastien found was a single lamp, its lone flame dancing cheerfully in a clear cylinder of glass.

Fury blinded him for an instant, his hands longing to shatter the lamp into a thousand pieces. In an effort to allay his rage, Bastien scanned the cramped space for anything that might help him find Celine. To one side was a cot, blankets folded atop it in a neat little pile, a basket of sewing supplies beside it.

His anger threatened to slide into despair.

Many of the things he'd treasured had been taken from him all too soon. These losses had taught him to hold fast to his heart, save for two exceptions: the love he had for his immortal family, and the love he had for his city. He'd refused to make room for anything else. Then a month ago, a seed had been planted in his mind, watered by the hand of Fate. By a wry smile and a fall of raven hair. By a girl who met him word for word, challenge for challenge.

Something unraveled in Bastien's chest.

It appeared there was now a third exception.

He should have told Celine she'd captured his heart, instead of allowing ridiculous social mores and expectations to stand in their way. If anything happened to her, the devil himself would answer for it. Bastien would take no mere pound of flesh.

Before he was finished, he would see the demon's tears turn to ash.

His lips pushed forward in calculation, Bastien paused on the large slate board running parallel to Michael's desk. He studied the collection of clues the detective had amassed, including the many insidious things the killer had said to Celine on multiple occasions:

Welcome to the Battle of Carthage.

You are mine.

Death leads to another garden.

To thine own self, be true.

Die in my arms.

A muscle ticked in Bastien's neck. He perused the old map affixed to a corner of the slate, his gaze catching on something he'd missed before.

Then Bastien straightened, his eyes going wide.

Michael's notes were incomplete. The killer had said a peculiar thing to Celine the night he had stalked her through the streets of the Vieux Carré. Bastien's attention had been drawn by its absence on the otherwise meticulous board.

Come with me to the heart of Chartres.

Chartres was a city south of Paris, famed for the beautiful cathedral at its heart.

Rue de Chartres ran through the center of New Orleans, in the very middle of Michael's map. At the street's heart stood the three spires of Saint Louis Cathedral.

Had the demon been arrogant enough to lead them straight to his safe haven? To be sure, the church was an unusual place for a killer to find refuge. But it was also the exact kind of detail that would delight most of the immortals in Bastien's acquaintance. To seek sanctuary in a house of God.

"What in God's name are you doing here?" a harsh voice demanded from behind him.

Bastien turned to meet the wily figure of his former friend. "I beg your pardon, Detective Grimaldi." He kept his tone light, despite a surge of anger. "I'll take my leave."

"Like hell you will. You broke my door, you no-account fiend. You and your godforsaken temper. Will you ever learn?" Michael cut his colorless gaze. "What brought you to my office at this hour, peacocking about like a shitty king of France?"

"I had a momentary lapse in judgment," Bastien said in a blithe voice, crossing in front of Michael while he spoke, intent on making a swift exit. "Which has since been rectified."

The young detective grabbed him by the front of his ivory waistcoat. "Balderdash. Answer my damned question. Why are you here?"

Bastien fought to keep his fury in check. He could not strike down the detective. He *would not* strike Michael down. Generations of bad blood forbade it. "I don't have time for this pissing contest." Gripping Michael's wrists, he twisted the detective's hands free of his absurd costume. "Send a bill to Jacques' for the damage." His grin turned arrogant. "Be sure to sample the vichyssoise the next time you're there. You always did favor life's simpler pleasures." Again he tried to leave.

"Did something happen to Celine?" Michael stepped in Bastien's path, his nostrils flaring like he'd scented chum in the water.

Her name on his lips rekindled Bastien's rage. If he told Michael the truth, there would be no way to contain the matter. The fool would order an entire garrison to descend on the cathedral, and precious time would be lost navigating his righteous idiocy.

"I have no idea where Celine Rousseau might be. Wasn't that supposed to be your purview now?" Bastien sneered, attempting to push past his childhood friend once more. The clock in Michael's office ticked away the minutes. At any moment, Boone would find Bastien, his uncle trailing in the Hellhound's well-heeled footsteps. And those moments were precious to Celine. Just as she had become precious to Bastien.

More precious than life itself.

Michael shoved him back, his features mottled. "Answer me, Sébastien. Before I call for the—"

Bastien lashed out at Michael. Something he'd promised never to do, many years ago. To strike the young detective was in direct defiance of his uncle's edicts. For a Saint Germain to strike a Grimaldi . . .

His blow broke the bridge of Michael's nose, blood spurting from beneath it. A howl of rage flew from the detective's lips, causing footsteps to race toward them from below.

"Take heed, Michael," Bastien said through clenched teeth. "Never stand in my way again." With that, he glided from the office, the beat of his heart thundering in his chest.

There was nothing to be had for it.

Sébastien Saint Germain had just violated the Brotherhood's treaty.

THE FINAL NAIL

——✦◇✦——

Celine woke on her side, her cheek resting against cold stone.

A cloying scent wound through her nose, her temples thudding with the slow beat of her heart. For a time, she struggled to focus on anything, her vision swimming as if she'd consumed too much champagne. Licking her parched lips, Celine tried to lift her head.

A cry of surprise flew from her mouth. Searing pain shot down her right arm, warm wetness trickling along her collarbone, dripping down her black bodice. The wound on her neck was still fresh, which meant not much time had passed since she'd been attacked on the terrace. The sharp scent of blood permeated the air, mingling with the perfume of . . . incense?

Again Celine attempted to shift position, but she was weak. So very weak.

At least the killer had left her alive. She supposed she should be grateful. For a harrowing instant, she'd been certain her last breath on this earth would be on that balcony.

Gritting her teeth through the pain, Celine fought to sit up, only to fail once more. Her hands were bound at her back, her feet tied at the ankles, the ropes like leaden weights. With her elbow, she checked to see if Bastien's silver blade was still concealed in the hidden pocket beneath her skirts. When Celine felt its comforting weight against her right hip, she let her head fall onto the smooth stone, wearied by even the simplest action.

Her eyes locked on the frescoed ceiling above as she counted to three in her mind. Then Celine heaved her knees to her chest, her taffeta skirts rustling through the silence, her brow beading with sweat. With herculean effort, she looped her wrists over her feet, snapping several of the wooden hoops at her sides and twisting her left arm in the process. She gasped—blinking away hot tears of pain—before taking in her surroundings.

To her left stretched a familiar floor of black-and-white stone, patterned at a diagonal. An aisle lit by long tapers ran down its center, bracketed by wooden pews.

Celine coughed, bitter amusement coiling through her stomach. Her earlier assumption had been correct. She was lying on the altar of Saint Louis Cathedral, at the very heart of Rue de Chartres. If she weren't so afraid, she would mock her attacker for his theatricality. Coughing again, she rolled to one side and fell from the stone surface, her teeth clacking together as her body hit the granite floor with a resounding thud. Shards of pain stabbed along her right side, a thousand tiny needles burrowing into her skin.

Celine bit her lower lip to keep from screaming.

There was no time for her to succumb to pain. She needed to

free her feet from their bonds so that she might at least attempt an escape. Celine sat up, drops of bright blood plinking against the cool stone. Then she tucked her knees beneath her chin and reached under the hem of her skirts to fiddle with the knots around her ankles.

"I admire your resilience, Celine," a warm voice pronounced from the shadows at her back, its accent refined. Distinct of the British upper class. "But you've lost a lot of blood. I don't believe you'll get very far."

Fear knifed through Celine, a ghostly chill racing down her spine. But she'd already made a promise to herself. Fear would not dictate her actions tonight. "Who are you?" Her voice was hoarse but firm. "Why have you brought me here?"

Footsteps circled closer, the killer's heels striking the stone floor with tantalizing slowness. "I'm somewhat put out that you haven't realized who I am, being so damnably smart and all," he continued, his tone mocking. "But in fairness, me love . . . I did sound a bit different before, I did." He eased into a vibrant Cockney accent. The accent of London's working class.

Its tenor caused Celine to tremble. Despite her bleeding wound, she turned her head to one side, disbelief splintering her thoughts.

Nigel?

"But you were dead," Celine whispered when Nigel strolled into view, looking hale and hearty and whole, the smell of earth suffusing the air about him. Shock began settling into Celine's limbs, causing her shoulders to shake. "I saw you. Your arm.

Your *head*." She gasped, realization cinching the breath from her body. "It was . . . *you*."

Evil did not look the way she'd imagined it would. Nigel wasn't the bloodthirsty villain of her nightmares. He was Arjun's good-natured friend. Odette's silly sweet boy. One of Bastien's closest confidants.

Nigel clapped twice with slow deliberation, his grey cloak falling away from his arms, revealing a rumpled waistcoat and stained shirtsleeves. "You saw what we wanted you to see, love."

"We?"

He ignored her question, switching back to the polished accent of Grosvenor Square. "You've proved to be quite the little detective." He changed his tone once more, as if he were donning or doffing a hat. "So smart. So bleedin' sharp, especially for a bird." His Cockney resonated into the rafters.

Dear God, he sounded mad. But Celine didn't sense any madness about him. His cheeks were pink, his eyes clear, his lips full. No, it wasn't madness.

It was pride.

Pride at playing to a crowd, like a revered actor on a stage. If Celine had to guess, Nigel was relishing the success of his deception, as if it offered testament to his greatness.

Determination etched across her brow. If pride was his downfall, Celine would distract him further by encouraging him to talk about himself. She'd done the same thing to the young man who'd attacked her that night in the atelier.

Never mind that it had very nearly failed.

"Please tell me why," Celine whispered, her expression

pleading. "I don't understand why you would do such a thing." While she spoke, her fingers worked at the knots beneath her skirts, willing herself to remain calm.

"Ever the brilliant little detective, aren't we?" Nigel said in the Queen's English. He moved closer to the trio of rounded steps leading up to the altar, pausing to rest his right foot on the dark granite base. "By the by, did you ever manage to uncover the meaning behind the symbols I left for you?"

"No," Celine lied, shrinking away from him, her back pressed against the altar's base, the bonds beginning to loosen above her feet.

"No matter," Nigel continued, a casual air about him. "Impressive how quickly you determined they might be from an ancient language." He braced an elbow on his bent knee. "You were only off by a few hundred years."

"The language predates ancient Greek?" Celine guessed.

"A totally different civilization." He switched to Cockney. "Even gave you a hint, I did."

Celine's shoulders slumped. "Carthage."

"Correct." He smiled, switching back. "As to why I did this . . . there are any number of reasons. Why does anyone betray their loved ones?" He straightened, his expression somber. "For power, perhaps. That's something to which the Medicis, the Borgias, the Tudors, the Ptolemies—any number of influential families throughout history—could attest." He paused. "Or perhaps it's because I never really loved them in the first place.

"Do you know why the Court of the Lions exists?" Nigel continued, his eyes shining with an otherworldly light. "Do you know why Nicodemus ripped me from my home in London's East End and turned me into a demon, cursed to share his fate?" Anger rippled across his face. "To obey my maker until the end of time?"

Celine shook her head, her first finger catching on a loop in her bonds, prying it free.

A muscle worked beneath the skin of Nigel's forehead. "The Court of the Lions exists for the sole purpose of protecting Nicodemus Saint Germain's legacy." He snorted. "Sébastien, the last scion of the Saint Germain family. I've guarded a mortal boy for nearly a decade. From the moment he sulked in a roomful of books to the moment he crowned himself prince of our dark court, I've been forced to do his bidding." Bitter laughter flew from his lips. "I—an *immortal being* with powers beyond your wildest ken—was yoked to a cursed breather, like a bloody watchdog." Distaste tugged at his lips. "It's no wonder the Brotherhood despises us so."

The loop loosened infinitesimally more, Celine's fingers chafing from the effort. "Why does Bastien need to be guarded?" If she could buy herself but another minute . . .

"Surely it hasn't escaped your notice that every other member of Bastien's family is dead. Do you think that's by accident or by design?"

A retort threatened to barrel from Celine's mouth. She bit her tongue, tasting the salt of her blood. She could not succumb to anger, just as she would not be consumed by fear. "It must be by design," Celine replied.

Nigel brushed a thin layer of dirt from his shoulders and

adjusted his shirtsleeves as if he were preparing for something. A knot of unease formed in Celine's stomach. "Bastien is the last piece of a retribution centuries in the making. And I—Nigel Fitzroy—will be the one to put the final nail in this coffin. The first of my kind to bridge the divide between the Fallen and the Brotherhood." He inhaled through his nose and spread his arms wide. Then he shouted once, as if in triumph, a fierce, guttural cry.

It sounded like the roar of a beast. Like the howl of a barely leashed creature relishing the spoils of his hunt. Its echo shook the very ground beneath Celine.

No. Evil did not look the way she'd imagined it would.

It looked far worse. It was hate wrapped in the guise of a friend.

Celine fought back a tide of anguish, despondency settling around her, its shadow closing in.

Before it could take root, she lurched to her feet and began to run. Her teeth chattering in her skull, she grabbed hold of the first pew, using it to propel her down the aisle toward the doors, expecting Nigel to stop her at any moment. Her bound hands itched to retrieve the dagger at her side. Itched to defend herself. To drive the silver deep into the place his heart used to be.

But once she unsheathed the blade, she would have only a single chance to use it.

Now was not that time.

Soft laughter trailed behind Celine, its echo searing through her soul. She could not stop to question why Nigel wasn't chasing her. There was no time to idle in curiosity. Choking back the rising bile, Celine continued racing down the aisle, her body taxed by every footstep.

Why was she so goddamned weak?

The doors to the cathedral stood sentinel less than ten paces away. All that mattered now was escape.

A rush of air gusted past Celine, her sight blurring from the breeze. She blinked, a cry of astonishment escaping her lips.

Nigel was standing before the cathedral doors. Only a second before, he'd been at the opposite end of the church.

Her senses dazed, Celine stumbled to a halt, grasping a pew to steady herself. "How?" She despised the way her voice trembled. *"What are you?"*

A beat passed in awful silence. Then a slow smile spread across his face. "I thought you'd never ask." His words were lethal in their calm.

Nigel began to change. His eyes darkened to black, the color spreading like a drop of ink through water. His features sharpened, the tips of his ears tapering to points.

Celine gripped the pew in her hands, swallowing her cries. Nigel's teeth had begun to lengthen, his canines resembling those of a wolf, gleaming like daggers in the low light of the tapers.

Panic gripped Celine's stomach. Acid collected on her tongue, its sharpness washing down her throat. She took a step backward, her heart hurling against her chest, demanding to be set free.

Then Nigel blurred toward her. One moment he was ten

paces away. The next he loomed a hairsbreadth before Celine, as if he'd manipulated the air around him, like a ghost or a spirit or a demon of the night.

Celine clasped her bound hands before her, as if she were in prayer. She leaned against the pew, struggling to hold herself upright. Hoping her perceived weakness would grant her an opportunity to draw the dagger from its sheath at her hip.

"Ask me again what I am." The scruff on Nigel's chin gleamed like molten copper, his eyes chips of obsidian.

Celine could not respond. Nor could she look away.

With a soft laugh, Nigel grabbed her wrists in an iron vise, pulling her against his chest. Then he leaned forward and licked the wound on her neck. Celine choked back a scream. When he tilted his head to the cathedral's rafters—to the brilliant frescoes of angels overcoming their demon brethren—his tongue was stained crimson with her blood. A sound of supreme satisfaction rose from his throat.

As if he found her blood delicious. As if he relished in meals of human blood.

Vampire.

A brutal shriek burst from Celine's lips. She tried to free her hands from her bonds so that she might grab the dagger at her hip, but Nigel laughed at her once more, reveling in her struggle. Toying with her as if she were nothing but a plaything.

"That's enough, Nigel."

The vicious admonition came from Celine's back. To the right side of the altar.

An air of triumph filled the space when Nigel glanced over her shoulder. He whipped Celine around, his skin vibrating with anticipation.

As if this had been his plan all along.

Bastien walked down the aisle toward them, his revolver trained on Nigel, his expression hewn from ice.

Nigel wrapped an arm about her waist, pulling Celine toward him, as if she were both a possession and a shield. Amusement tinged his voice. "The reckless Romeo has finally come to rescue his foolish Juliet. Tell me, Lord Lion, does our keeper know you're here?" His black eyes narrowed to slits. "What will Nicodemus say when he realizes you've risked his legacy for the life of a mortal girl?"

Bastien ignored him. "He won't harm you again, Celine," he said, his tone even, his words soft. "Not if he wishes to see another moon."

Nigel's arm tightened around her waist, drawing her back against the cool marble of his chest. "Don't lie to your love, Sébastien," he said. "For I haven't had my fill, and her blood tastes sweeter than sun-warmed honey."

The beat of her heart thudding in her ears, Celine nodded to Bastien, her bound hands inching toward her pocket.

With a subtle shake of his head, Bastien took a step forward, his thumb cocking the hammer of his revolver. "Your quarrel isn't with her. Let Celine go, and I'll do whatever you want."

"Perhaps all I want is to drain her dry before your eyes. To watch you live the rest of your short, godforsaken life as the Ghost."

The tips of Celine's fingers grazed the edge of her pocket, her breaths quickening in her throat.

Bastien's lips pursed together, something flashing in the depths of his eyes. "Don't waste a winning hand on such foolishness. No one goes to all this trouble for something so small and petty. I know we can make a deal." His smile was cold. Unforgiving. "Name your terms."

"You are in no position to make demands. Put down your gun, Bastien," Nigel said. "And perhaps I'll agree to deal in good faith."

"Fuck your good faith." Bastien's smile widened. "Let her go. Now." He took another step forward.

"Aim true." Nigel's icy fingers wrapped around Celine's neck, sending a shiver between her shoulder blades. "You may succeed in wounding me, but not before I rip the veins from her throat."

Celine's fingers closed around the handle of the silver dagger.

Before any of them could make another move, Nigel lifted Celine off her feet as if she weighed no more than a feather. Then he sank his teeth into her neck. Terror raked its sharp claws across Celine, the pain almost blinding her as she struggled to wrench his auburn hair from his scalp, her fingers flailing against a wall of stone.

"Enough!" Bastien commanded. For the first time, Celine sensed fear in his voice. "Let her go, and I'll put down my revolver."

Nigel licked his lips before he replied. "Drop it first."

Bastien said nothing. He disengaged the bolt on his revolver, though he did not lower it.

"Do it now, or I'll finish her off," Nigel taunted. "It won't take much. She has so little left to give. Her heart slows with each passing moment."

"Bastien," Celine whispered, letting her posture cave in on itself, hoping Nigel would mistake the gesture for helplessness. The same kind of helplessness her attacker had expected that night in the atelier.

But Celine Rousseau was not helpless. While there was still breath left in her body, she intended to fight. Nigel would not escape this church unscathed. She swore it to the heavens.

Trembling uncontrollably, Celine eyed Bastien sidelong, her fingers brushing across her right hip. "Bastien, please," she repeated, as if she were begging him to save her.

Though Bastien winced, he nodded once. Letting her know he understood her unspoken directive.

"It appears we are at an impasse, Sébastien," Nigel said. "What do you propose we do now? Fight to the death like civilized monsters?" He caught a trickle of blood dripping from Celine's neck and brought it to his mouth. "Some of us are better monsters."

"Some of us are better men." Bastien's fingers tightened around his revolver. Then he pointed its barrel toward the floor.

Nigel began lowering Celine to her feet. Dropping his guard. She waited for the instant her toes found purchase. Prepared herself to stab him in the throat, just as she'd been instructed to do the night Bastien gave her the dagger. All the while, Celine continued trembling, as if fear had found refuge in her bones. As if she were the pathetic little lamb Nigel had expected all along.

She was no lamb. She was a lion.

Bastien set down his revolver. Unfolded to standing as Nigel released Celine.

The next instant, the vampire blurred toward Bastien in a frenzy, his fangs tearing into Bastien's throat.

Celine hurled herself at Nigel's back, the dagger in her hand. Her fury past the point of reason, Celine stabbed Nigel at the base of his head and the side of his neck, over and over again, a snarl on her lips.

With an inhuman roar, the vampire whipped around, dark blood spurting from his wounds. He flung Celine through the air, her shoulders slamming into the edge of the pews, knocking the wind from her lungs and cracking something in her ribs.

Nigel staggered, the silver blade embedded in the side of his throat. Rage contorting his face, he stalked toward Celine, blood gushing down his body, his hands outstretched.

A breeze raced through the nave, the sound of beating wings trailing in its shadow. Then something grabbed Nigel, snatching him from sight, the shrieks of a wounded beast fading into the darkness.

Her body all but broken, Celine struggled to her feet, seeking a point of clarity beyond the pain. A sharp sensation radiated through her chest, her vision swimming as she looked forward. Bastien leaned against a wide column of marble, one hand pressed beneath his ear, a strange expression in his eyes.

He stumbled to his knees.

Then Celine saw the cascade of crimson dripping from his neck.

"Bastien." She rushed toward him, catching him before he struck the stone floor. Crouching by his side, Celine pressed her bound hands atop his, trying to stanch the gaping wound at his throat. Blood oozed from between their fingertips, flowing fast and hot, like a river bursting through fissures in a dam.

Several brushes of air gathered on all sides of them. Celine did not have to look to know who was there. The rest of the Court had arrived, not a moment too soon.

Bastien opened his mouth, the light in his gaze fierce. He tried to speak, but a trail of blood streamed from his mouth.

"Don't talk." Celine held him close. "You're going to be fine. Nicodemus will be here soon. Hold on to your strength." She placed pressure on his wound until the tips of her fingers turned white, but Bastien's blood only flowed faster, its warmth soaking through to her skin.

A small smile curved his lips. With his other hand, he gripped her fingers tightly.

In his eyes, Celine saw a sky filled with stars.

She saw a boy who would die for her, just as she would kill for him.

"You're going to be fine," Celine repeated, her words tremulous, tears trickling from the tip of her nose. "It won't end like this. I know it won't. I haven't even told you I'm falling in love with you." Someone was weeping softly behind them. "Damn it, don't cry," she yelled over her shoulder. "There's nothing to cry about. He's going to be fine. We are all going to leave here together. And I will love Bastien until the last star falls from the sky." Her voice broke. "Where is Nicodemus?" Celine shouted, her words resonating with imperiousness. "Find him at once."

The goddess within her smiled a sad smile.

And Bastien's eyes fell shut, his hand coming to rest on the floor beside Celine's feet.

Many Paths to Happiness

———◦◇◦———

Nicodemus Saint Germain stood over the dying body of his nephew.

The last surviving member of his line. The sole reason for his existence. Everything he'd striven for his entire mortal life—his *legacy*—was draining onto a church floor before his very eyes.

Fitting. For he'd destroyed hundreds of lives over the centuries. So many deaths. So much loss.

There would always be a reckoning. Time had taught Nicodemus that inescapable truth.

"Please," Celine begged, tears streaming down her cheeks as she clutched his nephew's head to her chest, blood pooling in a widening circle around them. "Save him."

The weight on Nicodemus' soul had already begun to settle. "No," he said simply. Brokenly. It had been the same after he'd lost Bastien's sister, Émilie. After their parents had paid for Nicodemus' greatest mistake.

"I refuse to accept that," Celine shouted. "Do something. Don't let him die."

To his right and left, Nicodemus felt his immortal children stirring. Boone openly wept. Farther away, Jae stared at a point of nothingness, his features wan, his fingers stained by the evidence of Nigel's final reckoning. A cloud of anger surrounded Hortense, Madeleine swiping a lone tear from beneath her sister's chin. Along the periphery, Odette inched forward as if to subvert his orders, her sable eyes wide. "Stop," Nicodemus commanded. They all straightened like soldiers. "I will not be defied in my wishes. Sébastien was always meant to live and die as a mortal. Nothing is worth the price of this curse," he said, his tone firm. "I swore to myself I would never turn a member of my human family into a bloodthirsty monster."

"It's worth any price in the world if Bastien lives," Celine pleaded.

A hard light shone in Nicodemus' eyes. "Sébastien has already proven he is too weak for this life. He did not heed my warnings when he fell in love with a mortal girl, and now his life is forfeit. If he were one of us, it would be the same. Our enemies would exploit these weaknesses. And there would always be something left for him to lose."

"Then protect him. Make him stronger. Just *save him*," she cried.

Nicodemus stared down at the cursed girl. The cause of his nephew's undoing. He knew Celine loved Sébastien. Could see the truth of it in her haunted gaze. And it left him cold. Bleak. Unfeeling. "I stayed away so my enemies would not be drawn to Sébastien. So they would not be tempted. I surrounded him with my immortal children so that they would always protect him. I sacrificed everything I loved to keep him safe." Nicodemus inhaled, a knot of pain taking shape around the emptiness in his heart. "My family has always been my weakness. And now my enemies have destroyed me with it." He shook his head. "Love is an affliction to our kind. I will not remake Bastien only to watch him fall prey to it again. I'm sorry."

"What do you want me to do?" Celine whispered. "What can I say that will make you save him?"

"Nothing. Whatever we are in our human lives becomes magnified by immortality. What Bastien loves now will be an even greater weakness." Nicodemus studied Celine, watching his words shatter her last hope. "Forget all this, child. Live your life apart from this wretched world." An approximation of sympathy laced his features. Nicodemus turned toward his immortal children, ready to take leave. To sit with his grief, pondering all he had lost tonight. To flee this cursed city forever.

"What if I promised to forget Bastien?" Celine said from behind him.

Nicodemus did not move.

She stumbled to her feet in a rustle of black taffeta, the wound at her neck filling the air with an intoxicating scent. "You told me you could help me forget. That Bastien would respect my choice. If I forgot him—if I was no longer a weakness—would you save him?"

Nicodemus took a step toward the doors of the cathedral.

"You said there were many paths to happiness," she continued. "If I can choose a different one, will you not do the same?"

He stopped. Turned to look at Marceline Rousseau over

his shoulder. Her hands were still bound, her body covered in blood, a great deal of it her own. Still the girl refused to capitulate. A part of Nicodemus admired her stubbornness. Her unwillingness to fold in the face of such odds.

His gaze fell on his nephew's battered body. On the last signs of life lingering within. Sighing in defeat, Nicodemus looked away.

"Bastien is the last of your kin. Are you ready to walk this earth alone?" Celine yelled. "Because I would rather lose him forever than watch him die."

Nicodemus met the eyes of his immortal children. Saw the weight of his loss reflected in their faces.

No. It is not meant to be.

He straightened and began walking away.

"Nicodemus!" Celine screamed, the anguish in her voice soaring to the rafters above. "Nicodemus Saint Germain!"

Again Nicodemus stopped, the echo of his family's name circling beneath the frescoed ceilings of the cathedral, the sound of her pain stirring the shreds of his heart. Bringing it back to life.

"Do we have a deal?"

Love Is Not Love

———◦◦◇◦◦———

The first of my people hailed from Carthage.

From a time when blood reigned supreme. When monsters and mercenaries ruled the known world. This was the beginning of the Brotherhood.

Not much has changed since then.

I stand along the pier, gazing toward the waters of the Mississippi, at peace for the first time in a decade.

When I first heard the news that Sébastien Saint Germain had been struck a fatal blow in the skirmish at the cathedral, strange pangs coiled through my chest. I know now it was the last vestiges of my weak human heart finally dying so that I might embrace the better, stronger version of myself.

There is no chance Nicodemus will have turned Bastien.

Not when he refused me ten years ago.

Amusing how tethered to his morals the great Nicodemus Saint Germain can be. Especially considering all the death and destruction he has wrought over the centuries. Bastien was the last living scion of the Saint Germain line. Now the one thing this four-hundred-year-old leech fought to protect above all is gone. His purpose has been taken from him, as mine was taken from me.

I have dismantled his legacy.

And it is sweet. The kind of sweetness that overshadows the bitterness, consuming it whole.

For I once loved Bastien more than I loved myself. I even gave my human life for his.

My beautiful little brother.

But my loyalties lie elsewhere now. With the creatures who offered me the gift Uncle Nico refused to grant me ten years ago. With the true immortal beasts of the Otherworld. The same ones the vampires have always cast aside, to be used as watchdogs and fed the scraps from their dinner table. Treated as nothing more than fodder in a centuries-long war with the Sylvan Vale.

But no matter, that is a tale for another time.

Once I walked among the Fallen. Saw them as family.

But I am no longer a Saint Germain. I do not need to mourn the death of my brother. He was complicit in my uncle's misdeeds. His impetuousness brought about my mother's death those many years ago. Bastien is the reason no one sought to save me, a mere girl, destined to become nothing.

My thoughts linger on Celine Rousseau. A formidable quarry, I will admit. She was close to uncovering the truth of what I have become.

But close counts only in cannon fire and horseshoes.

It was something my father used to say.

I move from my spot along the pier, slinking toward the shadows beneath it, comfortable in my skin for the first time in ages. The stars twinkle with abandon, oblivious to how they exist by the grace of the moon. But I am aware. She is our mother in all ways.

Luca will be waiting for me, as he always did, even when we were children. Beneath the silver light of our mother moon, we will run free together. Our families may have been mortal enemies in life, but it doesn't matter now. For I am among his kind. One of them. A member of the Brotherhood, evermore.

And Luca will always love me, as he has for over a decade.

I love him, too. In my own way. Just as I loved Marin.

Beneath the dock, the change begins. The magic burns through my bloodstream, sending shudders down my spine. My fingers curl into claws, my fangs lengthen, my long hair twists and reshapes.

And I become who I was always meant to be.

Émilie le Loup, an immortal wolf howling at the moon.

Ready for whatever may come.

———◇———

Celine opened her eyes with a start, as if she'd fallen from a tower in her dreams. Her body felt battered and sluggish, like the hull of a ship after a summer storm. A cloud hovered over her mind, causing everything around her to appear filtered as if through a haze.

She cleared her throat with a weak cough.

Immediately a figure moved to her side. "Celine."

It sounded like the voice Celine wanted to hear. But different.

In her dreams, it had been different. "Michael." His name cracked on her tongue. She cleared her throat again, realizing how dry it was. How long she must have slept.

"Do you want some water?" he asked.

"Please." Celine drank from the cup Michael held to her lips. Every movement he made was slow. Careful. Unmistakably tender.

Celine blinked hard, but the film clung stalwart to the edges of her vision. "What happened to your nose?" Her brow furrowed. "Did someone hit you?"

Annoyance flickered across Michael's bruised face. "I'm fine."

"Is Pippa all right?"

"Pippa is fine. Everyone is . . . fine."

"What happened?" She swallowed. "I can't remember how I got here."

Michael nodded. "You've been through quite an ordeal."

"It—feels like there are holes in my memory."

"That's normal after all that happened." Michael shifted a hand to cover hers. "Later, I promise we can piece everything together. But now you should rest."

Celine swallowed again, trying to banish the taste of metal and herbs from her tongue. She fell back against the pillows, the ache in her side causing her to cringe. "Thank you, Michael. It's comforting to know you are here with me."

"Where else would I be?" He squeezed her hand, his pale eyes warm. The openness in his expression soothed her. As if he had nothing he wished to hide from her, ever again.

Perhaps Celine had been wrong to discount his affections

as she had in the past. Michael Grimaldi had always felt like a piece of a puzzle that simply wouldn't fit.

Today? Something felt . . . different.

Michael continued speaking. "Pippa left less than half an hour ago to get some sleep." He smiled to himself. "She'll be furious when she discovers you woke in her absence." He turned toward the door, his strides long. Capable. Quick. "I'll send for her soon."

Celine sat up, her body screaming in protest. "Please don't leave. Not yet." She didn't know the reason, but she didn't want to be alone.

He curved a sardonic brow at her. Then reached for the wooden chair at the end of her hospital bed. "I'm simply moving closer."

With a grateful sigh, Celine sank into the pillows once more. She looked around. The cover strewn across her bed resembled the shawl she'd last seen on Nonna's shoulders. A vase of cheerful yellow flowers rested on a worn table beside her. At the foot of her bed was a small, well-worn tome. "What is that?"

Michael paused while he sat. "It's a collection of Shakespeare's sonnets. I've been reading them for research." An awkward smile tugged at his face. "A girl with a soul of iron told me I should write her a poem."

Celine blinked, the memory returning to her, indistinct at first, then slowly taking shape. When Michael reached out to grasp her hand again, she hesitated a moment, wishing the rest of her mind would clear of all its clutter. Wishing she could fill the gaps in her memory. Then she threaded her fingers through his. "Will you read one to me?"

Michael grasped her fingers tightly, then began to speak in a steady voice. "Let me not to the marriage of true minds / Admit impediments. Love is not love / Which alters when it alteration finds, / Or bends with the remover to remove. . . ."

Epilogue

—◦◦◇◦◦—

First there was nothing.
     Then . . . there was everything.

Acknowledgments

——◦◦◇◦◦——

This story has lived in my head since I was a surly teenager, with my head buried in Anne Rice novels until the wee hours of the morning. From the moment it became an actual reality, not a day has gone by that I haven't been thrilled beyond measure to have a team of people believe in me—and my work—without hesitation.

Barbara, I still remember your delighted cackle when I said I wanted to write a vampire book set in New Orleans. Nothing I've achieved in this career would have been possible without you. And that gorgeous cackle. Good luck, stupid . . . forever and always.

Stacey, there is no better champion than you. Your voice in my head pushes me every day to be better than I was the day before, and for that there are not enough words of gratitude. Also I've found us the perfect restaurant in the Quarter. I even picked our table already. New Orleans better watch out.

To the team of magic-makers at Penguin: your support and enthusiasm and work ethic have made the world and characters I created in my mind a beautiful reality. To Marisa Russell: thank you so much for your passion and enthusiasm. The day you told me you loved *Penny Dreadful*, I knew we were a match made in heaven. Endless gratitude to Caitlin Tutterow for answering every single one of my inane questions. A heart-felt thank-you to Carmela Iaria, Venessa Carson, Doni Kay, Theresa Evangelista for the stunning cover and design, Elyse Marshall, Felicia Frasier (I insist on another Brooklyn pasta night!), Lindsay Boggs, Shanta Newlin, Erin Berger (pasta night part deux, right?), Christina Colangelo, Colleen Conway, Caitlin Whalen, and Bri Lockhart. Immense gratitude to Laurel Robinson, Cindy Howle, and the inimitable Anne Heausler for their notes and edits. And a special note of thanks to Kara Brammer and Felicity Vallence for being the mad geniuses you both are.

A huge thank-you to all the amazing book bloggers, readers, and book lovers from all over the world. I cannot do what I do without you.

To Jessica Khoury for the stunning map and the gorgeous emblem. It's my desktop, and I am in awe of your talent and consummate professionalism.

To Daniel José Older for the New Orleans expertise, the notes, and endless support. Thank you, thank you, thank you.

To Alwyn for your precious emails and your enthusiasm and all the help perfecting my sad attempts at French. You are a delight and one of the most genuinely kind people I know. I adore you.

To Rosh, JJ, and Lemon: when I think of all the memories we've already made, I smile at everything destined to come. Thank you for gracing me with your love and endless talent.

To Sabaa for cheering with me, crying with me, reading with me, and inspiring me every day. And for watching *The Two Towers* Extended Edition and knowing every line by heart, just like me. Your friendship is a gift beyond measure.

To Gio Mannucci for all the help with the Italian. I love how this career has reconnected us in such a wonderful way.

To Carrie Ryan and Brendan Reichs for all the Cantina lunches, advice, and laughter. QC represent!

To my assistant Emily Williams: thank you for being the most organized person I know and keeping me—and my hare-brained ideas!—on track.

To Maggie Kane, Heather Baror-Shapiro, and the wonderful team at IGLA: thank you for all your endless work and unceasing professionalism.

To Elaine: I am so lucky to have a chosen sister like you. Thank you for fixing all the Spanish in the book and sending me curse-laden text messages at 3:00 a.m. and for loving New Orleans like I do. There is no one I'd rather gallivant down Dumaine with, searching for a tarot card reader or our next foodie fix.

To Erica, Ian, Chris, and Izzy: I love you all so much, and am so grateful to call you family. To my parents—Umma, Dad, Mama Joon, and Baba Joon—thank you for all your love and for always putting my books where everyone can see them, front-facing in bookstores.

To Omid, Julie, Navid, Jinda, Evelyn, Isabelle, Andrew, Ella, and Lily: thank you for our family and for all the times you never fail to show up and cheer for me. I'm so proud to share in this life with you.

And to Vic: for the way you look at me when you think I'm not paying attention, and for the way you make me smile even when you're not there, thank you, to the stars and back. There is no better man than you.